For

Hannah, Davis, Kira, Joe

with all my love

About the Author

Abbey Pen Baker is the great niece of Faye Martin Tullis. She divides her time between Yellow Springs, Ohio where she lives with children, animals and the title of Professor of English and New England, where she eats too much good food with good friends and collects rocks and sea glass on the coast of Maine. She is very busy editing the notes and previously published novels first penned by her great aunt.

In the Dead
of Winter

Abbey Pen Baker

First published in 2010 by
The Irregular Special Press,
for Baker Street Studios Ltd,
Endeavour House,
170 Woodland Road, Sawston,
Cambridge, CB22 3DX, UK.

ISBN: 1-901091-39-2 (10 digit)
ISBN: 978-1-901091-39-7 (13 digit)

Cover Concept: Antony J. Richards.

Cover Illustration: The Island Carnival at Brattleboro, Vermont from an original
watercolour by Nikki Sims.

Typeset in 8/11/20pt Palatino

Contents

Editor's Note

The story of Myrl Adler Norton and Faye Martin Tullis spans more than thirty-five years. Though their notoriety has faded and the legend of Myrl and Faye has all but evaporated, theirs is a singular story of two women who shaped their own world in a time when women's voices were not heard. My hope is that with this publication, their lives will once again take form and substance and reach out from the past to touch new readers.

Faye Tullis was my great-aunt, my grandfather's older sister. None of her books are in print anymore and when I was a small child I wasn't allowed to read her work. I met her just once, at a family reunion, and my sole memory of her is of a tiny white-haired woman sitting perfectly erect at the family dining table, passing me chocolate mint truffles under the table. Her hair was soft, fine, and wrapped in a tight, precise bun at the nape of the neck. She died in 1980 at the age of eighty-two.

Faye wrote twenty-seven books and eight short stories based on her relationship with Myrl Adler Norton. Some critics of the time have questioned her ability to stick to the facts and have suggested Faye fabricated much of her work. But history will bear out truth. Myrl Adler Norton was a genius, a logician of the highest order, and the only female private detective operating in New England in the twenties. She, of course, would never announce herself as a detective, though my aunt clearly saw Myrl's role as such. I have long believed the critics tried to find fault in Aunt Faye's accounts only because of her sex. I think men of the day, with few exceptions, simply did not believe two women could possess the mental and physical agility to put to shame so many of their own.

As her readers know, Myrl and Faye's cases involved murder, theft, arson, kidnapping, blackmail, and a mix of some of the above and took them overseas on several occasions: England, Japan, Switzerland, and India.[1] But I think her strongest stories are those which took place right in New England. Faye's style, though journalistic, often verges on the poetic and her careful descriptions of the times and places reveal an awareness that these stories would go on after her death.

That is why, after long and careful family discussion, I have decided to publish this remaining manuscript. It tells of Myrl and Faye's first meeting, of their relationship as teacher and student, of their ensuing friendship and their first case. I know Faye would have wanted it published. My thoughts on why it never was submitted to Lords and Winkler's are twofold: with her first efforts she must have felt unsure of herself as a writer; and, secondly, *In the Dead of Winter* contains a revelation of family history which I believe she felt uncomfortable disclosing.

The existence of this manuscript was a surprise. Three years ago I visited what used to be the Tullis farm in southeastern Vermont and spoke to the family who now lives there. Though just in their twenties, the couple had heard of Myrl and Faye, and were delighted to find out they were living in the very house where Faye penned most of her books. It was then they told me of an oak desk they had discovered in the barn right behind what used to be the two-holer.

---

[1] *Death at the Round Table* (1929), *Pacific Bound* (1928), *Murder by the Clock* (1930), and *Salt of the Earth* (1934), respectively. All were published by Lords and Winkler's, New York

The desk was an old roll-top, infested with carpenter ants, and had suffered considerable water damage. But it was also filled with papers and it had definitely been Faye's. Carved in the underside of the desk-top was the familiar, flourishing "F. M. Tullis" which graces her books.

I was ecstatic. I made arrangements to have the desk shipped to my home in California. A journalist myself, I was more than intrigued by this little piece of discovered history—histories both personal and cultural. On arrival, I began emptying the desk of all papers, clips, pens, etc., going over each item with great care. My husband helped me catalogue many of the things we found: old bills, an Estey Pipe Organ Company receipt, powdered Necco Wafer wrappers, trolley tickets, photographs, bills, several lovely feathered quills, completely useless now, but nice on my own desk. The bottom drawer was locked and I waited two weeks for a local locksmith to make a house call. Wrenching that lock was like breaking into a treasure chest.

Inside were two photos of Myrl and Faye, hand-painted photos I had never seen before, each one in pale patinas. Here they were, two young women early in their careers – Myrl: tall, thin, regal and inaccessible, eyes sharp and dark, staring right into the camera, her long thick red-brown hair shining in the famous roll along the back of the neck. And then there was Faye: eight years younger, impetuous, her face full and round like a little girl's, her waist small, her own deep brown hair carelessly gathered and pulled back into a looser bun than the one I was to see sixty years later. And under the photos, wrapped in sheets of waxed paper, was a manuscript. The unforeseen treasure.

The first time I read the manuscript, no one had to tell me what I had found. I recognised it for what it was – a piece of stolen history. There was no doubt in my mind Faye would have eventually published the book. I never found the first draft – the manuscript was in very nearly perfect form, with few margin notes. *In the Dead of Winter* was neatly typed, complete with a foreword, which I have included. As such, the manuscript needed little editing, and I feel like an opportunist attaching my name to the book. There was some water damage to the last twenty-two pages and I hope my restoration hasn't diluted the text. For devoted followers of Myrl Adler Norton, this discovered manuscript is a miracle which could not have been predicted – for those just meeting her for the first time, I trust this will be a rewarding introduction.

My hope is that I have done justice to my Aunt Faye and her companion, Myrl. They were two phenomenal women living in a time when phenomenal women were trapped in a vacuum, without the support of the past and with a vaporous future. They lived beyond the cycles of time.

Abbey Pen Baker
Yellow Springs, Ohio
2010

Foreword

It was just about a year ago that I stumbled across some of my old notes. Old notes. The words sound innocuous, conjuring images of dry paper and dust, but there is nothing banal or innocent about murder.

Over the years I have chronicled our life together, holding to the facts, setting pen to paper at the request of close family and friends. I laboured to put into a few words events which defy sanity but which are, nonetheless, part of human experience. I tried always to depict the truth, though I know some will strive to prove otherwise. As luck would have it, my labours were found to be saleable and thus, over the ensuing years, the long history of Myrl Adler Norton has become famous.

Our journeys crossed continents. We found the essence of morality often slippery and yet we never questioned the steady value of reason. Myrl's experience as amateur sleuth is legendary. She came to face cases of every nature: missing persons, jewel and art thievery, blackmail, counterfeiting, forgery. But it was murder which received such intense, horrific fascination from her.

Murder is in a class by itself. Though the catalysts for murder can be the same as those for other crimes – revenge, greed, lust – the formation of the plan and execution of murder involves a series of moral decisions and acts separate from those for other crimes. All murder, whether the result of calculation or circumstance, is premeditated, Myrl once told me. From this premise, the cause, motivation, and act became a notorious web of intrigue for her. Murder always demanded her closest attention and received her deepest repulsion.

Myrl and I were in each other's company for more than thirty-five years and I have described well over two-dozen other cases. But there has been one serious omission and this brings me to my notes.

I have yet to set in print the circumstances by which we first met – how we came to be friends and what began this long acquaintance. Myrl did not choose to be a criminologist; her path and mine crossed at a time when she had no inclination of delving into the darker side of the human heart. Her first love was her mind. Her second was logic. When I stepped into her classroom at Smith that September of 1918, neither one of us could have foreseen how chance and reason would guide us down a shared road for the next four decades.

In sifting through some papers last fall I discovered my old journal from college. There, neatly laid out on its pages in handwriting not much changed, was the account of our chance meeting – and the case which was to be our first.

This particular incident did not require travel to faraway places. Rather it was staged in our own backyard, on home territory in Northampton, Massachusetts. It was murder which brought us together. And it was an attempt at murder which nearly swept us apart.

Now, of course, I have the gift of hindsight and could, I suppose, wipe away all the girlishness and immaturity from the text, but I have decided against revision. With the exception of some very necessary editing, I have tried to keep the original version intact, complete with all the eager misconceptions that I possessed as a youth. I was twenty-one that fall. I was struggling with my sister suffragettes for the vote, we were hot and angry and ready to fight, and then Myrl Adler Norton stepped into my life. And everything changed, forever.

I have long chosen to guard this particular story. Readers will understand my reasons for silence and will see, too, why these reasons have faded over time. Though we are not yet free of the prejudice surrounding those with questionable parentage, social stigma has noticeably eased in the last forty years. I did not want to ever jeopardise Myrl's privacy or that of her parents, nor dishonour any member of her family. Myrl was devoted to the memory of her mother, Irene Adler, and to the man who raised her as his own, Godfrey Norton. Through all these many years and through each account, I was determined to keep submerged all events, descriptions, or allusions which might lead readers to suspect Myrl's true parentage. The name of Sherlock Holmes is famous and, in our day, pregnancy before marriage a moral crime for which all parties suffered. Finally, Myrl swore me to secrecy in this matter, and I would never break that promise.

For those who follow Sherlock Holmes, the name Irene Adler is synonymous with intelligence, courage, and beauty. She is the only person to have truly outwitted Holmes, and not for debased reasons. Her ability to keep him at bay and have her own integrity left intact was a play of genius.

Irene Adler was, indeed, "*the* woman," as Dr John Watson declares in both the opening and closing of *A Scandal in Bohemia*. In his introduction he continues:

> 'I have seldom heard him mention her under any other name. In his eyes she eclipses and predominates the whole of her sex. It was not that he felt any emotion akin to love for Irene Adler. All emotions, and that one particularly, were abhorrent to his cold, precise but admirably balanced mind. He was, I take it, the most perfect reasoning and observing machine that the world has seen; but as a lover, he would have placed himself in a false position ... Yet there was but one woman to him, and that woman was the late Irene Adler, of dubious and questionable memory'.

It wasn't until thirty years later Watson realised how completely deluded he had been at the time. Watson, for all his insight into Sherlock Holmes, never suspected. And he should have. When Holmes asked Watson to look up Irene Adler's name in his index, a warning should have sounded. For Holmes, a music lover and patron of the orchestra, to be ignorant of Irene Adler, the great contralto and adventuress, should have been a clue. The fact Watson did not play a very active part in the case but was forced to rely almost entirely on Holmes's recounting of the 'facts' should have been another. With the exception of his own 'death' at Reichenbach Falls, this charade constitutes the largest deception Holmes was ever to perpetrate on Watson. His reasons for deceiving his friend lay in the affairs of his closed heart – high stakes for one who prided himself on emotional restraint, one for whom passionate emotion was like, 'grit in a sensitive instrument'. As Watson explains, 'For the trained reasoner to admit such intrusions into his own delicate and finely adjusted temperament was to introduce a distracting factor which might throw a doubt upon all his mental results'.

It should be said, however, that it is certain Holmes had no inkling of Irene Adler's condition when she left England. Their last moment together was outside 221 Baker Street, where Holmes, dressed as an elderly priest, was passed by Irene, disguised as a young male clerk. Adler's 'Good night, Mr Sherlock Holmes' was the last he would ever hear from her. His admiration for her continued in silence. Though Watson tells us Holmes kept a photograph of her in his desk, it is clear the two never corresponded after her flight to America. It wasn't until Holmes was quite elderly that Adler's own secret was revealed to him.

Over the years, many of my readers suspected the truth, and I have remained bound by friendship and a sense of propriety to answer their letters in a polite, perfunctory manner. I never allowed myself to agree with their theories. But with Myrl's death, this chapter of her life may at last be opened.

Faye Martin Tullis
Saxtons River, Vermont
April 1968

Chapter One

At Smith College

It was a Sunday evening at the end of an unusually hot summer. The year was 1918, the movement was afoot, and the twilight air was thin and light. News of the day seemed far away and trivial: the publication of Zane Grey's *The U. P. Trail*, the release of *Tarzan of the Apes* starring Elmo Lincoln and Enid Markey, huge war bond rallies whipped into frenzy by Douglas Fairbanks, the theft of England's Duchess Royal Ruby, the unflagging popularity of the summer Chautauqua.

Shivering slightly from sunburn I waited with about three hundred of my sisters for the notorious Emma Goldman to speak. She was late. Two hours late. The Quad at Smith College was a faded green, its edges burned by the long season, and grass was worn away in spots from the summer concert series. The gazebo in the centre was oblong and the front of its wide stage faced us. The stage and banisters were white, the footings blue, and the roof red, painted patriotically for the past Fourth of July celebration. A large electric bulb was strung up on a pole to the right of the stage and it was just now casting light. Women speakers, mostly students from college, were taking turns onstage. Right now, a woman with long loose red hair, wearing a brown shirt and slacks was speaking through a megaphone and talking about working conditions.

The police had formed a circle around us, tall men with bland faces standing in blue-black uniforms twenty feet apart.

On arrival, they originally stayed close together and remained tight around us like a noose, but as more of us gathered they were forced back, like the outer ring of a ripple. The shiny billy clubs, the guns strapped into heavy black leather holsters, the metal buttons and black boots, polished the twilight with apprehension, dread, excitement.

I had come from the Smith Riding Club after a vigorous outing along the Connecticut River and had traded my riding boots for more appropriate footwear. I was concentrating on my feet, shifting my weight back and forth, easing the pressure of my shoes-new brown leather beefroll loafers with a slit for a penny. I had carefully placed a new penny in each and they winked pale pink and orange in the sunset. The voice in the megaphone droned on. A second voice whispered in my left ear.

"So, Faye, what do you think?"

I turned and saw Rachel White, a classmate from last term. She had spent the summer in Paris studying painting and I was envious of her excursion abroad. My dream was to see Shakespeare in England-rather, to perform.

"I don't know, maybe they've arrested her."

"Yes, that's what I've heard." She paused. "I bet they did. They always pick her up and lock her away right before a speech ..."

I knew this to be true. Emma Goldman was often jailed for the night just hours before a rally. It was then the woman with the long red hair waved a piece of paper at the crowd and held up the megaphone.

"Emma Goldman will not be speaking to you tonight," she began. The crowd was silent. Her voice was clear and loud and she walked up and down the stage, the white piece of paper fluttering. "She won't be speaking to you because she's sitting in a Boston jail. Sitting in jail because she believes in birth control, believes in sex education for your children, believes in your right to vote ..."

The crowd suddenly became agitated and began moving in closer toward the stage as if magnetised, and the police, following like a shadow, tightened their circle once again.

From the corner of my eye I saw one man on my right unsnap his holster. I shifted my gaze momentarily to him. The speaker onstage began talking louder, switching her hand on the megaphone.

"She is in jail because" – here she paused, lowered the megaphone for a moment, and then brought it back to her face –"because she believes in your freedom of speech!"

Someone from the back yelled, "Freedom of speech!" and the crowd called in return, "Speech! Speech! Freedom of speech!"

The woman with the red hair paused again, assessing her new resource. The megaphone was raised to her mouth. "Let us get her out. We can do it. All of us. NOW." And then she began the call: "Free Emma, Free Emma, Free Emma, Free Emma ..."

The crowd was moving like the sea and the call was turned into a chant, shouted by hundreds of women. The woman onstage was joined by several others and they were waving, encouraging the voices. I picked up the call and as I did, I heard Rachel join. Our united voice was daringly harsh, deep, demanding, and an electricity swept me, riveting, pulsing. I felt good, strong, invincible, light-headed inside my armour of being so terribly right.

Three or four policemen had begun pushing their way through the crowd, toward the stage. I could see them slice through our tight group like a blue-black lightning bolt. Their target was the stage and when they hit, another roar went up, a deep affront. No real words, but the sound of disgust and disrespect, a rumble of forewarning. The police were joined by more of their numbers. Several tried to climb onstage and were pulled back down. More police swarmed along the front of the gazebo and began encircling the stage. Then the woman with the red hair made a terrible miscalculation. She singled out one policeman as the bull's-eye for her megaphone and stepped a little too close.

He simply reached out, grabbed her foot, and she fell. The megaphone was dropped, the electric line toppled, and the bulb popped.

17

The rumble became a tremendous roar as tension from the crowd released. The women, all of us, turned to the ring of police and began shoving, pushing outward, and the meter of the chant was lost. In the fading light there seemed to be too much movement, and Rachel and I were at first pushed together and then swept up and separated. I saw one billy club raised but failed to see where it landed. I heard a woman scream and then more. It seemed only seconds passed and then wagons were on the scene, new black automobile wagons, and women were shepherded on like cattle. I stood as still as I could and watched for Rachel. Then a large, red, angry face was directly in front of me and I looked up. It was the young fellow who had unsnapped his holster.

"Get on the wagon, missy. Now." There was a wagon just several yards away. He pointed at it with his club.

"Are you arresting me?" I was still floating, and the call was in my heart. Someone crashed by me, a fight, pushing. I stepped aside.

"Get on the wagon, missy, or I'll have to carry you on."

I looked up at him and smiled.

"You're just a biddy little thing and it won't hurt me none to load you on."

Now, I have not been picked up by anyone since I was a child and I can only say that it was not pleasant. He managed to bruise one of my ribs and I felt rather tossed around like a potato sack. I saw a wedding band on his finger as he closed the wagon gate.

* * * * *

Jail did not frighten me. I'm afraid I was intoxicated with the realisation that I, Faye Martin Tullis, was a threat, wanted off the streets by the State. I was deemed worthy of imprisonment – I was a menace. We were all excited, seeing ourselves as flesh and blood suffragettes in the shadow of Emma. Our arrest was a kind of baptism, a public validation of our motives and we were thrilled with our power.

The jail in Northampton was small, used only as a holding area for drunkards and petty thieves. There were three cells, none of them large, and each was outfitted with two bunk beds. For us sisters, the first stopping point was for personal convenience. The toilets were all urinals and were the cause of much discussion.

I was hustled into the third cell. It was mouldy and smelled of clay and mildew. The humidity of the past summer had been high, and moisture condenses easily, given the right elements. The cells were half below ground, dimly lit, and the floors were of dirt. There were two small rectangular windows complete with bars above our heads. My new shoes were filthy, both pennies gone, and my ribs ached.

I kept searching for Rachel and stood by the bars, smiling to myself, trying to think of an eloquent statement full of poise and intellect that would stun my captors when they finally got around to booking me.

Unfortunately, they did not book us. Or at least not me. I was not that notorious. I felt quite envious of the woman with the loose red hair and slacks, who was ushered to the front desk and kept from the rest of us for the first several hours. When she was finally escorted into the cell next to mine, I saw her fingertips were slightly blackened and knew she had been fingerprinted.

Conversation among us was hushed. After an hour or so, excitement began to wane and I could hear several women crying softly. But for the most part, spirits were high. Then Rachel was brought to the middle cell next to me. I called out, and she made her way over to where I was standing. We were just inches from each other, clasping hands, but separated by bars. I suddenly thought of my parents.

"My father always told me ten glasses of water, a carrot stick, and a full eight hours of sleep per day would sustain a body. He never mentioned what to do if you're jailed."

Rachel's thoughts seemed more focused on our immediate predicament. "They won't feed us, you know. Nothing. Not even your carrot."

As she was speaking the metal door crashed open and two men and two women came down the steps into the hall. A voice, loud and clear in the quiet of the night, echoed slightly and I stood on tiptoe to see who was speaking.

"I am not about to be incarcerated in a building for which I pay taxes to support ..."

The group stopped by the first cell. Most of my sisters moved forward to the front edge of the cells to see, and greetings were offered to the two women.

"Do not, I repeat, do not touch me, you will not contaminate me, and do not use foul language in my presence." The voice gave these words as a command to the two officers.

"Who is that? Can you see?" Rachel whispered.

I shook my head. We could hear the first cell door being unlocked and opened and, by ducking, I caught a glimpse of a short dark-haired woman deposited in a circle of her sisters.

"I don't think that's the one who's talking," said Rachel, and we both resumed standing on tiptoe.

And then I saw her. She was tall. She was long, thin, towered over the black-haired woman, and stood eye to eye with her two captors. She had deep mahogany-coloured hair, brown with veins of red, turned under in a crescent roll behind her ears and along her neck in a fashion popular decades ago. She carried only a small white beaded purse and a pair of white gloves. Her strapless dress was in the newest fashion, of black velour or velvet, cut smoothly to the knee and fit her rather tightly across the hip. She wore no wrap. She looked fashionably dressed for the opera or a party, though she wore little jewellery, simple dangling pearl earrings and a matching string of pearls around the neck. Her face was sharp, angular-not a pretty face by common definition, but attractive for its boldness. Hers was the kind of face which reveals sudden flashes of beauty with time and intimacy. I saw her only in profile and I remember thinking how strong she appeared. It is an odd way to describe someone, I realise, but that was how she looked. Her strength, though apparent, did not seem to derive from tension – she was not a spring wound tight. Rather, her power was pervasive, steady, enduring like the equilibrium held by a rock. In the bad light she could have been twenty-five or fifty-five. I had no idea. But her voice, deep and even, carried well and resonated with a security that comes with age.

"I am not going to be incarcerated. I repeat this to both you gentlemen not for my pleasure, I assure you," she said, planting both feet solidly on the ground. The three stood outside the middle cell, the cell which held Rachel. One of the officers, an older man with greying side-whiskers, sighed audibly. The key was inserted and the cell door pulled open.

"Inside, miss."

"I am not entering. I have told you, I have explained in excruciating detail to your superiors, the facts of my being present at this –" Here she was pushed, and none too gently. She turned around, standing even straighter. The door was shut.

The crowd inside the three cells began a wave of boos. Ignoring her supporters, she raised her voice.

"I assure both of you that I can and will have a word with your supervisors, the state attorney general's office, and the governor's office, if need be. And you will be sorry. This is not a threat you should ignore!"

The metal doors closed. The booing stopped.

"Well," was all she said. She turned back to her new cellmates and rapidly scanned the lot of us. I cannot explain the intensity of her eyes or why I was so fascinated by her. She was a woman apart from the rest of us, a singular island. Her manner of dress was fairly spectacular, her stature breathtaking. But it was the poised self-assurance and regal presence which gave an aura both inspiring and humbling. She suddenly spotted Rachel and me clustered by adjoining bars, and she seemed to make a decision.

"Do you know her?" Rachel whispered.

"No, do you?"

"Never saw her before in my life-uh-oh, here she comes."

"I realise this is not your fault and I apologise," was how she began, "but I simply cannot remain captive in this bastion of filth. There is, no doubt, the stain and soil of vomit in these floors from drunkards and louts and I'll have none of it." She seemed very annoyed and kept her ivory linen gloves clasped in her hands. Her hands were large, bony, and not pretty, but they were very expressive and every move seemed calculated. Now she was grasping the gloves with one hand and striking them in the palm of the other.

Rachel said nothing and I could think of nothing to say.

The woman cast her glance about and then stared at us both.

"I repeat. I will not be incarcerated. I need you two for a very specific task. You in particular," she said, looking straight at me, "because of your interest in what I gather to be the theatrical."

I did not know what to say. Now it was Rachel who turned and stared at me.

"Although it is unfortunate that we are not sharing the same cell. I guess," she sighed at Rachel, "you'll do." Here she paused and looked down the hall for a moment. Then her gaze was back to the two of us. "I just do not belong here."

"Well," Rachel began, "maybe you could talk –"

"Oh, for heaven's sake," she said. "Enough drivel." She suddenly shut her eyes, took a deep breath, and said without the slightest waver in her voice, "I do believe I feel faint."

"What!" Rachel was not prepared for this announcement.

The woman gasped and dropped her gloves, gripping a bar with one hand and fanning herself with the other. "Oh," she gasped again and she swooned as I reached through the bars to grab her around the waist. Her head fell back and her eyelids fluttered and for a moment I carried her full weight. She was heavy. Rachel moved quickly, put a shoulder under the woman's left arm and I let go. The woman tried to take a step and I heard her mumble something. Then she collapsed completely.

Poor Rachel had the woman's full weight now, but within seconds others gathered and together they laid her gently on the dirt floor.

"Guard!" I yelled and several others joined in. I saw Rachel grasp the woman's wrist and feel for her pulse and a second woman raised her feet, holding an ankle in each hand. The cry for a guard fortunately met with immediate response and a gurney was sent for. A guard brought smelling salts, but they seemed useless. As the guard waved the vial under her nose, she would begin to stir, moving a hand by her face weakly, but as soon as the vial was removed, she would succumb again and sink back on the gurney. Two men carried her out of the cell and a third kept applying the salts as they left the jail.

I watched the metal door close behind the gurney and sighed.

"What was that all about?" said Rachel and sat down hard against the bars. I joined her on the floor and we sat shoulder to shoulder. I rested my head on the bars separating us.

"I haven't a clue. What could make someone so sick so suddenly?"

"She was odd. I tell you, I have met the oddest people ever since I got back from Paris." Rachel sighed and laid something next to me on the floor. "You keep these," she said.

I glanced down. By my hand was the pair of ivory linen gloves.

* * * * *

We were released in small groups beginning around seven the next morning. As the light of early dawn poured easily through the two small windows above our heads, we were escorted in threes to the urinals. There was no meal offered, or water, and Rachel and I were terribly thirsty. The tall woman with the mahogany hair was never returned to the cell, though both Rachel and I watched for her throughout the night. Rachel was released a half-hour before I was and we agreed our next priority was getting to class – we were not to wait for each other. My first assignment was an eight o'clock teaching assistantship in beginning logic.

As I stepped out on the sidewalk with a handful of other women, we were met by suffragettes. A small woman, rather plump and not much older than me, shoved a piece of bread in my hand and offered me apples from a basket. As I took one, I felt distant and melancholy and my cheeks were dry and warm from lack of sleep. The apple was hard in my hand as I walked toward campus. No words passed among us and one by one we each turned down different streets. I took a bite of the bread. The smell of yeast was strong.

By the time I reached my room at the Martha Wilson House I had less than five minutes to get to class. My room was small, neat, painted light green with a pretty French floral wallpaper. The bed was of brass, tarnished but quite comfortable. Sheets were changed once a week and that is more often than they were at home. I changed my skirt, quickly tied my hair back with a fresh bow, and splashed my face with water from the nightstand. I grabbed my pen and notebook and ran. I heard the bells chiming eight o'clock as I dashed across campus.

Taking the steps of Seelye Hall two by two, I didn't even pause to catch my breath on the landing, but swung wide the tamarack door and stood in back of the class.

I was in luck. Dr Norton was tardy himself. I swallowed, seeing the empty chair and desk at the front of the room in the far left-hand corner. These left-hand seats were always reserved for teaching assistants. I walked purposefully down the centre aisle, aware of the lower class-women watching me. I slipped behind the desk, sat down easily, and set the notebook strategically in the centre of the desktop with the pen resting alongside.

I heard whispering and the door in the back of the class closed once more as someone else was late. I turned around, performed a quick head count, and estimated the class at about forty pupils. The classroom had the luxury of a south-facing outside wall, so the room was brilliantly lit with sun pouring in from long paned windows.

There was an oak podium in front of the class, and on either side, wide, black chalkboards filled both walls. Directly behind the podium was a thin door and above the door was the clock. The time was four minutes past eight. Someone coughed in the rear of the class.

The little door between the chalkboards opened suddenly and a woman entered. For a moment I thought I recognised her and I felt my heart falter. So Dr Norton was a woman. But was she the woman? But no, I told myself, it couldn't be. I watched my posture, sitting as straight as possible, and picked up my pen. In that second, Dr Norton dropped something on the floor, stopped to pick it up, and I lost sight of her. When she reappeared from behind the podium, adjusting her round, wire-frame glasses and looking quite commanding, I held my breath. It was she. The woman from the jail cell. And she was a vision of health.

She was spectacularly dressed in a pale blue evening dress with a loose, low, round-necked bodice, and short kimono sleeves ending in flounces high at the front. The skirt was full at the hips, narrow and elasticised at the ankles. A single white feather adorned her hair, stuck rather haphazardly through the back of her heavy, thick, mahogany loop. She towered from behind the podium, glanced over the class quickly, gave a swift, perfunctory smile, and cleared her throat. When she spoke, her voice was strong and clear, her delivery a witness to good spirits and vibrancy, familiar in resonance.

"Good morning, everyone. I am Miss Norton and this is an introductory course in logic. Anyone here who shouldn't be, who thought perhaps this was an itinerary of Elizabethan poetry?" There was a pause, though she did not look up from the papers she was busily spreading on the podium. "Good."

My pen was sweating in my hand. It was a fine silver pen etched with tulips and swallows, given to me years ago by my mother just before she left with my youngest brother for Canada. Right now, it was hovering above my notebook with a mind of its own. My minor was Elizabethan poetry. I did not want to be in this position of confidence – to have the dubious privilege of having been a part of her ruse of last night. I felt the flutter of nausea in my stomach and I swallowed.

She looked up toward the back of the class. "To begin, I repeat what I just said, this is *An Introduction to Logic*, course number 371-A. Unfortunately, we can not proceed further with its study until we have performed certain rites of passage, i.e., the roll call. I would like to start with me. My name is Myrl Adler Norton. You are to call me Miss Norton and not Dr Norton, as I do not pretend to know a tibia from a scapula. My office is on this floor, room twenty-five, and I have office hours every afternoon, Monday through Wednesday, from one to three o'clock. If there is an emergency, you can always reach me though the office or by leaving a message with my teaching assistant."

She spoke quickly, succinctly, and for the first time I saw her look at me and I dropped my gaze to the flowers etched on my pen. I was so close to her that in my peripheral vision, I could see her hands reach up and grasp the side of the podium. I heard an almost imperceptible sigh.

"Please introduce yourself." Her voice never changed.

"Shall I stand?"

"Please," she said, waving me up with one hand.

I stood, pen in hand, and said clearly, "My name is Faye Tullis. Faye Martin Tullis."

"And what is your major field?"

"Of study?"

"Yes, yes."

"Theatre arts."

She stared at me as if trying to understand what I just said. "Faye Tullis," she repeated slowly. And then, "Theatre arts." There was a long silence. I started to sit back down, certain my tenure with her was to be short, but she stopped me.

"Remain standing, please, and turn to face the class for a moment so the students may see you."

She then addressed the class without so much as a glance to me. "Faye Tullis is a theatre major who one day hopes to perform Shakespeare in the round in England. She has lived abroad for much of her life and this gives her an outsider's perspective on many issues. She would be a good person to speak with involving personal matters as I have little aptitude in this area." She stopped and frowned slightly. "Faye is a serious student, but is without much sense of humour. She lives at the Martha Wilson House. If you need to meet with her outside her normal office hours, you can catch her in her dorm or in the library most days except Sunday mornings, when she's off at the Riding Club. You may be seated."

All this was rattled off so quickly I was unprepared for her final command and was left standing a moment or two. Miss Norton was frozen, staring straight ahead, her eyes never wavering. I was very confused, trying to remember exactly what I had written on my application for assistantship. And I did so have a sense of humour. I opened my mouth to say something and I realised I didn't know what to say.

"So you will announce your office hours when your own study hours are set? Please be seated, Miss Tullis."

"Oh yes, of course," I said and sat down as quickly as I could.

"And now, for attendance," Miss Norton said, slapping open her roll book and sliding an index finger down the columns. "Martha Tripley Adams."

A young woman stood up from the third row. "Present."

Again, there was a laboured pause, and then the name repeated slowly. "Martha Adams." Miss Norton leaned forward on the podium. "Turn around, please."

Martha Adams obliged and several girls giggled.

"Now, Miss Adams was a seamstress and I stress was – she is not to be persuaded to mend anyone's clothes or fit patterns for some party. She must learn to focus on her studies because her father has brought her up in the strictest of homes and her success here at Smith is very important to him. She enjoys dancing, and should, I think, learn to keep to her room Saturday nights. She is excruciatingly sharp. Please be seated, Miss Adams. Caperton Dawson."

A very round, small woman shaped like a butter-mint with thick, curly blond hair jumped from her seat in the second row. "Present."

"Mrs Dawson has, to the chagrin of her parents and in-laws, decided to first pursue a college degree before embarking on that most demanding of professions: motherhood. Her husband is a thoughtful young man currently serving our country in wartime as a naval officer. She will, no doubt, perform well in class. Forfeiting or delaying a personal goal always makes for a more determined student. You may be seated, Mrs Dawson."

And this went on and on. Each time a student stood Miss Norton would provide a short, precise description, which was always received in silence. Toward the end of the class, I realised she managed to close each profile by inserting encouraging phrases such as: "She will no doubt do quite well," or "There is no doubt in my mind that talent should always be coaxed and polished," or "Her greatest personal reward is her own mind." I couldn't help but believe this last comment referred to herself.

When Miss Norton finished the roll call, there was an incredible, stunned stillness. The sunlight was brilliant, my left arm hot to the touch. The air was electric-everything from the chalkboards to the oak trim on the desks seemed too bright, crisp. Miss Norton took a deep breath, smiled broadly at the class, and adjusted her glasses again. "What I have just accomplished is nothing more than an exercise of the capabilities of a trained mind. I take observations and file them as questions onto little mental note cards, then whisk each card through a prescribed logic loop. Once through the loop the answers become almost mechanical." She closed her eyes and continued. "I have learned to turn premise into question and force observation into answer. When you leave this class in January, you will be able to do the same. Now" – she paused to open her eyes and look at her notes –"the primary text for this class is by Maxwell Jones, *Logic: Its Method and Application*. It is a new edition. Please read the first two chapters for Wednesday's lecture. Questions?" She waited about half a second. "Good. Now, in a spirit of fairness, I will tell you something about myself."

The class stirred, people moving feet under desks, crossing and uncrossing legs: the magnifying glass had been removed, and we could all relax.

"I have been teaching logic at Smith for five years. I schooled at Radcliffe, studying anthropology as an undergraduate and finishing with my doctorate in philosophy at Harvard. My mother died when I was three. She was an opera singer in her youth – I cannot carry a note. My father, a successful lawyer, is now retired and he lives here in town. My parents made a terribly handsome couple. It is unfortunate I received neither of their superior looks."

A titter went through the class.

"I do not like parlour games. Parlour games carry the sting of too many random elements. I do enjoy a good game of patience or solitaire, however. And chess. I adore chess. I will be exquisitely fair in all my dealings with you and I expect the same. We have run out of time. I will discuss grading requirements tomorrow-and don't forget to read the first two chapters."

* * * * *

"Well, I thought I'd never make it through class. How did you do?" asked Rachel, sitting down beside me on my left.

I had invited her to dine with me at Martha Wilson and we were the first ones to sit down. Lunch was served at the tables, fresh flowers were set out, and linen napkins were smartly folded at each place setting. Today's lunch was beef bean soup and finger sandwiches with a fruit cup. I was famished and my poor stomach was grumbling. I have little tolerance for hunger and I was very distracted. Steam from the soup breathed up from my bowl. I plucked a second sandwich from the platter.

"I've got news for you, though," I said, swallowing. "You know that woman who passed out last night in jail?"

Rachel leaned over the table, "Shh. Keep your voice down!"

"All right, all right. Anyway, guess who she is."

29

"Guess?"

"Yes."

"Guess – Guess? I don't know. Why, did you finally realise you knew her or something? You know I thought you did, because she seemed to know plenty about you."

"I didn't know her, but I do now," I said, blowing steam off a spoonful of soup. "She's Dr Norton. The professor I'm assisting."

She looked at me and I could tell she didn't understand.

"You know, that boring logic course I got stuck with this semester. The teacher is that woman from the jail last night." Rachel stared at me. "No! Norton? Oh my. What did you do? Did you just want to die?"

I shook my head. "No, it went quite well, actually."

"And she wasn't strange or anything'"

"Strange? Well now, that's a funny question. I think she is a little strange, but not about last night. One thing's for sure. She's not ill."

Other students were beginning to fill the dining hall and we had to raise our voices slightly. Each table could hold up to six and our privacy would soon be invaded.

"Well, speaking of strange birds, I've got one." Rachel stirred her soup. "My landlady. Her name is Miss Alyssa Dansen. Do you know her? She rents out over on Courtney Place in that huge two story white house with the slate roof near the corner."

I shook my head. I had never lived off campus and was unfamiliar with the rentals in town. I did know that Courtney Place was in a very well-to-do part of Northampton, close to campus and quite desirable.

"Well, I moved in two weeks ago, after my three months in Paris, and I have met the woman who owns it only twice – once to interview, that was last spring, and once to pay the first month's rent."

"Why is that so strange ?"

"Because she lives there too. She lives on the second floor. My apartment is complete with a kitchen and bath and private entrance off the side, but even so, you'd think we'd run into one another sometimes. But we never do. And it's just the two of us in the house. We do all our correspondence through notes dropped in a basket by the staircase. I see her all the time, though, nearly every evening. When I come home from work –"

"Where are you working?"

"At the bootery off Main Street. In fact, she's the one who put in a good word for me there. Now pay attention," she continued. "When I come home from work I see her sitting at her window facing the street, having dinner or just looking out. I used to wave, but she never sees me. Usually the curtains are drawn by eight o'clock or so, so I know she's retired to bed. But she never comes downstairs to speak with me. And she plays this opera music every night. It's driving me crazy."

"She must be a recluse."

"Whatever she is, I think it's more than a bit odd. Watching that street every night-very strange. It's like she's looking out for something."

"It does seem a bit odd."

"Well, I haven't told you half of it."

"There's more?"

She nodded and leaned toward me. "There are dead animals all over the house. Trophies actually. They're everywhere." She leaned back again. "I've never seen anything like it. My father was a hunter but our house was never like this. There are trophies all over – from deer to zebras and –"

"You mean some are exotic?"

"Oh, yes, there's even a gorilla or chimpanzee or some big kind of ape, I don't really know what it is, but it's huge. I'm trying to tell you, it's like living in a museum."

"I'm not too sure I would like living with all those glass eyes staring at me."

"It's not the glass eyes that bother me so much," she said, and here she lowered her voice, "It's that they seem to move."

"They move?"

31

"Someone moves them. It is hard to explain, but they never seem to look quite right. Or the same."

"The place sounds haunted to me." I stood up. Our lunch was over and others needed our seats. Rachel picked up her books as well. "But seriously, Rachel, I'd think about finding another place to live. That is all very strange."

She shrugged. "Well, the rent is cheap, and it's in the nicest part of town. I'll just have to learn to live with ghosts."

Chapter Two

The Distress of Rachel White

It was now exactly three months since my incarceration and the whole episode had faded from memory. Not because of lack of interest or passion, but because too much of what took place played out under a film of exhaustion. There was, in fact, very little I could remember about that first day of class without help from my diary. The hot, moist summer air had turned dry, brilliant with fall colour, leaves dropped, and in those three months the campus turned from lush green, to red-gold and, finally, to the grey of bare bark.

I did not see much of Rachel and though I promised several times, I never had the opportunity to visit her and witness the odd menagerie she lived with. The war had ended, there were speeches, rallies, film strips of our doughboys, talk of shaming Germany forever. Some wanted a complete victory: Pershing marching down the Unter den Linden in Berlin. Those who opposed the war now opposed Germany's political fate. Everyone agreed, however, echoing President Wilson, that there would never be another war. In all this we kept at our studies. Rachel would meet me sporadically at Martha Wilson for meals, gossip, and laments and then embark on her own course. She was studying for a degree in art history. I was to receive a Bachelor of Fine Arts in the spring. And as far as I was concerned, the stage awaited and my future held only promise and opportunity.

I was crossing the Quad, preparing to spend Saturday

33

afternoon reading, when a long shadow wavered on the winter grass beside me, and a now very familiar voice said, "Faye, would you mind coming to my home for tea. I'd like to go over some discussion about next week's lesson."

I couldn't help but notice that though the first sentence was structured as a question, there was no accompanying inflection. It was a statement. This was very much a part of her personality. Though an expert in her field, I decided Miss Norton was a poor teacher. Her manner was not to embroil students in debate and discovery, but rather to regurgitate and lecture. I hoped to bring up this point as a favour to my students, who voiced regular complaints.

I assured Miss Norton she did not have to offer me tea and I would be quite pleased to spend the afternoon with her. I am afraid I was still very much embarrassed our first meeting took place in jail. Though exhilarating for me, imprisonment was obviously humiliating for her. She never mentioned that night in jail. In my subsequent dealings with Miss Norton, efficient manners and a shroud of seriousness were the sentries shielding my confused ego. I knew in my heart she believed as strongly as I did in a woman's right to vote. But for her, jail was obviously not an empowering circumstance – better to have been marching side by side than thrown together in a cell. Her discomfort translated into embarrassment and somehow that embarrassment was a wall blocking my entrance into her good favour. Not that she had been short or unkind to me in our first months together, but she remained aloof and inaccessible, commenting curtly on my observations of classmates, and had little patience with my questions about the learning plan. So this invitation to tea constituted a fresh beginning, a second chance, and a way to engage her outside campus.

She waved a hand to me to follow her, and in an instant we were off campus and walking swiftly toward Hope Street. Her legs were long and I, being rather short, was kept moving at a good clip. As usual, she was dressed in the newest and most exotic fashions, complete with a fiery red turban, complementary mid-calf tunic, slit up the sides, and long black high-button boots. Her only wrap was a short-waisted embroidered quilted affair for which I have no words to describe.

"You understand you may call me Myrl," she said. "Every day it's been Miss Norton this, Miss Norton that, and Myrl will suit me fine. Except, of course, in class."

I, however, did not feel comfortable with this arrangement. My father was a military man, a captain in the navy, and I did not chafe under clear lines of authority. I understood the necessity of order when accomplishing goals.

"New slacks?" she blurted suddenly as if preying on my unease.

I looked down at my black slacks. I was quite proud of them. They were new wool and lined with flannel. But before I could say anything, she burst out again. "So, did you enjoy your stint as a woman in shackles?"

"Excuse me?"

"Your incarceration. Did it meet with your expectations?"

"My expectations?" I did not want to pursue this conversation with her. I had witnessed her act. The confused configuration of trust in having knowledge about her that no one else possessed made me feel, oddly, at her disposal. My fresh beginning was evaporating.

"When we first met. We've never discussed it. Your evening out, shall we say. You and your friend were absolutely glowing with the excitement of ones propelled by mission and conquest."

I smiled. "Yes, I was. We were. It was very exciting, I must admit."

"Yes."

"Well, I wish Emma Goldman had shown up, of course. I heard she was released the next day around noon. Do you know anything about that?"

"Oh really, now," she said quickly, leaning toward me. I smelled the now familiar peppermint on her breath. "I was merely walking across the green in pursuit of some good reading. I didn't even know what you were all shouting about. I thought it was some distraught students complaining about something. Campus food, perhaps. I don't follow this Emma woman. My only crime that night was an early evening penchant for Don Quixote."

I could not believe she did not believe. "You did not come to –"

"For heaven's sake, no. I could never involve myself with so many narrow minds. I don't mean you, of course, or your friend. You were both propelled, you felt a calling."

I thought there was a bit of sarcasm in this. "In a way, yes, I suppose we felt a calling."

"A calling," she repeated and recoiled slightly. We crossed the street in front of a Windsor buggy. "Did it ever occur to you that those who follow a call have no voice of their own? Those women, these suffragettes as they call themselves, I just do not understand their reasoning."

I needed to make my point, but I also needed not to argue with her. I tried to speak slowly, quietly, in counterpoint to my frantic pace. "Our reasoning is simple. We want the right to vote. How is that so difficult to understand?"

She glanced at me and sniffed. "Please do not take offence, Faye," she said as we bounded up the curb, "I was merely stating that I do not understand their thinking, that is all. All the purse strings in the world are held by men, and I do not see their fists loosening. The 'cause' is futile because you do not have any way to change it."

"That's why we want the vote."

We were now in a footrace, and with the exception that I did not have a clue as to where we were going, it seemed we were both straining for the lead.

"Oh, now that's ridiculous." She gestured to the sky, with a broad sweep of her hand. "So they give you the vote. When something is given from a position of power to those not in power, there are so many strings attached that slow strangulation is assured. I repeat: so they give you the vote. What are the benefits of voting?"

"To change that power structure. To make things equal."

"Equal? That, my dear, will never happen. Men cannot and will not represent women. Politicians speak out both sides of their mouths. If they give you the vote, you will not hear the truth about issues-your ears will only ring. They will try to embroil you in their odd little schoolboy fights and legitimise war. They will try to make you believe all the excuses they have for keeping women in a place comfortable for them, and even though you and I may see through their ploy, others of our sex will agree with their ravings. Voting is merely a way of offering complicity in their power against us. It is muddy water, Faye, muddy water."

"I must disagree with you – it is so clear!"

She pointed a long finger at my nose, quite a feat considering our clip. "There is only one clear point in this issue: your mind is free. Your mind is free – it is not bound by men. They have power, but they will never be powerful enough to control the mind."

We were approaching Hope Street and much to my amazement she increased her pace. I was simply dumbfounded, for I felt a great loss, and my opinion of her sank in these few moments. I could sense my own feelings of betrayal beginning to smoulder.

I was quite sharp. "I don't see how you could possibly feel this way."

"Please don't take this so personally, my dear. It just seems to me, that remaining shut out of their world, the world of men, is the only possible alternative to avoiding hypocrisy. I cannot live with hypocrisy. Hypocrisy is one of the major evils of the world. Their world, mind you, and I'll have none of it. I say, let them squabble over banking and property. These are, ultimately, trivial matters. For the woman on her own is the freest of women. Free in her mind."

I could not stand it a moment longer. I knew in my heart she was wrong. "But that is ridiculous. We are bound by the laws of men! We cannot hold certain jobs or own property – how can we be free? "

"Playing by someone else's rules does not mean you have to believe those rules fair and just."

"But these rules are unjustly applied." I was speaking very quickly now, a bad habit I have when I become overwrought.

"The only reason I was in jail that Sunday night was because I exercised what I believe to be my right to free speech and assembly. Our Constitution guarantees freedom of speech."

At this moment she stopped suddenly in front of a white picket fence and in one motion bent over, unlatched the gate, swung it wide, and swept through. I was right behind her.

"And after a night in jail you believe in guarantees?" she said over her shoulder.

I could feel my breath quickening. We were running up the steps to a large two-story brick colonial with black shutters. We were charging the front door.

"Do you realise that I, a grown adult, an American, was forced to spend a night in jail simply because I believe in my Constitution! Forced! In jail!"

We were at the door. A key lay in her hand. She glanced at me momentarily. When she spoke, her voice was deep and low.

"And I," she said, turning the lock, "was not forced to do anything. You suffered needlessly. I enjoyed a cup of warm cream and went to bed."

I stared at her. "Your friend has caught up with us," she announced and pushed open the door.

I turned around. Rachel White was running across the street. Running and looking over her shoulder. She came through the gate and up the walkway.

"She seems to be troubled," said Myrl, and this was true.

"I have to see you, Faye. Now. I'm sorry. Can I come in? I think I should call the police."

"Yes, you may most certainly come in. Are you hurt?" Myrl watched Rachel with the utmost care.

"No. No. I don't think so."

"Rachel, what happened?" I said, growing alarmed by her appearance. Her clothes were crumpled and her hair was messed, but it was her eyes which made me realise the state she was in – they were fearful, worried, too wide and red-rimmed.

"We'll get you some tea," said Myrl. "My father's British and there's always a kettle of hot water for tea in the afternoons. Let's get you some."

She led us through the entryway, through a long dark hall designed during the Federalist period, with a wide staircase yawning in the centre. I noticed a winter coat hanging on the peg rack and dark moody pictures, family portraits, no doubt. The parlour was at the other end of the hall and as we entered, we went from dark to light. The room was full of sunshine, with white plaster walls and tall, deep schoolhouse windows, complete with roomy window seats. There were many plants, and a small parakeet in the far corner chirped from a wrought iron cage. Myrl waved us to a small blue divan next to the birdcage and then disappeared through swinging doors into what I presumed was the kitchen.

"What happened?" I whispered.

"Oh, Faye, you won't believe it. I just ran out of the house and kept running and then I saw you walking down the street. It was fate, Faye, fate."

"So what –"

"Someone broke in and went through all my things!"

"What do you mean?"

"I mean, some thief has been rifling through my personal belongings. Someone's been in my room and everything's a mess, and I think we should be calling the police."

"Rifling through your belongings," repeated Myrl, returning with a tray. She set it down on a small lion's claw table and poured hot water. I noticed how fine the cups and saucers were. From China, tiny and without any handles, the pattern a fine blue of rice fields and farmers, locust blossoms and bamboo. She set tea balls in two of the cups and in hers she dipped a sprig of mint. She passed the cups to us, turned, and sat down in a very old, very worn leather chair.

"I don't think you'll be wanting to call the police just yet, Miss, ah ..." she looked at me.

"Oh, I am sorry. This is Rachel White."

"Yes, Rachel. Not yet. After your stay in prison, you should understand the limits of the police. Was anything taken?" Myrl sat back in her own chair and her long legs stretched out in front of her. Her shoes were missing and her stockinged feet were crossed.

"Well, no. I mean I don't think so. I really didn't have time to check. You see, I'd come home from a study group, unlocked the front door and saw my bedroom door ajar. I didn't think too much about it and fixed myself a biscuit and jam in the kitchen. When I returned the door was shut."

Without removing the sprig of mint, Myrl began sipping her tea.

"Go on. So then you checked your room – very plucky of you."

Rachel smiled and glanced down at the floor. "I thought maybe, finally, it was Miss Dansen."

"The landlady," I interjected.

"But when I opened the door ... oh, what a mess. Everything was out, dumped on my bed."

"What do you mean by everything?"

"All the drawers in my dresser were dumped on the bed and on the floor. The mattress was moved and sheets and covers torn up. Everything's just a mess. A complete jumble. Miss Dansen doesn't have a telephone and I didn't want to stay there. I had this awful feeling there was someone still in the house. And then that's when I thought about Miss Dansen."

"That she might be hurt?"

"Yes."

"And I got really scared, but I walked upstairs and knocked on her door and she answered right away."

"Well, that's a relief," I said.

"Yes, except – well, I can't explain it, but her voice sounded strange."

"Strange." This was a statement from Myrl.

"Well, she is a strange woman, and I've only met her a couple of times, but her voice did sound different somehow – strained." Rachel went on to explain the oddities of the house: the stuffed animals from other countries, the absence of the mistress of the house, the perception she arrived at that the animals were occasionally moved.

"So you heard her voice and were not reassured," said Myrl, bringing the conversation full circle. She closed her eyes, tipped her head back slightly, elbows on the chair arms, and balanced her chin on her fingertips.

"No. And that's when I left the house. I thought maybe she might have gone crazy or something and sacked my room herself."

"And then you saw Faye here, walking with me down the street. Yes. But what is in your pocket that you keep fingering?"

Rachel hesitated a moment and then from her pocket she retrieved a thick gold chain. "I think I should be giving this to the police. It's not mine and I found it on the floor of my room."

"The police," said Myrl, her eyes snapping open, "as my father is so fond of saying, are often incapable of determining the difference between an acorn and a rock. You are doing the right thing, my dear. Now let us see the chain in full light."

Rachel spread the chain on the little table. Myrl did not touch the link of gold but peered at it for quite some time. It was heavy, two strands twisted into a rope.

"Well," she said finally, removing the sprig of mint from her cup and setting it on the saucer, "you were right to seek us first."

"I didn't really seek you –"

"You do need our help. Faye," she commanded, "what do you see? "

I looked at the gold. "Nothing, really."

"No, Faye. Exactly what do you see?"

"I see a gold chain."

"What type of chain?"

It wasn't a necklace or bracelet, but I couldn't come up with an answer.

"It is a watch chain," she urged me along, "which was cast by hand, privately, not for resale."

"Well."

"To be kept by the maker." She smiled at me.

"And you came to this conclusion because …" I paused.

"Because of what is missing," she said gently.

I looked again at the chain. "Because the watch is gone? No. What's missing?"

"The signature of karat. Any gold object sold in the United States must be stamped with the measure of gold to alloy and that stamp is always placed right here." She pointed to the closing clasp. Picking up the chain, she bit one end, and held it up to check teeth marks. "This is very soft, high quality. Probably twenty or even twenty-two karats." She turned to me. "Is there a particular type of watch associated with this kind of spiralled chain?"

"Well, I don't know."

"Nor do I," announced Myrl. "But I do think we should go back to your room, Rachel, and see what else we may find. Faye, I'd like you to keep this safe," she said, nodding in the direction of the chain, and I tucked it in my front pants pocket.

"Oh really, I wouldn't want to put you out," said Rachel, looking very pale.

"You would not, and I cannot stress this enough, be putting me out at all," said Myrl.

There was something in the way she spoke, the deep resonance of drama around these last words that gave me a sudden insight. She spoke them in desperation, as if our little outing was to save her life. I did not understand then how close to the truth I had come.

Chapter Three

In Which a Gun Is Fired

The Dansen home was just across the street and down around the corner, two blocks from Myrl's. It was fast approaching dusk, and I felt a sense of loss – autumn was truly over and the sun was already beginning its nasty tease of setting far too soon. Rachel and I were running along on either side of Myrl, and though the air was cool the brick path was still warm to the touch. Along the street several people had pruned away their flowerbeds, and the blunt, dusty green smell of turned earth and dead flowers streaked the cooling evening air. Though it was only around five o'clock, it was nearly dark. Heavy grey clouds lay overhead.

"Can I ask you something, Myrl?" I said as we hurried along and crossed the street. "How were you able to do that thing at roll call on the first day of class?"

"Thing? Thing? I am not aware of any one thing that I did. Now, Rachel. Exactly when did you arrive home?"

Rachel was having difficulty keeping up with her as well. "Oh," she gasped, grabbing her skirts as we trotted up the curb. "I think it was, oh, it must have been about a quarter past four."

"And this was unusual?"

"Yes, it was. I'm usually not home until five-thirty and on the evenings I work, I'm not in until seven or so."

We rounded the corner and I was on the outside. I felt much as if we were playing crack the whip and I was on the end, being readied for a spin. A low white fence fluttered by as we came down the home stretch.

"Which house is it?" I asked. The light was fading to dirty grey.

"The fifth one down on the right, across the street."

"Right," announced Myrl and we made another dash off the curb. That is, Rachel and I dashed – Myrl never seemed hurried in the least bit. Suddenly, in the middle of the street she stopped and held up a hand. "Now wait. Rachel, you've told both Faye and me that you haven't seen your landlady, this Dansen woman, since you took up lodging with her."

Rachel nodded, breathing hard. "Yes, I haven't –"

"Have you heard her speak?"

"Speak? Well, yes, just a while ago."

"No, I mean before that. In these last few months. Have you heard her sing, talk, whistle. Talk to the postman? Anything at all?"

"You mean without actually seeing her, have I overheard her?"

"Precisely."

"Well, yes, I think I have." An automobile pulled away from the road curb. It was a roadster and I urged my companions forward. The automobile roared by and I saw pure irritation on Myrl's face.

"I hate those things," was all she said. Then she was back to Rachel. "Are you certain? Give me an example. Tell me what you heard."

Rachel thought for a moment and then turned first to me and then to Myrl, shaking her head. "I can't say."

"You mean you have not heard her at all."

"Yes. You're right. I haven't heard a thing. Not her speaking to neighbours, not even a cough. Nothing. Not even the pipes upstairs or her brushing her teeth. I'd never really thought about it before, but it's really quite strange, isn't it? I do hear the phonograph every night. Some opera piece, an aria she plays all the time."

"And you see her every day," I reminded both of them. It seemed to me everything was growing mysterious and obtuse for no reason. "Maybe she's just a very quiet person," I said to Myrl.

"Now why would that be?" she responded, absently stopping and gazing down the street at the house. We were two lots away, and the house certainly appeared innocuous. A simple white Gothic revival with black shutters and a perfect gable over the front, lovely, glossy, box-bushes on either side of the door and empty flowerboxes along the front windows. A ratty little mongrel dog with tufts of reddish fur sticking every which way came trotting down the path toward us. I sighed. The soles of Myrl's shoes made a gritty sound as she began walking slowly down the sidewalk. When she spoke to Rachel, her voice was low, intense, and filled with a gravity I did not understand. Her long hands were pressed together as if in prayer and she tapped the tip of her nose with her fingertips.

"Let me confirm the following: you have not physically seen Alyssa Dansen downstairs in three months – since you've taken up residing in her home. You have not heard from her in that time. Yet you see her virtually every evening gazing out from her window –"

"Yes, yes, yes," said Rachel, still breathless, only now it was not just from exertion. "Like now, look. I can see her right now."

I looked to where Rachel was pointing.

It was a ghostly image. From the second-story corner window overlooking the side yard where we stood, I could see the profile of a dark-haired woman sitting quietly, looking straight ahead out onto the street.

"Because it's a corner room, you can see her from both the side and front of the house," said Rachel. "She just sits there, with the light on, eating supper, and then she'll draw the curtains around eight o'clock or so."

A soft white sash covered the window so it was difficult to make out the details of the woman's dress or her movements, but she was definitely sitting forward in her chair, looking for someone or watching for something.

"She sits like this every night?" I asked Rachel.

45

"Almost without exception."

I shivered.

Myrl abruptly turned to us and held up her hand again. Her voice was nearly a whisper. She did not look at us, but stared at the ground. "There is something terribly wrong here. You must both do exactly as I say, without question. I mean exactly, or we will all be in terrible trouble. I want you two to go this instant and –"

At that moment, the sound of a single gunshot – loud, violent, completely unearthly – ricocheted from the house and across the side yard. In the silence which followed, not a breath was taken, not a hair moved, not a flicker of consciousness shimmered between us. I was struck deaf and dumb.

With a sudden dramatic lunge, as if breaking surface from under deep water, Myrl began running toward the house. I was lost for a moment and then I grabbed Rachel's shoulder, "Come on," I yelled, and for whatever reason, whatever faith Myrl instilled in us, it caused us to follow her.

We were abreast of the house and I could hear yelling in the street.

"Myrl, look!" I said. The front door was opening and there before us stood a man not twenty feet away with a pistol in his hand. He was roughly dressed with a leather jacket and wool pants and bright red hair, which stuck out from underneath a very worn leather hat. Rachel screamed and the man ran down the steps, leapt over the box-bushes, nearly knocking Myrl over, and lit off down the walkway.

"Forget him," said Myrl and she raced up the steps. Then we were inside. The house smelled odd, like strong chemical dust, and in the front hall stood a bear, well over six feet, front paws extended out to forever attack intruders. I was momentarily startled, though Myrl seemed hardly to notice. She found the staircase and we all took them two at a time, not knowing what we would find, certain there would be blood. The thought that I might see a dead body never had time to seed in my brain. I rounded the corner in the upstairs hall with Myrl, and Rachel called from behind, "Second door on the left."

Myrl turned the doorknob. It was locked. She fiddled with the lock for a second and then threw her weight against the door, but it held firm. Part of her magnificent hair slipped from its knot. "Faye, you and me together. Put your shoulder to it," she said and I turned swiftly. With my back to hers, we heaved ourselves against the door. It gave slightly and I heard the jamb rip.

"Again," she ordered and again we threw our weight against it. The door snapped open with a loud crack and I nearly tumbled across the thick woollen rug. The room was lit by a chandelier in the centre of the ceiling. There was a brash floral wallpaper all in reds and purples, and the smell of crushed roses and spices in water.

Sitting quietly in a wicker chair with a tray in front of her was Alyssa Dansen. There was no blood. At least as far as I could see. Her body was not slumped. She never turned her head. Myrl touched my arm and walked past me to face Miss Dansen.

"Rachel, I want you to go downstairs and lock the front door. The police will be here in just moments and no one else should be allowed in here."

"But, but I think we –"

"Just go, Rachel. Now. Hurry before some neighbour lands in the dooryard. And I want you to stay there and let the police in when they come."

Rachel left and I could hear her running downstairs when Myrl said to me, "Come, Faye, I don't believe this will be unsightly for you."

Now, I have seen dead bodies in India, lined in shallow graves, the graves always appearing smaller than I thought they should be, and I once saw a man killed in a sword fight on the streets of Bombay when I was twelve. I have lived an adventuresome life, actually. For years, my mother lived abroad, caring for a sickly younger brother. As a consequence, I was raised by my older brother and a father, both of whom seemed to not notice my gender was supposed to be of the fairer. But to see death as a result of murder – to see death where only moments ago there was life …

"Come, Faye." Her eyes were a cool, depthless grey as she watched me cross the room.

I knew the woman must be dead, but I feared for what I would be forced to see. I came around slowly, and glancing up, I saw an odd system of ropes and pulleys set up against the sash on the window. As I lowered my eyes I saw a woman, quite pale, but with a kind of jaundiced complexion, staring straight ahead with eyes that looked nearly glass. Her face was unscathed, her thick black hair neatly curled, cropped short and waved. She was indeed dead, she had to be dead, and yet she seemed alive. Her pose was so very natural. I looked at her body and again there was no blood. I knelt down and gave a short gasp. Across her neck, curved from ear to ear was a monstrous slash, badly stitched with black thread, the skin gathered and puffed, the edges of the wound overlapping.

My mind was unfocused and I could not think for a moment. "What about the shots we heard? And that man? She's dead, isn't she?"

"Of course she's dead." Myrl was scrutinising the woman, without ever touching her. "Look behind her ear."

"What?"

"Look behind either ear," she said.

I bent down to get closer to the woman's head and looked behind her right ear. "I don't see anything at all."

Myrl peered behind the left ear and then shut her eyes and straightened up. "It is as I feared," she said simply and I quickly came around to look for myself. But I was still confused. I heard knocking on the door downstairs. The police had arrived.

"I don't understand."

"What do you see, Faye." Again, her tone was that of a statement, not a question.

"A hole."

"Correction. A gunshot wound."

"Well ... but there is no blood." She sighed heavily and looked very weary. She rubbed her eyes. "What is there instead?"

I bent down to take a second look. "I don't know, really. It looks almost like sand or –"

"Don't touch!"

I withdrew my hand.

"It is sawdust, Faye. Sawdust." Myrl paused and looked out the window, following the sightless gaze of the dark glass eyes. "The body has been filled with sawdust. The bullet went in behind the ear and came out –"she gazed along the front of the skull and then reached up with a finger and pointed at a spot about two inches above the hairline over the right temple "– here."

Above the black curl of the woman's bangs, as if someone had spilt ash on her, was the light sprinkle of sawdust.

*　*　*　*　*

"I am sorry to keep you ladies here so late. I know you must be exhausted," said Detective Frank Lorey.

"And famished," snapped Myrl. The bells of Smith began chiming eight o'clock. We were all sitting in the room where the body was found. Detective Lorey was standing and there were other officers coming and going. I did not pay much attention to the bustling around us.

Lorey, a thin man of average height and curly black hair peppered with white, looked at Myrl and then back to his little yellow pad of paper. His street clothes were neat and official, an overcoat and shirt of dark wool and grey tweed pants, all smelling softly of mothballs. It was, after all, the first really cold evening of the season. He scribbled a note to himself with the tiny stub of a chewed pencil and glanced back at Myrl. I could tell she had been irritating him all evening. I was realising the limits to Myrl's patience were definitive.

Myrl slipped a peppermint into her mouth and stared out the window. From where Rachel, Myrl, and I sat, on the divan by the side windows, we could still see out across the street. The bedroom was small. Beside Alyssa Dansen's bed and dressing table there was a standing Sheraton armoire, a sewing table, and a small table to the left of the door with a phonograph on top. Dust was thick on every surface. Roses, long wilted and dried, stood in a long brown knot in a glass vase on the mantel. The body had been removed and all that was left of the grisly sight was the wicker chair with a peacock pattern woven in the back where the body had been posed.

Lorey paused for a moment and looked again at the odd arrangement of rope around the window. Draping the perimeter of the window were two long pieces of twine, each with small sandbags at either end and held in place by two pulleys at the top left- and right-hand corners of the window. In the middle of the window frame, on top, was a gear mechanism with a slender rod, which was attached to a fine fishing line connecting the tops of the curtains, an interesting device, which Myrl already investigated and formed conclusions about. To me it looked just like the weights of a clock and I surmised it was some kind of timing device. A faint ticking from the gears notched small increments of time.

"I think I'd like to go home now," said Rachel. "I mean, I'll stay with some friends of mine at the school." I knew Rachel had some close friends at Talbot Hall and assumed she would spend the night there.

Lorey was peering out between the curtains, obstructing our view, when Myrl said, "I suggest you step away from the window, Mr Lorey."

"Excuse me?"

The bells echoed in the distance ... seven ... eight. As the last chime rang, a weight from one of the sandbags suddenly fell, the gear above the window made a quiet grating noise, the slender rod jerked out, and the drapes suddenly snapped shut. Lorey jumped back. The gear locked and the quiet ticking began again. At that moment there was another clicking sound and the phonograph against the far wall switched on. Rachel half rose.

"That's the piece, that's the piece of music."

The sudden music was loud, violent and intimidating, and as a woman's disembodied voice swelled in the spaces between us, I shivered.

Lorey walked over and quickly turned the phonograph off. "You will find another mechanism to lift the record and carry the needle arm across," said Myrl, still looking out the window.

Lorey bent over and squinted at the phonograph. Then he came back to us and watched Myrl very carefully. "Now how did you know all that was going to happen –"

"Mr Lorey," she began, not addressing him directly, but rather speaking to the room in general, "Rachel White has already told us that at eight o'clock the drapes close. Every night. How can the drapes close if there is no one to close them?"

"But that's the way it's been since I moved in months ago," said Rachel, sitting back down. She seemed a little feverish and her colour was very bad. She pressed a hand to her forehead.

"Precisely. The body has been here for a long time."

"Oh God," said Rachel. "You mean I've been living here all this time with her like that? But who's been taking my rent money? And when the pipes broke someone took my note and called a plumber."

"Yes, and someone has to sort of wind this thing," said Lorey. "Or put the weights back." He gazed at the system of pulleys again.

Myrl looked directly at Rachel. "Well, it's simple. Whoever did this has been vigorously keeping a charade that Alyssa Dansen is alive. You'd made arrangements last spring to rent from her, you were unavailable all summer because you were overseas, so the murderer had no choice but to run as go-between and use the basket in the hall as a means of communication."

"I really must go and I feel faint. I don't think I can stand it here a moment longer." Rachel stood and looked down at her hands. Lorey smiled. "You may go, but let me get you an escort. You'll have to exit through the backyard. Reporters are thick in the front and they're going to try and grab a scoop. Try to say nothing until you hear from me, all right? This is gruesome, gruesome business and the fewer rumours we have spreading around, the better." He lifted his head and called, "Perkins!" and a young man in a blue uniform entered the room. I saw his billy club and pistol and looked away.

As soon as they were out the door, Lorey reached down and lifted the peacock chair in one smooth, careless motion. He swung it around and sat straddling it, facing us. I realised with a start that no one had mentioned finding the gold chain and I glanced at Myrl nervously.

"Now, for you two. You seem to be made of tougher stuff. I want to know again why you were both so keen on coming here." Myrl gazed out the window as if in a trance.

I cleared my throat. "When Rachel came to us, she seemed very upset," I began.

But Myrl wanted to correct Lorey once more. "Let me assure you that Rachel White has suffered a shock, a justifiable shock, but one she will recover from shortly. Your comment about toughness is ridiculous and vapid."

Lorey whistled under his breath. "Okey-dokey. I'm sorry if I offended. I think we're all a little tired and in just a bit you can both go home. Now, getting back to where I was." He looked at me.

I began again, "She came to us because –"

"Yes, yes, I know all that. Someone was snooping in her room. But why didn't you call the police? Why come here on your own? Very brash of you both, I must say."

"I saw no danger and therefore took no risk," said Myrl, speaking very quickly. "I would never lead my friends into an unfortunate situation, Mr Lorey. My failure was in not foreseeing the extent of the crime committed – and that was not at all evident from what Rachel had told us." Myrl swung her gaze from the window to Lorey without blinking.

"No danger? No danger? What about the gunshot Miss Norton? Does that ring a bell? Excuse me." He coughed and began again slowly. "When you heard the shot and saw the man running away, you ran inside the house. That was quite brash, Miss Norton. And quite foolish."

This was not a description that suited Myrl and she blinked very slowly at him with one eyebrow cocked high. I could feel her holding her breath.

"I can't tell you," he paused and shook his head. "I don't know what you were thinking."

"Of course you don't and you never will," she snapped tartly and crossed her legs. "Mr Lorey, I had already deduced the woman was dead before we heard the gunshot."

"Oh, you did. I see. Well. How did you figure that out?" He smiled and it suddenly struck me that he thought she was a confabulator.

"Rachel White explained she had heard nothing. Absolutely nothing from the woman's living quarters except that bit of opera every night. No one lives that quietly, Mr Lorey, especially someone from the theatre."

"The theatre?" I said.

"Yes, Alyssa Dansen was with a theatre troupe. I saw her perform on campus last year. Anyway, the fact that there were no sounds, the fact that Rachel only saw her from a distance, the fact that the drapes close every night at the same time, and music played, all seemed very ominous to me. The stranger with the gun complicates things and it was his arrival on the scene I did not foresee."

"You were sure doing a lot of thinking on one little walk," he said, closing his notepad.

"I am paid to think, Mr Lorey." She looked out the window again. I watched my feet. After a moment's pause, she continued. "I am sorry, Mr Lorey, for all my banter. I am completely exhausted and sickened by this. I need to go home and have a hot supper. I am sure if you need to speak with me again, you will reach me at my home. You have the address and telephone number." She stood up and so did he.

He opened his note pad briefly and glanced again at the address she had given him earlier. "Yes, I know your father. A good man, and a fine attorney."

"Thank you, Mr Lorey. Now I feel I really must go."

"Why, Miss Norton, this is incredibly shocking – it's shocking for all of us. I just don't want you running, literally, into trouble again." He smiled. "You can go too, Miss Tullis – oh, do I have your address?"

"I'm at the Martha Wilson House," I said. "On campus."

Lorey escorted us down the stairs and was lining up two escorts for us. "Oh, that won't be necessary," said Myrl. "Faye will be spending the night at my home tonight."

"Oh – okay. Then you'll just need one –"

"It's really not necessary. I only live a block or so away, Mr Lorey, and I'm not –"

Lorey was not taking her refusal well. I nudged her arm.

"Oh, I guess I do feel rather weak," she said, sounding perfectly fine, but she held out a hand and leaned against the wall for just a moment. "Perhaps an escort would be welcome. I am a proud woman, you understand, Mr Lorey." She sniffed.

"Yes, I think I do," he said.

* * * * *

It was when the front door slammed shut and the hall light was lit and I saw the long brooding paintings on the wall that I thought I might cry. Myrl shut the door firmly in the face of the officer standing on the front step and graciously draped an arm across my shoulders. She patted my arm gently and with great care, but said not a word. She seemed very mature then, much older than myself.

"Father! I'm home," she called, and then to me, "You can wash up in the kitchen, there's no downstairs bath."

"You live with your father?" I said and she stared at me. It took me a few moments to realise what I said required no response. "What are you going to tell him?"

She smiled. "I hide very little from my father and you should do the same. Now, go wash up. The kitchen is straight ahead and I'll be right down in a minute. Father's held dinner, no doubt." With that, she turned and went up the stairs and I was left alone in the hall.

I walked through to the end of the corridor, made a jog to the left, and found a door. As I pulled the door open, the sweet smell of candied yams and turkey warmed the cool night air which had seeped into the hall with our entry.

The kitchen was small, everything done in black and white, with a chequered tile floor, white porcelain stand-alone sink and black cutting counter. There was a small table next to a shallow fireplace and two chairs. There, sitting in one of the chairs reading the afternoon paper was an elderly man with thick, absolutely white hair. He was reading without glasses, head tilted back, his carriage erect. He seemed in very good health, lowering the paper when I stepped in, smiling and rising immediately with his right hand outstretched.

"You must be Faye."

When he came forward into the light I saw how refined his features were and when he spoke I heard a strength in his voice. There was no mistaking the British elocution and upper-class emphasis on my name. We shook hands – and he shook my hand as he would another man's, firmly, decisively, palm to palm.

"Yes, how do you do. Myrl's coming right down, she said."

He pulled out the second chair from the edge of the table. "Of course. Here, sit." He smiled again as I sat down. "I'm Godfrey Norton, Myrl's father."

Chapter Four

Detective Lorey Pays a Visit

"This is so terrible to have happened right here in town. Or anywhere. Such an atrocity." Godfrey Norton was spooning chocolate pudding into bowls. We were finishing dinner around the small porcelain table by the fireplace. Before I sat down, I did not think I could eat a bite as I was so sickened by the afternoon's events. But Godfrey was quite congenial, comforting, in a vigorous way, and the yams and hot turkey were very good. In the end, I was able to help myself to seconds without having to forfeit interest in the pudding. Myrl ate very little and though I could see that Godfrey was concerned, he said nothing to her. He reminded me in part of my own father – allowing my older brother and me to do as we wished, watching with disinterest from afar. But with Godfrey, I sensed he strained against every fibre not to interfere with Myrl's way of life.

"Yes. It is. And I am hard pressed to believe that any human being could violate nature like that and perform such a heinous act upon another. It is hideous. Debased." Myrl set down her fork.

"Well. It's over now. The police and Detective Lorey, right? Yes, well, he'll take care of things. I bet we read next week that the murderer is found." Godfrey stopped spooning and took a sip of wine. I was grateful Prohibition was denied yet again this year and raised my glass as well.

"We shall see," said Myrl. "Since when did your opinion of

the police change?" She looked very young sitting by the fire next to her father. She was a good head taller than he. It suddenly occurred to me that with the exception of the way she carried herself, she did not take after him at all. "Now, I know Lorey. He's a good man," said Godfrey, passing out spoons for the pudding.

"Oh yes," I said, remembering. "You are a lawyer. I forgot."

"Retired," he said smiling. "Like the pudding?"

I nodded.

"Do?" Myrl said absently. "I don't know if there is anything anyone can do." She pushed her plate away.

"I said this was an atrocity," said Godfrey. "I wasn't asking you to do anything."

I was feeling quite robust and well fortified. "We could investigate this ourselves," I said, nodding in pleasant agreement to Godfrey's tipping the wine bottle into my glass. I noticed that while Myrl did not drink, Godfrey was keeping me good company, matching me two for two.

Godfrey seemed suddenly distraught and glanced quickly at Myrl as he poured my third glass of wine.

"Well," he said almost nervously, "I really think this ghastly mess is for the police to clear up, Faye. I mean really. For God's sake, there's a whole science to these things nowadays."

Myrl said nothing.

That night, after the dishes were done up, Myrl prepared herself a teacup of warm cream and showed me to their guest room. The bedroom was upstairs, right next to hers. It was quite nice, small, with a low ceiling and simple furnishings: a nightstand, a dresser, washstand, and a double bed. Now I have slept on dirt floors, woven straw mats, hammocks, train cars, and even on the hump of a camel. But this was to be the first time I was to sleep in a bed large enough for a queen. Myrl had laid out a flannel nightgown and a towel to wash with. The flannel nightgown was so long I had to laugh. I pushed the sleeves up past my elbows and watched my feet disappear under a good foot of extra cloth. But in an odd way

I felt very comforted that night. The flannel smelled of peppermint.

The next morning I rose at nine o'clock, washed, brushed my teeth, dressed, and wandered downstairs. I say 'wandered' because I really did feel at home, as if this house were mine. I attributed this feeling of ease to Godfrey's hospitality. I found a pot of coffee in the kitchen and cream and sugar set out on the little white table. In the morning light, the hall was lit and so I found myself perusing the portraits on the walls, sipping coffee and feeling in remarkably good spirits. I was also terribly excited. The flutter in my stomach was keeping me from breakfast. I wanted to go find Rachel. We needed to talk.

"So what do you think?" It was Godfrey letting himself in through the front door. He nodded toward the paintings. "Dour lot, aren't they? The only spark up there comes from those two. That's Irene there in the blue dress and her mother's in white."

I looked to where he was pointing, up on the right-hand side. There was a portrait of two women, both slightly built, small and elegant. The elder, in a white dress of lace, sat in a large chair. The younger woman, standing next to the chair with one hand resting on its spine, was obviously her daughter. She wore a floor-length blue satin gown and long matching gloves. There was the same tilt of the jaw, the same texture and style of hair, upswept into a rolling bun along the nape of the neck-simple and charming. Irene Adler's beauty was magnified by grace and intelligence. Godfrey pointed out the bear rug on the floor, in front of the women in the painting.

"Irene hit that one between the eyes," he said. "She was very proud of that. Did it at thirty feet."

I peered closely with great interest. I am something of a good shot myself and usually feel an affinity to women who can shoot true.

"And she sang? Opera, isn't that right?"

"Oh Lord, yes," he said. "She was very popular in England and Europe. She was very well known, famous. She retired from the stage before we left England."

"And you've never returned?"

"Oh no."

My gaze shifted to the row of paintings.

"The rest of these dreary things are of my family. Solicitors mostly, and crabby women. A foul group, really."

I laughed. Their faces were certainly not convivial. But that was the style then. There was a mystery around the paintings, however, that I did not understand. Something seemed amiss and it went beyond the solemn expressions and reserved poses of the subjects. There was something to be discovered in these paintings.

"Myrl's out on her walk, but she should be back any moment. Would you like an omelette?"

Breakfast was delightful. Myrl entered the kitchen just as Godfrey was slipping eggs onto our plates, and she seemed very excited. She took off her Russian-style three-quarter-length coat with the high, round Cossack neck to reveal a tailored grey costume positively conservative. I note her clothing only because I found her penchant for style so amusing. Her face was flushed and she all but slapped me on the shoulder when she demanded to know how I had slept.

"Great," I answered.

"I could have told you that," she said, and she and Godfrey burst out laughing. He poured me a cup of coffee and she had her sprig of peppermint for tea. Her shoes were off again, and in white cotton stockings her feet appeared quite large.

I felt slightly at the butt of some little joke and so I tried to pin her down with a question she had earlier evaded: "I want to know how you knew so much about me the first day of class."

"What are you talking about?"

I saw Godfrey smiling.

"Oh, Myrl, how did you know I ride? That I love horses? That I am a theatre major?"

Myrl stopped smiling and leaned forward. "I told you. Logic. Let me see." She thought back. "That day you wore a linen pleated skirt, matching jacket, and a plain white shirt. You carried a pen and a notebook. The night before, in that horrible jail, you wore the same outfit, except there was horse manure on your right shoe, inside the heel, and by the way you held me as I 'fainted', I could tell you had strength in your hamstring muscle. I also noticed the slight stain on the outside of each index finger caused by leather reins. Obviously, you rode often. The Riding Club is only free to all students on Sundays. Because you do not wear gloves when you ride and because of your pen, I assumed you were not of the means to join the club and therefore would be forced to take advantage of the Sunday morning open slot."

"My pen?"

"Pens are given as gifts. Your pen was of great expense but your dress was not – clearly your parents gave you this writing implement at some point in your life, probably just before you began at Smith. This gift demonstrates education and writing are worth expensive symbolisation in your family – assuming more importance than, say, fancy clothing. The pen was probably not purchased at a sacrifice, but is outside the realm of what they would usually spend."

She was right. On all counts.

"And what about the other students? With most of them you couldn't see their shoes, or their hands or whatever – they were too far away to get any real impression. So how did you do that?"

"It is not a trick, you know, Faye."

"I know, I know, it's logic."

"So how did I know when I could not possibly have seen the clues? Remember Roper's principles."

I paused. "You came to your conclusions by different means."

"Yes." She glanced at her father. "I actually read the personal narratives of my students, the narratives everyone must write to enter the school. I have a good memory for the written word."

"A photographic memory," corrected Godfrey, swallowing coffee.

"Well, –"she waved a hand "– some may say."

"So you just got it all … from student notes?" This was not as exciting.

"Yes. But wasn't it a nice effect?" She smiled over her peppermint tea.

"But in jail. You came up to me and said I was in the theatre –"

"No, I tempered my statement by saying you had an interest in the theatrical."

"Well. But still. How could you have guessed?"

"My dear. That was done without a clue. I was trying to flatter you into my confidence. Virtually everyone is enamoured of the theatre these days. What young college woman, self-possessed, and caught in the throes of leftist politics, would not be interested in the theatre? The stage is the pallet of politics. And then once I realised how squarely I had hit the mark, I simply pursued the direct line of thinking."

"And you then determined I would probably want to do Shakespeare in the round." I nodded my head. I could see the suppositions she made. She was truly amazing.

"Precisely. You are attractive, bright, well read, and there was no reason to assume you would shirk from a lead in Shakespeare. And those who are serious about theatre seem to always aspire to do Shakespeare in the round."

Suddenly, the bell rang over the front door. Godfrey once again appeared nervous. He glanced at Myrl and sat back in his chair. I could tell he was pretending to read the paper. Myrl grew composed and set down her cup. "That would be Mr Lorey, I'm sure," she said quietly.

* * * * *

"I'm just checking in with everyone this morning," Lorey said. We were sitting in the parlour on the east side of the house. On the west side was a formal living room, but given

Godfrey's acquaintance with Lorey and the intimate nature of the call, the parlour seemed a better spot. The canary in the birdcage sang when we four entered, and I took my seat again on the divan. Godfrey took a seat near the kitchen and Myrl sat herself squarely in the overstuffed chair across from me. Lorey stood.

"Now according to Miss White, and I confirmed this statement just an hour ago, she claims to have heard the victim speak about thirty minutes before the shot was fired," he continued.

"Yes, I am interested in that myself, Mr Lorey," said Myrl, sitting on the edge of her chair, back straight, hands folded in her lap. "What was said, exactly?"

"Let's see." Lorey flipped through his yellow pad for a moment. "Ah. Here it is, 'I said' – this is Rachel White speaking –'I said, "Miss Dansen, are you all right in there?" and she answered me after a moment by saying, "All is well," in a strange little voice.' It's quite obvious the murderer was still in the room."

"Obviously," said Myrl, smiling at him.

He smiled broadly. "You see, Miss Norton, that wasn't the murderer in the room."

"No?"

"No. Remember, the woman was already dead. So the fellow who shot her did not know she was dead. He thought he was committing murder."

"You are very clever, Mr Lorey." She folded her arms.

"Well," he began and glanced at her, sniffed and went back to his notes. "My concern is you two. That fellow who fired the shot is guilty by motive and deed. Though he did not actually commit the murder, he must be caught and tried. The room was locked from the outside. This means he had a key. So he knew her – he might be instrumental in finding out who did commit the crime. I want you both to try and remember anything at all about him. Any minor detail you might have left out. Miss Tullis?"

I began ticking items off, trying to remember what I said yesterday. "Well, as I said before, he seemed not well-to-do.

His clothing was dirty and torn. He was of average height. He had a large hat pulled low across his face and bright red hair. The hair was curly and full. I can't remember how long it was. Not too long, I guess. And he had a red beard as well. I heard one shot. Loud. Saw him on the step a moment later with the gun. And then he jumped off the stoop and ran up the street. That's really all I remember about him."

Lorey did not write anything down in his pad. I knew he wouldn't as my answer to his question did not add anything to yesterday's report.

"Now you, Miss Norton. And Miss Norton, I want you to be very honest. Is there anything about the man or the events of yesterday that you want to share with me?"

"Mr Lorey," she said and gave him such a stare. "You are accusing me of an oversight?"

"Let me be frank with you. Rachel White claims to have given you something yesterday, a chain. A gold chain, Miss Norton."

"Oh that," she said, waving her hand and relaxing back in her chair. "That was nothing. I don't even know what happened to it. Didn't you keep that, Faye? Didn't Rachel give it to you? You see, Mr Lorey, I am only good at mind games – I fail at the little practicalities of where things are and who put things where."

"She can hardly find her shoes," said Godfrey from the end of the room and went back to his paper. "I don't have it," I said, reaching in my pocket. And I didn't. "It must have fallen out when we broke the door down."

Detective Lorey closed his eyes for a moment.

Myrl tried to appease him. "Now, Mr Lorey, given our description of the intruder, it seems doubtful that the valuable gold chain could belong to him."

"Ladies. Please. That is for me to determine. If you come across any oddities again, will you bring them to me and not stuff them in your pockets."

"Lorey, they did as best they could," said Godfrey from the back. "I should remind you these are ladies with female sensibilities."

I looked at Godfrey, but he was back to his paper.

"I believe this chain might be very important to this case. I want you two to call me if you can think of any other bit of information. Even something which seems unimportant. Especially you, Miss Norton." He paused and made an attempt at small talk. "I understand you work at the college."

"I teach, Mr Lorey." Myrl stared at him. Chitchat was not her strength.

"Yes. Well." He closed his little pad of paper again. "If you do, by chance, find that chain, I want you to give it to me."

"I'm sure it fell out. I put it right in my pocket," I said, checking once more to be sure.

"I will have the fellows look around the door over there. Goodbye, Godfrey. It was good seeing you again. I hope we can get together under less ominous circumstances one day."

Godfrey tipped back the upper corner of his newspaper and then folded it and stood.

"Good day, Frank. I'll keep my daughter in tow, don't you worry," he said and the two men shook hands. Godfrey led Lorey out the front.

The instant the men left the room Myrl shot like an arrow out of her chair and sat next to me on the divan.

"Next weekend, will you travel with me to Brattleboro?"

I knew of the town. It was up north, just over the border, in Vermont. I had heard of the water cures and Island Park, both in Brattleboro, but other than that, I knew little of the town. I paused for only an instant. "Certainly. I mean, of course. But why?"

"Oh, I do like your answers, Faye," she said and jumped off the sofa. "I am just exhilarated by this." She flung open the middle pane of glass and leaned out the window. It had begun to snow lightly, and chilly air swept the room. The canary chortled. "I returned to the Dansen house early this morning."

"What!" I was both shocked by what she had done and dismayed I had been left behind.

"Yes. Well. I went and managed to get myself in. There was just one fellow guarding the place – so I was able to sneak in through the back. Anyway, all that is not important. I went upstairs to look at the scene of the crime." She tipped her head back and brushed a finger under her nose. "Yes, an interesting thought. It's not truly the scene now, is it? The scene was really somewhere else and played out over several locations. Anyway –" she waved her hand –"I thought I recognised the voice on the phonograph and I was correct. Her name is Mary Howe, an old friend of my mother's. She's long retired now and lives in Brattleboro. She only had a few of these records made and so I assumed she must have been an acquaintance of Miss Dansen·s."

"Or Alyssa received the record as a present or something," I said. "Or bought it second hand."

"Correct," she continued, undaunted. "So I tried to check the sleeve, to see if there was any notation on it proving they were friends. You know, like 'To Alyssa with all my best'. And there was none. No sleeve to be found anywhere in the house."

"What does that mean?"

"It's not her record. Whoever set up the phonograph to play precisely after the drapes closed, put the record on and took the sleeve with them. Or destroyed it."

"But why get rid of the sleeve?"

"I don't know. Obviously the killer did not expect visitors in her room. He was waiting for the right moment to dispose of the body. But there would always be the threat of being found out. So my guess, and this is just a guess, is that the sleeve was inscripted, but inscripted with something incriminating."

"But why not just use one of her own records?"

"Precisely," she said and stepped away from the window. "Faye, there was not a single phonograph record in the entire house. Obviously, Alyssa Dansen did not own a phonograph! The machine and the record belong to the killer."

"You are amazing," I said. "So now we are going to Vermont, to see this friend of your mother's. This will be exciting."

Myrl stood and began talking to herself in a kind of mutter. She walked back to the open window, reached out and closed the sash. "We must be very careful ..."

But there was a piece missing. "So what happened to the chain?"

"Very good, Faye. I'm proud of you. I took one more careful look at it –"

"And you dropped it in the house this morning." I was nodding as I realised how unfaltering her actions were. And then I understood what she must have done. "You came into my room last night and plucked that chain from my pocket!"

"This morning," she corrected me, "before sunup. You looked very peaceful."

I was shaking my head.

"And then I went there and tossed it on the stairs," said Myrl.

"God, how I loathe that man," said Godfrey, coming through the door. "What about the stairs?"

"Only minutes ago you were saying how great he was and the murderer would be found in a week." Myrl stood with her hands on her hips.

Godfrey sighed. "I find his manner irritating," he said and poked his finger in the birdcage. "What was I hearing about the stairs?"

"Oh, that slip of chain Detective Lorey was complaining about. He'll find it now on Alyssa Dansen's staircase."

"You went back, then?" Godfrey's face soured slightly.

Myrl seemed unaware of any change in her father's manner. "Yes, and I discovered a very interesting bit of information."

Godfrey shook his head slowly from side to side. "Myrl. I would hope you might think twice before involving yourself."

"Oh, Father, for crying out loud," she said suddenly. "Don't dither about." She left and went into the kitchen. In a moment we could hear running water in the sink.

He stared after her, at the door leading out to the kitchen. Then he sighed and sat down slowly next to me on the divan.

It was the first time since I had met him that I saw him as an old man.

I felt terrible for him. He seemed very sweet, really, and vulnerable and though I am young, I had a flash of what it must be like to be a parent and to have had to raise such a headstrong individual.

"You are the first person Myrl has ever brought home as an overnight guest," he said slowly.

"Well, the circumstances were so extreme. I'm not too sure she had a choice." I smiled.

"Myrl always makes certain she has a choice. No. Her bringing you here is very important. It was very deliberate and calculated." He rubbed his face with his hands and then leaned forward, put a hand on my knee, and spoke very low and quietly. "She is not well, Faye."

"Myrl seems fine," I said, and then for some reason the portraits in the hall came to me, draping a fine dark veil across my psyche. I shuddered slightly and the haunting passed.

"No, she is not fine. Myrl suffers terribly. She suffers from depression – what they used to call melancholy." He glanced over his shoulder at the kitchen door, leaned closer to me, and continued. "We have tried various treatments. None have worked. You've noticed, no doubt, that she does not drink alcohol or coffee or tea. She does not smoke, either. She is deathly afraid of any substance which might lead to an addiction. She's afraid of addiction. It is because of this fear, the chemical treatments we have tried fail with her. She just refuses to take medication for an extended period."

I remained silent and just let him speak. I was very self-conscious and nervous about hearing of her affliction and I was very uncomfortable with the secretiveness with which he told me.

He sat back. "I am telling you this so that you will take some responsibility when you are with her. She needs to be watched. I thought she was going into another spell just a few days ago. This murder, this ghastly, ghastly business-has revived her in some way."

"She wants to go to Vermont next weekend." I said, feeling awkward, chafing with the subtle shift of allegiances.

"I know. She told me that bit before breakfast. You must take care with her. Myrl is not as resilient as she appears. And Brattleboro is not a place filled with good memories for her."

I left the Norton home that Sunday afternoon. On my way out the door, I noticed a row of Myrl's shoes, a pair of stylish cream satin Louis heels, leather open-toed pumps, rubber galoshes, purple satin slippers with buckles of brilliants, and black leather mid-calf boots with side buttons, all resting in orderly fashion in the front hall. Her shoes were always where she could find them.

Chapter Five

We Travel to Brattleboro

On my way home Sunday afternoon, I called on Rachel, but she was out and so I left a note for her to get in touch with me at Martha Wilson's. But it wasn't until Wednesday that I heard from her.

"Faye! Faye Tullis," Rachel called in a loud whisper. I was in the library studying. I looked up from my book. Rachel was walking down the rows of books in my direction.

"Where have you been?" I said, half rising from my chair. "I've been leaving messages all over the place for you."

"I know, I know," she whispered.

"Let's go outside," I said, "where we can talk."

"But I don't want to talk about it. I can't believe I'm involved in something like this," she said and looked around as if someone might overhear us.

"Let's go outside," I repeated. We left the library.

But the change of venue didn't help matters much. We sat on a small hill overlooking one of the campus gardens, now just a strip of bare earth.

"Faye, is that woman through with this? I mean is she still talking to Detective Lorey?"

"I know he came Sunday to ask questions. But he called on you as well, right? And you told him about the chain! Why? If Myrl thought he should know she would have said something early on."

"This is a murder investigation, Faye. Murder. I'm not

going to hold anything back. I don't want that woman doing anything. She caused all this."

"She didn't cause it, Rachel." I folded my hands. "And she stuck up for you."

"She's the one who dragged us back to that house. Oh, I don't want to talk about it. I just want you to know that I think this is all too disgusting for words. My parents want me to leave school and come home."

I sighed. "So, are you?"

"No. I want to stay here, but it's getting difficult. I'm moving into the new dormitory across campus, because I can't live at that house. What do you two say? I mean, does she mention it in class? Does she talk about it? Does she mention me?"

"No, no, no. Really. What's the matter with you? Look, Rachel, Myrl has said nothing to me in public or private about what happened since Sunday. In class she's Professor Norton. Period. She seems to have no trouble dividing her life into compartments. It's almost as if she's trying to avoid me. We're supposed to go up to Brattleboro Friday night for two days and she hasn't even said a word about it."

"Oh good, so she'll be far away."

I glanced down at my shoes.

"What?" Rachel asked. "Don't tell me she's meddling."

"Well, she's going there to get more information. At least that's what I think she's going for."

Rachel moaned. "I don't want her doing anything!"

I bristled slightly. "You know, Rachel, she's trying to help. Not help you, not me, or Detective Lorey. She's trying to help the cause of justice. I thought that might appeal to you."

"It does as long as my name isn't bandied about in the details of a murder. I'd like to get married someday."

"Oh please," I said. We said nothing for several minutes.

"I don't want to argue," she said finally. "Maybe I should go home for a while."

"And what would you do? Help your mother pick out wall coverings? You would be bored in a week and dying to come back."

"I guess you're right," she said and picked a dead leaf from the sole of her shoe. "So you're going to Vermont with her?"

"Yes. We leave Friday evening and come back Sunday."

"So is this kind of a weekend hobby for her? Solving crimes?"

"No," I said, choosing to ignore the sarcastic edge to her voice. "She's never been involved in this sort of thing before. She didn't ask for this."

* * * * *

Friday, after class, Myrl came up to me and said, "I have tickets for the four-thirty train. Meet me at the station by the ticket window. There is no meal provided, which is a ghastly oversight given the hour, so be certain you are well fed before we leave. Pack lightly, please. We must be agile. See you then." She left quickly out the little door behind the podium before I could say anything, and it suddenly occurred to me her quick flight might be a signal of worry, and she thought I might not want to come with her after all. She didn't want a chance conversation to be the opportunity for me to bow out.

The station in Northampton was made of stone quarried from Maine, with an arch-bowed ceiling of maple from the local mill. The dimensions of the building were small, the station operated efficiently, and trains were quite punctual. There were vendors about selling long stemmed roses and carnations wrapped in baby's breath, warm rolls and roasted yams. We met as planned by the ticket window and boarded. Myrl was flamboyantly dressed in a loud satin red chemise dress complete with sequins around the collar, two broad straps at the shoulder, a satin tie at the waist, and a wide black bowler-shaped crown hat with a bright red feather stylishly tucked in the band. Her shoes were patent leather Louis heels, with a diamond strap, slick and shiny and lent her even more height. I wore my black wool pants, white shirt, and an overcoat. I carried one small overnight bag. Myrl, on the other hand, had two huge black leather suitcases stuffed, no doubt, with several outfits for each day. She was very energetic and loud, stomping up and down the aisles, trying to find our seats. When she determined we were in the wrong car she whisked us, suitcases and all, through the narrow doors. When she found our seats she smiled broadly at the conductor, ignoring his attempts to help us with our suitcases. She was smiling and laughing too much, making failed attempts at small talk with the poor man. When he left to tend to other passengers, she flopped down next to the window, hat off and in her lap, her long legs sprawled open in a very immodest fashion.

"I find this exhausting," she said.

I cleared my throat.

She looked up at me and saw my raised eyebrow, and crossed her legs. "You are hostage to decorum, Faye," she said and closed her eyes wearily.

"One of us should be," I answered and my comment was met with a faint smile.

"I must apologise for an error in observation," she said. "You do have a sense of humour."

The train pulled slowly out of the station and within minutes the geometric lines of town buildings and the white and brown paint of homes vanished. The train quickened. In their stead was a long smooth blur of grey punctuated with the green of a patch of fir trees. Autumn colour was gone. On some farms, summer hay still lay in tidy rolls, gathering mildew from the late rains. I had heard farm help was hard to come by this past summer and the abandoned haystacks were testimony to difficult times. No one wanted to stack hay or pick if they could get a job in town. The closer the towns grew to the edge of farmland, the harder it was for the farmer to survive.

"I have some notes I'd like to share with you," said Myrl. I turned from the window to face her. She was still sprawled and her eyes remained shut. "Mental notes."

I sat back and took out my journal and flowered pen. "Well, I will keep written notes, just so I can keep everything straight."

Her eyes fluttered open for a moment. "Oh, this is interesting," she said and the softness of her voice caused me to glance up at her. "Everything comes in cycles. Everything repeats. The speaker, the writer."

She was looking at my open notebook with vulnerability or yearning – I couldn't decide which. In a second her strength was stripped from her, and she was left exposed, wounded in some way, pushed toward painful thoughts. And then it vanished, whatever the moment held, and she was back, ticking off events, eyes closed.

"Mr Lorey is correct in one assumption. That the man we saw knew Alyssa Dansen. He had a key, he locked the door from the inside and vanished. In these older homes, all the locks are the same – the front door, the back, the bedrooms. So he was familiar with the house."

She paused. The train jostled my pen and I straightened my notebook. She continued. "I am sure you noticed the thick layer of dust which lay on everything in Alyssa Dansen's room. Obviously no one had been up there in several weeks, if not months. In fact, the only thing not dirty was the recording of Mary Howe's aria, presumably because the needle ran across the tracks of the record every evening and kept the dust from settling. I did notice Alyssa's clothing, both what she wore and what was in her closet.

"She was very neat. There were fifteen dresses, ten blouses three of silk, mind you – and six skirts hanging in her closet. That accounts for thirty-one hangers. But there were thirty-three hangers."

"She was wearing a dress," I offered. "That would account for one hanger."

"Yes, but that still leaves a missing article of clothing. My guess is that this was the dress she wore when she was killed. She also had four pairs of dress shoes, two pairs of galoshes, and one pair of riding boots. With the exception of the boots, each pair was in their own shoebox. There were, of course, two empty shoeboxes."

"That's right, she had laced leather shoes on when we found her –"

"Yes, I find that curious, actually."

"Really." I glanced at her from my journal.

"Yes. Why take the time to cover her feet? No one can see her feet from the street. The effect they wanted was to have her appear alive from the window where neighbours and Rachel could easily see her. In fact, why trouble to cure and stuff the entire body? I find this troublesome."

It did not appear to me all that critical. But something else she said snagged my interest. "You said 'they.' Do you think the murder was done by more than one person?"

Myrl yawned, set her hat back on her head, tipped forward across her eyes, and settled into her seat. She spoke very softly and with a smile. "Very good, Faye. No. I mean I don't know. Possibly. I do know that at least two people are involved in the conspiracy to keep her death a secret." She sighed. "We have a dress and a pair of shoes to look for," was all she said before she fell asleep.

A dress and a pair of shoes seemed a lost cause to me. Especially because we did not have a clue as to when or where the murder actually took place. It could have been weeks ago, or months ago, half a year or more. The dress and shoes would be long gone. It seemed to me her reasoning was good, but the resulting course of action somehow skewed. It would take me several more difficult lessons to learn to trust her implicitly. I sat back and looked out the window. As we neared Brattleboro, I could see the outline of several churches, steeples high against the early evening sky, lit by gas lanterns from underneath. Serving as the state line between Vermont and New Hampshire, the Connecticut River bordered the little town and in the early darkness the river swirled parallel to the train tracks, reflecting little, its black waters a silent presence.

We stepped off the train to the flash and pop of camera bulbs. Word had spread from Northampton that two of the women who had found the body were arriving by the six o'clock train. Myrl adjusted her hat, handed her bags to a porter and descended to a flurry of questions mostly about our mental health and how we felt when we saw the body.

There must have been twenty reporters, from as far away as Wardsboro and Keene, all here to question us. Myrl stood on the last step, adding to her height, and cleared her throat. I stood behind her and said nothing. After several minutes the crowd quieted and Myrl announced, "I have one comment to make," and the men drew even nearer.

"My companion and I are here to visit an old friend and have a suitable rest, for our nerves are shot by this hideous mess." The men all began to talk at once and she raised her hand. "My friend is very frail ..."

I stared at the back of her head for a moment before recovering enough to realise she was concocting some story to suit her needs.

"... and cannot suffer through persistent questions about what happened last Saturday. Now. It is terrible a woman was killed. It says nothing of virtue or goodness about us as human beings. Print that. As to how we feel about this personally" – here she actually began to tremble slightly, and I could see the sequins across her back shimmer under the station lights –"we really must not be asked to dwell. Come, Faye," she said, turning swiftly to me and offering me her hand while I stepped down. Myrl kept my hand as two porters came and took our bags. The reporters stepped away and allowed us to walk to the end of the platform. There, a heavy draft horse pulling a Blacksom carriage waited with a small white haired woman and her driver, a young man about my age, with black straight hair. He waved to us. Both the driver and the woman wore scarves, and while the man paired his with only a heavy sweater, the woman was bundled in blankets.

"Ho, Myrl," she waved.

Myrl turned to me and said, "That is Mary Howe. One of the finest sopranos of her time."

I watched her wave back, and within moments we climbed aboard. Myrl stood and waved once more to the reporters who stood in a cluster at the beginning of the platform, and she finally sat down only as the carriage pulled away. I saw one reporter apart from the group. Dressed in black wool

pants and a deep grey flannel coat, there was a subtle
challenge in his decision to follow us a short distance down
the platform. A camera strapped across his chest was pushed
to one side and his head was bent over a writing pad. When
he glanced up for a moment I saw a man in his mid-forties or
so, with wavy blond hair lightening to grey at the temples.
Below the brim of his hat, his blue eyes held the steady gaze
of one with purpose.

"How do you do," said Mrs Howe to me. I nodded to her
and smiled, but my response was cut short. "Myrl, you need a
wrap," said Mary Howe. "Look at those bare shoulders." And
from behind her hood of blankets, Mrs Howe winked at me.

* * * * *

The young man was Real Howe, Mrs Howe's nephew, and
he drove us all down Western Avenue to a large two-story
tavern set back well off the road. The stable was around in
back, and we were deposited by the side door. Mrs Howe
lived on the north end of town in what was called the Hayes
Tavern, the home of Rutherford B. Hayes, one of our
country's past presidents. I remembered reading how Hayes
actually lost the electoral vote to Democrat Samuel J. Tilden
by 20 votes in 1876, only to have the Republicans contest the
vote in three key states. Tilden had also won the popular ap-
proval by 300,000 votes. The final count in January of 1877
was 185,184, Hayes's favour. I considered Hayes something of
a rogue and was delighted to see a row of portraits lining the
entryway which depicted a host of scowling faces.

"I'm renting here in town for now," Mary Howe was
explaining to Myrl, "because I can take the trolley right to
downtown and not mess with having a carriage brought up."

"Who else lives here?" asked Myrl, noting several coats
and hats limply hanging on the stand by the door.

"Oh, that'd be Bigelow. Hayes Bigelow. He's a
photographer, just starting out really. He's a Rutherford, you
know," said Real, smoothing down his hair. Fog had swelled

above the Connecticut River on our short ride to the Tavern, and hung white and thick in the streets. It left us all damp.

"So this isn't a tavern after all?" I said. I had seen the sign out front – a horse and rider carved in oak and painted in oils, with R. HAYES above and ENTERTAINMEN below with the final T cut off and hovering above the N.

"Well," smiled Mrs Howe, "this is no longer a working Tavern and certainly not a men's club anymore. It's just me and Real, and Hayes. And if they ever get called to duty, I'll be by myself." She turned to me. "Come, you two, I'll show you your rooms while Real takes care of the horse."

For dinner, Myrl changed into a grey wool suit. Her blouse was of pearl silk, buttoned to the top, and a cameo of grey and white, a woman in profile, was affixed under her neck. I noticed she was comfortable enough here to shed her shoes as she did at home, but she did wear a pair of fleeced deerskin moccasins, with intricate beadwork in bright strips across the tops.

"So why are you here? I know you're not here visiting us country folk out of whimsy," said Mrs Howe, spearing a potato from the platter. Now that she was not swathed in blankets, I could see how small she was. Smaller than me, her face smooth, her skin soft. She had bright chocolate brown eyes. There was something strange about them and then I realised she did not have any eyelashes or brows. There was the faint outline of eyebrow pencil on her forehead – an attempt to correct the situation. I realised, too, she wore a wig when I saw her adjust it slightly as she sat down to dinner.

A large pot roast had been prepared for our visit complete with boiled potatoes, carrots, and a slather of onions. The meat was tender, the wine a biting burgundy, and I was touched to see a sprig of peppermint set inside a teacup for my friend. Mrs Howe knew her adopted niece well. I was very pleased to see the bottle of burgundy.

"No, we are not here for our health. You surmised correctly," said Myrl, pouring boiling water over the mint. "We are here for our own reasons."

"One of them being curiosity," said Mrs Howe.

79

"Yes, one of them being curiosity. Did you know her?"

"Before we get into this, I just want to be clear," said Mrs Howe, setting down her fork and looking very stern. "On whose behalf are you poking around?"

Myrl smiled and took a sip of her tea, far too soon, for she grimaced and set the cup down.

"That's fall mint. It takes longer to steep," said Mrs Howe.

"Yes, well. We are here because there's a puzzle to be puzzled," said Myrl. "And a woman was killed and her body desecrated. In addition, I'm bored." She looked swiftly at her friend and added, "And you know I do not handle boredom well."

"I see. Well," said Mrs Howe brightly, "yes, I did know her. I knew of her, rather, but I did not know her intimately."

"She was a figure in town?" Myrl dipped the sprig in the hot water vigorously.

"So to speak, yes. Alyssa was well known and recognised by most because she was so active in the town theatre troupe. She and Giles Wilcox nearly always had the lead roles and were seen together often in each other's company. Especially this last summer." She shook her head. "It was almost scandalous that the engagement wasn't announced earlier."

"They were that close?" I asked.

"Well, she had been ill in the early part of the summer and had returned to Northampton, down by you folks, for the duration of her illness. Giles would travel south and visit her and bring her gifts from folks –"

"Did she have influenza?"

"No. I think it were pneumonia," said Real. A door slammed in the kitchen. "That'd be Biggy. She got it right after her last show, before the summer season started off and her understudy, Marion French, had to take over her part in *Heart Throb*, the summer comedy they put on."

"Now, I've heard of Giles Wilcox," said Myrl slowly.

Hayes Bigelow waved to us from the kitchen, grabbed a plate and joined us at the table. He was about Real's age with thick brown wiry hair, glasses, and his manner was rushed. He sat down with great energy, scooting his chair up and knocking into Myrl. Whispering an apology he helped himself to some roast and then piped up, "Got some great shots of you ladies for tomorrow's papers. I've watched what's been going on down south. Smith really has the press off you two, don't they?"

Mrs Howe stiffened in her chair. "I think, Bigelow that not everyone knows who you are."

He grinned and set down his fork. "Sorry. She keeps me both humble and in line. Bigelow Hayes. Man about town. Wine. Yes." He jumped up from the table and disappeared into the kitchen again for a glass.

Mrs Howe sighed. "He was brought up without lacking anything but proper manners." She turned to Myrl. "Yes, you've met Giles Wilcox before. He was at the Putney farm two years ago when you came up for – your rest." Mrs Howe then explained to me, "That's where my husband and I kept a farm for years." She wiped her mouth. "Giles is fairly well to do. An outsider from New York, who's been here for six years or so and fits right in, I'd say. He can talk to anyone. He's a great benefactor to the town actually. You know, he gives to the fire department regularly and he revived the Wheel Club."

"What's that?" I asked.

"The Wheel Club is a group of sports enthusiasts who get together and cycle," said Myrl, attempting her tea again and Mrs Howe finished Myrl's thought

"Now with Island Park cleaned up – the ice floes did terrible damage to the park last winter – they often cycle there."

I had heard of Island Park. Brattleboro was known for its great boardwalks up and down the Connecticut and West rivers. In addition, there was a twenty-acre strip of land in the middle of the Connecticut between Brattleboro and Hinsdale, New Hampshire. Used mostly for farming, ten years ago or so a group calling themselves the Island Park Amusement Company built a grandstand, casino, dance hall, ice cream parlour, bowling alley, and a movie theatre. The summer Chautauqua was held on the green, and people from miles around would come to hear religious inspirationals, opera divas, poets, writers, see the fantastic, and listen to band music. The grand finale was usually an epic sermon on the majesty, grace, and goodness of personal success. Several years ago a hotel was also established. In fact, last spring, Rachel had vacationed on the Island with her parents for a canoe race.

"Have you ever been to Island Park?" asked Mrs Howe.

"No, I haven't," I answered, "but I know of it."

"Oh, for heaven's sake, you should definitely go. Biggy runs a ferry out there, or you can rent a canoe – it's just a nickel –"

"But please take my ferry," Biggy smiled. "Between the ferry and photos, I need the money and the river's going to ice over soon."

"Bigelow! Or you can have Real take you out. There's a bridge. They're building a huge carousel, a merry-go-round thing, and it's supposed to be finished in time for Winter Carnival. I hear it's quite a sight. Giles is a part of that project too, so I hear."

"Oh. Giles Wilcox. Yes, yes. I remember now. He carried two watch chains. Quite a big game hunter as I remember," said Myrl. "He's off on a hunt right now," said Real, helping himself to seconds. "Oh. So he's not in town?" asked Myrl. I could tell she was very disappointed. "Naw. He's somewhere in Africa. But he's due back in two weeks."

"Now, Real, he may come back sooner once word of this reaches him," said Mrs Howe. "Hollister did send him a telegram." She turned to Myrl. "That's Hollister McLean, a good friend of his. And if he gets the message, he may just come home."

"I doubt it," said Real, and he smiled at me. "I don't like him."

"Why?" I asked.

"He carries two watches, I guess. And he thinks he's pretty wonderful."

Mrs Howe laughed. "Yes, he does, doesn't he? Especially with the girls in town."

82

"Oh, he's harmless," said Biggy.

"That's because you have no trouble either," said Real.

"Boys!"

"Oh, that's just because the girls think I'm rich." Biggy winked at me and took a swallow of wine.

"That's enough."

"Where did Hollister and Giles meet?" asked Myrl, not observing the fray.

"Oh, I don't know. Hollister's family has been here for years. His father ran the jewellery store down on South Main Street. It's gone now. His father was a gambler, unfortunately."

"What is Mr McLean's business?" said Myrl, poking at the sprig of mint. Mrs Howe pushed over a tiny blue ceramic plate and Myrl laid the sprig down.

"He's the local taxidermist."

"Really," said Myrl, looking up sharply.

"Now, don't go getting all excited, Myrl. Hollister McLean is one of the most civil people I've ever met. He's really a very level headed person. I have never seen him angry or nasty to anyone. In fact, it's Alyssa Dansen who was the nasty one of the bunch."

"Now why do you say that?"

"Well, she was," sniffed Mrs Howe. "She was haughty, and thought she was a queen. She had her tight circle of friends and no time for anyone else. I say she was well known, but no one really knew her. But I do think her illness set her down a notch or two."

"Was she more gregarious after her recovery?"

"Well, actually no. Not outgoing certainly, but she seemed sweeter. I mean after she'd recovered somewhat, Giles brought her up to his farm – it's in Putney too – and we'd see them together out on the river in early summer before he left for Africa, canoeing and talking. He took her to Spofford Lake quite often. That's right over in New Hampshire – he's got a camp on the south shore. There's an island in the middle of the lake and they would picnic there sometimes with Hollister. Giles would always relay her messages of thanks and kindness to everyone, and I even received a note of thanks for a fruit and cheese basket I made when she was bedridden."

"Did you ever give her one of your recordings?"

"You mean one of my records? Good gracious, no. What a waste. She hated opera and took no pains in telling me that."

"I see," said Myrl slowly. "I see." She paused and wiped her mouth. "Is the Wheel Club still a men-only affair?"

"Oh, certainly not. Dr Burnett was also a benefactor and she made certain the ladies could have their fun as well"

"Dr Burnett?" I asked. I thought I recognised the name.

"An intriguing person, you would like her," said Myrl

"And a hot-tempered thing," added Biggy.

"Just because she told you off," said Real

"Well, I was sick. Feverish. Delirious with that wretched influenza last year – seeing my last breath practically – and she was there with me in my room and all I did was –"

"Hayes. You must stop this." Mrs Howe was quite stern. "I will not continue to board here if I must continually listen to this sort of thing." She sighed. "Yes, Grace Burnett. She's quite a celebrity of her own, of course, fits her practice off her horse – what's his name, Real? The horse I mean."

"Juniper."

"That's right. Juniper. She sees many folks who might not be able to get into town. She's also quite a shot herself and is always trying to get Giles in a match, but he pleasantly declines, as he should. It wouldn't be right, you know."

"True," said Myrl and smiled at me. In Africa where I spent most of my late teenage years, shooting was a sport of both sexes and I had my share of challenges in competition with men my age and older. "Would the Wheel Club be a good place to visit tomorrow, as guests?"

"I should say so," said Mrs Howe. "Many members of the troupe are also members of the Club, so there'll be plenty of talk around, I'm sure. I'll call Grace, she could get you in."

"And they would be willing to talk to us?"

"All those theatre people were born with long tongues," said Real, so pleasantly I had to laugh.

That night, we turned in late. Mrs Howe and I enjoyed some whiskey sours after dinner, she enjoying several more than I. Biggy was off on a date with a young seamstress. Myrl and Real chatted amiably about the coming winter and the ice business. He cut ice out on the lakes and on the West River for The Crystal Ice Company and Myrl seemed particularly interested in how the blocks were cut and hauled. Most families in larger cities now owned the new Kelvinator electric refrigerators, but out here, where it was still so very rural, the ice cutting business could still boast a profit. Stafford & Holden Manufacturing were the local providers of ice tools and equipment, though Real said that when he lived in Maine several seasons ago, he was fortunate enough to cut with Knickerbocker blades. I faded in and out of the conversation. When Myrl and I ascended the staircase it was well past midnight. She did not look tired, however, and seemed quite animated, talking about the weather up here, how different it was than further south, how the rivers ice over and break open at different times each year and how you could never tell when the thaw would come.

"Remember what Real said right before we went upstairs?" she asked. I was nearly asleep. The lights were out and moonlight sifted between the curtains and fell across our twin beds in cool silver strands. I thought I saw her pillow on the floor.

I yawned. "No, what did he say?"

"'We always get a January thaw, even if it doesn't come until March'."

Chapter Six

We Visit the Wheel Club

The Wheel Club was located in West Brattleboro, on Elliot Street across from the Brattleboro Opera House. The weather was warmer, the day bright, and the early winter air filled with the smell of smoke and baking breads. Myrl and I rose early, breakfasted and took the trolley, efficient and new, painted bright red and blue with shiny copper wheels, and arrived at the Club a little before noon. The perfect time to catch gossip, according to Mrs Howe – just as the morning riders returned and before they sat down to lunch.

Myrl wore grey flannel slacks, a matching coat with black trim, and a white blouse, complete with a man's black silk tie. Her shoes were men's Oxfords, leather heeled and black with fresh polish. I confess I felt rather juvenile in my knickers and coat, but I had expected to be wheeling around Brattleboro on a bicycle. We were to meet Dr Burnett, and as we entered, a short woman in a navy pleated wool dress greeted us. Her hair was dark and very curly, pulled back and restrained by a leather clip. It fell past her shoulders, though the bangs frizzed above her eyebrows and she pushed at them every now and then.

"Grace, this is Faye Tullis, my companion," said Myrl, and I shook the doctor's hand. "So good of you to meet us!" Myrl added, smiling widely and looking around distractedly.

"So good of you to want to come visit us at the Club and ride," said Dr Burnett. "I told you a little exercise would be good for you."

"Grace believes in flushing the system," said Myrl and then, after glancing around the room, "Oh, this is very nice. Not what I would expect."

"You mean in Vermont?"

"I mean in the country." Myrl smiled.

It was true. The main room was carpeted in deep blue and the front desk was mahogany. Behind the desk was a cork pushpin board with numbers and destinations bordered on either side with pen and ink drawings of cyclists, one of a man and one of a woman, out on the grass among maples. The wallpaper on either side of the front hall was a hand-painted mural of where the West and Connecticut rivers met, with cyclists of all ages wheeling up and down the banks on the boardwalks. The blue of the carpet was picked up in the clothing of the cyclists and parts of the sky, and the effect was truly spectacular. Gilded light fixtures, with opaque glass in the shape of shells, curled upward and cast light toward the ceiling. The Club could compete easily with any found in a large city. Grace led us around the corner to a small cafe-style dining room. The carpet changed to a deep gold and linen tablecloths were in place. Crystal and silver were laid out and each small square table had a single rose in a tiny porcelain vase resting in the centre.

"The clientele," said Grace, looking around, "is sometimes very full of themselves," and she wrinkled her nose. "But I must say, the Wheel Club does an awful lot for the town. There's always a dance or charity ball, dinner or parade going on around here. Right now the club is gearing up for Winter Carnival. So Myrl, it's been a long time since we've seen each other. How have you been? Well, I assume."

"Quite well, thank you," she answered and leaned forward to take Grace into her confidence. "Never better."

Grace laughed and patted her arm. "I'm glad to hear it, truly. Let's go on through to the lounge." We entered yet another room, of dark mahogany wainscoting, long low leather couches, a copper spittoon, ashtrays, and deep green floor ferns in silver pots. The floor was of red oak, quarter sawn and richly oiled. At the far end was a large stone fireplace, unlit, with eight leather chairs in a crescent moon yawning at the dark chasm. A heavy crystal chandelier with several tiers and hundreds of tiny prisms hung in the centre of the ceiling. We sat on the low leather divan and Myrl crossed her legs and tucked them under her. I had never seen her in pants. She looked thin, even gaunt, and as she leaned back into the thick brown leather, her strength vanished and she seemed almost sickly.

"But what is this I hear of you two and vampires –" said Grace, leaning forward and pinching Myrl's knee.

"No! Vampires?" I said. "Is that what people are saying?"

"Folks are saying. The body was found emptied of blood, right? What else could explain it?" Grace shook her head. "I tell you, some of what I hear around town puts me in fear of the future. People's minds – I can't fathom them sometimes. But that's been the talk. Vampires."

"How unfortunate," said Myrl. She sighed. "Better to believe in the supernatural than to discover a neighbour with an ability to murder. So what do they say about this vampire?"

"Well. The running theory is that Alyssa flirted with a vampire unknowingly and then he killed her. I'm sorry to say most of this has come from a woman in town who fancies herself a witch." Grace chuckled and scratched her nose. "She's a dear, rather touched I think, but harmless. Her name is Gladdis McFadden and you'll probably meet her today. She says the organs were eaten and there is no way to appease him except to offer him a second course. Appetising, isn't it?"

"What do you mean? You mean another victim?" I asked.

"Well, yes, but Gladdis isn't going to murder anyone. You see, according to her, in order to release the soul from the vampire's grasp, you have to remove the organs from the victim and burn them. Because the organs from the first victim were eaten, supposedly, there will be another victim and another and another, unless he is stopped. The town's job is to find the second victim, remove the organs before he does and burn them. Folks are spooked around here and talk is very mysterious." Grace looked up at a large lion's head

89

mounted above the fireplace. "In fact, what happened is no more mysterious than that," she said. "A little sawdust."

"Oh, I disagree, it's far more mysterious," said Myrl, unfolding herself and suddenly rising, strolling over to the trophy, hands in her pants pockets. "To kill an animal is somehow a person's right and it is accepted as such. When this lion was shot, the threads of our past – the need to hunt for food, the quest for survival, the call to pacify our neighbours with offerings of meat and fur – all came together in an act of what has now paled to sport. I can see the series of steps in human history that led to the demise of this poor beast. But Alyssa Dansen's death did not come from any history. There is nothing in our past as human beings which provide a framework for her death. There is no legacy of a right to kill her."

"But people have always killed people," I blurted, not believing my ears. "I mean, my God, excuse me, but we have a most bloody history."

I saw Grace laughing beside me on the divan.

Myrl appeared to not hear me. "Faye, come here for a moment, would you," she said sweetly. "My eyes are bad, but I think –" She was waving me up from the sofa. I rose and stood next to her, craning my neck at an odd angle to look up to where she was pointing.

"I don't see anything," I said. "What are you looking at?"

Grace came over as well. "I don't see anything either."

"Where did this trophy come from?" Myrl whipped out her glasses and slipped them on.

"Good old Giles Wilcox, of course. He's got his trophies all over Brattleboro. He bagged this lion in West Africa on safari last year."

"Who mounts them? Who mounted this one?"

"Hollister McLean. He's supposed to be very good. He's got a man working for him who does the tanning – in fact, I think it's Gladdis's son – but Hollister does the actual mount. Giles wouldn't trust his trophies to anyone else."

"Do you both see that this mount has been tampered with?"

I looked again, but my attention was diverted by footsteps.

"Grace! Oh, I'm so glad to see you!" A woman crossed the floor in a stylish riding suit, cap in hand, and behind her followed a half dozen friends, some with tall glasses of juice. Big boned, the woman was of medium height, her face pleasant, her manner cordial, and she seemed eager to see us. "And these must be your friends from Massachusetts."

Grace whispered quickly in my ear, "Uh – oh, there's Gladdis, right behind that woman speaking," then louder, "This is Frances Hall. She is one of the theatre troupe. Frances, this is Myrl Norton and Faye –"

"Tullis," I answered.

"Yes, I know. The town is just abuzz with your visit," said Frances. This comment persuaded Myrl to cease her fixation with the trophy above the mantel and turn to the assembling group.

"How do you do," said Myrl, smiling, exuding warmth, shaking hands and releasing with a flourish, looking past Frances to the entourage. More introductions were made. There was Mrs Hope Mitchell, a singer in the Congregational church and volunteer for the troupe. Her husband, Henry, was a local banker and solicitor. Both were pleasant and commented on the morning's good biking weather. Hope Mitchell kept giving furtive little glances at Myrl as if she knew her, and I found her manner curious. Gladdis McFadden was a character. Short, thick, with stubby little fingers and loud makeup, she was dressed in a kimono-style satin wrap which billowed a shimmery purple all around her, matching the odd square turban set atop her head. She was middle-aged, of independent means, and created costumes for both opera and theatre productions. Then there was Howard Adams, who seemed younger than the rest and carried an air of excitement and brash strength. Even at five paces I could detect the scent of cut limes and astringent. His forehead was high, his profile perfect, and his black straight, thick hair beautifully combed back. His back was strong and his skin a rich hue of brown. I confess that his hand was the only one I pursued in handshake. When we clasped, I felt

91

sweat on my palm and I was disgraced with the blush I felt warm my cheeks. But he seemed not to notice, and turned back to the group rather distractedly. An older gentleman, wide around the middle and nearing fifty or so, carried a cigar in one hand and a pocket watch in the other. He laughed loudly but seemed soft-spoken. After Myrl shook his hand he returned to whispering in Hope Mitchell's ear. When I discovered this was Hollister McLean, I nodded at him with a frown in an attempt to gather all I could in a glance – I was annoyed that Myrl, with her perfunctory handshake, seemed completely uninterested in him. And, finally, there was Marion French: young, stunning, heavy blond hair cropped neatly at her shoulders, translucent skin, perfect white teeth, and a sweet smile. She nodded in our direction when introduced and then went back to her conversation with Howard Adams. By the angle of her chin, the downward cast of her eyes punctuated by quick, lilting glances at Howard, the agile smile, and the fingertips of one hand lightly touching the bottom of her throat as she spoke, it was clear that she was flirting. I wiped my hands on my pants. I never could flirt.

"You know that you two are truly celebrities here," said Hollister, smiling as he sat down in one of the chairs in front of the fireplace. The others followed suit, with Henry and Howard sitting stretched out on the floor. Myrl and I took the centre chairs.

"Well, we should not be," said Myrl. "What was done was hideous business."

"But, you were there," said Frances.

"And now we are here and we need to stop thinking about it, don't we, Faye." Myrl shut her eyes for a moment. "Still, though, I can't put the image out of my mind ..."

There was a murmur of sympathy around the room.

"It must have been awful," said Frances, leaning forward and offering Myrl a handkerchief from her bag. "I simply can't imagine."

"And I find myself wondering," said Myrl, opening her eyes and taking the handkerchief. "Who would have done

92

such a thing? Who could do this to someone? And you all knew her ..." She wiped her eyes and sat up.

"It must have come as such a shock for all of you," I said, and everyone was quiet, the pause not pleasant. I became suddenly self-conscious. "I mean you all knew her, right?"

"I can say that we all knew her, yes. I guess you could say we all knew her in one way or another," Frances said suddenly. "She was difficult at times ..."

"She was not," said Hollister. "She was just independent." He turned to Myrl. "I was particularly fond of her. Probably more than anyone else here. She didn't come from money, and she worked hard as a seamstress right here in town. She did not go much for gossip." He cleared his throat and did not permit a glance to the group.

"One person's gossip is often another's truth," said Myrl. She leaned back in her chair and looked evenly at the little group. I could sense that they were all suddenly uncomfortable. "Mr Adams –"

"Howard, if you don't mind –"

"Oh, we're all friends here," said Grace. "Then, Howard, what could you say about Alyssa? But no. You probably don't want to talk about this." She waved her hand.

Howard sat up and put his hands on his knees. "I don't mind, really. I didn't know much about her. Can't say much. That she was confident of herself, perhaps. That she was a talented actress. That she had regard for others. That she kept to herself."

"That you had it for her," said Frances. There was a difficult pause. At least I found it strained. Howard recovered but his tone was cool.

"I was a little crazy for a while, I admit it," he said. "But I think I've got my head on straight now." Howard patted Marion's knee. "You just watch yourself, Frances."

"Henry?" Myrl turned to Henry Mitchell. The ring on his left little finger seemed out of place in this country setting, and I watched as it flashed with several diamonds.

Henry cleared his throat and glanced at his wife. "She was strict, someone who measured her words carefully ..."

"You were her banker, I presume?"

"Well, I handled her affairs. And yes, I did represent her interests, so to speak. But I did not know her personally very well at all. Probably much less than the rest of you." He looked at his wife again. There was still tension in the group and Frances looked at the ground.

Myrl turned to Hope. "Hope, how about you?"

"She was aloof, yes. But kind. I really can't say too much about her either. I hardly knew her. She was different. She could do terrible things to men, so I hear, and for one who was always short on cash, she was a dresser, and I think she liked cards."

"Oh, please," said Hollister. "Really, leave her alone."

"But she did, Hollister. I'm not saying she gambled away her life, but she certainly made our bridge games more interesting." Hope smiled sweetly.

"Frances?" Frances looked at Grace. "Alyssa was very smart. As to who might want her dead, I can't imagine. She had no enemies."

"Oh come, come," said Myrl. She dropped her legs to the floor, leaned forward and gave a slow, sad shake of her head. "Someone killed her. Someone did this for a reason. Who could have wanted her dead? It must be someone in town, don't you think? How hideous to be walking around with – oh, I can't imagine it. Really. None of you can think of any reason someone would want to kill her?" She searched everyone's face as if it would be a personal favour to her if someone could recall something.

Hollister shook out a pipe. "I should think the person responsible for this outrage would not be someone from town – good Lord, she only summered here. It was obviously some gypsy or drunkard down south. Not to affront you two ladies, of course, but I think some deranged city person did this. I mean, my God, the body was found down there. Why would you think anyone up here would do such a thing?"

"I don't know," said Myrl and shut her eyes again.

"She was a looker," said Gladdis. It was the first time I had heard her speak and her voice was deep and grating. Hollister

94

lit his pipe with a hand cupped around a match. He waved the flame out and stared at Gladdis, flicking the match-stick with an index finger. "She was a hard woman, demanding and beautiful," Gladdis continued. "And not full of talk. I could see how someone might want her dead. What with jealousy being what it is – a force. And she could flirt. Really flirt without a care." No one said a word.

Myrl's eyes opened and she glanced at Grace. "I suppose she had many fanciers?"

"She had the attentions of many men," said Marion, her hands clasped in her lap. Her voice was rich and cultured. She sounded almost British, and I concluded she was from Boston.

"Anyone in particular?"

"Well," said Frances and sighed. "Our own Giles Wilcox."

"What will he do when he returns? Poor Giles," said Marion.

"Yes. Giles will be desolate, I'm afraid. You know he told me before he left that Alyssa had begged him not to go this fall." Gladdis leaned forward. "In fact, he said she told him she'd had a premonition, and that he shouldn't go."

"Oh, pomp and glory," said Howard. "Isn't that pretty natural? The men go off to some foreign place and the women fret over health or fidelity?"

"Well, I wouldn't know," Gladdis said, not looking at him. "She was an odd one, though."

Grace sighed. "She was odd. And she could be a handful. I treated her once for scarlet fever. She was very secretive. She told me to hold a letter for her and not to open it unless she died. The night of the crisis the letter was in my bag. The morning the fever broke, I found the letter gone. I suspected she had risen from bed and burned the letter in the fireplace."

"Probably some kind of will," said Hollister, looking at the others and hefting his pants.

"She didn't have a will," said Henry. "At least I never drew one up for her."

"So there really wasn't any money, then?" Myrl looked at Henry.

"No. Not at all," he answered. "By law what little she has should go to her brother, Forrest. But I guess that won't happen until this is all cleared up." He paused. "Hollister's right. She worked hard for herself. I know Giles was giving her a cut of what she could bring him from the mounts, but I'm sure she lived frugally."

"Ah yes, the mountings. So Giles is a hunter?" Myrl waved airily at the trophy on the wall.

"Oh yes," said Marion. "He's done two safaris a year for the last four years."

"Keeps me in business," laughed Hollister.

"What a nice arrangement," I offered.

"It is. I take the skins, Marty tans the hides – that's the fellow who works for me –"

"My son," interjected Gladdis, nodding her head. Hollister glanced at her. "Yes. Well. I mount the trophy and pass the finished thing off to Giles. Sometimes he donates them, like this one here," and he pointed to the lion's head. "Most often, he'd ship them down to Alyssa's home in Northampton and she'd find buyers. She had contacts in New York, Boston, and the like and was closer to that sort of thing than we are up here. And I must say," he paused and puffed his pipe –" I swear she liked the things."

"Liked them?" I echoed.

"Yes. She had an affinity for the animals. For the mounts." He lowered his voice and wiped his upper lip. "She liked their stillness. She used to pet them and she'd gaze into their eyes. I told her they were just glass, a dime a dozen, but she said she always thought they held a personality."

I remembered the cold brown liquid glass eyes of the body, reflecting light, seeing nothing, and I lost the thread of conversation his voice carried.

There was a silence. Marion shivered and Howard rubbed her knee. Myrl turned to Frances. "So Alyssa and Giles were close ..."

"Very. Inseparable in the late spring and early summer before he left." Frances looked at her hands. "She moved her summer home into one of his rooms above the theatre several years ago, before things were serious between them. When the engagement was announced, most folks thought she should move out until the wedding."

"They were officially engaged right before he left," droned Gladdis.

"Poor Giles," Marion said again to no one. "He's coming home to such a shock."

"Any idea when he'll be in?" Frances said to the group. "What time is it now?"

Henry reached into his breast pocket and retrieved a beautiful gold watch etched with birds and flowers. It took me a few moments or so of seeing him cup the timepiece freely in his hand before I realised its chain was missing. Hope Mitchell must have noticed the lack of chain at the same time for she tapped him on the shoulder and then flicked the watch with her index finger. "I can't believe you went off and blew it again," she said with such a deep note of revulsion in her voice I was embarrassed to overhear her conversation.

Hollister, snapping his own watch shut, shook his head. "I telegraphed him in Sierra Leone and never got a response. I don't know if he received it or not. If he did, I'm sure he'll be in soon. If he didn't he'll probably return on schedule – toward the end of month."

"When does the Wheel Club close?" I couldn't imagine pedalling around in snow.

"It never closes," said Henry. "It's always open and there's always plenty going on. We don't bike around, though."

"You'd better not," said Grace, "or I'll be treating you all for cracked skulls and broken bones."

"So did Gladdis, here, tell you of her theory? About how Brattleboro is being rattled by a vampire?" Howard was leaning back, staring up at the mantel.

Marion kicked him softly in the back with her toe. "Oh, shut up. That's disgusting."

Gladdis just smiled and rubbed her arm.

"Well, I've heard the same thing," said Hollister. "You know Giles has told me of stories, strange stories from his safaris ... of cannibals and midget people. People who could

97

sleep on fire and talk to animals. Creatures so hideous that – well. And I know he has stories from the native peoples about vampires."

Grace frowned. "I can't take this talk seriously, Hollister – now button up."

"Yes," said Frances, "you're going to give this young lady here nightmares," and she nodded in my direction.

Henry turned to me to reassure the meaninglessness of Hollister's patter –"He'll talk the tin ear off an iron dog."

Myrl watched Howard staring at the lion's head above the fireplace. "Who has a key to the Wheel Club?" she asked.

Howard coughed and glanced around. "We all do ... I think. Right? I mean at least I do. Why?"

"Oh, I rise very early, and I thought if one of you had a key I might borrow, I might treat myself to a dawn ride."

Hollister McLean reached into his pocket and pulled out a ring of heavy keys. Some were skeleton keys, but most seemed custom made. On his key ring was a square metal device, hinged, with an ebony facing. He wrestled with the keys for a moment, and then leaned over and passed one to Myrl. "I won't miss this. If I don't see you tomorrow, just leave it at the front desk."

"Well, I'm ready to eat," said Frances.

Henry rose, taking Hope's hand. She pulled away from him.

"I'm famished as well," said Marion and Howard scrambled to his feet. We all stood, except for Gladdis.

"I don't know how you all can speak of vampires and then want to eat," she said and sat with her arms folded.

"Oh, Gladdis, now don't be rude," said Frances, and Hope laughed.

Hope whispered in my ear, "She wouldn't know how not to be," and elbowed me in the ribs.

* * * * *

"Now Faye," said Myrl, "what occurred back there is a perfect example of Hammerstein's rule. For example, did you

98

find yourself wondering who or what Hollister McLean is waiting for?" I was alarmed at how Myrl did not look at the ground, but appeared to be gazing up at the sky as she pedalled. Grace was several yards behind us on a Windsor bike. The lunch hour saw us three out cycling down Main Street toward the Opera House. Myrl wanted to see the reconstruction of the theatre. There had been a fire last year which gutted the place and she said she was curious to see the stage on which the troupe performed. And I assumed, of course, she wanted to see Alyssa Dansen's room.

"Waiting for?"

"Did you see how he kept looking at his watch? And in a way so as not to draw attention."

Grace caught up with us and then coasted. "Hollister's a funny man," she said. "I can't say anything nasty about him and yet I can't say that I know him at all."

"Who is the man who works for him?" I called back to her.

"Marty McFadden? Sort of a rough cut. Few words. He has seizures, minor ones, and they wouldn't let him serve in the war. No education and something of a drinker."

"I'd wager he brews his own," Myrl said.

Grace smiled and nodded. "There's a lot of bathtubs in the hills around here," she said.

"Could he be put up to something?" I asked.

Myrl interjected with, "Anyone can be put up to anything, given the certain balance of risk and reward," a comment I found abrasively cynical. "I presume he has a mop of thick red hair and a red beard?"

Grace threw her a startled look and then laughed. "Yes, you can correctly presume that."

"I would say too that Frances Hall had a love interest, in Giles Wilcox?" She leaned her head in my direction, "You did notice how her neck reddened nearly every time Hollister looked at his watch? It will be interesting to see at what time today Giles Wilcox makes his appearance in town. He is, apparently, already late."

"So you think Giles is returning today, then," said Grace.

"Undoubtedly," she said and tilted her head farther up to the sky.

"What else did you note?" I asked, still smarting from the risk and reward comment.

"Ah – well. There's Henry pronouncing Alyssa to be one with few words, when he himself is very restrained."

"And what about the missing watch chain?" I asked.

"Yes, I noticed that myself. An interesting observation," said Myrl.

"I have trouble with Henry," said Grace. "He is not someone I would choose to associate with."

"Really, he seemed pleasant enough," I said.

"When the Men's League for Women's Suffrage tried to get a chapter started here, he whipped the town into a frenzy of antagonism. Said they were run by Wobblies and reds. And when I returned to town four years ago from medical school, he was still talking about Leo Frank and trying to get folks riled up to lynch a couple on High Street named Steiner. They eventually moved."

"That's terrible," I said. *The Masses* had done a whole series on Leo Frank, which I had read with a great sense of tragedy.

"Yes, yes," said Myrl, not interested in the least. I could not fathom her apathy toward these subjects.

"Myrl, what do you mean 'yes, yes'? That's absolutely hideous. How can you just say 'yes, yes'?"

We were outside the Opera House and the bicycles rolled to a stop. Myrl kicked down her stand. She touched her chin to her chest for a moment and then looked at me, and I saw the same look my father would give me when he thought I was being naive.

"These things will always exist," she said softly. "They are the utterly disgusting products of evil and ignorance. There is nothing I can do about them. Not all the talking in the world will convince Henry Mitchell that lynching Jews is a bad thing to do. The best weapon at my disposal is a conscious decision not to use his bank for my deposits."

Grace laughed. "Well spoken," she said. "Believe me, I've tried to talk to him, Faye. You could talk a blue streak and it won't make a bit of difference. Being right isn't enough. He's probably a member of the KKK. I mean, my God, what about all those people deported illegally, rounded up last January and sent out of San Francisco?"

"Well, if we get the vote next year, there will be twenty-six million new voices saying no to these sorts of crimes against humanity," I said and my heart beat hard.

Myrl spoke very slowly. "I know you care deeply about others and their plight, Faye, but you will find that voice of twenty-six million full of discord. In fact, I venture you will find few women who will agree with you on these issues. Most will become the dupes of both politicians and their own history, and they will align themselves with all those who want to keep women and others oppressed. Your Emma Goldman is often the subject of rueful comments and not just by men, my dear."

"But if they were just educated ..."

"Aha. You are dealing with those who believe in fallacies – the premise on which they build their view of the world is rotten, Faye. No matter how much truth you show them, you'll never change their minds."

Grace pulled out a small sheet of newsprint from her skirt pocket. "She's right in a way, though I don't take such a glum view of things, but read this," and she handed me the slip of paper:

> The suffragists are bringing us to the culmination of a decadence which has been steadily indicated by race suicide, divorce, breakup of the home and federalism, all of which conditions are found chiefly in primitive society. – *The Woman Patriot*

"What bullshit," I said, then clapped a hand over my mouth. Myrl threw her head back and her laugh was throaty. It ended in coughing. "Well, it is," I continued, folding my arms in front of my chest. "I don't know where to begin with a statement like that. The person who wrote this knows nothing of so-called primitive societies. I was with Daisy Bates, in Australia, and let me tell you –"

"No, Faye, you're off the mark here, come back to the line," said Myrl.

I could not. "Beryl Markham – this British girl I went to school with over in Africa – we were amazed at the culture. And we were just girls. This is all built on fear and ignorance."

"Exactly, and how do you persuade a child not to be afraid of the dark?" Myrl said as I handed the clipping back to Grace.

"Why do you keep that?" I asked.

"For fun," she said and tucked it in a shirt pocket.

"Faye, you are a very perceptive and confident young lady," said Myrl, "and that is a gift you do not recognise in yourself."

She swung one leg over the bicycle seat and stood outside the front doors of the Opera House. The building was of red brick, square and imposing, with beautifully turned maple double doors, bevelled leaded crystal ovals centred in each.

"The owner, Mr Fox, wants to start showing flicks in here as well, but some of the townsfolk are not quite taken with that idea," said Grace.

"I love the movies!" said Myrl and clapped her hands. "*The Perils of Pauline, The Hazards of Helen* …"

"*The Fates and Flora Fourflush*," I offered.

"Excellent parody," she said, undeterred.

I was dismayed. The movies were a soiled subject at my house. Made by men just this side of the law. My father forbade us children to attend them. "Oh, Myrl, how can you watch those things?"

"You will see that the movies will become the pillar which shapes this country, mark my words," said Myrl. "A dark room filled with flickering light, images not of ghosts, but of flesh and blood people. Truth is up there on the screen, and people will believe it – they'll believe it far more than a treatise in a book or newspaper."

"Oh really, now, Myrl you are such a pessimist."

"Pessimist? No! I love the movies. I thank Thomas Edison every time I go to see a flick. What a genius. Films are architecture in motion. A cowboy atop a mounted steed captured on film at full gallop is a sculpture in motion."

"Oh, for heaven's sake," I said. "You're hopeless."

"I am. And I freely admit it," she said and threw an arm across my shoulders.

We walked around to the back of the Opera House. Train tracks ran along in back of the brick row. As we climbed the steps, Myrl glanced up at the top of the building.

"Are all three stories part of the theatre?" she asked Grace.

"No," said Grace, fiddling with the lock. "I swear Gladdis gave me the wrong key. No, there," she said, and pushed the small metal door wide. "In fact, the top floor has two rooms, both lent by Giles. Alyssa rented the one on the left."

"What about the room on the right, with all the windows boarded over?"

"I don't know about that. I guess Giles just uses it for storage."

I entered the building and turned to see Myrl tilting her head way back, gazing up at the window. She paused for a moment outside the door. She lowered her voice and spoke directly to Grace.

"I shall need to visit the town clerk's office after this," she said. "Do you have a way in?"

"Now, Myrl, no. The townsfolk just don't go around giving me keys to their homes and land records. Why do you need to get in to the town clerk's office?"

"What is done in secret is often right under our noses. We need only to look."

"I see. Well, I can't get us in on a Saturday," said Grace.

"Then I shall reward Captain O'Keefe with a visit. He will certainly let us in," said Myrl and disappeared into the building.

"Who's that?" I asked.

"Oh, he's someone who helped her out when she was up here last time. During her recovery. Captain O'Keefe's at the top of the local police, one of our men in blue."

"You know, she seems to know a handful of people really well and then nothing about the others," I said. "It seems odd."

Grace sighed. "Brattleboro is known for two of its cures: the famous water cures, and its mental cures. The Retreat is here, with an excellent reputation, and this is where Godfrey –"

"Where she went during her last bout," I finished, beginning to understand all the references to Brattleboro and why Godfrey mentioned the town was not filled with good memories for her.

Grace looked at me. "Yes. So she knows people well, like me and Patrick – Captain O'Keefe – who were involved with her on her last visit." She paused and then continued. "I put a call in to Godfrey after Myrl telephoned me to announce your trip up here. He told me how level headed you were."

"It would be difficult. I think, to have a child suffering so," I said. I felt awkward again. Knowing we were speaking of Myrl's dark problem, and yet pleased in some way that Godfrey had chosen me in whom to place his confidence. "So what did Captain O'Keefe do for Myrl?" We were still standing outside on the stoop and the sun was very bright. I heard a female cardinal in a maple right above our heads. Grace sighed and bit her lower lip. She sighed again and looked at me with such a pained expression I cannot describe.

"He found her canoe overturned on the Connecticut and dived in and saved her."

"She can't swim?" I asked. Somehow, I was surprised by this.

"She swims," said Grace. "But she had tied stones around her ankles."

104

Chapter Seven

In Which We Are Followed

"**W**hy, this is lovely," said Myrl. I stood behind her onstage and watched her, arms outstretched, embracing an invisible audience. Grace turned on the lights to reveal a large house, beautifully designed and finished in deep purples, lavenders, pinks, and white. The seats were chocolate brown velour. After the fire, the building was commissioned with the financial support of prominent town folk, and was built to compete with the best of what any city could offer. The stage was ample for modern productions, though the orchestra pit seemed small. Grace explained how the pit actually extended under the stage with sound bells placed way in the back to bounce the music to the front. It was the design of a local architect.

We turned our attention to the backstage. Here, there were sets from last season still intact, two storage houses, and eight small dressing rooms. The first four rooms were unnamed, but on the fifth door I saw H. ADAMS, and then F. HALL, A. DAKSEN, and finally, G. WILCOX, all with large gilded gold stars painted above the nameplates. Myrl cocked an eyebrow at Grace and glanced at Giles Wilcox's dressing room door.

"I don't think so, Myrl. That's private and there are locks on the door."

"True," she said and sniffed. "Who will take over Alyssa's dressing room?"

"I don't know. I guess Marion. I hadn't thought about it

actually," said Grace. She watched Myrl staring at the locked dressing room doors. "You know," she said gently after a glance to me, "Alyssa's room is right upstairs and we have a key. We could see if the lock on the room is the same as the back door. I bet it is."

We hurried back out to the hall and climbed the two sets of stairs to the third floor. At the top of the stair, there was a shallow landing with a door on the right and one on the left. A large cut rum barrel full of bright purple and white violets sat on the floor separating the two doors.

"Number one," said Grace, handing Myrl the key. Myrl turned to her left, fiddled with the lock for a moment, there was the click of tumblers, the door opened, and we entered.

The room was small, and modestly furnished with a bed, dressing table, and closet to our right, and a loveseat and chair to our left with a low table between them. Ahead of us lay a breakfast nook and two chairs, and around a partition was the kitchen and bath. Floral wallpaper of an intricate and bright design covered the walls in the main room. The kitchen area was finished in cream tile. The place smelled damp.

"May I?" said Myrl with her arm ready to pull the chain on the electric light in the centre of the room.

"Please," said Grace.

I had not been with Myrl when she returned to Alyssa Dansen's home in Northampton, so I had not witnessed how she canvassed a room. She was fluid, like a wave, beginning at one point and rolling to the next. She swung wide the closet doors, entered, and after no less than a minute, came back out and pulled open the dresser drawers, one by one. She then went on to wipe surfaces with her fingers and check behind furniture. I could hear her in the kitchen opening canisters on the small counter shelf and she seemed to spend a long time in the bathroom, wiping the floor with her hand. At one point she reached down into the bath and rubbed the small grille over the drain. Frowning, she popped the cover off and pinching her index finger and thumb together she reached down into the drain hole, but found nothing. She stood up and with a final glance inside the medicine chest, she came back to the central part of the room, glanced at Grace and me, and scooted down on her belly, disappearing under the double bed. It was really quite a sight to behold. Grace began to laugh.

"Myrl, what are you doing?"

Myrl's head reappeared from under the bed.

"I am trying to discover where Alyssa Dansen was murdered."

"Under the bed?"

Myrl paused, with still only her head showing. "No, she was not murdered under the bed."

"Well, I know that," said Grace.

"Good, so there's one location for the crime we can eliminate," she said, scooting out from underneath. She stayed on her knees and pulled out a medium-size flat wooden box. "Now, this could be interesting." She flopped down on the bed, lifted the lid, and began pawing through what appeared to me to be personal papers, receipts, and bundles of letters.

"Wait," I said. "What are those numbers?"

On the underside of the lid was a list of a dozen or so telephone numbers, the first three of which were underlined. Of these three, two had a New York exchange and the third was in Boston. Myrl picked up the lid and peered at the numbers for a moment. It wasn't until much later I realised she had committed them to memory. She tossed the lid aside and continued rifling through papers.

"I don't think we should do this," I said. "We could get in trouble."

Myrl paused, her hands still inside the box and closed her eyes. "Grace, how long have the local police known of this crime?"

"Oh, the papers were screaming about it last Monday. The Vampire Killer and all that, and every day since there has been some follow-up story postulating what happened and why."

"And have the police been here?"

107

"Well, I don't really know. Wait. Yes, I think a detective from Rutland came down to go over the place with Patrick, but I don't know for sure."

"So you see, Faye, the police have squandered their time. They have made a choice not to see what is here." She handed me a bundle of letters. "Go through these, please."

So we set to work. While Grace and I sifted through Alyssa Dansen's papers and tried to keep them organised, Myrl stood around looking impatient. Soon the bed was littered with piles of papers. But it seemed we were going to find nothing.

"These just seem to be business papers," I said. "There's even old movie receipts in here. *Love and Danger*." I sat back and looked over at Myrl.

"Don't give up yet," said Grace. "See – speaking of love, look what I just found." She waved a piece of paper.

It was a letter printed on smooth brown paper. The printing was rough, the spelling poor, but the intent of the letter was clear. "I waynt yu to be myn for allaways. I cant stop seein yuu in my dreemz. Yoo r a swt fluwr I must smel. I begg of yu to mary me. I will kep beggin yu til you say yes." It was signed "Mrty McFaden."

Myrl took the letter from Grace, studied it for a moment, and then folded it in half again and slipped it into her breast pocket.

"Marty McFadden must have been a frustrated man," I said. Grace nodded.

"Maybe. We can't be sure his affections were never returned, however," said Myrl.

"Despite his poor spelling. Let's clean this up," she said and Grace and I lifted the small piles of notes back into the box. "I am disappointed." Myrl stared at the floor with her arms crossed.

"Disappointed? Really? I thought that letter from McFadden was a pretty good find," I said, shifting my weight to lower the box back under the bed.

"I was looking for something else." She picked up a wooden inlaid letter box off the dresser and absently opened and closed it. Suddenly she stopped and sniffed the red velvet interior. With a glance at the perfume bottles atop the dresser she sniffed again and then closed the letter box.

Grace bent down and shoved the big box under the bed, behind the pink and black chequered bedspread. "Sorry this was so disappointing for you."

"I'll survive," Myrl said. "Is this a box spring?" I asked, remembering Rachel's room and how the bed had been torn apart.

"Good thinking, Faye." Myrl jumped and I rose from the bed. As she and Grace held the mattress high, I stuck my fingers underneath and lo! there was a bundle of papers.

They were letters, a half dozen or so, stacked between two sheets of black heavy paper and tied with a pale blue satin ribbon. In the light, the faded etching of typeface could be seen through the paper and it was clear these were letters and not receipts. Counting the sharp folds, I made out seven notes.

Myrl breathed in a long breath of air. "Now these, my dear Faye, may prove interesting. Do you see how the ribbon has been worn at the knot? That's from tying and untying. She was receiving these letters from someone regularly."

I put the bundle down on the bed. "Oh, I don't want to read someone's love letters."

"I'm sure these are not of love," said Myrl and picked them up. "Wait – listen." From the street level we could hear the backstage door open and close and then footsteps on the staircase.

"Prepare yourselves, ladies," said Myrl and stood.

"What the hell is going on in here," boomed a voice and even though we knew someone was arriving, we three still jumped. A man entered, rifle in hand, booting filthy and worn. A huge man, with tiny sharp eyes and a rough greying beard, hatless, but with a heavy buckskin coat, western style. "I said, what the hell is going on here. Who are you?"

"I," said Myrl standing, "am Myrl Adler Norton and this is my companion, Faye Tullis."

"Well, who gave you permission to be here?"

"And you are Forrest Dansen," said Myrl, extending her hand.

"Do I know you?" he thundered and stood like a tree in the middle of the room. "You" – he shook his gun at Grace – "who are you?"

"Dr Grace."

"Oh, I've heard about you – the lady doctor, yeah. Right." He still held the gun in front of him like a metal stick. "So, are you just being nosy or what? Going through my sister's things."

"Mr Dansen," said Myrl. "Your sister was murdered most brutally, and I can understand, or attempt to understand, your anger and outrage. But we are here" – she stumbled over her next words – "on an investigation."

"Investigation? Investigation? On whose account? Who asked you here?"

"On our own account at the moment," said Myrl. "It was Faye and I who discovered your sister's body in Northampton."

The gun was lowered. Her statement seemed to reassure him. "Now I remember your names."

"Your sister was killed in this very room," she said. "I would say she had her throat slit and that she knew her attacker. Though there may have been one killer there was at least one other accomplice."

"But Myrl, how can you be so sure of all that?" I asked and was instantly sorry I had questioned her.

She stood next to Mr Dansen in the centre of the hardwood floor. She kept her gaze on him. "Do you see the small carpet-tack holes in the floor, Mr Dansen? There used to be a large carpet here. Am I right, Grace?"

"She did have a carpet here, imported from the Orient. A big, thick, flowery thing. You're right."

"A brand-new floor – remember the fire here last year – so the floor was brand new, these are not old tack holes. Why would a carpet be taken up? Because it was stained with blood. Floors can be wiped clean. But a carpet, no. There's no way to get the stain out. And who rolled up the carpet? It looks to be twelve feet by eighteen or so. One person? Never. They could never carry it. But two people surely could. So you see, Mr Dansen, there is much to be learned from this room."

"And she knew her attacker?" I ventured.

"Would you say your sister was neat, Mr Dansen? A finicky housekeeper? "

"What? Hell, no. She was always too busy to clean up. I always said the fellow who'd get her would be sorry. Busy with her fancy life and her fancy friends. She was like a child. Spoiled rotten."

"So you see, not only are there no signs of a struggle, the room is spotless. And according to Mr Dansen, his sister carried a more relaxed attitude toward housework." She began to slowly pace around in a small circle. "What is missing from this room are signs of life. Alyssa Dansen was living here when she was killed. Yet there are no dishes out, no spoiled food in the ice chest, nothing to suggest she was staying here. Even the bathroom sink has been wiped clean. The person who killed her did not have to resort to struggle. More importantly, they were comfortable enough to remain here and scour the place down when they were through. The bath drain is of singular importance."

"What are you?" he said, tilting his head at her.

Myrl stood very tall. "A professor of logic."

Forrest Dansen smirked. That's the only way to describe the impudence behind his smile. "So, you're a teacher then at some college, ay?"

"At Smith, Smith College, in Northampton."

"Seems people waste a lot of time and money on fancy colleges when they could be earning a decent living."

"Let's stay on course, Mr Dansen," said Myrl. "We are here to discover why your sister was killed and by whom."

"You'll never find out," he said and moved over to sit down on the chair. He looked coarse, dirty, and quite oversize sitting in the dainty, needlepoint-covered Queen Anne chair.

"And why do you say that?"

"Because she was into something way over her head, that's why."

"What do you mean, precisely?"

"I mean she was up to doin' something no good, that's what, and she was loath to tell me, and believe me I tried to make her tell me too. But she was always quirky."

Myrl's tone changed and was less confrontational. "Why did your sister have a home down in Northampton?"

"That was our older sister's house and she left it to the two of us when she died. Alyssa bought me out."

I was surprised. "She was able to buy you out?"

"Well, she wasn't married so it was legal," he said. "The property could be in her name."

"I think Miss Tullis was referring to monetary considerations," said Myrl, wiping a hand along a windowsill.

"Oh, she's got money," he said and his eyes grew even smaller and very sharp with an intelligence I'm not too certain he meant to reveal. "Don't let nobody tell you otherwise. She had plenty of money. Too much of it if you ask me."

Myrl gazed out the window for a moment. "I suspected as much." She paused and folded her arms in front of her. "Mr Dansen, could you please do something for me?"

"I don't do nothing for nobody unless it lines my pocket," he said squarely.

"Mr Dansen, she is trying to help you!" I said, and Myrl held up a hand.

"All I would like you to do is allow Miss Tullis and me to represent your interests. In this manner I will be provided an excuse to investigate your sister's death. Right now, I am only here out of curiosity and people are willing to talk to me from novelty. But when the novelty wears thin, I will have no reason to continue a line of questioning."

"I don't know you from a cord of wood, miss, and frankly, I wouldn't trust a woman to feed garbage to a pig."

There was a stunned silence in the room. Somehow this statement, so clear, as if his prejudice lay right under glass, was more difficult to grapple with than the obtuse, slippery injustices women are asked to survive in the fabric of day-to-day life. His ignorance was up front and honest, and the brilliance of that honesty blinded me for an instant. Myrl was the first to recover – though this isn't quite true. To recover one must first be daunted, disarmed, or laid flat by something. His words carried no weight for her, and must have flitted about her ears much like the buzzing of an irritating fly. Her response, however, was carefully measured and was not lost on him at all. Her head snapped around, and she took several steps toward him, arms folded.

"You may not trust me to feed your pigs, Mr Dansen, but you can be assured you do not want me as an adversary. Let me remind you of something. Your sister was brutally murdered. Her throat was slit from ear to ear. Her internal organs were ripped from her and discarded. Her skin was then tanned and stuffed. This is the work of what some might call a mad mountain man. The people in town look down on you as it is for your lack of education and disdain for their town life. You are a trapper. You are used to slitting throats, skinning and carving up animals. If you stand to inherit a lot of money, Mr Dansen, and I'm sure you do, you will be more than just a suspect. In this town you are the outsider, and I trust you are correct in having little faith in the court system of a small town where many tongues can wag as one."

This time the silence flared, alive with a sense of excitement, as if we had named and caged a beast. He stood, passed the gun to his other hand, and passed a slow stare at the three of us.

"I can't believe I'm sitting here, listening to a bunch of females yack about something they know nothing about." He turned around to leave.

"I know quite a bit about the art of blackmail, Mr Dansen."

That stopped him.

"Ay? What?" He turned back around abruptly. "What do you know of that?"

"In terms of your sister, very little, at the moment, but I suspect I could discover far more than you." Myrl sniffed and walked over to me. "The letters, Faye."

I handed her the bundle wrapped in black paper. She pulled the blue satin ribbon, the bundle loosened, and she opened the top note. " 'May 20, 1918. This time there are two dozen. I want a hundred dollars. Same place. Remember the consequences'." She opened the next. "'September 12, 1917. The number now is forty. You are all so busy. I want five hundred dollars. Same place, same time. You know what will happen'." Myrl glanced up at him. "Should I go on?"

He was silent.

"I see this means nothing to you." She wrapped the letters back in the paper. "I'm taking these as evidence, Mr Dansen, and I will investigate them to satisfy my own curiosity. I see you do not care to be informed. Faye –." She handed the bundle back to me and I slipped it into a pocket in my knickers. Myrl walked right past him, and I followed with Grace behind me.

"Good day, Mr Dansen," Grace said.

"Ay! Wait there," he called to Myrl as she was on the fourth step.

"Yes?" She turned and looked up at him with irritation.

"I knew she was bein' blackmailed by someone. There were hints of it. That's why I know she's got money somewhere."

"Precisely, Mr Dansen. Your point, please, I'm very hungry and I have a lovely turkey and cheese sandwich waiting for me."

"Well, if you do find out anything about this blackmailer, I want to know about it."

"And why is that?"

"Because I want that money back!" he bellowed. "It's my money now and they've been milkin' it from her." Myrl stepped back to the landing. "Are you saying you would like me to represent you?"

"Do I have to pay you?"

"Technically, yes. I will only charge you a nickel, however, as I am concerned for the legitimacy of your claim."

"What does that mean?"

This time it was Grace who spoke. "It means she believes you may not get anything at all."

This agitated him. "What? Why do you say that? I will!"

Myrl spoke calmly. "Mr Dansen, I will work to the best of my ability to ensure you get what is your due."

He scowled and brushed past her, waggling the gun by his side. We watched the back of his head as he started thumping down the bare wooden stairs.

"So, Mr Dansen?" she called after him.

"Uh, what." He kept walking.

"Mr Dansen." This was said more sharply and it slowed him down slightly.

"For a nickel," he called over his shoulder. He was at the bottom of the stairs and then we three heard the outside door open and close.

"Well done, Myrl," said Grace, flipping the lock. "We finished here?" Myrl nodded and she closed the door. "Most of the time folks are pretty polite, even if they don't trust you, but once in a while …" She walked past Myrl and me, shaking her head. "And then I get called out to treat them for fever or to stitch them up and they won't even look at me." Grace paused for a moment on the stairs. "I hope he stays healthy for as long as he's in town."

"He'd be a cinch to treat," I said, wiping my hands on my pants.

"Yes, once I hobbled him."

I laughed.

Myrl frowned slightly. "What?" she said, deaf to the conversation and unaware of our need to lighten the mood.

"What's the matter?" I asked.

"That was not who I expected."

Grace laughed again. "You could have fooled me. How did you guess it was him? I've never seen him around before."

"The clothes, the manner, the fact he came up the steps with familiarity and was so affronted." Myrl frowned, not revelling in Grace's request for an explanation of her powers. "I don't mean to alarm you both, but we have been followed ever since we left the Wheel Club."

I stood very still.

"What?" said Grace.

"It's only a reporter. I recognise him from the horde which met us at the station yesterday. He was sitting in the lobby at the Wheel Club and he followed us here. I was expecting him on the stair, not Forrest Dansen."

Grace gripped the banister. "What does this guy look like?"

"Tall – average build, older than myself. Blond"

She relaxed. "Oh, that's Curran Holt from the *New York Times*. He covers all of southern Vermont. He's very city if you know what I mean. Likes everything just so. I'm actually surprised it's him. Are you sure? Very blond?

"Yes, and a grey flannel coat. Slight limp. Left-handed."

"Well, I wouldn't know about being left-handed," said Grace. "I treated him once for headache. I didn't ask him to write his name." She glanced at me again. "But that's him. He's got a piece of a bullet in his knee and it gives him trouble. He's not especially adventuresome. In fact he's rather lazy. That's why I say I'm surprised. He's not one known for expending much effort on a story."

"Well, we shall see," was all Myrl said and I knew she disagreed with Grace. I, too, had a different impression of the man standing on the platform. She glanced at the door to the room across from Alyssa Dansen's. "Who lives there? In number two?"

Grace paused and frowned. "Like I said, no one. Maybe Giles rents it out. I don't really know." She glanced at her watch. "I'm sorry, ladies, but I've got rounds at one o'clock."

"And we have work to do," said Myrl.

Grace descended the stairs. Myrl started to follow, but I laid a hand on her arm. "How did you know?" I whispered.

"Know?"

"That Alyssa Dansen had money and was being blackmailed and that those were the letters?"

Myrl lowered her voice and spoke very quickly. "Faye, what I know and don't know are sometimes the same. A person is killed out of lust, for money, or out of anger or

116

revenge. There was a reason the body was stuffed and that reason had something to do with the element of time. Someone wanted to create the illusion Alyssa Dansen was alive. They were picking a particular time to expose her death. This does not sound like a crime of passion to me. Someone in a jealous rage does not then gut and skin the victim. So that leaves money or revenge as the motive, though there is some thing very macabre which stretches these parameters, I admit. When Forrest said she had money, I had already suspected her modest income was a charade. Her clothes, her shoes, her complaints about poor finances. Coupled with the letters –"

"But they could have been love letters, that's what I thought they were."

"No. Firstly, why have them stuck under a mattress? If they were love letters she would want them in a desk drawer or her bureau where she could read them over and over again, not hidden away under a mattress."

I chose not to argue with her on this point. She obviously had never received letters of adoration.

"Which brings me to my second point: The paper was not wrinkled. She obviously did not read them over and over again as one would do with love letters. Third, there were seven of them. The paper of the first was much more yellowed than the one on top, meaning they must stretch back over several years. When we return to Miss Howe's, we shall read the rest, but I suspect they will go back at least four years. Last, black paper is not the sort of thing one would wrap love letters in, wouldn't you say?"

"No, I guess not."

"So, I believe she was killed for money and that this blackmailing business has something to do with it."

"Do you think she refused the blackmailer and that was why she was killed?"

Myrl paused and rubbed her chin. "One does not usually remove the source," she said. "But there are two things which puzzle me more right now."

I made a wild guess. "Why she kept the letters?"

Myrl closed her eyes and slowly smiled. She patted my shoulder and her eyes opened. "Yes. Very good, Faye. Kleinman's dilemma! Why? Why not burn them?"

"Are you two coming?" We heard Grace from downstairs and could see a swath of sunlight spilling into the dark hall from the open door.

"Coming," called Myrl and then she smiled again and reached out her hand to rub the downy green of a violet leaf. "And Faye," she said very softly, "don't you think it's odd that a plant should be so green and robust this time of year?"

"Well, violets are good winter flowers. You've got to keep them damp though. I'm terrible with plants, actually."

"Damp?" she said as if she had not heard me.

"Yes, they need constant moisture."

"Don't you find this interesting, then?"

"What?"

"The fact that no one lives in either room and hasn't maybe for months, yet someone comes here regularly just to tend to a potted plant?" She touched the soil with an index finger and held it up for my inspection. It was smudged with moist dirt. "And that person has visited here fairly recently."

* * * * *

We parted, Grace pedaling south toward the hospital, Myrl and I pedalling north to the police station. Though we both kept careful watch, we did not see our mysterious Mr Holt and I was relieved. Perhaps Grace's description of him was correct: he was not the most aggressive of his kind.

"Patrick. Is this office always in such disarray?" Myrl was sitting on the floor of the Brattleboro town clerk's office with stacks of papers around her. The office was small, with WANTED posters on the cork board along with announcements of land transfers, stud bulls, and head of dairy cattle for sale. There was one phone in the hall and the place was unheated.

"If you could've waited till Monday I could get Cheryl in here to help you," said Captain Patrick O'Keefe, a very young man, not much older than me, but with an easy manner toward Myrl, and a person who I thought seemed very self-assured. He had bright red hair, parted on the side, curly and combed flat with grease. He had the sort of skin that one would expect to freckle, but instead he was simply pale. When she first announced herself at the police station he gave the strapping hug of one man to another. Myrl seemed slightly taken aback and straightened her tie. He laughed and had given me the wink of a conspirator. He seemed genuinely pleased to see her. Though he stood taller than she, his stature was not mature. Thin and gangly, one was not quite sure if he would ever fill out. He looked boyish next to Myrl, and now he sat on the floor beside her and rubbed his eyes with the fingertips of both hands and yawned.

"And you know nothing of this?" said Myrl.

"Look, if it's here we'll find it," said O'Keefe. He dropped his hands. "All I know is what I've already told you. If they were married it was never announced in the paper, never officially recorded, and there was no license – and in that case, it weren't legal."

"Maybe it was filed under her name," I said and they both looked up at me. "Are any of the theatre group in key town positions?" continued Myrl.

"Like what? Mayor? We don't have a mayor, Myrl, unless you'd like to run." He grinned at me and there was that wink. Myrl unfolded herself from the floor, and scanned the rows of oak filing cabinets across from the window and the front desk.

"That is not what I mean. Something a little less formal."

"Oh, I know. Yes. The answer is yes. In fact both Henry Mitchell and Hollister McLean are justices of the peace. And Gladdis McFadden is a notary public. Don't ask me how she managed that one." He turned to me. "She stamps for the theatre and the opera house folks mostly. They needed someone to be able to do their papers. The Wheel Club uses her too."

There was a tapping at the door.

"Come in!"

Howard Adams and Marion French stood somewhat breathless in the centre of the room. I could see their bicycles outside the door, flung to the ground, and the couple looked as if they had pedalled hard.

"There's been an incident at Giles Wilcox's," Howard said. "Someone broke in and took a gun."

"He's back, you see. He came back on the eleven o'clock train and he discovered this," said Marion. "He called the Wheel Club when he couldn't find you. He wants you to come out to the house right away."

"He's got plenty of guns," said O'Keefe. "Which one was taken?"

"A pistol," said Howard.

Patrick O'Keefe tapped his upper lip with a finger. "Thanks for running me down," he said. "I'll call Wilcox," and he stepped out into the hall, rang the operator and placed a call to the Wilcox farm. The couple left as abruptly as they had arrived, no doubt to alert the rest of the town as to their efforts. There was something about their harried manner which told me they rather enjoyed the unfolding drama. It was as if they had forgotten this was all linked to murder. Or if they did remember, the murder was unreal, like a plot from one of their plays.

I strained to hear what Patrick O'Keefe was saying on the phone when Myrl whispered loudly, "Faye, come here," and waved me furiously over to the file cabinets where she was standing. One file was pulled forward and written in neat script was McLean, Hollister. Myrl's face was impassive in triumph but I could tell she was quite pleased with herself. She slapped the file on the desk, dramatically throwing open the manila flap.

"There," she said. "See for yourself." She launched her gaze out a window.

I looked down. There, neatly filled in, dated June 21, 1918, was a marriage license signed by Giles Wilcox and Alyssa Dansen, witnessed and filed by Hollister McLean. I felt my face flush.

"Interesting isn't it? Yes, I feel the same way. A sterling example of Chapper's Corollary."

I found Chapper's Corollary difficult. These rules of logic she kept deriving theories from were esoteric mathematical formulas found in a German treatise entitled *Rules of the Mind and Man* which she would make carbons of and hand out in class. I was certain no student would ever find applications for these rules and the text was a point of contention in class. Myrl, however, found the rules not just useful, but necessary. I knew the corollary she mentioned had something to do with the components of a premise, but I didn't want to press. "So she was alive in June," I merely said and shivered.

"We are getting closer to uncovering the date of her murder," said Myrl. "But we also need to know why. When these two pieces are fitted together, it will be self-evident who killed her. Like a Barbara statement. If both premises are true, the conclusion is inevitable."

Chapter Eight

The Stolen Gun

The Wilcox farm was a gentleman's farm – an estate with little property, only twenty acres, and mostly wooded. Wilcox's interests lay beyond Brattleboro, in other continents, and though he claimed to have no aspirations to public office, O'Keefe shook his head and shrugged to say Wilcox played that card close to his chest. We were on the road and I was gathering information, doing most of the talking, sitting up in front with O'Keefe. Myrl, who sat in the back seat, spent her time reading the Ford joke book she had spied on the dashboard.

I was surprised we had been invited out. It did not seem the best circumstance to engage entertaining two women, but O'Keefe explained Wilcox was desperate to meet us. To see the faces of the women who had discovered his fiancée. Excuse me. His wife. I was already building my suspicions about Mr Wilcox.

The drive out was long, at least forty minutes. Putney Road was dirt and not well maintained. As we bumped along, bundled head to toe in blankets, I was beside myself waiting for Myrl to announce our discovery at the town clerk's office. But she never said a word.

In Putney, we made a left at the butcher's on the corner and O'Keefe shifted into a lower gear to ascend Kimball Hill. When we reached the top, there was a wide curve to the left and then on our right was a sign painted with THE

WILLOWS. In echo were two massive willows, odd in this part of New England, to be sure, standing on either side of the driveway. In the countryside, where autumn finds elms turning brilliant gold and maples flame to orange and red, the only claim of the ever-green willow is that it is the first to shoot buds in the spring and the last to lose its leaves in fall. Where snow falls six months out of the year, the willow, in its own way, defies time. Now with all leaves gone from most of the other deciduous trees, the pair of willows stood drooping, holding a vigilance of waning green against the onslaught of winter.

I have always enjoyed looking at people's homes, the style of house and what they choose to surround themselves with. Years spent in the bush, living in tents or small cabins, have left me appreciative of the finer lifestyles I'm afraid. We circled up to the doorway, past a low stone wall. Beyond the row of stone, a flower garden lay tiered in five levels by stone retaining walls. Rushing down the hillside, away from the house, the flower beds levelled off into what must have been an enormous vegetable garden in the summer. Out the back, we could see pasture, and beyond that, green, thick woods. A stream ran parallel to the road and along the back of the field. Truly a pristine farm.

The house was Victorian, probably built thirty years ago with a turret on the right side and a long porch on the left. Though three stories high, its white paint and black shutters, the empty flower boxes, and four smoke-stained chimneys gave the impression of comfortable ease. For someone so wealthy I would have expected a massive brick and stone Gothic or a home like the famous Fletcher castle up north.

As we pulled up to the front door and O'Keefe cut the motor, the Ford sputtered and then fell silent. There was a roadster in the gravel drive, in front of the house. The front door opened onto the porch and Wilcox himself stepped out to meet us. It was growing cold in the late afternoon and he breathed on his hands. He was of average height, of muscular build, and had a tan of richer hue than Howard Adams's. His skin was coppery brown, the kind of tan one receives in the bush, from sunlight filtered through dust and sweat. His black hair was curly and unkempt, matching a pair of rather bushy eyebrows. His hands were strong, wide, and finely shaped, nails meticulously clipped, but as he shook my hand, his palm was of ice and I felt a tremor in his arm.

"It is very good of you to come all the way out here with no notice," he said, smiling slightly at Myrl and me. He nodded at O'Keefe and led us inside. Though he seemed in prime physical shape, he walked with a stoop and there was a weariness to his step. I could not help but feel protective toward him. To arrive home to find his loved one dead and his house burglarised ... I could not imagine.

He turned to take our coats.

"Where's Jordan?" said O'Keefe. "And Clarissa?"

"They're not due back until the end of the month. I didn't want to call them back earlier."

"It might be good to have them around."

Wilcox shrugged. "It's not necessary." Wilcox's words were deep and resonating. Even when he spoke quietly, there was a rumble and wave which penetrated. Cultivated for an audience, his voice was smooth and assured. In the even light of the hall I could see circles under his eyes and behind his tanned face there was a pallor in his cheeks which left him looking rather ashen. He dropped Myrl's coat on the floor.

"Oh, I'm so sorry," he said. "Forgive me. I'm not doing well and –"

"I understand, Mr Wilcox," she said and pressed a hand on his arm.

"We have met before? I seem to remember you ..."

"At Mary Howe's farm, several years ago."

He nodded and his dark eyes were like black water, framed by heavy lashes and troubled with deep sorrow. When he spoke again his voice shook.

"I have to say that I really can't bear to hear too much of this business right now. I understand you found Alyssa – I mean the body – and I don't or I can't really think too much about what happened to her. I really just wanted to meet you two and somehow try to grasp something ... but I don't know what."

He shook O'Keefe's hand, "Thanks for coming out, Patrick. I need you to see what happened down in the library."

We all stood rather awkwardly in the hall for a moment and then Wilcox motioned us to follow him. "Well, come. This way," he said.

* * * * *

Glass lay in long shards on the thick carpet and though a fire snapped in the deep fireplace across the room, the broken light in the outside porch door left the library cold and draughty. More glass lay to the left of the fireplace, where a gun case, six feet long or so, was smashed open on the floor. The top was shattered.

"I guess you should have kept your coats on," said Wilcox. "I don't know what I was thinking." I shivered slightly and he apologised again.

Myrl had moved over to the door and was poking at the broken pane with her finger.

"Patrick, will you be taking fingerprints?"

"Well now, I suppose I should," he said and winked at me. She brought out a pair of black leather gloves and pulled them on, distractedly looking at the porch door. She stepped outside for a moment and tested the lock. It was obvious the intruder broke the side-light to get at the lock. O'Keefe brought out a small vial of what looked like white talcum powder and a wide roll of clear tape. "If I find something, I'll let you know," he said. "Now excuse me." He knelt down to take a closer look at the lock.

"What a beautiful rug," said Myrl, brushing the toe of her Oxford across the plush nap.

"Yes, I got it in India at market."

"And did you also bring one to Miss Dansen?"

"Why, yes. It's a floral print, hand woven. It's in her room, above the Opera House."

126

"No longer, Mr Wilcox," she said. "It is gone. Faye and I were just at your Alyssa's and there is no rug. Was it of value?"

"No. I mean some, yes, of course. Not much, though. Why would someone steal the rug?

"Because, you see, it was where she stood when she was murdered." She paused. "I am sorry, Mr Wilcox."

Giles had sat down in a chair and now he stared at the fire.

"I can't believe how hard this has hit me," he said. "I'm sorry."

"Giles, we have to find out about this gun." Patrick stood and put a hand on Wilcox's shoulder.

Wilcox sat for just a moment longer, and then gripped the arms of the chair and stood again, walking over to the glass case. "It was in here. It was a Winchester Palmer, four cylinders, and a box of bullets was taken as well. I don't know why they left the two rifles and the Bonny pistol." In the case there remained two rifles with very long barrels and one rather large pistol with a white mother of pearl handle.

"A Winchester Palmer. Isn't that considered a woman's gun?" O'Keefe was wrestling with the roll of tape.

"No. Not really. A cardman's gun. A gentleman's gun. It is small. I suppose a woman might carry one. I just don't understand why it was stolen."

"Was anything else taken?"

"No. Not that I know of. I've walked the rooms and it looks to me as if the person didn't even go upstairs. There's a lock on the downstairs door leading up and that was not disturbed."

"Mr Wilcox. Was there anything else at all?" asked Myrl.

"No. Really. Not that I know of."

"Would you mind if I just looked around, Giles?" O'Keefe asked. "And checked everything out?" He had given up on the tape.

"Certainly. Go ahead."

"Mr Wilcox, is your house visible from your neighbours'? In particular, this door – can your neighbours see it?" Myrl peered out the panes of glass.

"In winter yes, in summer and fall, no. The foliage is too thick."

I glanced out the door and could see up as far as the next bend. Several large houses were scattered along the road, but unlike The Willows, these were set close to the road. As I turned away, Myrl touched my arm and pointed. I kept my gaze on the white farmhouse directly across the street. There was Curran Holt, walking quickly down the path, folding his notebook shut.

"There must be adhesive on our backs," said Myrl under her breath. She turned away from the door. "Giles," she said gently, "Faye and I went to Alyssa's room to see what we could find –"

"Which wasn't much –" Both men looked at me.

"Yes. Well. We did find certain letters suggesting that she was being, well ... I fear I cannot be delicate about this, but these letters suggested she was being blackmailed."

Giles stood very still for a moment. Patrick O'Keefe, on the other hand, roared "What the hell," and stood up. "Would you ladies please hand those letters over. You're not supposed to do things like that. You could get in trouble."

"I assure you we did nothing illegal. The letters remain under her bed." She paused, without even a glance at me. The letters remained in my pocket and she knew it. "I don't mean to offend you," began Myrl, but Giles held up a hand.

He watched the fire and I could see his hands shaking slightly. Giles cleared his throat and ran a hand through his hair slowly, deliberately as he spoke. "I thought she was in some kind of trouble. I tried to have her confide in me – but she was so proud. We became very close this past year, and I begged her to marry me." Here he stopped and dropped his hand. He turned back to face us. "I can't tell you how she refused. She said she loved me. But she said there was something from her past which she would never divulge and that I had to trust her. She told me repeatedly she was not a bad person, but that I already knew. She was an angel. But she did say there was nasty business –"

"Is that how she described it'" Myrl was watching him very carefully. She held her chin cupped in one hand, her right arm supported by her left.

"No. No." He sighed and gave O'Keefe a glance. "She told me repeatedly that there were people who were trying to destroy her and they would try to destroy us if we married. Or words to that effect."

"Did you ever feel" – O'Keefe cleared his throat – "threatened? And why didn't she come to me? She knew me well enough."

Giles shrugged. "I took it all to be fabrication. I mean, well, yes, maybe she did something in her past which may have been unfortunate, but that did not matter to me. I knew she had this half-corked brother – a loose cannon – and I thought maybe he was involved in something reprehensible. I did not take any of what she said seriously, except insofar as it kept her from her commitment to me. She believed herself. And now. Everything she said was true." He returned his gaze to the fire.

The clock above the mantel struck and a gilded cherub turned three times in a slow dance above the face of the clock. It was then I noticed the two pocket watches. Giles brought out a silver one from his left breast pocket and then, moments later, a gold one from his right. Both were secured with long chains, and I was relieved. He checked the time, and then snapped both shut.

Myrl gave Giles a small smile. "I am truly sorry, Giles. If we discover anything in our travels here, I will certainly alert you … and Patrick. And when you are more ready, we should talk."

Giles showed us out and as O'Keefe helped us into the Ford, I saw Giles start the motor on the roadster, hop back out, and lift the door on what used to be the attached barn. He waved goodbye and as the door lifted I saw a row of four-foot-high white painted horses baring their teeth, their necks arching out from shredded packing wood. I nudged Myrl. Giles edged the roadster inside the converted garage and the door closed.

O'Keefe, slamming the door, noticed my interest. "He's got something to do with the carousel going in and those are all the carvings. It's supposed to be the first of its kind in the country. All horses. All stallions. Fifty-two of them. No giraffes or tigers and lions or that sort of thing. Don't ask me why."

"I read somewhere that children always want to ride horses and ponies, that the other mounts scare them," I said.

O'Keefe shrugged. "Maybe that's why Giles picked all horses, then. He loves to talk about the carousel. You should ask him sometime."

The ride south to Mrs Howe's was uneventful. Myrl picked up where she was in the Ford joke book and I was left to weather O'Keefe's tongue-lashing about the blackmail letters. Right in the middle of the most humiliating diatribe Myrl piped up from the back seat:

"– I hear they are going to magnetise the rear axle of the Ford."
"– What's the idea?"
"– So it will pick up the parts that drop off."

O'Keefe did not appear amused. Myrl, however, just cackled.

* * * * *

As soon as we were back at Mrs Howe's tavern, Myrl flew up the stairs to change. I followed suit. She descended long after I did in the most outlandish outfit. The dress was of palest burgundy silk, shimmering to the knee, slit up both sides with a gathered ivory lace bodice. Scooped low across the back, a smooth arching shadow fell across her bare shoulders, cast by the severe tilt of the matching wide-brim hat affixed to her head. She did not seem the least self-conscious about her choice of dress and descended the stairs deeply invested in a game within her own mind, a moving of parts and players and she appeared oblivious to the present –

130

a victim of her own mental agility. The actions of her mind did not slow the actions of her body, however, and she was a flurry of distracted movement coming down the stairs, her low heels making a smooth even patter, pivoting at the foot of the staircase and launching herself down the hall. I was almost afraid to speak directly to her for the first several minutes we were all in the dining room, for fear conversation might be too jarring.

"Myrl," I began softly and she spun around.

"Faye, I've told Mary this morning that we would all be dining out tonight and she suggested the Wheel Club, of course. Very elegant, don't you think?"

Mrs Howe was sitting at the head of the long dining table playing Patience and slapping down cards dramatically. "Eh? We're not going there this evening, Myrl. And you're not either," she said, referring to me. She continued to scan her rows.

"Oh," said Myrl, snapping a fan into a neat half circle across her face. "There has been an invitation somewhere else?" Myrl did not seem surprised in the least. She collapsed the fan and tapped a card in Mrs Howe's hand. Mrs Howe placed it on the table.

"You see," said Myrl, "The game of solitaire has a set of random elements restricted to just one person. A good player can nearly always overcome the hurdles set up by these elements."

"I just enjoy the game," said Mrs Howe. "We did indeed receive an invitation, by the way." Mrs Howe looked up from her cards. "Howard Adams is having a little gathering at his house. And everyone's going to be there. He asked me whom you'd like to have and I said Grace, though I don't know if she will be able to come. It seems Marion has taken quite a liking to you two. He invited me, to be polite. I think they just want it in the papers that they hosted you."

"They like the publicity," I said.

"They like anything that will help them find their names bandied about town."

"You don't much care for them?" I asked. Mrs Howe pushed herself away from the table. "Oh, they're all right. They're just awfully young and I don't have much patience for that sort of thing anymore. And now that they've become something of an item, they're just ridiculous."

"Mary, who have you given copies of your records to?" Myrl smoothed a pair of gloves on the table.

"Me? Oh, anyone who asks, though I don't have many copies made. I don't mind a little attention myself, you know." She looked up from her game again.

"But of the key players in this?"

"Key players? How am I to know the key players? Oh well, all right, I'll make a guess. Let's see. Grace got a copy of *Aida* after she helped me through bronchitis last year. Hollister, of course. He loves opera. Hope Mitchell, I think has several recordings. I know she's got Carmen. Henry hates opera – I know because he never talks to me about it. Patrick O'Keefe's mother, Lily, enjoys opera, I believe. I know he's bought several of my records in town. You know, anyone can buy them."

"Yes, but I want to know who you have personally given them to. With perhaps a signature." Myrl fanned herself.

Mrs Howe looked at me for clarity.

"An autograph," I said. "On the cover."

"Oh, I always write a little something on the jackets, for friends you know. It makes it all less awkward."

"Anyone else?" Myrl was slipping on the pink silk gloves.

"Of your little theatre group? Well, Frances has nearly the whole lot – eight recordings, and all of them gifts, though she certainly could afford to pay me for them."

"What about Gladdis McFadden?"

"No. Not her. Wait a minute, though. Yes. Yes, I do believe I gave her a copy once years ago, some time ago. I don't remember what it was, though. The recording, I mean."

"What time is the party?" asked Myrl.

"Myrl, you make my head spin," said Mrs Howe and went back to her cards.

"Is Frances Hall very rich?" I asked.

Mrs Howe continued to watch her cards. "Rich? You mean wealthy? Yes. Rich in spirit? No. She can be very petty and she is never happy with how comfortable she is. I don't know how much she is worth, but it's quite a bit, I can tell you. Her distant uncle is a Sotheby. She's had her eyes on Giles for a long time and not for love, I must say."

"I'm glad you are coming this evening," said Myrl adjusting the delicate lace shawl on Mrs Howe's shoulders. In one swift movement she bent over and kissed her on the forehead.

"Oh, so am I," sighed Mrs Howe. "We'll have Real take us in the coach. Howard lives off Elliot Street, right in town." She smiled up from her cards. "I wouldn't miss this for the world, Myrl – to see you in action. Your mother would be proud."

There was a pause. "Yes. Well. Shouldn't we be going then."

Mrs Howe slapped down another card and kept her gaze on her rows of royalty. "Myrl, sit down and do take off your gloves. We must be fashionably late – not frightfully early."

* * * * *

Right before we left, Myrl put in a call to Patrick O'Keefe. I could hear her in the hall speaking very quietly and then she signed off with "I'll see you very soon."

As the Blacksom made its way down the street, Myrl leaned forward and whispered, "He didn't find a thing."

"Who?"

"O'Keefe. He didn't find a single fingerprint."

I watched her for a moment. "Myrl, how much did you help your father with his cases?"

She seemed startled by my question. "Why do you ask such a thing? I think I hear the nasty tinge of suspicion in your voice."

"Well, if Mary Howe gave you a love of solitaire and your mother inspired your hair style" – here Myrl touched her knot – "then I would like to suggest that in assisting your father and researching cases, you have been exposed to esoteric knowledge on a wide variety of subjects."

She smiled at me and patted my leg. "You are very observant, Faye. I'm so glad."

Chapter Nine

We Attend a Party

Howard Adams lived right in town, in a small, modern-looking rectangular house with a flat roof, which I imagined would not be terribly practical given the severe winters in this part of the country. Our ride in the Blacksom was fun, we three were all dressed up, and I felt very alive, becoming part of an unravelling mystery. Myrl was ignited with the quest, and she entered the role of guest of honour with grace and a seeming gift for chitchat that I knew exacted an utmost effort and was as calculated as a balancing act.

"You see, this was the library of the Allen estate – not Ethan, of course, one of his cousin's. See the beams. Hand-carved mahogany." Howard held Myrl's arm and was leading her up to a picture window that looked out over the yard. The black of night held fast against the window and I saw their reflections in perfect detail as they looked up toward the ceiling. Eight-inch arch beams crossed the ceiling every five feet or so, curved up like the inside of a boat. Beams also ran down the corner walls of the house and along the windows from ceiling to floor. These vertical beams were carved in intricate detail, cherubs and gargoyles, vines, flowers, gods and goddesses in what was truly fine workmanship. Myrl oohed appropriately, and then bit her tongue. I knew she wanted to ask about the references to Homer and Greek mythology chipped in the wood, but was certain Howard Adams would not be able to respond.

"So, this part of the room was the main library and then the bedrooms and bath were built on later?"

He nodded. "I had to commission them ... Yes?" Marion had stepped behind him and whispered in his ear.

"Excuse me a moment," he said to Myrl and dropped her arm. He clapped several times and announced, "Giles is coming. He just telephoned."

Frances Hall who was standing behind me by the crystal punch bowl on the long table caught her breath. I heard Hollister mutter, "He doesn't have to do that," and watched him jab a cracker in the small porcelain bowl of black caviar. Mary Howe placed a hand on his arm and they began a conversation. Patrick O'Keefe, whom I was surprised to see sitting and chatting with Marion French on the divan, paused in his conversation and shook his head. Marion laid a hand on his knee. She was lovely, lovely, lovely and from even a few feet away I could smell the soft, lilaced waft of scented powder.

Myrl, with her arm still outstretched, looked lost, abandoned by Howard. She was stunning, majestic in a blue hydrangea chiffon peg-top dress, the folds climbing from her ankles and gathered in curving rows like a clam shell to above her waist. The short jacket was of the same light blue, of heavy silk brocade, the intricate handwork of small swirls and twists of silver rising to a textured pattern of glittering feathers. Double-looped glass beads of pale yellow set off her very long neck, and she wore glass earrings to match. As if in defence of her height, the blue flower pot hat held a single yellow feather waving at least a foot above her head. It occurred to me that she really did not understand that others were not as interested in her as she was in them. And that's when I realised the elaborate costumery she was always involved in was indeed just that – a costume. As she did not fit in, clothing and stylish accoutrements were her means to infiltration. I do believe Myrl thought that if she dressed the part for every situation, she would be accepted. But given her penchant for the theatrical, she nearly always ended up overdressing.

I went over to her and was startled to see a whiskey sour in her hand.

"Myrl." I was rather aghast.

"Faye," she said swiftly and her lips hardly moved. "I want you to take this to the kitchen and fetch me some juice. Grapefruit. Anything. Please wash the glass first." She smiled broadly at Patrick O'Keefe, and as she passed me to sit on the other side of him, the glass was mine.

I walked through the swing doors to the kitchen, dumped the whiskey in the sink, rinsed the glass and found the icebox. It was a modern refrigeration unit and I could see pipes leading to the basement where the compressor was housed. There was a large fruit bowl in the pantry and by chance a good supply of citrus. With the cutting board out and a sharp knife, I selected the largest grapefruit and slit it cleanly down the centre. The swing doors opened. It was Hope Mitchell. She glanced in the sink and saw the ice cubes.

"You know, I'm not supposed to drink either," she said. "I was watching her to see what she would do."

Hope had a wineglass in her hand. She took a long drink and smiled, swirling the burgundy. She was an attractive woman, but for someone in her mid-thirties, she did nothing to enhance herself. Her clothes were rather shabby and unpressed and her brown hair, which she wore tied back, never looked freshly combed. Her features were handsome but not attended to, and she seemed unaware of her potential for charm.

"She hasn't mentioned me, has she?"

"Pardon me?" I said, squeezing half the grapefruit. I couldn't find a juicer so I gripped it in both hands and pressed.

"Myrl doesn't remember me, now, does she?"

"Remembered you from what?" I shook my head. "I'm sorry."

"Don't apologise, especially to me." She sighed. "We had such wonderful conversations. I truly admired her." She paused and quite matter-of-factly supposed aloud, "She must have been really doped up on medication."

It took me several seconds to deduce the implications of her statement. I glanced quickly to see if this admission embarrassed her but Hope appeared oblivious to her own comment.

"When was that, precisely?" I said, hearing Myrl's stressing of *precisely* coming from my lips.

"Oh. Let's see." She sighed and leaned against the pantry door. "Two years ago this past summer. I've been back twice since then. But I really can't see how this one little glass can hurt, can you? But she was there for something else. Her nerves or something. It's all pretty hazy actually."

"Well," I said, squeezing the other half.

"You know she wouldn't take her medication at the end. They had to force her. They had to hold her down and make her. It was awful."

My heart began to beat hard and I realised I did not want to hear what she was telling me. My interest in this subject was minimal.

"One time she was so medicated she couldn't even sit up and they had to strap her in a wheelchair. But she could still carry on the most fascinating conversations. About the stars and time, and how if you walked through a pasture and then scraped the mud off your boots into a potting bowl you could grow the most wonderful bunch of wildflowers."

I laughed. I thought of Myrl's shoes lined up by the front door back at the Norton home.

"But it's true," she said.

"Oh, I'm sure it is," I said, rinsing my hands. The faux whiskey sour was complete.

"You know Henry is a stiff," she said. "Oh, I shouldn't have used that word. That's so rude of me after what you've been through. Too many gangster movies."

I shrugged. "No apology necessary." She was standing between me and the swing doors and there was no escape. I stood my ground, grapefruit juice in hand.

"You don't seem as shattered as the papers make you out."

I attributed the wine to her sudden, confrontational tone.

"I'm sure it was difficult for you, though." She smiled. "I wish other people would treat me regular. Like Henry. He's a stiff, ooh, I said that again, didn't I? But he is, and he's so careful with me. He treats me like I'm made of glass. Like every little thing might break me. I think he's afraid I'll go off my crock and poison him one day. But I'm stronger than that."

My eyes must have given me away.

"Really, I am." She took a long drink of wine, breathed out a long stream of cigarette smoke and looked over her pink fingernails. She did not look up when she began speaking again.

"What was it like? I mean to see a real dead body? You know everyone here has such a morbid interest in it all and no one will really ask what's on their minds. But I'm not like them. Was it just awful?"

"It was pretty awful," I said.

"But why would somebody shoot her after she was already dead?" She suddenly looked at me, a little startled, like a deer testing the wind and whispered, "Maybe she was murdered twice!" Then she laughed. "Only Alyssa could get murdered twice." She downed the rest of her drink and walked past me, a little unsteadily, to the sink, setting her wineglass on the counter. "I guess I'd better leave it here – I don't want to get in trouble." She paused. "I know why she's here. Why you're both here."

"What?" I said, a bit nervous. I did not know what our role in town with this business was or what I was to say about it, and now I was about to be asked to verify or refute a statement concerning our motives.

"You heard me," she said, taking a step closer. "You're not here for your nerves. She always liked a problem. She's like that Houdini everyone's talking about. She could get out of anything and figure any puzzle. That's why you're here. Everyone knows."

"We really did want to get away," I said lamely. "And Mary Howe is like her aunt."

"Yeah, right."

Her dismissal of my answer made me feel somewhat childish, but I said nothing. She leaned back against the pantry again. "Well, I'll give you lots to think about. Anyone out there could have killed her – you do know they're a lot of verifiable lunatics." She rubbed a finger along the rim of the glass and made it ring a soft low note. "Crystal. I didn't know Howard would actually buy crystal. You see, Howard's a tightwad and a prig. He took a bullet you know, right at the beginning of the war, and lost his spleen. You think that would change him a bit. But no. I think he's also doing more than necking with Miss Marion. And she's a trip. She is just about gaga over Howard to the point that it's sickening to watch. And do you know that Howard would have nothing to do with her up until a month ago?"

"What happened a month ago?"

"Who knows? Oh, I suppose he discovered he could afford a girl. You know, courting's so expensive these days." She stopped her finger on the glass and folded her arms. "And Frances is a witch, just a witch. She's got a heart of cold stone and tons of money, and all she wants is Giles so they can become king and queen. Never mind growing old together, just double that income."

"I understood she was comfortable."

"Comfortable!" she said in a loud whisper. "My God, she's the niece or something or other of the Stetson family or Winchester or somebody like that."

"I thought she looked like hats or guns," I said, trying out the comforting, conspiratorial wink Mrs Howe had given me several times. But one should not attempt too much in the area of social mannerisms unless the measure of comfort is quite high. The wink felt forced, and it backfired.

"I'm serious, she's rich. You don't understand at all," she said suddenly, and her lips were drawn down in a thin, tense grimace. She began coaxing the low ring from the glass rim again and her face softened. "Even Henry. Henry. He gambles too much and he doesn't win often. He does the strangest things. I used to think he was having an affair."

140

Hope said this without the slightest trace of self-consciousness or anger. It was a statement made with the light overtones of one who quietly ponders questions of philosophical implications rather than the flailings of an outraged heart. Her tone puzzled me, and I was left with nothing to say. She sighed and looked at me. "But the real odd one out there is Gladdis."

"Gladdis? She seems a bit rough ..."

"Rough! Rough! Ha. She fancies herself a witch. I mean a real witch. You know the kind? Bubbling caldrons and all that. Hocuspocus. She's nuttier than a fruitcake. But," she said, nudging me before she walked out the swing doors, "so am I, they say."

Henry was talking to Hollister McLean when I returned to the room. Hope slipped up behind her husband and looped her arm through his. He absently patted her hand. She smiled at me and mouthed 'stiff'. I handed Myrl her grapefruit juice. She seemed relieved at my return and propelled me quickly into the ongoing conversation. Hollister was speaking.

"It was a fabulous performance, from both of them. She was breathtaking, in a role she was well suited for. He was charming, witty, and boyish. The script was adequate, but the joy was watching the two of them battle it out on stage."

"This was Giles and Alyssa?" I guessed.

Myrl nodded. "Their last performance together. *The North Wind Blows*, do I have that right?"

Hollister nodded. "The climax of the last scene is a shooting match between the brothers," he turned to me, "Giles and Howard, and her. And in the end, true love shoots her dead."

"It was lovely, wasn't it?" said Marion, floating over from her place next to Patrick.

"I'd say 'gripping' would be a better way of describing it," said Henry.

"Where was her character shot?" asked Myrl, adding, "I have such a morbid interest in all this now."

"Right here," said Hollister, tapping behind his left ear. "Alyssa's death was tragic, excellent theatre to be sure."

Marion cut him off. "She was quite good. I daresay my agent would have been interested in her." She smiled at me. "I did just get an agent, from New York. I don't like to tell everyone, but it's so exciting!"

"Oh, come, Marion, I can't believe you've waited so long to announce it in the paper," Hollister said. "'Marion French, part-time actress awaiting success, lands contract with talent agent. Please call her if you need more details'."

"Now you take that back," said Marion, but there was a nervous edge to her voice. "I have every right to be proud. You're being mean, Hollister."

"So I am," he sighed, and chuckled. "You are so easy to inflame, my dear, you are such easy fodder. You see," said Hollister, keeping his eyes on Marion but leaning into my ear, "poor Marion here suffers from a lack of self-confidence. She started with us as a lowly makeup artist and now she's making big trouble as a star –"

"A very good makeup artist," said Marion. "I have no regrets," she said and walked away, her back stiff.

Hollister winked at me and I saw his face up very close, his cheeks pink with small broken veins under the skin, and I was reminded of my father's brother, a solitary man who hunted elephants and drank too often, and sported the same seemingly robust complexion. "Guess I took it a bit too far," he said. "I should go and apologise or I'll have hell to pay later."

There was a knock on the door and a small pause in the overlap of conversations. Gladdis McFadden, who had been sitting at the piano all evening, continued playing a Strauss Waltz as the door opened and Giles Wilcox entered, looking a little worn about the edges and frazzled. His hair, mussed by the evening breeze, was not properly brushed back, and there were still faint dark circles under his eyes.

Howard greeted him and Marion floated over to offer an additional welcome, securing her position as Howard's woman. It was odd how perfectly matched they seemed. I watched her extend her arm to Giles and then lean her head against Howard's shoulder just for the briefest moment – long enough for Howard to slip an arm around her small waist. From the back they were polar opposites: his tall, dark stature and polished slick of smooth black hair, contrasted with her diminutive size, fair complexion, and fine sheath of shimmering blond waves. I felt a small kernel of jealousy in my stomach – at twenty-one I had had my share of tentative relationships with men, but nothing which approached the aura of intimacy these two so easily cultivated.

As everyone paid their respects to Giles, Myrl and I stood in the corner of the room by the piano and Gladdis. It was his first public appearance since his arrival home and I suddenly felt a little out of place. Mrs Howe, however, seemed to enjoy herself immensely, flitting from group to group and entering every little intimate conversation with such sincerity and warmth that surely could not have been conjured. And everyone responded. She was treated like royalty, a humble queen before an adoring public. She, after all, had accomplished what they all sought: an international career onstage, fame, and success. I was glad she had come and pleased to see her graciousness toward Giles. There was something affirming in watching her give condolences-seeing the wisdom in her eyes, and her face soften in the way someone quite elderly talks about the death of someone quite young.

Giles was very graceful and poised. A small man, he carried the illusion of great stature, but there was something oddly familiar in his grace and it nagged at me – it was as if I had seen him before, but long ago. Patrick O'Keefe waited until Giles had a drink in his hand and was moving over to sit next to Gladdis on the piano bench before he rose from his place on the sofa and laid a hand on Giles's shoulder. It was at that moment Giles's reservation of movement snagged my memory and I watched him pause, stand, and follow Patrick into the kitchen.

"Now what's that about?" I said to no one in particular.

"I suspect they've found the gun," said Myrl, sipping her grapefruit juice, and batting crumbs off her bodice.

"No! Already?"

143

"You are a devil, Miss Norton," said Gladdis, her gravel voice grating against the waltz's melody. "They have found it, you are right. They've found it down at my son's house. Under his back stoop." Her turban this evening was black and studded with sequins.

Myrl and I both stared at her.

Gladdis saw our faces and smiled sweetly up at us. "I work the switchboard Saturday afternoons. Sometimes you have to stay on the line with out-of-state calls." As she ran her short stubby fingers over the keys, a charm bracelet clicked against the ivory ever so slightly. "I suspect they'll be handing up somebody for the gallows soon. Poor soul." She closed her eyes and breathed deeply. "Mozart is so transparent."

"But that's Strauss," said Myrl. "Exactly why I play him," snapped Gladdis and pounded the keys. "Aren't you worried about your son?" I was incredulous she was so calm.

"I know he didn't do it," she said and her eyes remained closed.

"I'm grateful to see you two here – see you again, I mean," said Giles. He had returned from the kitchen and O'Keefe was at his elbow. Myrl extended her arm and Giles gently took her wrist, turning her hand over to kiss the soft cup of her palm.

I saw a slight quiver along her bare arm and she pulled back from him quickly, saying, "I only wish we were here under less tragic circumstances."

Giles sighed and glanced at O'Keefe. "I still cannot believe it happened. I'm going down to Northampton Monday to see the body. I'm seeing she has a proper burial, too. But Lord knows how long they'll want to keep the body. Maybe when I see her it will finally hit home."

"Do come and visit us then," said Myrl. "We would be very pleased if you would care to join us for the evening. Faye and I are in class until three or so, but here, take this, and do come for a visit." To my complete horror, she reached under her front left lapel, right down into the bodice, extracted her card, and handed it to him. He, too, was a little taken aback.

"You are a most resourceful woman, Myrl." He smiled. "I think I will take you up on your offer. I was planning on coming straight back up here, but visiting you might be a wiser decision."

Frances came over and put an arm on his shoulder. She was dressed in shimmering silver, wrapped tightly, sari style. As sure as I was the cloth was from India I was equally certain she was wearing no corset. Her long cigarette glowed on the intake, and she breathed out languorously, a bluish stream of smoke from red lipsticked lips. Truly a woman I could never be. Except, I mused, onstage. I would love to play a character like her. Rich, sexy, beyond typical marrying years, desperate for a legal arrangement and children.

Giles kissed her on the cheek and turned back to Myrl. "Again I am grateful you both came."

"And we are grateful to be included in your little group," said Myrl.

And we certainly were included. I felt drawn into their closed club with a sense of tremulous excitement tempered by my own aversion to elitism. I was thrilled to be not just accepted but elevated to some status by complete strangers. Having always lived as the outsider, as one looking in on another culture, not even feeling a part of my own, it was flattering to be one of a group and not have anything to prove. Without the responsibility of having to define myself, I was able to enjoy myself, and after several glasses of the most robust burgundy I've ever tasted, I found myself sitting on the sofa with Howard and yammering about trying to get a camel in Istanbul, all the while attempting, quite badly, to flirt. Conversation around me was of Winter Carnival, the opening of the carousel, and an ice-fishing contest, but all I thought about was Howard's hand so very close to my knee. Myrl retrieved me, placing a firm hand on my shoulder, and leaned over slightly to Howard.

"Thank you so much for having us this evening. Faye and I will be going now. Come Faye, your tongue is all purple wine stain." This was not what I would have wished her to say.

* * * * *

145

We stood outside the house, on the sidewalk, waiting for Real to fetch us in the coach. Mrs Howe had called ahead of time but he was late. The streets seemed icy and I guessed he had trouble getting the horse out of the barn.

"So, what did you think?" said Myrl, gazing up at the sky. It was beautiful, the air cold, the night black and clear, with crystal white star-points of light. There was no moon. The air was curling with the burnt scent of woodstove smoke. The hollow sound of horse hooves echoed from Main Street, and the gaslight under which we stood hissed with its burn.

"They're a fun bunch," I said. I was feeling very sincere about everyone.

"Don't be deceived," she said. "Remember Reichart's fallacy. Everyone in that room was nervous. Jumpy. Everyone, except Giles Wilcox."

"He was too exhausted to be jumpy."

She said nothing, sighed, and shoved her hands in her coat pockets.

"I've always liked Giles. It seems a shame he should be going through this," said Mrs Howe. "There is something very charming about him. It's Gladdis I can't stand. She has just a horrible disposition. Did you hear her talking about poor Alyssa and her vampire?" She shook her head. "It was just despicable. And all in that nasty voice. To hear her speak is like nails on a blackboard." Mrs Howe shivered slightly and turned up the collar of her coat. She was like a diminutive fairy, white hair shining silver in the starlight, a small tiara casting delicate, infinitesimal flashes of diamond light.

"It is the curse of being a vocal artist," said Myrl. "Your ears are too sensitive."

"I am no artist, but I'm with you," I said. "Her voice is awful."

Mrs Howe laughed. "I did overhear something which might be of interest to you, though."

Myrl looked up. "Ah, so the evening won't be wasted."

"Well, I don't know about that," said Mrs Howe. "It might still have been a waste, but I did hear Hollister and Henry talking about several mounts at the bank."

146

I yawned. "Mounts?" All I could think of were horses.

"Yes. Mounts. Animal trophies."

Myrl listened with great interest.

"It's hard to say exactly what they were talking about because I kept missing parts of the conversation. I heard Henry say something like 'It isn't my decision, Hollister' – that's when I pricked up my ears, you see – and Hollister said something I couldn't hear and then Henry just stared at him and said, 'I don't see what the interest is in this, they are fine. Speak with Mr Janice if you want'. He's the bank manager. I still didn't know what they were talking about until a few minutes later when Hollister caught up with Henry again and said, 'You know, it's my craft and they're looking a bit scruffy. I just don't want scruffy mounts advertising my business'."

"What do you make of that, Faye?"

"I don't know. He wants the mounts for some reason."

"Where are they located?" asked Myrl.

Mrs Howe rubbed her chin. "I think there are three right over the front balcony overlooking the main floor of the bank. You'd need a ladder to get up and take a look. But he is right. They are rather dusty. And Hollister is a perfectionist."

"I wonder if he's noticed the lion's head at the Wheel Club," said Myrl.

A coach was coming up through the cold fog.

"Ah, here's Real." Mrs Howe gathered her shawl.

I yawned again as we stepped inside. I sat next to Mrs. Howe and across from Myrl. "Oh, don't tell me you're tired now," said Myrl. I rubbed my eyes. I was tired – very tired and I wanted to go to bed. Myrl, however, was glowing. She pulled down the shade inside the coach and leaned toward us.

"Did you both notice anything odd about this party?"

I thought over small details of the evening – Henry holding Hope's hand a little too tightly upon her return from the kitchen, Hollister never really speaking to Giles at all, Patrick O'Keefe spending far too much time with Marion French. I frowned.

147

"Look at the big picture," she said. "Look at the universe in which the dilemma occurs."

I shook my head. "I don't know. We were so welcomed."

Myrl raised her finger. "We were excluded by our speedy inculcation to their group. They are like an organism, and though they pretend, we remain on the outside."

Mrs Howe closed her eyes and leaned back against the padded seat, closing herself to our conversation.

"You mean everyone there was keeping us at bay? Come now, Myrl, that sounds a bit paranoid."

She smiled at me and sat back. "Doesn't it strike you as odd, Faye, that a group of people would have a frivolous party at the death of their friend? And yet, no one really spoke of her?"

Chapter Ten

Our Crime

The church bells on Main Street were tolling midnight as the front door closed. Mary Howe kissed her nephew on the cheek and floated into the kitchen to prepare some tea. Myrl forwent her cup of warmed cream and we both trudged up the stairs after Mr Howe. The decision to forgo the cup of cream should have been a warning.

Our room was cozy and Real had set warm bricks along the foot of the beds, under the blankets. I was very impressed. Myrl seemed oblivious. She disappeared behind the partition to change. I draped my nightgown over my arm and started to sit down on the bed to wait my turn, glancing at a small stack of books she had unpacked, when she called from behind the partition.

"Faye, I want you to read those letters aloud."

"Letters?"

"The blackmail letters. They're in the top dresser drawer between the beds."

I sighed, laid the nightgown on the bedspread, rose, and rummaged through the drawer. In the back were the letters, still wrapped in black paper. I sat back down heavily on the bed with the letter from the top of the pile.

"May 20, 1918 –"

"No, no. We've read the last two, just scan the rest. I am particularly interested in the initial request."

I tossed the two dated May 20, 1918, and September 12,

1917, on the bed and glanced at the rest. They were all about the same, the language nearly identical. There was always a reference to a number of objects and the price the blackmailer wanted. As she had suspected, however, the first letter was more elaborate.

"Myrl, listen to this:

'June 2, 1914. You, Miss, do not know me, but I know you. I also know that there are seventeen items worth quite a bit to you all, arriving on the 15th of this month. In order to keep your secret I am advising you to check your account for $100.00. Do not hesitate in this matter. Place the bills, which should be small, into a brown paper bag and leave it on the bench on the grass right outside of the police station. Return to your home. I will place a call at ten minutes after to you and your friends at their respective homes. If you or they fail to answer, I will assume trickery and will go to the papers with evidence you will be unable to refute. Do not toy with me. There is no point of negotiation'."

"So this was the first letter. There's a reference here to other people. At least two. Did you catch that?"

She came around, fully clothed in a pair of green wool hunter's pants, a black cashmere sweater and black leather riding boots. She was pulling on black wool gloves when she glanced up and saw my face.

"Come now, Faye, we have work to do. And bring the letters."

* * * * *

The trolley did not run past six o'clock so we walked the three miles into town. I had not prepared my wardrobe as well as Myrl's and so was forced to wear her grey flannel pants with the bottom cuffs stuffed into the tops of my wool socks. Our breath came out thick and white, curling vaporous and ghostly, disappearing into the night. Myrl was loose-jointed and supple, her stride long and gangly and I was growing weary with having to sprint, let alone carry the oil lantern. I could not hold the light steady and its glow danced frenetically on the icy street. I was suffering with a stitch in my side when she suddenly clapped her hands, and flung them behind her back, linked them together, and began a kind of diatribe.

"Now, Faye, let us review. Review is always a good device in lesson plans and lectures, and summary statements are the fodder of the unprepared student. So, let's review the events in Northampton: firstly, of course, we have a body and a room devised with gadgets to give the appearance that a murder did not occur. We have a missing dress and pair of shoes."

My mind turned over slowly. "And someone pretending to be Alyssa. Remember Rachel said a deep voice answered her from Alyssa's room."

"Yes. A gold watch chain on the floor. A break-in of the house and a rummaging of items. The sound of a single shot and a man with bright red hair and beard leaving the house."

"What about all the strange goings on Rachel described? Like the stuffed animals looking as if they'd been moved around?"

"What? Oh yes." She unlaced her hands and brought them up to her face, blew on her gloves, and pressed the warmed wool to her cheeks. "Rather nippy, isn't it."

"Yes," I agreed. My face was numb, though I also knew it was not just the result of cold. The burgundy was making a slow but steady impression on my perceptions and I realised its power was latent.

"And now, in Brattleboro: we have a spotless room with no carpet, a box of papers containing among them a list of phone numbers and a profession of love. A mattress hiding letters of blackmail. We have a trophy lion head in the Wheel Club, which has been tampered with. We have a love affair leading to a secret marriage and a marriage certificate dated for June. We have a group of people so incestuously involved with one another that motives between them become amorphous."

151

"And we have a stolen gun. Who knows when that was stolen too? "

"I would say within the last day or two," said Myrl.

"Why?"

"To frame Giles Wilcox."

"Yes I know, obviously, to frame Giles Wilcox." I was alarmed at my lack of patience. "I mean, why do you say just a day or two ago?"

"The carpet, my dear, the rug. The rug came right up to the broken door and yet there was no water stain, no hint of damage from rain or the elements. Obviously, the theft occurred very recently."

"So those are the facts," I sniffed.

"Now Faye, Faye, we cannot list facts because we do not have enough information to classify these items as facts – but we can list them as observations, correct?"

"Well, we know Alyssa was murdered, that's a fact." Being uncooperative seemed to make me feel better and I shifted the gas light to the other hand and stabbed a finger in my side.

"Well, of course we know she was murdered. It wasn't an accident. I do believe wine has flared your emotions, Faye."

"And we know her throat was slit. So we know she was killed with a knife."

Myrl did not say anything for a moment or two, her leather riding boots hitting the cobblestones with determination. I could not see how she could remain so light and agile on her feet and yet have her step carry such a sense of purpose. She stopped. She turned and looked right into my eyes and for a moment I sensed an urgent spark of energy. She clapped both of her gloved hands to my face and squeezed my cheeks.

"Faye, you are a jewel! A diamond in the rough. Do you know what you just did?" She flung her arms down.

My mind was fuzzy and I blundered into a guess. "The fallacy of Gruiner's choice?"

"Precisely!"

"But her throat was slit."

"Faye. Listen. Her throat could have been slit at any time."

"You mean after she was murdered?" This made no sense to me. "But the only other mark on her body was the gunshot wound, which we heard the shot for and –"

"No, Faye. We did hear a shot – but there was no bullet. What we heard was a blank being fired. It was not the shot which left that little perfect hole behind her ear."

I rubbed my forehead.

"Think, Faye. Alyssa Dansen did not die at the peril of a knife. That blank was fired to cover up the real cause of her death – a bullet to the back of the skull. Her throat was slit to hide the cause of death and to aid in the taxidermy of the body. The best piece of evidence in a murder is the body. If one can create the illusion that a shot was fired after Alyssa Dansen was dead, the chances of coming to the conclusion she was killed by a bullet are nil."

"And whoever stole Giles's gun knows all this and is trying to implicate him."

"Exactly. You see, I have been befuddled by this business of having a dead body in a room and then having someone come in and shoot at it. Rachel heard that voice behind the door and then we returned half an hour later to hear the shot. Obviously the person in the room had plenty of time to figure out Alyssa Dansen was not alive – so the person must have known she was dead. But then why fire the shot? And now I have the answer."

"Hope Mitchell came up with a theory tonight as well. She said Alyssa must have had two murderers. One who slit her throat and another who shot her."

"No. The person who fired that blank wanted to hide the fact she had been shot. This was quite clever, quite clever." She put an arm around my shoulders for a quick hug. "So you see, Faye, we must be careful what we list as facts."

"So why are going to the Opera House? That's where we're heading, right?" She just smiled at me.

* * * * *

153

I waited in the landing, outside the door to Alyssa Dansen's room. Inside, Myrl was returning the letters to their place under the mattress. The barrel of violets waved deep purple velvet in the darkened hall. I had shivered as she disappeared inside the black chasm of the open door. When she stepped back into our weak light, I began descending the stairs. But she held me back and nodded toward the second door, key in hand.

"But Myrl, this is breaking and entering. Couldn't you just ask Giles to go inside?"

"And what reason could I give him? No, Faye, all this must be done in secret and with the freedom privacy affords."

I couldn't tell if this statement referred only to our immediate act or was a philosophical observation about life in general.

The key that opened the back door to the Opera House and Alyssa's apartment did not fit the door to this second room. From her pocket Myrl retrieved a stiff piece of cardboard with what looked like strands of thin wire wrapped tightly around it. This wire gave the cardboard flexibility and a smooth surface. She slipped the piece of cardboard inside the doorjamb and within seconds I heard the lock give way. Myrl straightened up and smiled at me and then opened the door ever so carefully.

Because the windows had been boarded over, the room was very dark, and where light did not flow easily there was only fathomless black. The place seemed to be a kind of workshop, with a long wooden table across the back, and a marvelous black ebony box with small drawers in the centre. In front of the box was a smooth piece of black polished stone, cut like slate, perhaps two feet square and an inch or so thick. Above this working surface and attached to the table by a jointed metallic arm was a magnifying lens, like one might use to complete very detailed handicrafts. There was no furniture except a footstool and a swivel chair, and the place smelled musty and earthy. Cobwebs along the ceilings and in the corners moved with the current of our passage, their wispy shadows dancing in smooth arcs, in counterpoint to our lantern.

Myrl approached the workbench very carefully, running a finger along the edges of the black marble and then diving underneath the table. I followed suit and I saw her rubbing whitish powder between her fingers. She took off her glove, pressed more of the powder from the floor to her finger and raised it to her lips.

"Cocaine?" I whispered. I had seen much of opium and cocaine use in Asia and parts of Turkey, and I knew of the terrible stupors it could induce.

Myrl looked at me. "Salt." And she rose from under the table.

There was salt everywhere. Along the back of the table, between its crevices, and on the floor salt lay thick. In the left-hand corner was a foot-wide pile of salt, carelessly swept. The broom still leaned against the wall.

"Can you think where you have seen this before?" Myrl asked. She walked over to the box and its series of tiny trays. "Faye, come here," she said, replacing her glove and pulling out the top tray.

There were glittering tools of the jeweller's trade. An array of fine chisels, several silver hammers, a series of brushes, a polishing stone and wheel, a dopping stick. Along the back was a tin of shellac and several glass containers of boric and sulphuric acid as well as smaller glass jars with nameless liquids of various hues.

"Hollister McLean's father was a jeweller in town," I offered by way of explanation.

"But Hollister McLean is not," stated Myrl. "This salt explains so much, so much," she said softly. "And now. Look at this." She pulled a small metal canister, a trash can, from under the table and removed the lid. Reaching down, she brought up what looked like a handful of cotton and motioned me to the magnifying lens.

"Look here, Faye, what do you see?" She placed the stuffing under the lens and moved the lantern very close.

I rubbed my eyes and adjusted the distance so I could get a good look. Before my eyes I saw the glossy gold and black of tiger hide. Another small snip looked like dense weasel, a wispy brittle snatch of spider monkey, and the rest were indistinguishable to me, a clumping of small clips of skins and fur.

"But isn't this what Hollister does? He's a taxidermist, right? One would expect to see this sort of thing."

"But he brought the skins here. Why? He has his business shop, so why the intrigue? You see, Faye, he has much to hide here. My understanding of taxidermy is that skins that are to be shipped great distances are salted first to preserve them. Rock salt, like this is used," and she held up a large nugget of dirty salt about as big around as a penny marble. She tossed it back to the floor. "This is all growing quite complicated."

Silently, she motioned me out of the room and we escaped with our light. She pulled the door hard behind us, and I heard the lock click in place.

"So you think whatever Hollister is doing here has something to do with Alyssa Dansen's death?" There was a pause. I could see her watching the shadows cast by the lighted lantern and then she sighed and looked at me.

"I believe the motive for murder lies behind this door."

* * * * *

Our next venture was to the dressing rooms. The performance hall was hollow and black, cavernous, and as we crossed the forestage in front of the orchestra seats, our light cast dramatic shadows against the curtains and in the wings. I must say I did not enjoy walking backstage, underneath all the fly lines and counterweight pulleys and two light battens. The theatre has always filled me with the flutter of excitement, but in this case, under our shroud of secrecy and in the dark, it seemed ominous.

The dressing rooms were all the same. Small, cramped, roughly nine feet square and identical in layout: a small wardrobe with swing doors to the right, three padded wrought iron chairs, one pushed under a dressing table. A mirror above each dressing table was surrounded by electric lights, big round clear glass bulbs. A shelf with hanging pegs ran across the back wall above the two remaining chairs. There were no wall coverings and the interior of each was painted a simple white. I was interested in that Myrl did not pick out one particular person's room to enter first, but went right down the line, beginning on the left with Frances Hall's.

The wardrobe was crammed with costumes. Many had metallic or shimmering textures, and the light from our lantern was reflected back in glistening hues of gold, silver, cool pinks, and purples. Hats and scarves hung from the pegged shelf, the top of which hosted several wigs. Cosmetics were placed strategically in order by colour and application. Lipsticks, for example, ran from left to right along the back edge of the dressing table beginning with deep red and ending with glossy pink. Face powders followed, and then an array of coloured wax pencils. There was a small china bowl filled with ticket stubs and though Myrl glanced at these, little in the room seemed of interest to her.

We found nothing, nothing which might be of interest in Alyssa's murder. Myrl shut the door and slipped her card into the lock of Howard Adams's room. Here the personality was one of prudence and restraint. Costumes were very carefully hung so as to not touch each other. A small stack of books lined the top of the little pegged shelf. Though Howard's tabletop was sparse when considered in comparison with Frances Hall's, it was equally well organised. In his top drawer was a long, sheathed knife, with an intricate design carved in the handle, and it appeared very old. There were also gambling notes and old cigarettes, but again nothing to shed light on our search.

The next dressing room afforded little in the way of disclosure as well. Alyssa Dansen's was nearly barren. Several costumes, all dresses, hung in the wardrobe and Myrl searched each one carefully, running her hands up and down the material and checking labels. She was equally attentive to the shoes. "These are from Fuller's. The bootery where Rachel

157

works part time. Interesting." She held up a pair of grey satin shoes and compared them to the other four pairs in boxes on the floor of the wardrobe. "Nice work – machine-turned." The drawers of the dressing table were nearly empty except the bottom one, which held silk hosiery and the top of which housed an assortment of pens and pencils. There was also a list of dates and times of performances for *The North Wind Blows*.

Giles Wilcox's room was a mess. There were costumes piled in one corner, obviously torn off their hangers and left on the floor. His dressing table was in shambles, drawers pulled out, papers sorted through in haphazard stacks. Everything off the pegged shelf had been tossed to the floor. A small satin pillow which rested on the chair in front of the dressing table had been pierced, and soft down spilled across the seat, onto the floor.

"It appears," said Myrl as I held the light higher, "that someone has been rifling through Mr Wilcox's belongings as well." She slipped what looked like a trip itinerary under her sweater into her waistband.

"For what, though?" I sifted some down between my gloved fingers.

"That cannot be said at this point. The person who did this may be searching for the same article which led to poor Rachel's room being sacked. Or this may be the result of a task with a much more devious purpose than a simple search. Instead of finding something, they may have wanted to leave behind something." She slid her hand in the back of the wardrobe, close to the ground and slowly, with great care, she brought out a long, thin blade, identical to that found in Howard Adams's room. The knife handle was ivory, the blade wrapped in a white strip of sheeting, smeared with blood. There was so much blood on the linen that it stuck fast to the blade and Myrl held it up to the lantern.

"Is that real?" I asked. "Real blood?"

She nodded. Light from the lantern turned the dried blood chocolate-orange. "This is not a prop, if that is what you were implying. The handkerchief was used to hastily wipe the blade and then wrap it." She turned the knife over, scrutinising the tip of the blade. I watched her frowning and pulling gently at the cloth. It was stuck as if with thick tar.

I said nothing. The knife shocked me more, somehow, than the discovery of the body – the texture of thickened blood took my breath from me. Myrl glanced at my face.

"Faye, this is murder, not a parlour game. You mustn't ever forget that."

"I know," I said. "It's just that that is her blood."

"Incorrect," she said. "More than likely it is the blood of a chicken or some such animal. If this knife was planted in his room to cast suspicion on Giles Wilcox, the knife, the blood, and the handkerchief may not be authentic." Very carefully, she slipped the knife back behind the wardrobe, pausing to stare at the wall and say slowly, "We shall leave this for Captain O'Keefe to find."

"I am beginning to see what you mean. This is an elaborate plan to frame Giles Wilcox, isn't it?"

"It would seem," she said. "Look behind me on the dressing table."

I raised my lamp and she turned as well. With two sources of light, the original and the one reflected, the wig which sat atop a dummy head was illuminated from both directions. The wig was of red hair, dishevelled and long. Side whiskers drooped down both sides, coming to meet in a thick, ruddy beard.

For a moment I did not understand.

"Faye," she said slowly, "What was the one outstanding characteristic of the gentleman we all saw leaving the Dansen premises last week?"

I heard the intake of my own breath as I gasped and I took a step back. It was the red hair. The same mop of red hair, only this time it wasn't attached to a person. I shifted on one foot. "If someone were trying to frame him, why make it all so subtle? Why not just – oh, I don't know, just make it all so much more straightforward?"

She nodded. "Like take the knife, complete with his fingerprints, toss it behind the police station, with a note attached to the wig saying 'Giles Wilcox did it'! You see, Faye, the person must deal with the issue of motive. If Giles Wilcox had no motive, framing him would make little difference." She glanced at me and waved me from the room.

We left the Opera House as we came in, through the back door and I, for one, was glad to be outside again. I breathed deeply and blew on my hands.

"But still, if someone were trying to frame Giles Wilcox, wouldn't there be an easier way about it?" Myrl took a deep breath and I could feel the astringent quality to the chilled air. I was very alert now.

"You mentioned the word subtle in there. A good word. But subtlety can be a somewhat less than honourable attribute. Honest subtlety is held in the eye of the observer. Dishonest subtlety is controlled by the observed. You and I, for example, notice the smallest details of people's dress and the manner of their countenance." She waved a hand at the stars. "The fact that Henry Mitchell is deathly afraid that his wife will learn of his probable singular affair with Alyssa Dansen was determined through our observation of subtle traits and behaviours between the two of them. Subtlety which is cultivated only for the sake of controlling people's perceptions –"

"Is acting," I said, still trying to figure out the affair situation with Henry and Alyssa.

"Yes. Yes. You are right. How I marvel at how well you restrain me, my dear." She returned to the topic at hand. "And because it is acting, because these actions knowingly conspire to lead us away from truth, it is false."

"And you like the movies. The 'purveyors of truth,' you said."

She stared at me and then continued. "Which would you believe? A clue which falls from the sky and whacks you on the head, or one you uncover, bit by bit, until the entire story is revealed? There is someone at work here who understands the seductive powers of subtlety and is trying to guide us down a dead end." She closed and locked the door. I turned the wick down on the oil lamp and we ducked back around the corner to the street side. Here, she put a hand on my shoulder. The light fell across her face without casting shadows and washed her in an orange glow. She looked very young. Her hair was beginning to come undone at the nape and she pushed at it with one hand.

"I think, Faye, that when we go home, we must shop for shoes." She clapped me on the shoulder and began walking.

"All right," I said, not really hearing her, "But if someone's trying to frame Giles – with – shoes? What are you talking about?" I caught up with her in an instant.

"It is an interesting question," said Myrl and suddenly stopped. "But I think it wise not to say much more right now." I looked at her and her head was cocked at a funny angle as if listening for something. About the same time that the smell of paper and tobacco caught my nose, I heard the faint, thickened breath of someone exhaling cigarette smoke. Turning, I saw the rounded glow of ash floating eerily in the dark of the little alley we had just emerged from. Myrl cleared her throat.

"Mr Holt, you may reveal yourself." Her voice was loud.

There was the gritty sound of leather heels on dirty stone and the tall, thin, blond man stepped out of the shadows and tossed his cigarette to the ground. He was a figure in grey tones, his skin and clothing the colour of mist.

"We really must talk, Miss Norton."

"And we are. Right now."

He smiled at her, and she tucked a strand of hair behind her ear.

"Simply put, you and I want the same thing," he said.

"False, Mr Holt. Far from it. I want personal satisfaction. You want a story. By your attempt to demonstrate a shared goal between us, you give away your assumption that I don't appreciate your position. That I may, in fact, even have dispersions as to your profession. Let me assure you, I do not. I am quite sympathetic. I admire the press as few do. The fourth estate is the cornerstone of our democracy –"

"Well –"

161

"And you and your colleagues are the footmen. Accolades aside, however, I understand the double edge of wanting to break a story. A sort of odd marriage of narcissism and duty."

"I wouldn't say –"

"Let us just say that if you break this story, your name would be dusted off and made to shine once again. Perhaps you'd even be asked to return to New York and report on real events instead of whose cows broke out of Farmer Cobb's pasture."

"I know a lot about the people in this town, Miss Norton. Miss Tullis," he said, tipping his hat in my direction. "Plenty which could help you. I am eager to break this story, for reasons both professional and personal. We could help each other."

"This is where I must admit to disappointment. I have word that you would not be of assistance because your edge is gone, and that you are, in fact, not eager."

"Don't believe everything you hear."

"I never do, unless it sustains a premise."

"Well, we don't have to be adversaries," he said, and smiled again. I did not understand Myrl's odd positioning – her words seemed so sterile and contrived. Like an orchestrated dance. And she seemed, I suddenly realised, very uncomfortable.

"Well, to the contrary, Mr Holt, my friends don't usually run around following me all over town."

He laughed. "You've got a point there," he said and lit another cigarette.

We began to walk together. The night was cold and we were wrapped tight, but there was a thin coating of snow and dirt on the sidewalk. I shivered. Holt carried his own lantern, which he left unlit.

"I do have some interesting titbits," he began. "Did you know, for example, that Giles Wilcox's neighbours saw Alyssa Dansen nearly every day for a week last summer, in July, sitting on his porch? But she refused callers. Now what does that tell you?"

162

I remembered what Giles said about foliage around the house. "But the neighbours can't see the entire porch."

"Correct. Looking down the slope, they saw her feet, and, if a wind blew, they could catch a glimpse of her sitting and reading."

"Just like at –" I began.

"Yes. Just as you found her. Conspicuously placed." Holt nodded.

"That would explain why she was entirely clothed from head to toe. If people were seeing her from afar –" I was very excited.

Holt continued. "You see, I think even in summer she had been dead for some time. Then I spoke to folks who live downstream from the tannery, McLean's tannery, and several people reported brush fires at night last spring, long brush fires that were burning hard even in the morning. Marty McFadden said Hollister was burning stumps."

"And have you investigated, Mr Holt?"

"You betcha. Early yesterday morning. I found this." He held up a piece of silk cloth, pale and gauzy in the moonlight. My heart skipped a beat. "I found it wrapped around a splinter of a burned out stump before good old McFadden sicked his dogs on me."

"What is it'" I whispered as Myrl took the thin shimmery piece of material and held it next to the light. It was a slip of pale ghost and as it fluttered against the black of night it sang a silent song of horror and blood.

"I would say, Faye," she said quietly, "that this is a piece of our missing dress." She handed the piece of material back to Holt. "Do you have any other bits of information? Anything which can be useful?"

"Nothing concrete. Just the regular stuff, the gossip. Who's sleeping with whom and that sort of thing."

"And who is" – here an eyebrow was cocked – "sleeping with whom?"

"Well," he took a long drag on his cigarette, "Howard and Marion are about as hot as duelling pistols right now. And everyone knows Marion's counting her blessings that Alyssa's out of the picture because Howard had it bad for her."

I spoke up. "You mean Howard was attracted to Alyssa?"

"She's cute," he said to Myrl and at that moment I thought I would forever hold a grudge. "Yeah. I'd say so. Howard used to write her love poems and throw flowers her way, candy, the usual. The whole town got to hear him moan and groan about it at the Club. She ignored him. She was very good at ignoring young men. She wanted the older ones."

"And Marty McFadden?"

"He never had a chance. She was too good for him. No. I don't know who she slept with. Her name was notorious, but I couldn't tell you why."

"Well, she slept with Giles," I said.

"Don't be too sure about that," Holt replied. "Everyone else saw them as an item, but I didn't. I never bought it."

"But it would make sense," said Myrl. "He is charming, rich, and single. Given her tastes, as you've outlined them, it would almost seem to be an irresistible situation."

"I know. I know. But even last winter when they really started being seen together –"

"How long had they been friends?"

"Years. I don't know. Maybe three or four years. But as I was saying. Even last year when they supposedly suddenly looked at each other with new eyes, they never seemed to act like lovers."

"What do you mean? Exactly," said Myrl and I saw him take her 'exactly' very seriously. It was several minutes before he responded. "I guess I would have to say that they just didn't act stupid enough."

Myrl laughed. "I see you hold romance in high regard!"

Curran Holt shook his head. "Look, they were just too perfect with each other. Too practical."

Aha, I thought, there's a bit of jealousy here. We were nearly to the tavern and my cheeks were numb with cold. Myrl kept the pace invigorating.

"Now, let me ask you some questions."

Myrl glanced sharply at him. "Off the record," she said.

"Off the record," and he agreed so quickly that I assumed his sincerity. "What did you find in there?"

"Where?"

"Oh, come now, ladies. I know you broke into the Opera House."

"We had a key."

"Oh, fine. You had a key. So what did you find?"

"We found nothing truly of interest. A blade with blood on it, obviously planted in Giles's dressing room in a continuing attempt to frame him. Nothing in the other dressing rooms."

"And that's all you did? The dressing rooms?"

"Well, of course," she lied. "We had the pleasure of canvassing Alyssa's room earlier today."

"So I've heard. Now this is for the record. Are you really representing Forrest Dansen?"

There was a very long pause while I waited for Myrl to speak.

"Yes," she said finally. "Yes. I am representing his interests."

"And why is that?"

"He hired me because he believed his sister was being blackmailed at the time of her death."

"You have proof she was?" The shortness of his questions and the sudden aggressive quality in their delivery made me suspicious.

"Not really," I said.

"Now Faye, we most certainly do. We have seen copies of the blackmail letters Alyssa saved."

"Oh, I'd love to get my hands on them," Holt said.

"I'm sure you would, Mr Holt, but at this moment, I'm afraid you will have only your longing to tend to." She paused. "What does Forrest Dansen have to do with this?"

"I'd say very little. He's a tough customer, but he's not very smart. Just one of the letters?"

She shook her head. "They are in Alyssa Dansen's apartment, under her mattress. I'm sure Patrick O'Keefe will be picking them up tomorrow morning. Talk to him."

"This is a very complicated piece," he said, and dropped his cigarette to the ground. "Very sophisticated. My bet is that Marty McFadden is going to be hauled in –" He paused. "Or maybe Forrest – who knows – and either one will get it."

"Well, let us hope so, Mr Holt, let us hope so. At least let the wheels start in motion and let the momentum build."

"Why are we hoping so?" I asked, blowing on my fingers.

"Here, let me take that," said Holt and lifted the lantern from my cramped hand. I rubbed my knuckles.

"Because once someone is charged," Myrl said, "wrongly charged, the real murderer will sigh and lean back, relax a little, and his guard will come down. It will be at this point, when there is a flash of guilt, a glimmer of something just not right, an instant where two halves do not fit together, that pieces will snap into place and the machinery of logic, greased by observation and supposition, will grind on to an inevitable conclusion. The lines of the puzzle will disappear and the whole of reality will lie before us."

Curran Holt watched my face to gauge the proper reaction to her diatribe. He nodded solemnly and furrowed his forehead.

"Miss Norton," he said, extending a hand, "I am grateful for the opportunity to work with you." He handed me back the lantern and tipped his hat. "Miss Tullis. I bid both you ladies a good evening and trust that you will refrain from breaking into any more rooms tonight."

We had arrived at the Tavern side door.

* * * * *

It was while I was slipping into bed, my eyes nearly closed, that I realised how much alike they were.

"He seems nice enough," I said, trying to keep up with some conversation Myrl was attempting to have with me. She was sitting straight up in bed, furiously brushing out her hair. An empty teacup wetly dabbed in the centre with cream was all that was left of her bedtime ritual.

166

"Nice? Nice? Faye, the fourth estate is a slum. At its best, the press is an insinuating dog at the heels of the rich and powerful, and at its worst, it panders to the feckless, prurient interests of the lowest denominator."

I yawned. "You're the one who lied about not going into Hollister's room."

"I did not want to give that up. That room is key to the case." She leaned over, reached for a book, decided against reading, and turned off the bed light instead. I heard the soft thud of her pillow hitting the floor.

"Don't you sleep with a pillow?"

"No."

"Ever?"

"No."

"Why?" I chuckled, pulling the sheets up under my chin.

"I do not want the blood draining from my head into my heels," she said.

"Oh, Myrl." I lay in the dark for a few moments. I remember hearing the wind-up clock tick and chime three o'clock and then nothing.

Chapter Eleven

In Which Poison Is Discovered

Sunday was to see us out on the early winter fields of Rankomana, Frances Hall's estate. A note had been delivered that morning requesting our presence at a clay duck shoot. My sleep, without the confines of time or consciousness, was dreamless and black, and when Myrl woke me, her hand on my shoulder and her whisper in my ear, I roused slowly, unable to talk or do more than simply gaze stupidly around the room. She let go of my arm, sat on the edge of my bed with a smile on her face, and slapped the back of the note with one hand. It was, she announced, the beginning.

I lay back, my head in the pillows for a few more moments. She was smartly dressed in a layered hunter green wool skirt that so ballooned I suspicioned there was a small hoop underneath. Her jacket of matching wool sported shoulder pads, gave an austere set to the gingham shirt and narrow black tie. She had pulled her hair into a tight bun and there was the slight hint of rouge on her cheeks. Smelling of powder and soap she reminded me for an instant of my mother, who after spending the early morning washing out diapers in cold spring water would wake me by sitting on my bed and smoothing my warm sleepy face with her strong, icy cold hands. Now my face felt thick and I ran my tongue over my teeth.

I cleared my throat. "The beginning of –"

"The end," she said, and waved her hand, the note

fluttering above her head. "We must have made quite an impression last night," she said and read the invitation out loud.

"To Miss Myrl Adler Norton and Miss Faye Tullis," she began and opened the parchment.

"Dear Myrl and Faye, You are cordially invited to a clay duck shooting party at my humble estate this glorious morning. Several of our friends from last night will be joining us. I am sending a driver along at eight-thirty to pick you up. If my offer finds you at an inconvenient time, let me extend my disappointment in advance and simply send the driver along. We will all be attending church directly after the hunt and I trust you two will join us."

I sat up and peered at the tiny Swiss clock on the dresser between our beds. It was five minutes past eight.

"Bring those legs around, Faye, and hurry."

* * * * *

The car was a 1917 Bullnose Morris Oxford, topless and out late in the season, past the time it should have been garaged. Our driver was a man of middle age named Robert, who was amiable and seemingly relaxed but who drove very fast. Myrl kept a hand on her felt cap and I tied my wool scarf securely around my head. Fog lay thick in the streets, cold and damp, and I wished I had thought to bring gloves. From my seat in the back I could barely hear what Myrl was saying to the poor man, but she appeared to be having a delightful conversation, looking around, pointing, the two speaking over each other in their overlapping quests – hers to glean hard information about the estate; his to supply an outpouring of as much anecdotal and harmless gossip as possible in a fifteen-minute car ride. She was barely able to direct his flow of conversation, but in the end, she gathered what I thought were some basic facts. It seemed the house supported fourteen domestics, most of whom lived in the eastern portion of the house. Morale was good and Rankomana was considered a fortunate place to find work. There

170

was a carriage house, smoke house, well house, ice house, sugar house, four lakes and five streams, more than a thousand acres, and little in the way of farming. With the exception of an apple orchard leased to a couple down the road, and sugaring in the early spring, the land was not utilised. Most of the property was wooded with maples, birch, and pine. Several pastures were home to sheep, a few cows, and some horses.

The house itself sat on top of Black Mountain and as the car slowly began the incline, I ceased eavesdropping, sat back and enjoyed the ride. Black Mountain was steep, and Robert had to forfeit his love of wind and speed to the force of gravity. He downshifted twice before we could enjoy a steady progression up the hill. The Morris Oxford was at a crawl. I do believe we would have been at a faster clip with a buggy and horse. The trees, bare and waiting for snow, stood thick in the forest, and the air was ripe with the smells of dirt and grasses, manure and mud, all drawn like a poultice from the wet of the heavy fog. As we came around a corner, the fog immediately thinned, and we were surrounded by a bright yellow haze, which in just a few short minutes burned off, evaporated, and there above us, atop the mountain in brilliant sunshine and against a bright blue sky, sat Rankomana.

Rankomana was built to tell the story of success and stability, of comfortable wealth, a fortress where people could gather and be safe. The outside world stopped at her wrought iron gates, a tall imposing structure with two S's coiled along the top. Once Robert returned from opening the gates, I noticed the road went from dirt to crushed granite. Inside these gates time could be made to stand still, and I could picture long summers spent reading poetry on the grassy knoll in front of the house, drinking champagne and lemonade, with distant family visiting, children in white starched cotton jumpers playing tag in the side yard, a dog slumbering in the thick grass. This time of year the building still carried an air of graciousness but with the trees bare, there was also a restraining sense of regal austerity.

171

The house was very large, from the second empire, painted a dark chocolate brown with six bedroom windows upstairs flanked by black shutters. Four chimneys broke the roofline, all in the centre. Massive maples stood as sentries along the sloping front yard, several perennial beds lay carved out in the grass along a stone pathway leading to the front. The front entrance was hidden behind an arboretum which spanned the entire length of the house, and I could see the green of vegetation and splash of colour from flowers through the glass. The side doors were massive, protected from rain and snow by a large porte-cochere, held up with colonial pillars. We drove underneath this impressive structure, past the carriage house and off down a back road which then circled around. Myrl turned to me and shouted, "We're going to the southern pasture," as if she were the guide.

It was at that moment I heard the crack of a rifle and, despite myself, I jumped.

* * * * *

"Come now, Myrl do have a shot," said Hollister McLean. He was standing elbow to elbow with her, rifle in one hand, champagne glass in the other. Marion and Howard were also enjoying a bit of champagne, as was Giles Wilcox. Only Henry and Hope abstained, and each carried a large glass of orange juice. A small folding table covered in white linen held a large crystal pitcher of juice, several half-empty bottles of champagne, several extra glasses, an ice bucket, and a basket of tender scones. A servant, a young man probably just eighteen or so, stood white-gloved and statuesque by the table, poised for the moment our thirst needed attending.

We were standing at the top of a large, gently sloping pasture of fallow clover, perhaps forty acres or so, surrounded by a thick forest of maples, birch, hemlock, and poplar. The pine trees were so thick that huge expanses of green could be seen on the hills across and below us. These swaths of green were a relief to the eye from all the grey bare bark in town. From where we all stood, cradled against the

172

mountain in the thin, brilliant, cool air of a bright wintry morning, we could see the wide valley below still thick with a pure white fog that churned and lapped up into the smaller hollows and crevices like a primeval sea. The view was spectacular and as Myrl took the rifle from Hollister, she waved a hand at the sky, the mountains, the valley below.

"Frances, this is such a fantastic view. Truly breathtaking."

Frances Hall, who was standing to her left, turned and smiled. "It is, isn't it. I am very lucky to have found this spot." She sighed. "So are you ready? Should Henry toss?"

Hollister had already loaded the rifle and as Myrl raised the butt plate against her shoulder, she warned us all, "Now, I am, you understand, a terrible shot."

I stood a few paces behind with her glass of juice. Frances held a little red flag above her head and dropped her arm. Henry, down in the field just several hundred yards, bent over, selected a clay duck and tossed it high in the air.

The barrel of the rifle followed the bird, and as its dead flight was cresting, in the moment before the descent began, her shot rang out. The bird returned unscathed, bouncing in the thick clover, and Myrl laughed.

"So you all see you can trust my word," she said to everyone. Frances reached into a burlap bag on her shoulder and held out another cartridge. We were to each get three shots per round. Out of three Myrl missed all and Hope's turn was next. She declined and passed to Howard who took the friendly challenge very seriously. He pulled the bolt handle, slipped in a single cartridge, and closed the chamber. He took a deep sigh, and I caught his look to Marion. He set the heel of the rifle against his left shoulder, shooting left-handed. He nodded to Frances and the flag was raised and dropped again. He sighted the clay duck, the trigger was pulled, and clay fragments splintered against the sky.

"Bravo!" clapped Giles, setting down his glass on the table. "Bravo! That's the first real hit of the morning." He retrieved his glass, raised it to his lips and said to Hollister, "It seems we have a real talent in our midst."

Howard returned to the burlap bag for another cartridge and then for a final one. He fired the two additional shots, both as carefully measured as the first but not as well placed. The birds fell to the ground just winged. He seemed distraught and wiped his forehead with a hand.

"Now it's Faye's turn," said Frances. "So far, it's Hollister two for three, Henry three for three, Myrl zero for three, poor Myrl, Howard three for three with one bull's-eye and I'm at two for three. Would you like Howard to load for you?"

"I can manage," I said and reached into the burlap bag on her arm pulling out three cartridges at once. I slipped two into my skirt pocket and held out my hand for the gun. Howard's hands were soft and warm as our palms brushed together for an instant on the rifle barrel. I lifted the rifle easily under my left arm, opened the bolt, loaded, and sighted a pine cone off a distant tree just to get my bearings. The rifle was a Winchester and light, a featherweight compared to the elephant guns in Africa, and I was feeling very adroit this raw morning. The flag went down. I fired before the duck reached its full height, on the swift ascent, and it shattered.

There was a round of applause and Myrl, in particular, was amused I think. I was slightly embarrassed. Henry tossed again. There was the crack of the rifle and then the dense crinkle of more clay splintering.

"Good grief," said Giles. "We've got a regular Annie Oakley," he said and chuckled.

I quickly loaded a final time, the acrid smell of gunpowder stinging my lungs, lacing metallic and warm in the morning chill. For the final shot, I waited until the descent was nearly at full speed before I fired and clay rained down on the field once again.

"Faye's had quite a bit of training with a gun," said Myrl, "I should have warned you all."

Marion came and grabbed my arm, "That was wonderful! I just think you are wonderful. I would love to learn to shoot like that. Good show!" she gushed and I felt awkward. She glanced over at Howard, who seemed rather moody, and she then retreated slightly and whispered, "Don't worry about him, he just wanted to impress me."

"Giles," said Myrl, taking the rifle from me, "your turn."

Giles never even put down his glass. He just laughed easily, flicked ashes from his cigarette and said, "Oh I never get involved in these things. Besides, how could I follow up on Miss Tullis's performance? "

"He doesn't think it's fair to compete with us lowly folk," said Frances, gently teasing.

"Well, it's what I do for a living. It would skew the scores."

"Yes, dear. We understand," she said and gave him an air kiss.

"He probably can't even shoot straight," laughed Hollister, raising his glass to Giles and Giles laughed back too, a moment later throwing down his cigarette and grinding it into the grass.

"How is the big-game hunt these days? I hear animals are hard to find." It was Myrl's turn to shoot, and the question caught Giles off guard.

"It's certainly not what it used to be," said Giles, shaking his head. "The herds must be properly managed and there is quite a bit of poaching. Elephant, in particular, have dwindled."

"Because of the ivory trade?"

"Yes." He stuffed his hands into his pockets. "Some would say I shouldn't hunt at all, but there is something which happens out there in the jungle, a sort of coming to terms with one's own mortality. There is fear and pain and sweat, and then great relief when the animal is down." Giles looked out over the field and lit another cigarette. "Sometimes, even tears."

The wind was stronger. Conversation ebbed to silence as his listeners tried to follow his thoughts. Myrl ignored the lapse and said loudly –"much the same language used by women after childbirth, Giles – in particular, fear, pain, sweat, and then tears. Interesting, don't you think? Faye?" She raised the gun and fired.

I agreed lamely, "Oh yes. Yes."

Giles pulled hard on his cigarette.

"It must be a wonderful opportunity for organisations when you donate a mount," Myrl said, peering, trying to see where the duck had safely landed.

I loaded for her.

"Well," breathed Giles, "I like to give something back. Some are worth quite a bit. I do sell, though, to museums mostly. Museums of natural history."

"And Hollister's work must be well respected."

"It is. Marty's a good man too. Excellent with solutions. I could never work with that stuff – degreasers, oiling solution, borax, formaldehyde. He works plenty with arsenic. I'm no chemist. But I know you don't want to hear this, Frances."

Frances was wrinkling her nose. "Marty's a pest."

Giles laughed. "You don't forgive easily, now do you?"

"He shouted at me in a very impolite manner. There is no avenue for forgiveness. I merely went to the tannery out of curiosity. I was really there to see Hollister anyway, about supporting the Women's Auxiliary. That Marty acted like I'd dropped from the sky to rummage through his rotten little lair. The tannery smelled. He was more than short with me."

"Well, that's Marty's place. The tannery, Frances, and you were poking around. Anyway, Hollister has made quite a name for himself – off of my luck with a rifle."

Myrl turned to Hollister, who was offering scones. "My dear friend Mary couldn't help but overhear you speaking to Henry about the condition of the mounts at the bank."

"Oh? Yes, well, they are my craft, you know, and I want them to look presentable."

"Is there a problem with the three at the bank?" asked Giles, smiling at Hollister. He turned to the rest of us. "He's so finicky. I've got a pair of bullfrogs in my bedroom poised with swords in a fencing match and he dithered about those for months before getting it right. In fact, I swear he came over while I was gone and reposed them again."

Hollister laughed. "Well, the three at the bank do look scruffy to me."

"As long as you are doing cleanup work, I suggest you take a look at the lion's head at the Wheel Club," said Myrl, sighting along the barrel and firing again. Another miss.

"What's wrong with that one? That was donated just last spring," said Giles a bit shortly.

Myrl fired once more. "Well, I couldn't help but notice that the neck cavity looked as if it had been tampered with, pulled apart or something."

There was silence. "Oh, I probably just imagined the whole thing." Myrl handed the gun to Frances.

There was a total of five rounds and I did miss a couple of shots, more for lack of concentration than anything else, for I was too busy trying to hear what Myrl was chattering with everyone about. She did get several hits over the course of the morning, but she seemed amused and gave chance the credit. Twice her glasses hit the butt of the rifle as she sighted the barrel.

"You know," Myrl said, pushing her glasses up, "I was speaking to a woman in town – one of your neighbours, Giles –"

"Oh, who? Mrs Catering?"

"Yes. Maybe. I don't know. I'm just terrible with names, but one of your neighbours at any rate, and she said she saw Alyssa out on your porch in July, every day for a week."

"Well, she had a key, and I told her to come up and visit as much as she wanted, if she felt well enough," said Giles. "Hollister here was supposed to be taking care of her."

I saw Marion glance at Hollister. "Did she ever write you?" asked Myrl, gazing down the barrel out over the field.

"Write me?"

"While you were in Africa."

"Well, yes, of course she did. At the beginning, of course, but then, once you're out in the bush, letters become impossible."

"When was the last letter you received from her?"

There was a lapse before Giles spoke. "What is your point?"

"Oh, I am just not putting this well," she said. "Forgive me. I'm just trying to figure out when Alyssa was last alive. No one seems to know."

"Well, I saw her when she came up in August," said Frances Hall.

"How was she then?" Myrl stood with the gun pointing down.

"Fine, I guess. I mean I didn't really speak to her, I just saw her from afar."

Just as before, I thought.

"But I waved and she waved back cheerfully. She was getting into the roadster with Hollister."

"Yes," said Hollister, "that's true. She was up in late August. She wanted some things from her apartment in town and I was helping her."

Late August. I was confused. This made no sense to me and I was stunned. The assumption all along was that the murder had taken place in early summer. Myrl was marvellous at charades, and though I knew she, too, was befuddled by this news, she moved away from questions and became the giddy listener of parlour jokes.

We had just finished the morning shooting, the fog below had burned off, and the easy curves of the Connecticut River could be seen as it stretched to mix with salt water three hundred miles away, glittering blue-gold, reflecting a mid-morning sky. I was starving. I had just eaten one of the scones, dusting crumbs from my bodice when Frances Hall suddenly went white. I was standing across from her. I saw her reach out to try and grab something. The burlap bag fell from her shoulder. Giles came forward.

"Frances?" he said and offered his hand. "You don't look well."

"I feel miserable, I don't ... I think ..." Her arm came down against the small table, the linen pulled to the ground and everything fell softly into the tall grass. Giles caught her, Henry came running up, Hollister as well, and as I bent over her she was trying to speak when an awful foam began at the corners of her mouth.

Her body began to jerk spasmodically, as if with severe cold. She cried out, holding the back of her neck. "Germain, run to the house and call the doctor, quickly, go!" said Giles.

The boy froze for a moment, looking down at his stricken mistress with his mouth open.

"Go boy, now!" Giles shouted at him and pointed at the house.

He turned and fled.

* * * * *

We were all sitting in the east parlour when Grace Burnett descended the spiral staircase, black bag in hand and a frown on her face. We all stood, hoping only the best for our hostess.

"Is she all right?" asked Marion. She was extremely shaken and kept wringing her hands. She even shrugged off Howard's solicitous arm and sat apart from the rest of us in the room.

"Of course she's fine," said Hollister quietly. "For heaven's sake, Marion, what are you so worried about?"

Marion ignored him.

"Well, she will be fine now," said Grace. She looked exhausted, and it wasn't until later we found out she had delivered two babies the night before and was called out of a dead sleep for this emergency. She looked at us all and then spoke very slowly. "I don't know for certain yet, but my fear is that she was poisoned. I can't tell what exactly poisoned her. It is not arsenic or strychnine, or any other kind of substance I've seen, but her system has definitely been violated. I've emptied her stomach and she's sleeping now. I've called Patrick O'Keefe and he's coming over immediately to speak to you all. This was very close, I'm afraid. Very close."

Myrl spoke first. "A point of clarification. When you say 'poisoned', you are not referring to food poisoning or tainted water, am I right?"

Grace nodded.

"You're talking about attempted murder," said Myrl.

Patrick O'Keefe did not allow his boyish constitution to betray the seriousness of what had just occurred out in the field. His manner was solemn, his glances at people untempered by friendship, and I realised what a difficult job he must have in a town so small – always remaining separate from friends, neighbours, and the rest of the townsfolk for the sake of impartiality. We all simply rehashed the morning's events, which were frighteningly simple given their horrendous conclusion. Myrl was very quiet and did not pursue any questions of her own, which I found notable. I listened to the facts as they were presented around the first half-hour before our arrival, but they, too, offered little. It was unfortunate, Patrick O'Keefe remarked, that the tablecloth and everything on it had been pulled to the ground. It would have been nice, he explained, with an eye on all of us, to see what was in the champagne and the scones. But in the course of the drama, nearly everything was crushed in the grass. At this point Henry got a bit miffed.

"Are you implying that one of us tried to poison Frances?" He was standing with one arm on the mantel, an ornate affair with carved oak roses and rosettes, bows and ferns. Representing the art of Grinling Gibbons, the mantel was probably worth thousands of dollars.

"Either someone tried to poison her, or there was a serious mistake made down in the kitchen this morning," said O'Keefe, his humour empty.

"Could it have been something she ate earlier in the day?" I asked.

Grace shook her head. "I don't know. The effects could have been latent, I suppose, or immediate. As I said, I'm not certain really what was ingested."

"Well, why in the name of God would we want to kill her?" Henry lit a cigarette. His hands shook.

"I don't know, Henry. Let's see, her skin isn't a different colour from yours and she's not Jewish. But she is rich. And maybe she knows something about Alyssa Dansen's death and someone doesn't want her to tell."

Henry smiled at O'Keefe. "You've never liked me."

"Like or dislike, it don't matter much to me, Henry. You're the only one of this group who talks about killing people like it's nothing."

"That is unfair," said Henry, "and unjustified, and if you don't watch your ass, young man, the town will do away with you."

"You and your friends don't scare me one little bit. I know which of you selectmen are KKK and you're a small bunch, believe me. A small, small bunch."

"Henry, stop it," said Hope and took his hand and pulled him next to her on the sofa.

"But Frances?" said Giles. "Who would want to hurt her? It just seems preposterous. I mean, obviously, it wasn't one of us. Could she have done it to herself?"

"Well, you tell me," said O'Keefe.

There was a pause. "No," said Hollister. "Frances would never do any such thing. But," he added after a long silence, "perhaps it wasn't meant for her." He looked around the room at everyone. "Perhaps another one of us was supposed to be silenced."

Myrl glanced at me and I saw how troubled she was. I started to speak, but she put a finger to her lips and I sat back.

* * * * *

We were the only ones who needed a ride down the mountain, and Giles Wilcox was there to answer our call. We bundled into the front seat, which was wide enough for the three of us. I sat in the middle and watched his hands on the steering wheel.

"Is it like Patrick O'Keefe to go after someone like that?" asked Myrl.

"You mean what happened with Henry? No. It was very much out of character, to be sure. I think Patrick's feeling some pressure. This whole rash of incidents is making the town notorious and he doesn't have any answers. Plus," he sighed, "the Klan has been riding him too."

"About?"

181

Giles shrugged, "About leaving the members alone. It's just a touchy subject for Patrick. He wants to get them and he can't. There was an incident right over the border in Massachusetts just a month ago. The body of a young Negro man was found mutilated and thrown in the river and I know Patrick thinks Henry had something to do with it. And they're also involved in a lot of illegal gambling. Big stuff. Property, thousands of dollars."

"What does Hope think about all this?"

Giles shrugged again. "I don't know. I don't think she's happy. You know, I leave here, it's the beginning of a beautiful summer, I'm engaged, my life is stretched out before me, the path is chosen, and I leave to the applause of my friends. When I return my life is in shambles, complete shambles. And now this happens with Frances. I don't know who to trust."

We were off Black Mountain and he turned right, onto Putney Road. We would be home in minutes.

"You can trust us," said Myrl

Giles smiled, an exhausted sort of smile that seemed to allude to unspoken misery. For a moment, I felt as if we owed him something, as if his trust in us should be tested so that we might remove some of that pain. And that's exactly what Myrl meant.

"You can trust us enough to tell us why you have kept your marriage to Alyssa Dansen a secret."

We had pulled up to the Tavern and Giles was just preparing to stop the motor, his hand on the key. He turned his head, leaning over the steering wheel to look at Myrl, and for the briefest moment I thought I saw anger in his face. But then he sighed and glanced out the window for a moment, gripping the steering wheel again. In profile, he was shaken, and his lips trembled as he spoke.

"We were married. I don't know who told you. I didn't think anyone knew."

"No one told us, Giles." She smoothed her dress. "Faye and I discovered this at town hall."

182

"Well, then, I must thank you for your discretion." He cleared his throat. "Something came up and Alyssa and I were married secretly, last June, just before my safari to southern Africa. Hollister performed the ceremony, if you can call it that, and we signed our marriage certificate. Legally we were married. But we decided to keep it secret until my return when we could stage a proper wedding."

"So time was your only consideration?" Myrl kept her hands carefully folded in her lap. "Was the pregnancy that far along?"

He looked at her. "Nothing escapes you, does it? But to answer your question, no. Well, I don't know. Alyssa never sought a midwife, but we both suspected she was with child. That wasn't the primary reason for keeping the union a secret. It was this thing she was involved in. This secret!" At this point, he struck the steering wheel with the palm of his hand. He sighed and closed his eyes for a moment.

"She begged me to marry her before the safari. It was such a turn. I told her it didn't matter to me if she were pregnant, that I held no shame in that. But she felt something awful was going to happen to me. She kept saying they would find me out. She kept repeating this over and over, and at first I thought it was the ravings of a woman with child, that she was simply distraught. When I finally got to the bottom of things, she said she was afraid I would die, that they would do away with me to torment her. She thought she would be left financially unable to care for the baby, and have to turn it out for adoption. She became hysterical and said to lose me would be a blow she could hardly stand, and then to lose our child would kill her. I, of course, was ready and more than willing to marry her. She had held me at bay for the longest time, and now she suddenly wanted to do it. I saw it as a gift. I saw her as a gift. I think she thought she might be able to straighten out what trouble she was in before my return."

There was a silence and the motor ran loudly.

"And no one knew of this marriage, no one at all?"

Giles shrugged. "Not that I know of. She could have told her brother, though if she did, it would be more out of spite

183

than anything else. They did not get along. But I can't imagine anyone else finding out."

"What about Marty McFadden."

"Hollister's tanner? Him? Oh, he's harmless. He had it bad for Alyssa, that's true, but he wouldn't hurt her. Oh, that's preposterous."

"I didn't ask if he was capable of murder, I asked if there was any way he might have found out about the marriage."

Giles shook his head. "No. Absolutely not. Hollister's very loyal and was very sympathetic to our plight."

"Could McFadden have spied something in Hollister's files or on his desk? A slip of paper, a note to himself perhaps?"

Giles was thoughtful. "I suppose. Though I don't know. Why would McFadden be snooping around Hollister's personal papers?"

"If, and I say if, McFadden had an inkling that Hollister McLean was up to something not quite legal and was searching for proof –"

"You mean to blackmail him!"

"Precisely."

"McFadden no more has the brains to blackmail –"

"Yet you know now that Alyssa was being blackmailed by someone. There is someone in this town who is up to no good and who is profiting from the weakness of others. I don't think any conclusions can be drawn at this point about anyone, Giles. What about Frances? Has she ever spoken of blackmail?"

"Frances? Good God, no. She's a dear, but she'd rather cut off her own arm than give a cent over to anyone. I don't mean to sound cruel, but she just wouldn't stand for it."

This time I cleared my throat, feeling a bit awkward stuck in the middle between them. "I would think the next thing would be to find Marty McFadden and speak to him."

Myrl nodded. She had her hand on the door handle and Giles moved to get out and open her door. She held up a hand. "Don't bother. So we will see you tomorrow for dinner? Around four o'clock or so?"

Giles smiled and said, "It will be nice to be with friends afterward, that's to be sure. I have never been to a coroner's."

We stood on the curb watching the roadster continue on up Putney Road. Giles was heading home. Myrl stood apart from me watching the back of the car.

"Again, we are reminded that this is a mystery about what is not."

I looked at her.

"What is not there." She waved an arm. "Who is missing. It's a mystery built on all that which is absent." Myrl held her gaze on the car a moment longer. "I called this morning, and checked the passenger list for departures to South Africa last July and Giles Wilcox was on that ship."

Chapter Twelve

The Arrest

Our train was to leave at four-thirty and it was nearly three o'clock before we were deposited in front of the Tavern by Giles Wilcox. Biggy, who had lit the parlour with dish lights, ran around trying to coerce Myrl and me to sit for a photo for the Brattleboro Reformer. Mrs Howe, who promised to keep all reporters away, nonetheless hovered around us while we packed our bags, getting in the way and causing Myrl some irritation.

"Really, Mary, we are quite fine. I just have a few things to pack," she said, and I looked with a frown at the large pile of clothes thrown on the bed. Mrs Howe stood in the centre of the room wringing her hands and I knew the morning's events had left her shaken. This was a very small town. People did not get poisoned.

There was a tap and Grace pushed the bedroom door open.

"Biggy let me in, but he made me sit for a picture," she explained. She frowned and folded her arms. "So what do you make of this?"

"I don't know," said Myrl.

"Well, I don't like it. I don't like it one bit. Did you know Patrick O'Keefe has gone up to the tannery to question Marty McFadden?"

Myrl cocked an eyebrow and snapped a cotton shirt out in front of her before neatly folding it on the bed. "About Frances?"

Grace nodded. "Well, about a gun-which Marty claims to have found – in a burlap feed bag thrown under his back step – and yes, about Frances."

"Now why does Patrick think Marty is involved with that."

Grace sat on the bed and picked a piece of lint off the shirt. "Because Hollister McLean told him Marty had a book on poisons. Now Myrl," she began, "this isn't a parlour game where the players all just drink tea after the match, chuckle about bad luck, and go home. There is a desperate person out there and you are muddying up the waters."

"Is there any chance of seeing Frances before we leave today?" Myrl picked up the shirt.

"Absolutely not. She's sleeping, and with any luck she'll be out for several days. She should be in the hospital, but I'd rather not move her. She's getting excellent care where she is."

"But what if someone makes another attempt on her life? Shouldn't the police be watching her?" I was slightly taken aback.

Grace sighed. "I guess they do have an officer at the front door and he's supposed to stay there for a day or two. I don't really know for sure."

Myrl flipped the top of her suitcase, turned, and sat down hard to close the latches. After wrestling for a moment with the second latch, she sat with her hands in her lap and looked at both of us. "I'm sure Frances Hall is safe."

"What makes you so sure?" I asked. "It sure seems like someone wanted her dead." I was already packed and was sitting on a pleasant little footstool at the end of her bed.

"No, I do not think that's the case. Grace, you believe this was some kind of exotic poison? Perhaps with a delayed reaction?"

"Exotic maybe, but definitely coated with something to change the time it acted on the body. I have sent a sample of the contents of her stomach to Boston for close analysis, but I doubt they will come up with anything concrete."

"But someone knew enough chemistry to put together some very sinister potion."

"Not just put it together but to also administer it. My feeling is that it was smeared on one of the biscuits like a paste and then offered to her. Or it could have been in a liquid form and diluted with her drink somehow. My first guess is the paste – a liquid would have been absorbed too quickly. According to her the last thing she ate or drank was a good half-hour before the spell."

"And someone with that kind of knowledge of chemistry would be certain to know precisely how much to use to render the dosage lethal, am I right?"

"Well, yes, I guess. In fact, if the dose was large enough to kill her, I'm not certain I would have suspected poison. Her fit was caused by a massive flow of blood to the brain, and if she had died, it would have looked as if she'd had an aneurysm. At least those were the symptoms."

"So," Myrl said, moving off the bed and hoisting the suitcase to the floor, "it seems whoever did this thing to Frances did not want to kill her. They obviously did not want to poison her enough."

"Just warn her?" I said.

Myrl frowned slightly. "Warn? Warn? I don't know about warning Frances. It could have been a warning to someone else."

"In that case, the warning could have been for you," said Grace. "Myrl, I want you to be careful. Very careful. You're not from around here and people have their prejudices about out-of-state folk, no matter how pleasantly they smile. You're mixing the batter up and someone's getting mad."

Myrl looked at her evenly and smiled, putting a hand on Grace's shoulder. "Grace, my friend, I am just here out of duty to my client."

"Forrest Dansen? That oaf? He's just a crass opportunist."

"Nonetheless."

"Well, you haven't even seen him since you started, have you?"

"True, but he has not dismissed me either. I am certain he is following the proceedings in the paper."

* * * * *

Curran Holt was breathless as he stood on the loading platform under our train windows. Boarding the train, we had braved a swarm of reporters and Curran was the only one who remained. He was waving his hat and yelling at Myrl, but the sash was up and locked. Steam from the engine, pulled in tufts by the strong evening wind, blew in thick gusts past our window. I could see his face bobbing beneath us. But she was not interested in him at the moment. She was speaking to me.

"Faye, do you see that if it wasn't a warning, then the only possible reason that the dose was too small would be because it was meant for someone else?"

"Well now, Myrl. That is quite a leap." I glanced down at Curran Holt. "Ah, Myrl –"

"No, it isn't. Please bear in mind Rimmer's convention."

Rimmer's convention dictates that the cause of an action can exist separately from the result. A cause exists solely for one result. If the result is faulty, one should not attribute the fault to the cause – the cause was meant to have another outcome.

"Why don't you think it was a warning?"

"There are other ways to warn people than to make a public display and institute poison."

I waved politely to Curran. "Okay, so who was supposed to get it?"

"Someone smaller than Frances. Remember, the science of pharmaceuticals is based on weight."

"Well, she's a big-boned woman –" I began, "It could have been anyone, then."

"Now Faye, still, she underweighs all the men on that field this morning. Think about the women."

I suddenly realised whom she was alluding to – "Marion! Marion French! And she was so nervous afterward. I mean we

190

were all a bit nervous – who wouldn't be – but she, in particular, was just a wreck. She didn't even want Howard touching her. Yes, I see – but why poison her in front of all those people?"

Myrl held up her hand. "Remember what Grace said – if the dose were large enough, she probably wouldn't even have guessed poison – it would have looked like a stroke, an aneurysm. Tragic, to be sure, in someone so young, but not suspicious. And not unheard of."

With that, Myrl suddenly stood, lifted the clasps and hoisted the window open. She leaned out and I was a little alarmed at how revealing her dress suddenly became. She had saved her best piece for her exit, and now wrapped tightly in crushed purple velvet, black glossy high heels, and fox stole, her plunging neckline seemed a bit too summery.

"Myrl ... ah, Myrl ..." I tried, standing rather mother-hennish at her side. Curran Holt came right up to the train as she raised the window, and then retreated a few steps when Myrl leaned out. At least he was a man with manners. I could barely hear his voice above the grinding of the engine.

"Marty McFadden is missing. He's been missing since last week."

"What do you mean, missing?" She seemed irritated.

Curran squinted up at us, brushing smoke from his eyes. "He was supposed to be off hunting all this week with this guy, Orrin Staples. Marty must've called Patrick O'Keefe from someplace yesterday when he said he'd found the gun, because Orrin came back from the woods just an hour ago with four turkeys and no Marty. Said Marty was never with him."

* * * * *

When we arrived back at the Norton house, Godfrey met us at the door.

"Hello, dears," he said. It had been snowing slightly, and he brushed our coats before he hung them in the hall. "I got a

191

call from Mary saying you were on your way and you had some news."

Myrl turned to him. "News? Well, I shouldn't think we do. I'm no further along than when we left. In fact, I'm more befuddled by this whole business. Missing persons. This is uncalled for." She wandered into the kitchen. Godfrey turned to me and I felt the responsibility of having to provide an explanation. Remembering her loose rule of hiding nothing from her father, I launched myself on a capsulated explanation of the last two day's events.

"Frances Hall, a woman who was Alyssa Dansen's friend and an actress, was poisoned this morning, though Myrl thinks the target was Marion French, another actress with the theatre troupe. We discovered Alyssa Dansen and Giles Wilcox, a gentleman farmer and theatre star as well, were secretly married. Wilcox had a handgun stolen, we found a long knife with bloodstains in his dressing room, a wig of red hair, and Myrl thinks someone is trying to frame him. We met Forrest Dansen, Alyssa's brother, who is something of a brute. Myrl's working for him, in theory, that is. For a nickel, so she won't get rich. Another gentleman, named Hollister McLean, is doing something not quite right, but I don't know what it could be, in a separate room owned by Giles Wilcox. Then there is this man named Marty McFadden who works for Hollister, whom we haven't met yet. The stolen gun was found at his house after he himself reported finding it, and he also was seen with a book of poisons on his person. Unfortunately, it turns out he's actually been missing for a week and nobody knows where he is. Did I leave anything out, Myrl?"

She had returned from her foray in the kitchen with a piece of bread and a hunk of cheese. She kicked off her shoes and her height seemingly remained unchanged. Popping a piece of cheese into her mouth she said, "You've left out the diamonds."

"I think I'd like a drink," said Godfrey.

We moved into the parlour and the bird in the cage twittered and squawked when she saw Myrl. Myrl walked over and stuck her fingers through the bars of the cage for a moment and made little cooing noises, stroking her finger against the downy little head. Her actions were out of character, but I was afforded little amusement because of the wave of aggravation which suddenly washed over me. She reached up, unzipped her dress under the arm and down the side, and flopped onto the divan.

"What are you talking about, diamonds? What do you mean, diamonds?" We had never spoken of diamonds. I stood, refusing to get comfortable. I felt a headache coming on and Godfrey put a hand on my shoulder.

"Myrl, it sounds like you got plenty done, maybe more than you should have," he began but she just waved a dispassionate hand. She seemed suddenly quite exhausted, her stores of energy spent, and I realised that for once this weekend I was ready and primed for action, adrenaline coursing, and she was ready for rest.

"Hollister McLean is cutting diamonds in room number two at the Opera House," was all she said before she yawned. Her eyes closed and her body was limp, completely relaxed. I stood for a moment trying to figure out how she came to that conclusion, given the barrel of violets, the salt, and the tool station, and concluded it must have been the black box on the workbench which cast this light of illumination on what was going on in there.

Myrl opened her eyes for a moment and patted a spot on the divan next to her. As I sat, she spoke to Godfrey. "Dear Father, don't upset yourself. It is not some inevitable curse of fate which drives me in this mystery."

"But Myrl, it is uncanny and if you knew –"

"I don't wish to know and you must stop upsetting yourself about this matter." Her eyelids fluttered a moment and she shifted deeper in the soft cushions. I was very irritated.

"Diamonds." I sat straight, in rigid counterpoint to her.

"Oh, yes. Well," she said, her eyes still closed, "it is quite simple. The tools in that black box on the workbench were the tools of a jeweller. Older, yes, but a complete set. The bottom four drawers were unused as was the small torch – remember how dusty everything was. But the top drawer, the one you pulled out yourself, Faye, was clean from use and in that tray was a set of chisels of incremental size and matching hammers. The dopp stick and shellac are used to hold the diamond while the cuts are made. The dopp was sticky. The magnifying lens also would be used. Remember, Hollister's father was a jeweller and so it seems natural he, too, would be skilled in the trade. Also, did you notice his key chain? The fob was a jeweller's eyeglass. He obviously keeps it around as a good luck piece. A final note – I do believe he is in financial trouble, possibly the result of gambling debts. I could not help but notice he keeps the most recent racing form in his breast pocket, complete with the names of favoured dogs checked off. It appears he engages Henry Mitchell in his folly as well. Twice now I have overheard the two men discussing wagers."

Everything she said was true, though I had not noticed the dog racing form. The track in Hinsdale was famous for dog racing, however, and it seemed likely Hollister McLean might have inherited more than a jeweller's eye from his father.

"Maybe this is a side business for him, resetting stones, and the like," I offered.

"From a room with boarded windows? I think not. I don't believe Hollister McLean wants people to know of this particular side business." Here she patted my knee and said quietly, "I do need to sleep a bit, Faye, do you mind? Can you find your way home this evening and I'll see you tomorrow in class."

"See here, Myrl, it's nearly eight o'clock at night. I think Faye should stay the night, for heaven's sake," said Godfrey and I felt my face growing flushed. I was put off a bit by her dismissal of me and was grateful for his rescue.

"Oh yes," she mumbled, "I didn't mean to be rude, dear Faye," and with that she was asleep.

"Well, I never!" I started to say.

"Her mind is like an engine, grinding away, all stops out, and then she runs out of gas. Sudden, kaput." Godfrey had his hands on his hips and was looking down at her, shaking his head. "She is the strangest child."

"Should we move her?" I asked.

"Good God, no, girl, she weighs a ton, you ought to know that, no, here, I'll just get her feet up," he grunted as he lifted her legs and pulled her around straight. I picked up a cotton blanket from the back of the overstuffed chair and threw it across her. We went into the kitchen.

"Other than being tired, she seems in fine spirits," said Godfrey, sitting down at the porcelain table. I sat across from him and nibbled at the cheese and bread Myrl had left out.

I nodded my head. "She was. But she didn't sleep a wink, not a wink. We were up late both nights – Saturday until three in the morning ..." I paused, breaking her rule by not divulging we broke into a building in the dead of night, "... and I'm not sure she ever fell asleep."

Godfrey got up and put a pot on for tea. His back was to me and I could not see his face. "Faye, you have broken the cloister this house has been operating under for many years."

"Oh Godfrey, really," I began, feeling embarrassed.

He turned around, and I again saw an old man, teary and spent, a man harbouring a past which he thought about perhaps too much and gave himself too much guilt for.

"Come sit down," I said and he came and sat across from me, looking down at his folded hands. I was reminded of how Myrl clasped her hands when readying for a speech.

"Myrl has had a difficult life, and she is all the world to me," he said. Then he swallowed and leaned forward, not looking at me and still focused on his hands. He pressed his thumbs together. "Her mother, as you know, died when she was just a very young child and swore me to a secret." He paused again. "You see, I am not really her father."

I could tell he was watching my face for some reaction, but I remained merely attentive.

He continued, "When Myrl was twelve years old, I tried to tell her the truth. I thought it her right to at least know that, but she beat me to the punch line. I'll never forget that little face looking at me as she said, 'Why, Daddy, I've known

195

about that for simply ages, and it doesn't matter'. She's never been an affectionate child, but at that moment she threw her arms around me and I knew she was really mine."

The ghostly faces from the portraits in the hall haunted me now and I knew why they seemed so vaguely disturbing.

"No one is privy to this. No one. Not even Mary Howe, Irene's best friend. Irene and I married quickly when she was first with child, before she began to show her condition, and everyone was pleased we were starting our family right away."

I didn't know what to say. I thought it had been he, not Myrl, with the difficult life. "Oh, Godfrey," I said softly, touched by his compassion for this woman I never knew, "you are such a noble person."

"Noble? Oh Faye, if you were to meet Irene, you would see I had no choice. I was in love, desperately in love. Her only mistake was one indiscretion. We were separated in England for several months and she met someone."

"But to forgive and then to raise her child as your own, not knowing the father ... Godfrey, I must say," I shook my head, "you are a modern man."

"But I did know the father. Not personally, but I had heard of him. It almost didn't matter. Irene's indiscretion can't even be described as a moment of weakness. When she confessed to me, in tears, her tears were because she did not want to hurt me, they did not come from shame."

"But this man, to turn his back on his own child!" This was an age-old dilemma and one for which I had little patience. Godfrey shook his head. "The father was a famous man, well respected in his field."

I stabbed an index finger on the table with every other word, punctuating my sentence. "That is the poorest excuse of all." I sat still for a moment. "Why should the woman bear the financial burden just to spare the man's name? And let me guess – he was married? "

Godfrey looked shocked. "Oh no. It was nothing like that, Faye." He sighed. "I am not explaining this well at all."

"It doesn't matter, no matter what she thought of him, he was still some kind of selfish brute to let her go like that with no –"

"He did not know she was with child."

I paused and laid my hand flat on the table. "She never told him?"

Rubbing his forehead, he began again. "She was in love with me, not him. She had but one liaison with the gentleman, and later she told me she thought theirs was the only intimacy he'd ever engaged in and that he probably abhorred himself for it."

"But this makes no sense!"

"Irene and ... this man were attracted by like minds. Irene's mind was like a trap. She was not just clever, she was brilliant, as was he. The two of them, despite themselves, saw this in each other and were overcome – you must forgive me, I've never spoken a word of this to anyone and words are difficult. But this man, his profession, you see, and why I am growing so upset with Myrl over this murder. He was – well – he was a consulting detective." As if escaping from a heavy burden, Godfrey sighed deeply and straightened his shoulders.

"And Myrl still doesn't know who her father is?"

He shook his head again. "No. Nor does she care to. I am thankful in a way because that is what Irene asked me never to divulge. Myrl senses this promise whenever the subject comes up, which is very rarely, I must say. But she respects her mother's judgment and dismisses my attempts."

I thought of Myrl lying on the divan slumbering, her mind troubled with the events of the day, the phantoms of depression and mental illness flitting about her like dark angels, sapping her strength, leaving her vulnerable. I realised how deep my affection for her had grown, and how protective of her I felt. It was an odd combination: fondness and friendship tempered with a sort of objective fascination and sense of guardianship. I realised this was perhaps the first true adult relationship I had embarked on, seeing her for who she was, and accepting her as such.

Reaching across the table I placed a hand on top of Godfrey's. "Thank you for taking me into your confidence. I really like Myrl. And this all helps to understand her better."

Godfrey laughed and wiped an eye. "Well, that can't be done. No one could possibly understand her!"

* * * * *

I stood before the class, fuming. Myrl was absent and had left me notes to lecture from. When I rose from my wide bed at the Norton home, she had already left for school. When I arrived at class there was her careful script across the blackboard, directing me to check the podium where her notes lay and give the lecture. I was so put off that the lecture went rather well, as I didn't give a hoot. Distraction wasn't such a blessing in Dr Collins's class, however, and I missed most of what he was saying about the advent of monotheism. I ran into Rachel at noon walking across the Quad and this time instead of avoiding me or the subject, she ran right up to me flushed and breathless, books in one hand, newspaper stuffed under her other arm.

"I heard Brattleboro was a hot spot. It's in the morning papers, that woman being poisoned and all and they think it's connected somehow. Oh, Faye, you're very brave. And that Dr Norton, what a cut! She came into the store today, this morning, actually, and I was just leaving and she ended up making me late to class, but I didn't mind a bit. She is so funny. She was just buying shoes. Buying shoes at nine o'clock in the morning! And she's got huge feet. I kept trying to get her into a smaller size, you know, but she just waved me away and took a pair of elevens off the shelf and ordered two more pair. We don't keep anything like that in stock so Bruniel's going to have to cobble them and I told her it would cost a little more and then do you know what she asked about!"

I shook my head. What was Myrl's interest in Alyssa Dansen's shoes?

"She began asking about Miss Dansen and what kind of shoes she ordered. Well, I didn't know and I was late to class anyway, so I couldn't really help her when Bruniel comes from the back of the shop and tells her that all Miss Dansen's shoes were custom made. And then she asks to see all the order forms and, of course, Bruniel's about fit to be tied, he's so disorganised, but he gives her a wad of order forms and she sits down and proceeds to ask about this order and that, why Alyssa Dansen wanted shoes with hand-stitched pearls, why purple satin. Why was one order a whole size larger – that pair was a gift – why was another order cancelled, and I know Bruniel's making up most of the answers because he's got a terrible memory. Anyway, I just had to leave then, but I was desperate to tell you. What is she up to?"

Despite my foul little mood, I had to laugh. "I don't know, Rachel. I haven't a clue. She wasn't in class today. I got up, and ran to class to find out that I was to do the lecture." My shudder was belated. "And then I had to sit through Collins."

"So you haven't seen the papers at all?" I shook my head. "But I'm surprised Frances's story made it in so quickly."

She set her books on the ground and withdrew the morning edition from under her arm, snapping it open. "That's because that story is running next to this one."

Dual headlines screamed up from the paper. On the right was a picture of Frances, beautifully coiffed, and above her: THEATRE STAR POISONED, and in smaller print underneath, *Possible Connection to Alyssa Dansen Murder*. On the left was a drawing of a man's face, thick and heavy set with curly hair, a beard, small dark eyes, and a sullen, pouting expression. This headline read: MAN ARRESTED IN HIDEOUS DANSEN MURDER! *Suspect Caught While Escaping Police!*

"You've seemed to have forgiven Myrl her curiosity about this case," I said, cocking my head around trying to read the story. Curran Holt had written the piece on Frances Hall. The byline on the other story was Waltham Silverman, a local writer from Amherst.

"Here," she said and shoved the paper into my hand. "Oh, I was just a wreck last week, that's all."

I whistled softly. "This is why she wasn't in class. Listen to this: 'Northampton, Mass. Police apprehended Marty McFadden, twenty-eight, of Brattleboro, Vermont, this morning in connection with the murder of Alyssa Dansen, thirty. Miss Dansen's body was discovered November 14 in her home on Courtney Place. McFadden, a tanner, had been seen by neighbours loitering about the house for several weeks. His disappearance last week ago left authorities in Brattleboro suspicious and when a neighbour alerted police in Northampton that a man fitting McFadden's description was prowling, police investigated'." I glanced up. "How convenient that a neighbour would call. New paragraph. 'Police Detective Frank Lorey'" – I cocked an eyebrow, "our dear friend – 'began the chase on foot with five men. McFadden was apprehended on Norbert Road after a short chase which ended peacefully. McFadden has not secured counsel and it is not clear on what charge he is being held'." I shook my head. "I bet Myrl elbows her way in to see him," I said, scanning the rest of the story. There was more – laid out in black and white just as Myrl predicted. "'So far the case against McFadden has been written by his own hand as he attempted to throw suspicion on Giles Wilcox, thirty-nine, of Putney, Vermont, and Alyssa Dansen's fiance. A stolen gun was discovered on McFadden's premises and a book extolling the application and mixing of poisons was found on his person at the time of the arrest. The gun belonged to Giles Wilcox, and police believe McFadden was preparing to frame Wilcox with it. In addition, a bloodstained knife was placed in Wilcox's dressing room'." I handed the paper back to her. O'Keefe must have searched the dressing rooms right after the poisoning.

"Faye, this is so exciting. It's wonderful they've got the man who did it already, don't you think? And it's perfect, him being a tanner and all."

I thought about Marty McFadden, and wondered if Gladdis knew her son was in hiding the past week.

* * * * *

I stopped in to check my room at Martha Wilson and deposit my suitcase. I had a little over an hour before my next class, and I was anxious to unload my bag and change clothes. I nodded to Mrs Lawrence, the house mother, and walked briskly to the bottom of the stairs. From the shadows next to the stairwell, from a Queen Anne chair tucked against the far wall, a person rose and called my name.

"Faye!"

I paused with one foot on the stairs. "Myrl, where have you been –" I turned around. "No, wait, let me guess." I viewed her up and down, and set my bag on the floor. "I see you've not been in class today, but went instead to the cobbler's. There you bought a pair of shoes and ordered two more ... size elevens I would say, by judging your foot. I would venture you asked about Alyssa Dansen's shoe preference –"

"I see you ran into your little friend Rachel," she said with a small tight smile. "I do believe you are mocking me. Pick up your bag and come with me."

"I have class in an hour."

"I know that, Faye, but sometimes one must sacrifice. That said, however, I will do everything I can to deposit you in your class seat in sixty minutes."

She began to move toward the front door. I grabbed my bag. "But where are we going?"

"Marty McFadden was arrested this morning."

"I know, I read about it in the papers."

"He's being held right here in town, and we are going to see him." She held the door open for me, but before I scooted through I ran back and left my bag with Mrs Lawrence at the front desk.

"We are?" I was running out the door.

201

"The newspaper report said Marty McFadden was seen lingering around the Dansen home for weeks." This was offered as if the conclusion was evident. It was not. At least to me.

"So?"

We were hurrying down the concrete steps.

Myrl touched a finger to her nose. "If he has been secretly spying on the Dansen home, doesn't it follow that he may – and I stress this is a *may* statement – have witnessed something which might be critical to discovering the truth?"

Chapter Thirteen

The Arrest

The jailhouse carried a sense of menace and doom, far different from the air of tenuous excitement and shrill elation which echoed in the halls during my brief stay. Myrl rang in at the front desk. The policeman on duty seemed very doubtful that we would be let in to see McFadden, and called his superior. Both gentlemen were thoughtful and pleasant and they seemed familiar to me, though their solicitous manner was a sharp contrast to their cold dismissal that Sunday evening three months ago. Myrl, who was set off in a man's suit and tie, her Oxfords polished to the nth degree, was stiff and cool, throwing the men pained small smiles, and looking put off.

"I am here representing my client, Mr Forrest Dansen, and I do not see the harm in asking a few private questions." She shook the captain's hand.

"Well, miss, we can't just allow anybody to go in and question a suspect. Now what if you were really a reporter? What would happen to our case? "

"Let me reiterate again. I am not a reporter. I am here in the interests of my client. Why don't you go and ask Mr McFadden if he would care to see us. Tell him there are two women from Northampton who would like to talk to him for just a few minutes about a certain, particular, letter."

The man scratched his head. "A letter, ay?" The captain was a ruddy Irishman, with a fair complexion, wide girth and a red mouth. He could, no doubt, cast off quite a rendition of *Bonny Lass* or *Down the W'orty Thicket* in no time. I shifted my weight.

"Mr ..." began Myrl.

"O'Donnell."

"O'Donnell," she sighed and closed her eyes for a moment. "You have had a hurried lunch not quite up to your expectations and heartburn has set in. The day has been rigorous. With the chase this morning, you've suffered a twisted ankle which will shorten your temper for the remainder of the day. With luck, you will be off duty at half past, and you will return home to a fine meal of perhaps gravy and dumplings or fish and chips and kiss your wife. You'll down an ale and head off to your meeting of the Masons over on Church Street, where you will be plied with questions about the arrest. You will have to remain strong and not give in to the dual pressures of drink and nosy friends. Very few will truly understand the position you've been placed in, and several friends will grow grumpy with you for not divulging facts about the arrest, charging you with self-importance. The evening will begin to stale with these accusations and you will return home early, finding a nightcap waiting by your bed." Here she paused and looked him in the eye. She was slightly taller than he, and she did nothing to lessen her stature. "Do you see that my client has chosen me carefully? It is imperative I speak with Mr McFadden. If he'll have us, of course."

O'Donnell wiped a hand across his forehead. "I don't know how you did that, miss." He seemed to relent for a moment but then shook his head. "I ... I really can't let you ladies in to see him. It's against the rules."

Myrl drew close to him, "Mr O'Donnell, you cannot refuse us."

"What are you actually?"

"I am trained in law –"

"So you're a lawyer?"

Scepticism was heavy in his voice. There were only a few more than a thousand women attorneys in the United States and many served with limitations on their practice. I cleared my throat. "She has training in legal matters. Frankly, Mr Dansen is of restricted means –"

"Faye, I think you've said quite enough about our client."

"I think the captain is due the facts." I continued, "And he can not afford to hire a private attorney at the moment. But he has secured us to do some background work along matters of probate and that sort of thing."

"Probate? What has that got to do with McFadden? Did the victim have some kind of relation – oh …"

"That is not for us to say," snapped Myrl as I opened my mouth. I stood quietly chastised.

"I'm beginning to see," said the captain. "You want to ask a couple of questions of a private nature about certain intimacies?" The corners of his mouth pulled down with the word 'intimacies' in such a way I felt a pang of sympathy for his wife.

Myrl moved closer to him, a hand on his arm. Her tone matched her beseeching posture. "I beg you, Captain O'Donnell, let us meet with him in private. There may be a guard right outside – in fact, given his violent nature, we would feel much protected if you were to secure a guard within calling distance."

"Well, I was going to plant me-self right in there with you –"

"Oh, that won't be necessary – that would be a waste of your valuable time and you need to nurse that ankle." She smiled. "You are truly helping two women in need," she said poignantly, and then added with a choke to her voice, "It is hard, you know, when one is beyond marrying age, to make ends meet. There are few honourable professions left to a barren woman."

Captain O'Donnell blushed at the word 'barren'. It was at this moment of vulnerability that she struck.

"Now, do go ask if he will see us – we have little time."

He turned obediently, almost sheepishly, and asked over his shoulder, "I'm to ask about a letter?" After he left, Myrl smiled a quick smile to the duty officer and turned her back on him.

"Now Myrl, really," I began.

She kept her voice low. "The fact that he failed to take the time to remove his jacket and so splattered it with heavy grease gives evidence of a hasty meal. Given the size of his girth, and the oil and sauce spotted across the front, I assumed indigestion would begin almost immediately. That assumption was further supported by the series of small belches he offered upon entering the room. The newspaper story featured a quote from our captain, so he was indeed one of the arresting officers. His limp and grimace was evidence of a new injury, not an old one, and as he could not chase our poor Mr McFadden with an injured ankle, he must have injured it during the chase." She paused and took a breath. "Do I go on?"

"Please," I said. "Let me marvel at you."

"Oh, Faye," she laughed, "you are so good for me. Well, the captain's shirt collar has been heavily starched, his cufflinks and buttons polished, and his left sock freshly darned. This neatness would fly in the face of his manner of eating, so I assume, after checking the direction of his Claddagh, his ring, that there is a proud, attentive wife who devotedly makes heavy, rich meals. He wore a second ring, five stars of the Masons on his right hand, and the only Masonic meeting house is on Church Street, where meetings are on Monday nights, tonight. The rest comes from conjecture coupled with a self-serving need to appear in need so as to make him more sympathetic to our cause. And, Faye, bravo to you for your flawless complicity. Probate indeed."

The door opened and Captain O'Donnell led us into the jail.

Marty McFadden was sitting on a chair in the middle of the third cell, the same one I had had the pleasure of visiting. The room was dark and what little sun filtered in through the tiny window above did not stray from the ceiling and left most of the room in shadow.

One could tell he was a McFadden. He had his mother's stocky build and the same round face. I would have not recognised him from his picture in the paper, however. There was no set to the jaw, no look of heavy malevolence. Instead, he sat on the edge of his chair and looked up like a berated farm boy when we entered the corridor. His hair was his most outstanding feature: bright red curls boiling up off his forehead, flowing into a scruffy beard, and ending in long shaggy spirals down the back of his neck.

O'Donnell placed a guard at the entrance of the hall, as a precaution against verbal abuse, he said. He would not allow us in the cell with the prisoner, but he set up two chairs for us to sit on four feet or so from the bars. We were not to take one step closer.

We sat and Marty McFadden inched even closer to the edge of his chair and wiped his nose with the back of his hand. "Have you come to help me? What do you know about this business?"

"Mr McFadden," said Myrl, clearing her throat, "I am here on a quest for the truth."

"I didn't do it. I didn't do what they're sayin' I did."

"You are in a bad position, Mr McFadden, to be sure. My name is Myrl Norton and this is my friend Faye Tullis." Our names seemingly meant nothing to the man, so he had not evidently kept up with the week's news.

"We are here on behalf of Forrest Dansen."

McFadden's eyes narrowed and he scowled. "He'd be no friend of mine."

"Friend or not, that should make no difference to you. Miss Tullis and I discovered your letter to Miss Dansen in which you basically proposed marriage. This is damaging enough –"

"I didn't write no letter."

"– without the added fact that Giles Wilcox's gun was found at your home."

"So someone pinned that gun on me, I didn't steal the friggin' thing."

The officer in the back yelled, "Hey!"

McFadden scooted back in his chair and slouched a bit.

"Why would someone want to do that to you'"

"Who's she?" he asked, looking at me. Then he glanced back to Myrl. He leaned forward, "And who are you?"

"Mr McFadden, we know you wrote the letter and we know you were in love with Alyssa Dansen. Eyewitnesses have reported seeing you hanging around the house on Courtney Place for several weeks."

"I thought you was here to help me. When that captain fellow said 'letter' I thought you were talkin' about something else."

For the first time, I saw that his nerves were a bit frayed. He gripped the bottom of the chair and tipped so far back that the front legs were a good five or six inches off the dirt floor.

Myrl cocked her head to one side, "This would be –"

"– none of your business."

"Perhaps a telegram?"

He folded his arms across his chest. "I'm not sayin'. Look, I don't need to talk to you." He threw his head back slightly and yelled "Guard!"

"Mr McFadden," said Myrl in a tense whisper, "don't be an ass. There are forces at work here beyond you – you are merely a dupe." She stood up and leaned toward the bars. "I know you were in love with Alyssa Dansen. I know you suspected something was amiss. I also know someone is going to let you dangle at the end of a rope in their stead." The guard was just a few paces away. Her voice dropped even lower. "And I know about the diamonds."

At this, McFadden's gaze slowly came back to her and he stared for several seconds. "It's all right," he said to the guard.

"We'll need about ten more minutes," said Myrl without even a glance at the officer. I tried to smile pleasantly and he returned to his post.

The chair came back down. Leaning forward, McFadden hunched down, elbows pinned to his knees, hands folded in the middle. "Now looky here, I didn't know anything about no diamonds. What's she writin' down?"

"Faye is taking notes, that is all, Mr McFadden. Please continue."

"I don't want no notes."

"Mr McFadden, please. Notes are permissible in court under certain circumstances. This could be to your advantage."

He said nothing. I laid my flowered pen down inside the notebook and closed the cover. He glanced at me and then stared at the ground.

"Shall I begin?" asked Myrl.

"I don't know what you want me to tell you –"

"I want to know about you and Alyssa Dansen."

"Now?" And with that question I saw much of McFadden's stubbornness fade into despair. His head hung low and his voice dropped.

"I'd seen her before, you know, it's not like I didn't know who she was. I mean everyone knew Alyssa, and her face was all over town 'cause of that theatre show she did. Anyways, she'd come by Hollister's quite a bit, and they were friends, and then she'd stroll down from the shop to the tannery and sit a spell with me. She knew I had it bad for her. She could tell, and she would say one thing and do another. She'd milk you dry. She was like that."

"So you gave her your attentions and she did not reciprocate?"

"Reciprocate? Hell. When I was with her I was wearing a ten dollar hat on a ten-cent head. I was sending her flowers, cards, letters, we ate in town a couple of times last winter – she dared to be seen wit' me. Oh" – he let out a long, low chuckle – "she ran me in circles. And then, nothin'."

"You mean she stopped answering your calls?"

"I mean I never hear a word from her after the thaw."

Last spring. I made a mental note. That would have been about the time Alyssa and Giles began seeing each other seriously.

"Did she get another suitor?"

"I'm not sayin' we were a couple, if you know what I mean. I mean, she'd talk to me and we had our two dinners out in town but, Gawd, I knew she was the one and I knew she couldn't care a horse's hair for me. But she stopped comin' 'round the tannery and when I got enough nerve to call her she never answered. I did write her that letter proposin' marriage, but that was early on, before I saw it was a lost cause. Then my mother told me she'd gotten sick and went south."

"And then what happened?"

"Well ..." He rubbed his hands together and stole a look at Myrl. "You were right, though I don't know how you knew't – but there was a telegram. Hollister asked me to fetch a key out his drawer in the shop for the barn – he had a spare in his desk – and I pulled out the wrong drawer and was halfway through it 'fore I saw it was wrong. And there was this telegram and I just saw it for a second but it made gooseflesh on my arms." He rubbed a hand over his forehead. "I ain't ever gonna forget it – it said, 'Blood on way. Stop. Heart bagged. Stop. Let's see what worms crawl out now. Stop'."

"Who was it from?" I asked after a pause.

"There was no name and I didn't think to see where it come from. I just shut that drawer and got the hell outta there."

"And then you began to worry about Alyssa?"

"Well, now, that was separate. I mean there's Giles, goin' down every weekend to visit her, takin' baskets of fruit and Lord knows what all and then she comes back all sweet and pleasant to everyone but me. I don't hear a word from her. Nothin'. Not even a 'Hello, sorry but I'm engaged', and that's not like Alyssa. Some folks thought she was snobby, but I think she was just careful. Anyway, I begin writing her all kinds of letters. I try callin' more and more. Nothing. So finally I decide I'm goin' to see her myself. By then, the season's closed, you know, the theatre season, and she's back down south again, so I start comin' down here. But she won't see me either. I try callin' her by phone, I come up to the house, and I see her boarder girl, but never her. Except in the evenings, when she sat by that window." McFadden sighed and leaned back in his chair. "And really, that's all I know."

"Did anyone else ever visit her?"

He shrugged.

"Did you ever see anyone from Brattleboro come down besides yourself? "

He shook his head.

"What can you tell us about the stump burning?" Myrl was putting on her gloves.

"Ay?"

"Last spring. Last spring, neighbours have reported night burnings of brush and stumps which went on all night." Again McFadden shrugged. "I don't see anything special about that. McLean's got a flat bed of land back there that needs clearin'."

"I think you did see something a bit unusual, Mr McFadden."

"Well, that reporter fellow was tresspassin', if that's what you mean."

"Games are for children and virtueless attempts at riches can be lethal. If this charge sticks, and there is every likelihood it will, you will never have your chance at extortion."

At this point, Marty McFadden seemed to relax and he slumped back in his chair. He glanced from side to side, and while he spoke I had fleeting thoughts of all the "virtueless attempts at riches" throughout history which ended, unjustifiably, in horrid success. I decided Myrl was either a secret optimist or terribly naïve – or both.

"I didn't see a thing."

"You are being foolish. I will not tell you what I suspect you saw, because my statement will make you believe you have a chance to win this game of blackmail you are so desperate to set up. You will never get beyond these bars, McFadden. Don't you see? Can't you see you are being framed and that I am possibly the only person in the world who understands this? You will hang because of your own obstinance. They will say you killed Alyssa Dansen, desecrated her body, and then tried to poison Frances Hall."

McFadden's face remained impassive.

Myrl continued, speaking quickly, lightly, the words tripping out her mouth in succinct succession. "You poisoned Frances Hall because you thought she knew of your deed – that she'd come by the tannery one Saturday night, months ago, on a friendly call to Hollister, and found you up late in the back of the tannery. By her admission, you were surly with her and ordered her out – because, perhaps, she saw something incriminating. The town will turn against you like wolves when the case is made that you tried to frame poor Giles Wilcox by stealing his own gun, and had planned on planting it in Alyssa's front yard. The man seen leaving the Dansen home had bright red curly hair and a beard, Mr McFadden. Faye and I are eyewitnesses. You seem to be unable to escape your fate."

"Now wait a minute!"

"Goodbye." She turned to go, as did I, but his next words froze my heart.

"I saw some bones."

Myrl turned slowly and took a step toward the bars. He remained seated and looked up into her face. His expression was of a boy caught with his hand in the cookie jar – all guilt and little defence.

"I did love 'er, you know. I wanted her for mine and when I first saw them things, those bones last summer, I didn't think anything of it. But then when I'd heard what happened last week, I put two and two together, you know, and –"

"Hid away."

"Yep. I was scared at first. At first, I was. Then I thought I'd go back for a look myself and there was that reporter nosin' around and that's when I realised there might be a pot of gold at the end here."

"So what, exactly, did you find in the stump?"

McFadden sighed, and his voice dropped to a whisper. I sat and opened my notebook to no objection.

"Well, I was out dumping trash. It was a Sunday, the end of last June – June, I think, yes, it was before the fireworks on the Fourth, and I was supposed to be off, but" – McFadden wrinkled his nose – "the tannery was a mess so's I thought I'd come in and straighten up. So anyway, I was dumping trash when I see smoke you could smell it too. I kept walkin' back through to the meadow – there's a little meadow beyond the backyard, and at the far end there was a brush pile still smolderin'. A big brush pile. I didn't know nothin' about Hollister clearin' brush that weekend and I was sort of dupin' around, when I saw three or four big stumps burned out. Now the stumps had always been there, I thought. They were about so high" – he held a hand slightly lower than his shoulder, about a yard from the floor. "The ash in them were white and chalky and there was coals still hot to the touch. I poked a stick around and that's when I found 'em. At first I thought it were just some animal, but there were bone bits in all four stumps. It was really queer, but at the time I didn't think so much of it. Not until last week. So's I go back and try pokin' around but I couldn't find them."

"They were gone?"

"Gone," he said. "I didn't know what to think."

"But you did think enough to contemplate harassing Hollister McLean about it all."

McFadden leaned his head back and folded his hands across his chest. "I thought it might be worth my while."

Myrl stood. I assumed we were about to leave. I stood as well.

"Not a very charitable story, Mr McFadden. Not one I would be proud of."

He stared at her and tipped the chair back once again. "I didn't ask for your 'pinion."

"By the way, why did you have a book of poisons on your person when you were arrested?"

"Oh, for cryin' out loud," he said, spitting on the ground. "That belongs to my mother."

* * * * *

On our way out, we ran into Detective Lorey, who was up at the front desk on the telephone. At his side was another man, who I later realised must have been Waltham Silverman, the reporter who was running the story on the murder. Lorey caught sight of Myrl and me, subjected us to a sorry double-take and slammed down the phone.

"Miss Norton, I am troubled by seeing you here, frankly. I'm glad, of course, because it saves me the trip out to your home to bring you down here. But I do wish you had waited for me before consorting with the prisoner."

"And why would you be whisking me off to the police station –" asked Myrl.

Lorey clenched his jaw for a moment. "Because I want you and Miss Tullis here to identify McFadden as the man you saw leaving the Dansen house last Saturday."

"Well, you may ask Faye for her opinion, of course. But let me assure you that I will emphatically state McFadden was not the man I saw fleeing the premises."

She turned to me. "Faye? Your observations?"

From behind her I heard Lorey muttering, "I knew she was going to say that."

"I'm afraid I have to agree with Myrl, Mr Lorey. I'm sorry. I know you want a different answer, but I just don't know. I don't think it was the same man."

I realised it was one of the few times in my life I have allowed myself to be swayed from voicing the truth as I saw it. Because I did believe Marty McFadden was the man with the gun.

Chapter Fourteen

Strangers on a Train

"I must say, I am so grateful for your invitation this evening," said Giles, raising his glass. "My nerves are shot. Look at that." The port in the glass quivered slightly as his hand shook. This was the first mention of his visit to the morgue that afternoon, and the small dining room fell quiet. Godfrey cleared his throat.

"I do have my sympathies with you, my boy. This was awful business. I am truly, terribly sorry." He leaned over and placed a hand on the younger man's shoulder, and I was again impressed with the breadth of his warmth. Godfrey was sincere, affectionate, very kind, and he harboured no self-consciousness expressing himself – a rare quality in men and one I much admired. Giles gazed down at his plate. He hadn't much of an appetite, and food was pushed around for the sake of being polite. I rose and began clearing the table.

"I am beginning to feel angry about it now. I don't think the police are working fast enough." He glanced at Myrl. "You seem to have a keen mind about all this, what do you think? I spoke with that Lorey fellow today after our visit and they don't seem to have much evidence against Marty. It all seems very flimsy to me. And if he gets off" – his voice shook slightly and his hands, always so expressive, became fists and slammed the table – "I'll kill him."

"I would not be so quick to condemn an innocent man," said Myrl. She sat across from Giles, a feather hat bobbing up

and down as she ate voraciously. She was in a rare mood –
her face animated, nodding, frowning, eyes widening,
winking, or squinting when her mouth was full, and chatting,
gesturing, and sighing when it wasn't. It was truly a
remarkable performance. I'm not certain she actually knew
what she was eating. At this moment, she was coyly turning
her cheek to him and buttering a piece of bread.

"Innocent. Why do you think he's innocent?" Giles could
not look at her.

"I do not think," Myrl said, setting down her knife and
taking a bite. She shook her head and then looked at him,
swallowed, and declared, "I know. The problem we face,
Giles, is that the police need to make an arrest. In this way the
public is assured the police are doing their best. But there is
not enough evidence to hold him, and I am sure he will be out
on the street by next week."

"I don't think I can stand to believe you, Myrl, forgive me.
I want to believe they have found their man."

"Giles," she said, slamming down her fork and wiping her
mouth, motioning Godfrey to pass more mashed potatoes,
"there is not just one person involved in this mess."

"What are you talking about?"

"Myrl believes there are at least two conspirators." I was
waiting for Myrl's plate, I had no idea she was about to help
herself to thirds.

"Two! You mean to say two people did this?"

She nodded vigorously. "Oh yes, definitely. You see, well,
how shall I put this delicately?" She glanced around the table
as if there was some tool which could aid her. "I can't think of
a way, so I'll say it – I believe your friend Hollister McLean is
involved."

Giles stared at her for a moment, just a swift moment, and
then he leaned over the table and said, "Miss Norton, your
hospitality is much appreciated, but I take offence at your
suggestion. Hollister is an old, dear friend of mine."

"And one you presumably know very well – intimately.
All that said, is there nothing about him you can't answer
for?"

216

Leaning back from the table he said, "Well, of course, every man has his secrets, I presume, but Hollister is a fine man. I've known him for years ..."

"How long, exactly?"

"Five years. Five years this past summer."

"Certainly long enough to learn everything about a person."

"I see where you're leading, but yes. I mean I presume to know –"

"What does he take in his coffee?"

"What?"

"What does he take in his coffee?"

"This is ridiculous!"

"Well? Cream? Sugar? How much?"

Godfrey couldn't stand it any longer. "Myrl, please, get to the point."

"Well?" she insisted.

"I don't know!"

Myrl smiled and sat back, waving for me to take her plate. "See, you presume to know and yet you know nothing. I understand it is difficult to suspect your dearest friend, but what I say is true."

"That Hollister murdered Alyssa?" I asked, a bit incredulous myself.

"He is involved in some cover-up. You see," she said, turning back to Giles, "Hollister is also being blackmailed."

"I can't believe that."

"I am not positive, but I carry a high suspicion that this is, indeed, the case. And I believe it is related directly to his gambling debts of which I am certain you are aware."

Giles raised his head, "Christ! Everyone knows he gambles! But who would want to blackmail him? What's there to blackmail him about? So he gets in a little over his head. Excuse me," he said, fumbling with his napkin.

Myrl suddenly brought out a cigarette and placed it between her lips. In the same instant I found myself staring, I heard Godfrey sit back in his seat and gasp with a swift intake of breath. Giles bent one arm over the table, the lighter ready in his hand.

"He is dealing in stolen diamonds," she said before bowing her head toward his hand.

He flicked his thumb, the flame flew, and she drew in the smoke. She quickly placed a fist over her mouth to fight the urge to cough and closed her eyes against the haze curling around her.

Giles laughed and sat back. Relieved. "Why, that's preposterous! What do you think he's doing? Creeping around in the dead of night burglarising the rich of Brattleboro, confiscating their jewels?"

"Far from it," she said. "He does not need to creep. He is merely one link in a chain. His role is to cut diamonds into new ones."

Giles watched her and shook his head, "I don't know what to say."

Now it was her turn to lean forward. "I beg you to say nothing. Nothing at all. Faye and I will return to Brattleboro Saturday morning, and by then I hope to have several questions resolved."

"But shouldn't you tell the police your suspicions?"

Myrl looked at him severely. "The police, at this point, do not want to hear anything which might derail their case. Perhaps, by next week, Detective Lorey will be in a better frame of mind to hear what I have to say."

"Is this all part of Forrest's idea? I mean, are you really working for Forrest Dansen? I read that in the paper, and I find it remarkable."

"Not remarkable, Giles, just practical."

"He wants his inheritance, doesn't he."

"I would think that a fair statement," she said, pulling once more on her cigarette.

"You know he has a motive of his own," said Giles suddenly, paling slightly and, though he tried to make light of it, his hands began to shake again. "If he thought we were to be married, he wouldn't inherit a thing."

"Nothing?" I asked.

"Nothing," he said. "Alyssa despised her brother."

"He is," Myrl said, smiling, with that coy turn of the head, "my first client, Mr Wilcox, and I bid you to bite your tongue."

He laughed amiably and slipped the lighter back into his pocket. As Myrl rubbed out her cigarette in her saucer I caught him watching her. I had the sudden, uncomfortable impression that she had inadvertently given something away.

"To change the subject to something less morbid," he said easily, "the opening of the carousel is next weekend at Winter Carnival. I'd like for you all to be my guests." He fished around in his coat pocket and drew out five tickets.

"Oh, I don't travel much," said Godfrey. "But thank you anyway."

"So the horses are out of your garage?" I asked.

"Long gone," he said "and they've been working night and day to get the thing in working order. It's top of the line, from the Philadelphia Toboggan Company, a fifty-four-seater, all horses, white stallions at that. One hundred and twenty-eight pipes in the pipe organ made to order at The Estey Organ company right in Brattleboro. Three hundred electric lights. So how about it? Myrl? Faye? And see here, there are two tickets for Mary and her nephew – I do hope you'll come. Everyone will be there."

* * * * *

"Faye, could you open the window," Myrl moaned and I rose obediently from my seat next to her bed and raised the sash. Lying flat on her back, two pillows under her feet, a hot water bottle on her forehead and a bag of ice on her feet, she waged a war against a headache.

"It was that horrid thing," she mumbled.

Godfrey stepped into her room for a moment. "How's the patient? "

"I think she'll live," I said. Then I looked down at her. "Do you need anything else before I go?"

219

"If I ever raise a cigarette to my lips again you are to slap it out of my hands. They are hideous. I have been poisoned," she said, eyes closed.

"Well, what was the point of all that?"

"I wanted to test his reactions. Mr Wilcox is a fine actor, Faye. I wanted to see if I could catch him acting with me. But the flame did not quiver when I made the accusation against Hollister, and I held his gaze. Giles Wilcox is a man of steady nerves." Her eyes flew open. "How many letters were there?"

"Letters?"

"Alyssa's blackmail letters."

"Seven."

"Oh yes, that's right. Nearly double four."

* * * * *

Tuesday began a cold snap which continued all week. Thursday afternoon a blizzard hit that carried over into Friday, classes were cancelled, and we were forced to delay our trip. I spent that Friday at the Norton home and enjoyed figuring table puzzles with Godfrey. At lunch, the three of us engaged in an excellent game of double chess. Two game boards were brought out and set up, and Myrl played Godfrey and me simultaneously. It was quite an exhibition and she downed me in eight moves. Godfrey was a more equal opponent and I heard her reasons for her love of the game.

"It is a game of perfect information," she said, sending her rook forward. "Both players, spectators as well," she added, glancing at me, "have the same information available to them at all times. There are no random elements. Luck does not even have a finger-hold in this game. One plays chess either to win or to draw and one's strategy falls into one of these two categories. Chess is meant to be solved," she concluded, adding, "checkmate," to her speech. "And no one has solved it yet."

After her double victory, she remained cloistered in her room for much of the time, emerging to the kitchen to place several phone calls, and waving us out if we dared to enter for food or drink. I learned not to take her manners personally. In fact, the better she knew me the fewer niceties were employed. All airs gone, she puttered around the place talking to the canary and calling for me from various rooms of the house – not to engage me in conversation, but to have me stand and listen. And her thoughts on this white frigid day were varied and fell into distinct logic patterns:

"… The extortion was not a singular case, therefore there could be other victims."

"… A triad forms three contiguous parts – all dependent on one another."

"… If Hollister McLean is being blackmailed and if he has a partner in his conspiracy, then it follows the conspirator, too, would be blackmailed."

"… Evidence of an embarrassing nature is nearly always destroyed unless it can serve another purpose."

"… 'Blood on the way. Heart bagged. Blood on the way. Heart bagged'. What on earth could this mean? Faye? Faye, your thoughts."

I was moved out of my reverie. We were upstairs in her room and she was packing. The snow had stopped and were to take the 6:25 tomorrow morning, arriving at eight o'clock. "Well, that line about the worms crawling out – that sounds like someone wondering –"

"If someone is going to find out. That is nearly a direct reference to blackmail, or some kind of pressure exerted on the two people involved. That line I'm not as interested in. But the first two –"

"You keep saying two people, Hollister and who? Who was his partner?"

"Think, Faye. Who else was being blackmailed?"

"Alyssa Dansen! She was involved in stolen diamonds? Now Myrl, I find that hard to believe."

Myrl flung open her walk-in closet door and disappeared into its depths. From the back, amidst the rustle of dresses I heard, "Now why is that so hard to believe?"

"Well," I stammered, a bit flustered. She emerged holding her set of books.

"If she were a man, now Faye, you'd have no problem coming to that conclusion. The clues all fit just too nicely. She was close to Hollister, she made frequent trips to Boston and New York, she apparently has some wealth hidden from others, she was afraid of someone and she was being blackmailed."

I sat down on the bed. "Myrl," I said, "I hate to change the subject, but what are these little books you carry around?" I stared at the titles: *Upon the Distinction Between the Ashes of Various Tobaccos*, *160 Ciphers Demystified*, *Influences of Trade on the Palms, Fingers, and Wrists*, and several more tucked underneath. I couldn't make out the author, just two initials: S. H.

"These," she said, tossing them into the suitcase, "are monographs. I find them interesting." Staring at the slender books for a moment she paused and then seemed to remember I was in the room. She moved to her dresser. "I took the liberty of making a few phone calls this morning to several numbers from those two cities, numbers from her black box, remember," said Myrl, slipping a piece of paper from her skirt pocket. "The first was a Mr Bleckdom, who seemed very interested in a diamond necklace I purported to have, and quoted me a serious price, unseen. The second was a Mr Whitingham, who quoted me a similar price after I gave him a lengthy description of the necklace. The third was a Mr Marchalle, who, interestingly enough, quoted a price a third above the first two."

"Why?"

"I told him I might repeat business and he wanted to ensure my satisfaction with his services."

"So you called these people – Myrl," I said, shaking my head.

"Faye, I told all three that discretion was of the highest order."

"So they thought the necklace was stolen."

"Precisely."

222

My mind was going over and over the facts. "So she fenced these diamonds for Hollister and the two of them were being blackmailed."

Myrl tapped the end of her nose with her index finger. "I am still puzzled as to why she kept her letters. So neatly tied and bundled. That does not make sense."

"Unless," I jumped in, "she was getting ready to expose the blackmailer and wanted proof!"

"That might work," said Myrl, and I felt a rush of excitement. "And on the eve of exposure she was murdered."

But this line of thinking did not erase the frown on her face. "There are still questions to be answered."

* * * * *

The train was packed. We were bounced around, everyone wrapped in heavy winter coats, wool and fur, and no lap space for carry-on baggage. We were lucky to find two seats together, with everyone travelling as we were, making up for a lost day. Myrl actually carried a smaller bag as we were to stay only one night, and I realised the inclement weather would serve to restrain her wardrobe.

Godfrey had sent us off with toast and eggs and I enjoyed several cups of coffee. I had stayed up late Friday night studying, finding that I had somehow been selected to perform in the winter production of *As You Like It*. I auditioned for the part of Rosalind two weeks before, and was surprised to find that I was accepted. Somehow the excitement I thought I would revel in was absent, and I spent Saturday evening going through an uninspired recitation of my lines.

Myrl was very quiet the first half of the trip, and I found myself nodding off. The snow was thick, three to four feet in places, lying down heavy and still, giving a hush to the landscape. The blizzard came with strong winds, which had blown snow into drifts and left none layered on tree branches. The trees stood very thin and naked sprouting up from this white blanket. As the train gathered speed, the heavy white

223

became a blur. Above, pure white cumulus clouds, blustery and wild, were set against a single depthless, expansive charcoal grey cloud spanning to the horizon. I coughed and closed my eyes.

The train stopped in Greenfield, just south of the Vermont border, to pick up passengers travelling from Boston. The shift in speed and noise stirred me from sleep, and I yawned and straightened out my legs. Our car, already packed, was growing warm and I tried to shed my coat. A young couple vacated their seats in front of us to disembark and within seconds the seats were taken. I struggled with my coat and Myrl, who could have very easily afforded me some help, remained transfixed, staring at the two gentlemen who were trying to get settled in front of us. After a bit of wrestling, I finally was able to shrug off my wrap. I was wiping my forehead with my hand and preparing a sarcastic remark when her hand came down on my knee with such force that I jumped.

She pressed a finger to her lips, and with her eyes beckoned me to observe the two gentlemen. I did not see anything out of the ordinary.

"What?" I mouthed, with, I am afraid, some irritation. "Observe," she mouthed in return, and then shook her head and sat back.

Both gentlemen were nicely dressed, a bit foreign in manner and presence, the thick tweed and wools not American. They were both elderly, similar in years, though the fellow on the right, directly in front of me, seemed more frail. He sported a long grey travelling cloak, an Inverness I thought, and gripped a cane. It was difficult to see them, and all I was doing really was watching the backs of their heads. I did not understand her sudden fascination with the pair. The shorter one wore a bowler hat and the taller one an ear-flapped travelling cap. With a second glance, as to their scarves, I realised they must be British. The train whistle blew and we pulled away from the station. As the engines shifted into high gear, the noise of the train covered our voices.

"What do you want me to see?" I whispered fiercely.

Myrl watched them for a moment and then seemed to shake herself. "I don't know," she said. "This is all more complicated than I ever had imagined." She opened the magazine on her lap, a glossy fashion tabloid I am abashed to say, but I saw her hands shake.

Half an hour later we were at the Brattleboro station. As usual, I was in an unwarranted panic to get off. After all the years of travelling I have undergone, I am still desperate, for no logical reason, to exit the bus, train, ship, whatever, first. But Myrl held me back, and it wasn't until the two gentlemen in front of us rose that she suddenly sprang to her feet and followed them out.

I have never seen her so distracted. She left her bag on her seat and I doubled back quickly and retrieved it. When I caught up with her she was halfway up Bridge Street, watching as the two men crossed Main Street and entered the Brooks House. Real was patiently waiting in the Blacksom right up next to the loading platform, and as I tossed our bags inside I said, "Where's she going?"

"I was told to wait," he said.

"Well, I'll offer a good morning first. Good morning, Real."

"Good morning, Faye. Why don't we turn this around and snatch her off Main Street?"

"Sounds good to me." He turned the horse and carriage around, making our way silently up Bridge Street. The road was a bit steep coming on to Main Street and the horse struggled in silence, the sound of its hooves muffled in the heavy snow. We were lucky the snow rollers had just gone by and the snow was well packed. It was still dusting slightly, and the light, infinitesimal snowflakes gathering along the horse's back told of the extreme cold air. The colder the air, the smaller the flake, and these flakes were like a spray of fine confetti.

When we pulled onto Main Street, the wooden wheels sliding and leather suspension creaking, the horse nickered and I looked up to see Myrl standing directly across from Brooks. I was surprised at how quickly the man with the cane travelled. Just under the awning, he stooped and said something to his companion, who then turned and gave a glance to Myrl. The shorter man said something in return, and took the elder's elbow. They stepped into the lobby.

Myrl suddenly broke out of her trance and waved to Real and me. I was growing weary of this intrigue, and wanted to get to Mary Howe's. I'm chagrined to say that at the time, I was famished – a situation I need to learn to manage better.

"What is she doing now? Oh, for God's sake," I said when she hurriedly ran in front of us and disappeared into the hotel. I sat back and waited.

"She is a flighty thing, isn't she," Real said and he clucked to the horse, letting the reins droop.

Our wait was short. In just a few minutes she appeared from under the awning and ran back to the carriage, blowing on her hands. I flung open the door and she stepped inside.

"Thank you both for your patience." She sat down and arranged her heavy skirts. "I wanted to check the registry."

"Well?" I said.

She looked a bit startled. "Well, what?"

Above our heads Real clucked and the carriage began to move.

"Now Myrl, come! You are entranced by these two men all the way from Greenfield, follow them off the train and into the hotel. What does this have to do with the case?"

"Faye. I will speak to Godfrey about making you a more substantial breakfast."

"That is beside the point!"

"Those two men are –"

"British. Yes, I was able to gather that. I still don't see why you are so interested in them."

"Did they strike you as sightseers? Did they leave the train burdened with cameras? Large amounts of luggage and gifts for family and friends? No. Our Mr Escott and Mr Morstan each carried one small bag. Obviously, they are here on business and do not expect to stay long."

"Maybe they're here to seek medical attention."

She thought about this for a moment. "Perhaps," she said. "We must get to Marion French immediately. I'm afraid her life may be in danger."

I was alarmed by her change in thinking. "But you said earlier you thought they wouldn't try again."

"I'm afraid. Terribly afraid that this whole thing is taking on proportions I had not foreseen."

"You think these two men really have something to do with this business?"

"They are, I believe," she said, looking out the window, her face in dark silhouette against the white snow, "here on a mission."

Chapter Fifteen

The Attempt

"Do you know where Marion French lives?" called Myrl as the horse gathered speed up Main Street.

"Marion?" Real called down. "She lives over on High Street. Why? You figuring on visiting her for breakfast?"

"Take us there at once."

"Now?"

"At once," she repeated.

Marion lived in an apartment on the ground floor of a Victorian house, replete with turret and wide porch, gingerbread moulding, and stained glass. There was no answer. A sash was raised from upstairs, and a round-faced woman smoking a cigarette poked her head out.

"You lookin' for Marion?"

"Yes," I called. "Is she home?"

"She's gone off to Winter Carnival on t' Island. You family?"

"Friends," said Myrl. She turned to Real. "I'd like you to go and pick up Mary. Here are two tickets to the carnival. We will meet you at the Pavilion door at eleven." That was a little over two hours from now. "How long of a walk would it be from here?"

"Oh, not much. A mile or so," said Real, pocketing the tickets. "Thanks."

"Then let's go."

"I can give you a lift partway and that'd cut down your walk."

* * * * *

In the half-hour since we'd arrived in town, traffic had grown heavy with automobiles and carriages, and a uniformed officer was out directing travellers on the corner of Bridge Street and Main. The Carnival officially began at nine and it was ten of now. The steel bridge linking Brattleboro and the Island was gaily decorated in red and blue cloth ribbons, and a welcome banner over the first arch said SECOND ANNUAL ISLAND CARNIVAL. The air was thick with exhaust and the breath of horses and I was reminded again of how swiftly the machine was taking over. Even here.

The boardwalk leading down to and then paralleling the Connecticut was thick with pedestrians, and Myrl and I joined them. I was surprised the turnout was so heavy on such a frigid day. The wind was damp and very raw, so cold I found it difficult to breathe, and I had to keep a handkerchief in hand to wipe my nose. The heavy grey and white clouds were parting, however, and the promise of at least a sunny day was beginning to unfold. As we approached, I saw that the river was frozen over, with a thick wedge of ice encrusted along the banks, presumably thinning in the middle. It was clear of snow, due to the storm's high winds, and the ice lay white and blue-grey over the deepest river in New England. Now the sun began to poke through the heavy gray clouds, and in places where they swirled apart, a raw, blue sky winked through.

Myrl, oblivious to the cold, stepped on the footpath on the side of the bridge and kept watching the crowds. "We must find her. Soon."

"Myrl, why do you think she's in danger?" I said, grabbing her arm and pulling her close. She stopped suddenly on the bridge and people swarmed around us. "If Alyssa Dansen was killed in late spring or early summer –"

"Well, it would have to be after June 20 – the marriage certificate –"

"– then that means someone –"

"But Frances said she saw her, remember, in August."

"Saw someone, Faye. She saw her from a distance."

"But she was walking and she waved –"

"Let me correct myself. They saw someone dressed as Alyssa. Someone painted and costumed as Alyssa."

"Someone?" I put a hand over my mouth. "You mean Marion."

"Exactly. Remember – she began with the theatre group as a makeup artist and is, in fact, an actress. She could easily play the part of Alyssa. Yes, she is involved, but only to a point. I am certain she did not understand Alyssa was dead."

"And she was seen with Hollister that time – but you don't think she was part of the murder?"

Myrl shook her head. "I don't know, but I don't see how."

"Why hasn't she stepped forward, then?"

Everyone was in high excitement. There was much chatter and laughing, the sharp crack of firecrackers bursting, and several wayward dogs weaving their way through the crowds added to the pandemonium.

Myrl took my arm and patted my hand. "There are, my dear, dark secrets of the heart which do not look pretty in the light of society." She dropped my hand and we joined the movement of the crowd again. I was very confused.

"You mean Marion was having an affair with Hollister? No. With Giles! And Hollister found out!"

"No, my dear. Do you remember the small letter box, empty of letters, in Alyssa Dansen's room? Again, a case of the significance of something missing. The strong flowered fragrance in the letter box was not to be found among Alyssa's perfumes. That powdery scent is Marion's. And there must have been many letters – the perfume of lilac was quite strong. Those letters were taken during a search for something else, and used to coerce Marion."

It must have been clear from my face I still did not understand.

Myrl sighed. "You see, there was an affection between the two women. Alyssa and Marion." She paused and looked at me. "Lovers, Faye. They were illicit lovers. An unnatural love, the less tolerant would say. And Hollister McLean found out, and used Marion for his own devices."

I was stunned. "But what about Marion and Howard?"

Myrl smiled. "Faye, they are actors. They are very skilled at putting on a play. Didn't it ever occur to you that Marion and Howard are almost too easy with each other? What is missing from their liaison is sexual tension."

* * * * *

The Island was beautifully done up. Twenty acres or so of land, and from the bridge you could see it in its entirety. At the entrance sat the Pavilion – a large, round domed wood and stucco structure with beautiful latticed arches which could hold five hundred wooden bleachers, sported a bowling alley, a bar called the Brewery, a ballroom, and a vaudeville stage. I remembered Rachel saying she'd seen a circus in town at Island Park. The Pavilion was so immense that part of it was cantilevered out over the river, and a terrace ran down behind it to the green where in summer there was baseball and ice cream and the Chautauquas. In the centre of the Island was a smaller, round, covered building, where I presumed the carousel was to be unveiled. On the far side was a betting track for greyhounds and I was again reminded that this Island was really a part of New Hampshire – not Vermont. All the buildings boasted brilliant blue and red flags, snapping in the breeze off the water, and banners knotted with tinsel were strewn across thresholds and windows. Stakes sunk in deep snow had streamers linking them together to help shepherd the throngs of visitors.

We stepped off the bridge, walked along the path to the Pavilion, and were swept under the WELCOME banner. We offered our tickets and entered the Pavilion. Inside, there was the heavy smell of pork ribs and cooking fat, breads and sugar pastries, and roasting corn. Booths were set up and down the Pavilion showing off local crafts and businesses, from linens and silks, to tattooing. I was overcome with hunger and wanted nothing more than to buy a dozen cider doughnuts and eat them on the spot. We were shedding gloves and scarves when I spotted Henry Mitchell. He waved and came over.

"Good morning, ladies," he said, a bit loud. "Back in town, I see. Can't seem to get away from us?"

"I'm looking for Marion," said Myrl, shouting a little herself above the clamour.

"She's here, I've seen her. I think she's outside in back. She's with Howard, of course."

"I must speak with her," Myrl yelled back.

He was nodding as Hope Mitchell, laughing and chatting with a friend, walked up, saw us standing there, and said, "You've got to come and see Gladdis." She was snickering and I was nearly certain of the ether-smell of Scotch. "Come, come," she said again and Henry grabbed her arm.

"Gladdis is having a rough time. You let her be."

Hope's eyes grew wide. "Oh, and when have you been so concerned for other people? Besides," she said, waving a hand, "she's the one in the booth. I mean no one's making her do it."

We followed her to a small booth shrouded with black silks and crystals. Inside, dressed in black, and with a rather loud red turban wrapped about her head, was Gladdis McFadden. She smiled when she saw us and reached down to turn over three hideously printed oversize cards. The cards had a black and white etching in intricate detail depicting people clawing over one another with their mouths open in silent screams, their faces in wretched horror. When she turned over the cards the print on the reverse side was in colour. The first card was of the sun all in flames of red and orange, the second was a nightingale with its long tail feathers elaborately curved, and the third was of a naked eye, the iris blue, sitting balanced on the point of a brown pyramid.

"We're trying to track down Marion," I said, watching in complete fascination.

Gladdis stared at the cards for a moment and sighed.

"What?" I asked.

"She's out in back. With Alyssa's murder, I bet everyone buys a lottery ticket."

Hope explained, "Marion and Frances are taking turns manning the booth for the theatre company. They get plenty of donations at this sort of thing, you know. And they have a drawing and give away free tickets."

"Hello, Miss Norton, Miss Tullis," said a familiar voice. I turned and there was Hollister McLean resting a hand on my shoulder. I very nearly shivered, and it took a concentrated effort on my part to appear convivial and not self-conscious.

"I've spoken to Giles and Howard and Marion and they are desperate to meet you out on the terrace down by the water. Or now, I suppose I should say ice. Frances is over there," he pointed, "doing quite well as you can see. All week long she's been the jewel and we are merely the setting." He stressed merely in a way that did not evoke mirth – rather he seemed annoyed, and he crossed his arms and fingered his cufflinks, twirling them nervously, and I saw they were lion teeth set in silver.

I could see Frances Hall sitting in a wicker lounge in front of the booth, graciously accepting handshakes and kisses from her admiring public. She was an elegant figure in front of the black and white billboards, with photos of recent productions plastered to the frame of the booth. A large glass bottle held lottery names and it was already half full. Hollister caught my glance. "You see what a big pull she is right now, and she loves it," he said. "Say, Henry, there's a race this afternoon – would you care to make it interesting?"

"Don't you dare," said Hope. Henry glanced at Hollister with some irritation. "I don't believe we've squared off since our last wager."

Hollister just chuckled. "Oh now, come, come, Henry, since when are you so honourable? I hear you've had to sell off more land. I know you've got the cash, my boy."

Hope hung on to Henry's arm. "I swear to God, Henry."

Hollister laid a hand on Hope's shoulder. "Now don't fret, my dear. Henry and I have a few business details to work out and a hearty wager might put things a bit right, wouldn't you say?"

"I don't think so, Hollister. I'm afraid it's too late."

Hollister was perspiring. I could see the sheen of sweat on his forehead, and his eyes were very bloodshot. He laid his hand on my shoulder again and squeezed rather hard, and I felt a tremor run through his arm. "Faye, you feel as though you are built of muscle – what a strong little thing you are," he said and rocked my shoulder slightly before letting go. He turned to Gladdis. "Gladdis, you want to join us outside?"

"I have to stay for demonstrations," she said, her voice somehow more grating than the cough which followed. Hollister offered Myrl his arm, and I was alarmed by the ease with which she joined him.

"You know," whispered Gladdis as the others started off, "he and Henry go back a long time. That was all talk about the Klan." She smiled benignly and reached out a stubby hand. Her fingernails, bitten down to the quick, were little half-moons painted bright red. She looked around as if someone might overhear us and leaned forward in conspiracy. "Hollister owes them money." She sat back.

"Owes who money?"

"The Klan. Henry bankrolls Hollister. Marty knows. They meet at the tannery, I saw them once with their white hoods and fire."

She leaned back around and picked up a small purple glass bottle. "Oil of vitriol and desiccated calf liver. That fixed them. Though Hollister's suffering now."

"So is Henry protecting Hollister ..." I said, remembering the comment about selling off land.

Gladdis shrugged. "How can he, really – Hollister should come to me. I could protect him."

I glanced up and saw my friend pausing to wait for me and I waved. I bid Gladdis luck on her demonstrations – I could only imagine what they might be – and saw Myrl's black gloves still resting on the table. I grabbed them, stuffed them in my coat and followed, walking past an organ grinder and his monkey, a booth offering exotic and unseasonable fruits such as pineapple, mangoes, bananas, and oranges, a medicinal booth filled with tinctures with names like Pratt's Healing Ointment, White Pine Compound and Tar, and Holman's Iodine Cure, booths with fine clothing of all kinds from light colourful silks and summer dresses to machine-knitted scarves and gloves, work pants, and boots. There was livestock for sale and to marvel at like Cherry, the Half Ton Pig, and Duke, the 3,000 Pound Horse, and then booths with tintypes, Miller's ice cream, Estey Pipe Organs, Crosby Flours where pies sat for sale, eggs and butter booths, soda and cigars, and booths offering services varying from water witching to bank appraisals for one's home. I nearly stopped at a pastry stand, but Hollister and Myrl were moving smoothly again through the crowd with Henry and Hope right in line, and all four were so far ahead I did not want to be left behind.

When we stepped outside the Pavilion, the breeze which had been so biting had ceased, and the warmth of the sun was welcome. I was happy to go hatless and saw Giles, Marion and Howard, Grace and Patrick standing together on the terrace overlooking the water. I felt a certain tension released seeing Marion. I saw her avoiding Hollister and I knew she was safe for the moment. The Connecticut lay in back of them, unmoving, a thick sheath of white thick ice. And I have to admit to a real sense of relief when I saw gawky Patrick O'Keefe towering among the group. For the moment, everyone was safe. I felt I could relax knowing the steady hand of the law was within reach. When I touched his shoulder in greeting and gratitude, I'm afraid my face must have given away my feelings and he was slightly taken aback. His manner became quite aloof and I realised my touch was too intimate.

Everyone was chattering, mostly about the storm and the carnival and how well Frances was doing. I was nearly faint and I really needed to eat. I could feel a headache coming on, and was trying to bow out gracefully so I could go back inside and buy a muffin or a bowl of hot cereal. Every now and then someone would exit the Pavilion, and when the door was opened, a fresh wave of the smell of good food would warm the air. We were all lined up along the edge of the terrace where it hung over the magnificent river and Giles was talking about the carousel.

"I just have always loved carousels, ever since I was a little boy," he was saying in answer to Marion's question as to why he had such an interest in them. "I really don't know why. They are an art form, you know. The master carvers are Italian. The fellow who worked on my horses is Frank Carretta from Milan. A fine fellow and I bet he will go far. His horses are hand carved, solid. Not like those hollow Parker horses. The Philadelphia Toboggan Company was against putting on all horses, but they finally relented. The engine on this one is steam and it is clean, very clean. Precision workmanship. All the glass and mirrors are done by hand. Now that is hard to find nowadays. And I was able to get old Estey behind the project – I thought it would be good for the town to showcase our local boys. Estey was able to reconfigure one of his pipe organs, in fact, he put Roger Small on the project – do you know Roger? No? Fine man. But as I say, the true test of a carousel is the horses. I commissioned them more than a year ago and these horses were shipped last spring."

"Before you even knew if the carousel was a go," reminded Henry, taking out a pipe.

"Yes," laughed Giles. "That is true. Well, I was sure of it, even if some present here were not," and he looked down the line of listeners with an eyebrow raised sarcastically. "Faye, have you ever ridden a carousel?"

"I have, on several occasions."

"And which was the most memorable?"

I thought for a moment. "I guess I'd have to say there was one in Holland – they call them *Stomcaurossels* – but I'm afraid it wasn't that I was so taken with the ride itself, but the huge facade you had to pass through to get to the carousel. I must have been about twelve or so."

"And what kind of mount did you select?"

"A horse."

Giles was pleased. "See? The animal of choice. Myrl, have you ever ridden?" Myrl shook her head. "I never have," she said. "I have never thought to."

"We will have to correct that, then, won't we?" said Hollister. "The grand opening's at noon, and Henry here will be happy to give you a leg up. And Marion too. She's never ridden one."

Myrl was standing between Giles and Howard and, as far as I could tell, had not made a move to speak to Marion. We would have to get her alone for just a moment and I trusted Myrl to take this action. Giles returned to talk about his carousel.

"The paint is all enamel. The glass and beadwork on the bridles and saddles – which are all of English leather, mind you – are set or blown by hand. And the tails and manes are of real horsehair. Hollister, you ought to like that. Sort of like pseudo-taxidermy. Anyway. They truly are beautiful and I'm sorry to be so boastful."

"When's the unveiling again?" asked Hope, biting her thumbnail. Henry pushed her arm down.

"At noon," said Giles, checking his watch. "It's ten-thirty now. Say, why don't we all go have a peek – I'm sure Small wouldn't mind. He's still tinkering with the organ, I think."

Seizing the chance, I excused myself from the group.

"Yes, Faye needs to eat or she will become frightfully grumpy," I heard Myrl say as everyone moved away from the terrace.

I ran up the shallow flight of stairs and entered the warmth of the Pavilion. I turned to my right and saw nothing but livestock pens: chickens, pigs, sheep, goats, and a pair of hooded falcons. I saw Curran Holt for a brief moment in the crowd and then he disappeared. I looked to my left and there, six or seven booths in, was a matronly woman, plump and smiling, handing out sweet breads wrapped in brown paper.

I bought two blueberry muffins, huge and warm, and watched as butter melted, adding a fatty scent to the sweet fragrance of blueberry. The woman also was serving warm cider and I helped myself to some, dipping in a stick of cinnamon. Standing against the wall I could see out the large pane of glass, and though drafty, the spot was a perfect place to wolf my food, and the view out over the river was pleasant. I could see our group standing away from the terrace and watched with interest as Myrl took Howard's arm for a brief moment, holding him back as the others walked along down the path. She spoke in his ear and then released him, and Howard stood very still for just a moment, not moving until Myrl took his arm again and began to walk with him. Marion was coming toward the Pavilion herself now and paused for a moment, turning back around. I saw Hollister point to something in the river below. Myrl walked up to the railing, following the direction of his finger. Myrl seemed to check herself for something, reaching into pockets and such, and I bit into my second muffin. When I glanced up again, there was Myrl walking down the main path toward the carousel's arena, waving to the little group halfway there, and then winding back on a secondary path down to the riverbank.

"Oh good, you found something to eat," said Marion, coming up next to me.

"Where's Myrl going?" I asked, nodding to my view out the window. She was nearly at the bank's edge.

"Oh, that's the footpath to the boat launch. She dropped her gloves out over the ice."

"Oh."

"Yeah. Hollister offered to get them for her, but she wanted to fetch them herself. Your friend is a stitch, that's for sure. Boy, I need something to eat too. How are those muffins?"

"Marion, has Myrl spoken to you?"

"About what?"

I lowered my voice. "About the case."

Marion laughed brightly. "No, why? You mean today?"

As she spoke, I took another bite. And then I could not think. Time stopped for as long as it took me to shove my hand in my coat pocket and bring out Myrl's pair of gloves.

"What are those?" said Marion.

"Myrl's gloves," I said accusingly. I held them frozen in my hand. "Her damn gloves," I said again. "Then what is she doing?" Marion suddenly paled and gasped. "Oh no. Not again."

My heart leapt to my throat and beat painfully. I couldn't breathe. All I could see in my mind's eye was Myrl, moving as if in slow motion, and I was powerless. I turned back to the window. I could not move. There was nothing I could do or say to stop what was about to happen. I saw her step out onto the ice, and from my vantage point there was indeed a small dark spot visible on the stretch of ice about twenty feet out from shore, directly under the terrace. She leaned forward to balance herself as she walked.

Action, action, action. I pushed myself out of paralysis, suddenly found strength in my legs, and sprinted. I ran down the aisle of booths, past the chicken and pigs, and flung open the door, slipping on the icy landing at the top of the stairs. I waved my arms and yelled. I don't know what I yelled, but everyone looked up at me, even Myrl, but I was too late. Too late to help my friend. She was just a foot from the gloves, when suddenly I saw her try to right herself as the ice broke. Somebody screamed. It broke again and black-green water, thick and heavy like oil, opened around her. I saw everyone else running too – Giles was halfway down the path with Patrick right behind.

I hit the bottom of the stairs and ran to the railing. Fifteen feet below me she stood for a split second, cold black water moving around her, and then she was gone – pulled under ice by a swift current drawn by gravity to the sea.

Chapter Sixteen

Diamonds

"Someone get a rope!" yelled Giles, and I was throwing off my coat, hurling past the group, sliding as I launched myself across the ice. I heard Patrick behind me, and he grabbed me around the waist only after I was a good ten feet from shore. People shouted and several screamed from the boardwalk across on the main shore.

"Get back here," Patrick yelled in my ear and I sank to my knees, pulling him down with me. "You'll never get to her."

Hollister had a rope and was hurrying down the embankment. My chest felt hollow and I was sick to my stomach and all I could see was the dark liquid hole she had disappeared into.

Suddenly everything was quiet. Everyone stood in a small cluster on the bank. The breeze kicked up for a moment, and above the hole of broken ice was a wide blue sky, sheer, wintry, quivering with sun and my own tears. I blinked and began an uncontrollable shaking. Patrick let go of my waist.

The wind off the river filled my ears with a small roar and I failed to hear the first crack of ice. I saw everyone look toward the main bank to my right, and I followed their gaze.

It reminded me of the slow, surreal movement of ice in Alaska, when great mantles of ice would grind against each other from the force of the ocean, pushing heavy shards up into the air. There the groaning of ice was a hollow, primordial sound which could be heard for miles.

The ice was breaking up several yards from the main shore.

Something huge and curved was coming up from underneath and the crust of ice opened and broke rhythmically. We could all see huge fissures opening. I was up and on my feet. So was Patrick, and we were both slipping and sliding on ice covering shallow water, staying close to the overhang of the terrace. I could hear my voice calling Myrl's name and then the others were moved to action, a thin line of people shuffling on the ice. Several people on the other side of the Pavilion were sliding down the hill from the boardwalk, and I saw Curran Holt step out onto the river.

Right in front of me the cracks widened and ice suddenly heaved up and there she was, on her knees, gasping, drenched. I grabbed one of her hands and Curran grabbed the other, and now ice broke under me. Patrick got down and flattened out on his stomach. Black and freezing water swirled around my legs and I gasped at the sudden numbness, the penetrating cold, and my strength was sapped immediately. But at least I could stand – the water was shallow. Curran still held her arm and Myrl was trying to get on her feet as well, but she couldn't, and kept slipping back into icy water. Patrick scooted around to Curran's side and then stood, grabbing my arm as well, and together we three got her coat off, hauled it onto shore and then, seconds later, got her up on the ice. She lay on her side coughing for a few moments, struggling to breathe and I held her hand, kept her head up, and her grip on my fingers was strong. Within moments, Curran and Patrick picked her up, Curran at her head and Patrick down by her feet, and carried her to shore.

* * * * *

"Well," said Grace, patting Myrl's shoulder, "I'm not going to tell you how lucky you are."

Myrl was sitting in the centre of Mary Howe's bed on the ground floor. A fire roared in the fireplace, an iron kettle had been brought in and hung on the swing arm over the fire.

Wet, warm air kept the room steamy. Propped up by big pillows, Myrl was buried under blankets. Her hair, loose and lank, hung in heavy twists and though it was nearly dry, she still shivered uncontrollably every few minutes. Her lips were blue as were her hands. She had said almost nothing since her rescue an hour ago. The missing pair of gloves, retrieved from my pocket, lay on the nightstand next to her. I sat wrapped in blankets myself with my feet in a large pan of warm water chalky with Epsom salts. I sipped strong black tea, the same strong tea Grace was plying Myrl with.

"Drink up, my girl. You need this." She held the cup up to Myrl's lips. "It will leave my nerves shot," chattered Myrl as another wave of shivers overcame her.

"Well, good," laughed Grace. "Then you'll be just like the rest of us. Poor Faye has had ten years taken off her life."

I nodded. "This was not fun, Myrl. Please don't do that again."

"Yes," agreed Grace. "Never, ever, go out on a frozen river. I can't believe Hollister let you go. He of all people should know better. He ran an ice-cutting business years ago and lost a man just that way."

Grace packed up her things, and left me with a set of instructions: basically to have Myrl sleep, and there were pills to help her with that if need be, and to call if any fever or wheezing developed. Myrl lay with her eyes closed as Grace whispered goodbyes to me. I heard her go down the stairs, and then the soft murmur of her voice as she spoke to Mary Howe down by the front door.

I snuggled in my chair. Myrl was asleep. Warm and content, sipping my tea, my eyes closed in the bliss of safe darkness, I could hear Mrs Howe taking away the cup and saucer, felt her tucking blankets in around my waist, and heard the pop and sizzle of the wood as it burned. I was off, falling into deep sleep.

I do not know how long I slept when I heard, "Faye. Faye. Wake up."

Myrl's voice penetrated through layers of consciousness.

"Faye. Come to. For pete's sake."

My eyelids fluttered and I turned my head, only to feel a stab of pain shoot down my neck. I had fallen asleep with my head bent over my chest. I rubbed my sore neck, and looked at her from under heavy lids.

"What time is it?"

"Three-thirty. Time is slipping away from us."

She was sitting straight up in bed, her hair dried in mats around her face. She looked very young, her cheeks far too pink, and I realised she was overheated. At any moment I expected her to fling off the quilts.

"Myrl. I forbid you to move. Doesn't anything affect you? Don't you see you just nearly lost your life?"

Her eyes were fixed on my face, and in a moment she lost her composure. She closed her eyes and lay back in the pillows. "Faye, you are the dearest friend I have ever had and the fact you have been drawn into this, have very nearly lost your own life – you could have gone under as well – is a cross I will bear throughout my life." Here she opened her eyes. For the briefest of moments they were very bright, heavy along the bottom lids, and I could have sworn there were tears. She cleared her throat. "But what happened down there as you well know was no accident." She reached over and sipped some tea which had to be cold by now. She held the cup in her hands, on a pillow in front of her. "The ice had been cut in places to give way. A pair of gloves were tossed out there on purpose, I assume they were purchased during the carnival. It was only sheer luck that the dam had been opened."

"What do you mean, the dam?"

"It was how I escaped." She closed her eyes again, and raised the cup to her lips. "This is a hideous brew. I don't see how people can drink it."

"Well, it's cold. It's supposed to be hot." I removed my feet from the now tepid basin of water, and began drying them with the towel on the floor. "So what about the dam again?"

"The level of the river goes up or down depending on the release of water from the Vernon dam. Ice formed over the river at a certain height days ago and then, this morning probably, water was released at the dam. If thick enough, the ice remains in place like a shell. So you see, when I fell through, the surface of the water was actually several inches below the ice."

I shivered. "So you could still breathe."

She nodded. "And I knew if I could get on my feet in shallow water, I could stand and break through. I also could see blade marks in the ice where someone had made cuts." She closed her eyes yet again and I could see how tired she was. "I merely had to swim under the ice toward the direction of the main shore."

Under ice, with no light and no way to find direction.

"So what do you want to do now?"

"Marion is still in the gravest danger. I told Harold to stay with her at all times. I believe I know what –" She was interrupted by a gentle tap at the door. It was Mrs Howe, looking very flustered and very sweet.

"There's a Detective Lorey to see you, Myrl. I heard voices so I came up. If you want me to send him away …"

I half expected Myrl to sigh and lean back, languishing in the pillows as she can do apparently on cue, but she surprised me with her answer.

"No, please, send him up and can you do me a favour? Will you please give the *Reformer* a call and have Curran Holt meet us at Alyssa Dansen's room above the Opera House? Say in three-quarters of an hour?"

"Myrl, you are to stay in bed." Mrs Howe pulled at her wig.

"Go, Mary, and do a good deed."

Detective Lorey was courteous and only moderately condescending as he interrogated Myrl. He arrived with the suspicion the incident out on the river was a deliberate attempt on her life, but he could not find anything to back up his inkling and Myrl refused to help him in this matter. No, she kept repeating, it was purely her own stupidity. I kept quiet and actually excused myself to change into more suitable clothing. When I returned, he was standing above her and she was sinking back into her pillows, looking very wan. His tone was not affectionate.

"You are toying around in matters which are international," he said, shaking a finger at her. The effect was almost comical.

"Detective Lorey," she said, her eyes closing and her voice low. "If you truly want to explore the reasons why I know Marty McFadden had nothing to do with this murder, then you will accompany me to the Dansen apartment. Regardless of the feudal war of jurisdiction you must be fighting with Captain O'Keefe, I do assume you are here in the interest of justice – even if that means somebody else will have the pleasure of the arrest and prosecution." She continued to lie quite still. I had grave misgivings about her getting up and about.

This stopped him. "You are going there now?"

"As soon as I have changed. I am sure you will want to attend this."

"What's there that Patrick hasn't found already?"

"Patrick is a nice soul, but he is very young, wouldn't you say, Faye?"

He was, I am certain, probably just my age, but I nodded knowingly.

"I know what the person fleeing Courtney Place was looking for."

"You do?"

"Yes. Now, will you come? We don't have much time. You had better get Captain O'Keefe and have him join us as well."

* * * * *

Myrl paused twice on the staircase leading up to the second-floor apartment. And she was not acting. Her colour was off and she perspired freely. I really thought she should be in bed, but I did not feel in the position to be making that argument. Patrick O'Keefe and Detective Lorey were behind us, and Patrick carried the key. When we reached the landing, Patrick shuffled by to unlock the door and he paused, leaned forward, and then faced us with a finger to his lips.

"Someone's inside," he whispered, pointing at the door. Lorey bounded past us, Patrick jammed the key in the lock, and they burst inside, with Myrl and me standing a good distance back.

The room was dark, shades pulled, and there was a heavy scent of rosewater and pine and burning hair – that is how I must describe it. The odour was strong and pungent and at once sickly sweet and acrid. Candles burned all around, and sitting on the floor, in the centre of the room, was Gladdis McFadden.

Patrick pulled the electric light chain. "What the hell are you doing here, Gladdis?"

Lorey was even more outraged. He turned to Patrick. "This is the kind of shoddy operation you run up here? You let just anyone come in on a case site and mess things up?"

Patrick ignored him.

Gladdis, dressed as she was for Winter Carnival, was a sight. She had seven small twists of hair in a half circle laid out in front of her in a fan around a piece of broken mirror. There were three candles lit as well and that's when I noticed some of the hair twists were burned, singed at the tips.

"And what is all this muck?"

"Pipe down, Lorey," Patrick said, hastily adding, "please."

Gladdis McFadden did not rise from the floor. She remained seated and began to talk, her voice low and reverberating. "I have come here to repent."

Myrl and I had followed the men inside. I steered her over to the divan and we took two seats.

"Repent?" I heard Patrick ask.

"You mean you're seeking forgiveness?" said Myrl.

Gladdis looked down at the floor. "Yes. Forgiveness. It wasn't Marty's doing, it wasn't my boy. It was me. I did it." She said this without emotion.

Patrick raised an eyebrow. "You killed Alyssa Dansen?"

"Yes."

"Why?" he asked gently. She remained sitting on the floor, legs crossed. "Because she was a cold woman. Cold as stone and she was killing my boy. Killing him. She was evil."

Patrick continued with, "And how did you kill her?"

247

Sighing, Gladdis reached down the 'V' of her bodice and held up a small crystal bottle on a chain. Removing the stopper she took a whiff and held it up to us. "Dragon's breath and ferret's blood," she said. "It makes the strongest potion."

Lorey was suddenly impatient. "What's she talking about? Is that some kind of poison? What's this dragon's breath?"

Patrick didn't even pass a glance to Lorey. "She's saying she cast a spell on Alyssa."

"You cast a spell on her?"

Gladdis replaced the stopper. "My apologies to you," she said, nodding to Myrl. "I had no idea this one would be so strong. That it might include others. Somehow Frances fell under its power as well, and now you."

"Oh Lord," said Lorey.

"I think you should just go home, and not worry about this, Gladdis. Go on and get back to the carnival," Patrick said, helping her up.

"But I'm not finished."

"You are finished here, Gladdis. Now don't worry about things."

"But you do see, right, that he didn't do it?"

Her exit was anticlimactic compared to our bold entrance, and we could hear her shuffling down the stairs, a carpetbag slung over her shoulder tinkling with the glass of the candle holders. She had taken the twists of hair with her – twists of Alyssa's hair retrieved from her brush on the dresser.

"Well, what are we waiting for now?" said Lorey, jingling keys in his pocket. "You know McFadden claims that book on poisons is his mother's. That's going to be easy for him to prove if she gets on the stand." He rolled his eyes.

"She doesn't hurt anyone," began Patrick.

"Yeah. Not that you know of, anyway," said Lorey.

"Detective Lorey," Myrl said suddenly. "Did you eat well today?"

"As a matter of fact, I haven't. But I don't really think that matters right now. I want to know why we're all here."

"Well," said Myrl, "I will show you." With that she rose and walked to the closet, pulling open the door. Bending over she rummaged for a few moments along the bottom and then straightened back up, a hand to her temple. "I have to sit down."

I hurriedly came to her side and Patrick and I helped her sit down on the edge of the quilted bed. She swallowed hard and then seemed to become resolute. "Patrick, will you please take out a pair of shoes?"

The door downstairs slammed and we heard someone taking the steps two at a time. In a moment Curran Holt stood breathless on the threshold.

"They had trouble finding me at the carnival … Oh, I'm too old for this," he said, rubbing his knee, and trying to catch his breath.

Lorey was not pleased. "Who invited him?"

"What is about to happen must make tomorrow morning's papers," said Myrl. "Now Patrick, listen carefully. Mr Bruneil, Alyssa Dansen's cobbler, said she had a pair of shoes made one size larger as a gift. We are looking for that pair of shoes."

Patrick knelt on the floor. Curran took out his yellow pad, removing the pencil from the crease of his ear. Holding up a red satin shoe Patrick looked at Myrl expectantly. "Well?"

"Now take every shoe in there and compare the size."

"I don't see what you're aiming at here, Miss Norton," said Lorey.

"You don't have to at this moment, Detective Lorey. The purpose of our little quest will become apparent in just a minute." Myrl sat with her hands folded in her lap.

Patrick unboxed several pairs of shoes and they all were the same size. Then he reached in, way in the back, and found a pair of light blue velvet high heels, with double ankle straps, very elegant and modern. They looked quite new. He held one up. And the toe was a half inch longer than the others.

We all looked at Myrl. She was sitting very tall on the edge of the bed; not a muscle moved in her face. "Break the toe, Patrick. Break open the toe of the shoe, but do it very carefully."

Patrick gripped the toe and pressed down hard.

"No, no, no, gently," she said, remaining statuesque. "Have you a pen knife?"

Placing the shoe in one hand, he cut around the toe, several inches down. He sawed through the velvet and the canvas shell, and then suddenly, as if exploding from under great pressure, diamonds – pure white and shimmering – spilled across his hand.

"Jesus," said Lorey. He dove down and retrieved the mate and made his own cut, laying the second shoe on the bed for safety. Again, as the canvas separated and the toe point was peeled back, diamonds sprinkled out, a small fistful, and they twinkled, tiny specks of pure carbon so priceless their history included murder. Curran Holt was writing furiously.

Lorey turned on Myrl. "How the hell did you know that? How did you know there'd be shoes like this and they'd be full ofdiamonds?"

Myrl sighed and looked up at him. Her shoulders actually sagged for a moment and then she pulled them back. Her voice held a dead weariness which could not include sarcasm.

"Women's intuition, Detective Lorey."

"Women's intuition?"

"A gift you do not possess." Myrl turned to Curran, who had sat down on the bed next to her and was scribbling away. "I trust this will make the morning edition?"

"Oh yes. It will be on the front page. I've got clout at the *Reformer*. Right between the carnival story and the story of your fall."

"This is to be at the forefront, do you understand?" she said, rising from her place on the bed. "Could you run us back to the Tavern, Mr Holt? I am not feeling well."

Chapter Seventeen

The Chase

"So you see, someone had already gone over every inch of both places – the apartment above the Opera House and the house in Northampton – looking for these diamonds. My guess is that it was Hollister." Myrl said this carelessly and pushed away her bed tray. It was six o'clock and we were all ready to retire for the day. I felt ridiculous wandering around in my bathrobe, but I was also grateful that Mrs Howe was not strict in her code of modesty. Mrs Howe took the tray out, frowning at all the food left on Myrl's plate.

"That's why the rooms were so neat," I said, remembering how well kept each apartment was.

"Exactly. Hollister rummaged through everything and then spent time putting the place back in order. That's why her bedroom in Northampton was so pristine, except for the dust, of course. He had already gone over it."

"But why suddenly break in to Rachel's room?"

"From what you've told me about his financial arrangements with Henry, my guess is that he had grown desperate. In the end, he decided to search every room of the house, probably for a second time. It was Rachel's luck to come home early and surprise him."

I shook my head. "You know, I saw him too that afternoon. And I can't believe that was Hollister. I could have sworn, and I nearly did, mind you, that the man leaving the house was in his late twenties, with a full crop of red hair, and of medium build."

Myrl smiled. Mrs Howe brought in a teacup of cream, a dish of chocolate mint truffles, and the warm smell of cream and chocolate was strong.

"Oh, Mary, you are a dear," said Myrl, shifting up in her bed to take the warm cream. She popped a mint in her mouth and took two more. Carefully setting the two chocolates next to her teacup she explained, "They achieve a glorious melted consistency like this. Yes, well. In the height of excitement, the mind can play funny tricks. You probably thought he ran light-footedly down the road. His pace was, in fact, that of an older, stocky man, probably in a corset, unaccustomed to physical exertion. The wig and beard were an attempt not only to hide his face, but to frame Marty McFadden from the start, and I fear it might have worked. You and I could have played a huge part in putting an innocent man to death, had we testified Marty McFadden fit our descriptions."

"So you think Hollister was looking for the diamonds to pay off a debt. But how does Henry fit into all this, then? And the watch chain?" I poked at the fire with a piece of wood and then threw it on the flames. Embers rose in a wash of bright yellow sparks and the fire crackled. It all seemed unreal to me that we were discussing this case as if it were a parlour game. "And there were so many diamonds. If Alyssa Dansen was the go-between why did – oh, I see. These were the diamonds she didn't have a chance to sell? I mean, these were the next batch to go. But there were so many!"

Myrl shook her head. "The ability to lie here and think a bit on all these problems has been, indeed, a luxury," said Myrl. "Remember the problem of the letters? Why did Alyssa Dansen keep her blackmailer's letters? Why not burn them?"

I shrugged.

"Why does someone keep something? Anything. Good or bad."

"Well," I said, thinking of mementos, "as a keepsake. To remember an event or person. Out of love, and sometimes, to show other people." I was not on secure ground and Myrl sensed this.

"Think concretely. People keep things for proof."

"Proof? "

"Ultimately, it is proof – proof of love, of hate, of duty, of the past, and this is the case quite literally with Alyssa's letters. She kept them as proof."

"Oh, we've been through this before." I shook my head. "You thought she was getting ready to corner the blackmailer and that's why she was murdered."

"If that were the case, she certainly had to think far in advance to have the wherewithal to save that initial letter. And that would have meant she would have waited four years to finger her tormenter. Why wait four years? This brings us back to the first question. Why did she save those seven letters? No, Faye, this is a bigger problem. You see, Alyssa Dansen herself was the blackmailer."

I thought about this for a moment and saw the glimmer of the line of reasoning Myrl was following.

"She was blackmailing Hollister?"

Myrl nodded. "Hollister and herself. She told him she was being blackmailed, just as he was, and kept the letters as proof in case Hollister ever suspected her. By setting herself up as a victim as well, she could exonerate herself. If ever suspected, she could pull out the letters as real proof of being blackmailed."

I jumped ahead. "But yet the ruse didn't work with Hollister."

"No. No. It didn't. Somehow he found out and how he did is indeed a puzzle. But Alyssa was very clever. She hit him on both sides. Not only for money, but for diamonds."

"These diamonds were part of the ransom?"

"No. I think not. Hollister stuffed the diamonds in the skins of his animals and shipped them down to her, at which point she would retrieve and fence them to her contacts in Boston and New York."

"If you want to sell something –"

"You sell to the highest bidder."

"Very good."

"Aha," I said, as the picture became very clear. "So she would sell a few diamonds to the person with the highest bid and keep the rest for herself, and then turn around and tell Hollister she got a lower price for the ones she did sell."

"Well done." Myrl savoured the last mint on her saucer, and then sat up and helped herself to two more. "Try one, Faye, they are truly glorious. Hand dipped from Bennington and" – she licked her fingertips – "smooth, smooth, smooth."

I was shaking my head. "Alyssa Dansen was very, very savvy."

"Not savvy enough," said Myrl. "Something went wrong. I suspect Hollister found out the blackmailing was fraudulent, and then he did what I did ... discovered her contacts and placed a call himself."

"So the motive becomes clear." I sat down in the rocking chair again and stared at the fire. "He killed her for revenge and money."

"And the diamonds. Hollister McLean is a dangerous man, to be sure," said Myrl.

I continued to stare into the fire. "But to kill Alyssa and then skin her and fill her full of sawdust. It is horrific."

"It is the work of someone completely, horribly, violently insane, or someone who considers women simple animals, and thinks nothing of giving them the same kind of treatment. The line between is grey and vacillates with shifts in public outcry and public complicity. Every day women are beaten, chained, violated, and forced into situations in which a good man wouldn't leave his dog. You know this, Faye. This was part of why you were out on the Quad three months ago."

There was a loud, percussive pop from a log on the fire.

She went on. "First thing tomorrow we must have a chat with Marion French, and discover exactly the date Hollister asked her to impersonate Alyssa. That will give us a better time frame to determine when the murder actually occurred. Marion is the only person who knows Hollister is involved in this and she probably hasn't a clue to how incriminating her testimony could be. I think the fact that Frances Hall was poisoned shook her up, but I don't think she realised that the target of the poison was herself."

The next morning, I rose early and made my way downstairs. I was stiff and very sore and I realised I must have been very tense. I thought Myrl was still in bed, but I heard her laughing in the kitchen with Mrs Howe, and moments later she came barrelling through the door in a grey wool hunter's dress, layered and flounced, heavy and impenetrable. I half expected her to be in stocking feet, but here she stood in black high-lace boots, the toes polished and pointed. Her hair was pulled back in its original loop along the neck, and I was glad to see her up and about.

"Faye, grab a little something to eat. Mary has a tray of biscuits and jams and some fruit – oranges and pineapples and such like that – Biggy stole some from the carnival – I think he's trying to score some points with you, Faye," she said, uncharacteristically poking me in the ribs.

"We are off to Marion French's. Take a look at the morning paper." She whacked the newspaper against my chest as she walked by. "Ah, here's Real now with the carriage. Faye. Get some food. Scoot," she said, yanking open the front door and sailing out.

The day was brilliant. The temperature remained steadfast, below zero, and there had been no melt from the storm. Snow lay heavy, white, and thick across the road, covering bushes, obliterating crevasses and bumps, making everything round and smooth. Even the road had remained fairly pristine, with street cleaners working overtime because of the carnival. I sat in the buggy and read with interest the story about the diamonds. Curran Holt was an excellent writer, I could see how the *Times* would want him. The story was simple, stuck to the facts, and was devoid of conjecture. It ran opposite a large story about the carnival with great photos – Biggy had all the photo credits. A small box at the bottom of the first column alerted the reader: *Woman Falls into Connecticut, page 2.* I flipped the page and there was Myrl, from a distance, being hauled up on the ice by Curran and myself, though you couldn't make out our faces. The story was very short and stated that the episode was an accident, and should serve as a reminder to everyone to stay off the river in winter.

255

"I have been publicly chastised," said Myrl as I closed the paper. "Made an example of. Well, fine."

We pulled up in front of Marion's apartment. I saw Howard's car there too, and hoped this would not be awkward. Standing on the stoop, the door opened almost immediately and Howard stood before us, smelling heavily of musk oil and soapy shaving cream. His hair was wet, and it was obvious he had just showered.

"Where's Marion?" he asked, looking surprised.

I glanced at Myrl for a moment. "We were going to ask you that."

"Well, she left to meet you two. About ten minutes ago."

"I told you to stay with her at all times," said Myrl.

"Well, I did and I have. Except this morning when your letter came. She was off. Out the door in a flash. Said you told her to come alone."

"I wrote no note. Where is it?"

Howard turned back to the apartment for a moment. "Drat. She took it. She took it with her. I remember seeing her stuff it in her coat."

Myrl stood very still on the stoop, her arms folded in front of her. Her voice was low and uncompromising. "Where in God's name did she go off to?"

"She said she was going ice skating. She said you told her to meet you at the Retreat Meadows."

"Have you a gun, Howard?" she said smoothly.

He shook his head for a moment and then stopped. "Yes, in fact I do. I have a pistol."

"Get it."

"What?"

"Get it," she said. "Now. And give it to Faye."

* * * * *

We tore through town, past the Common, with its snow-covered gazebo sitting silently waiting for summer. The buggy made the right turn toward the Meadows, sliding in a wide curve, and I gripped the inside strap with one hand and hung on to the door handle with the other. The buggy was old, and cold air whipped in through the tops of the windows. Though the snow rollers had been through town, the snow was soft and pushed down into ruts because of all the recent travelling. The ride was hard and I set my jaw.

We pulled up in a spray of fine snow, the horse's steamy breath floating on the air. Myrl and I ran down to the stands, where there was an elderly gentleman renting skates. Myrl came right up to him.

"Has a young woman passed here this morning? Maybe you know her? Marion French."

"Pretty little blonde, pesky?" He spat and rubbed his beard, silver grey flecks which ought to have been shaved off. "Ayup. She's out there on t' Meadows. She said she'd be lookin' for some gentleman. You sure you want to be messin' wit' her right now?" He grinned.

Myrl turned to Real. "Go get Patrick, tell him to come to the Meadows and to bring a gun – he must have a weapon." To me she said, "Do you skate, Faye?"

"You sure you don't want me to wait? I think I should go with you. What are you doing anyway?" Real was standing on the floor of the driver's box, reins in hand. The horse chewed her bit.

"We need someone to fetch Patrick. Just go and get him. That's the most you can do."

We strapped on our skates and took off moments later, skating directly out from the reedy bank. I could see Real turning the buggy around and heading back toward town. It would only take him ten minutes or so to get to the station.

Skating was difficult going at the beginning. Old cattails, bent and broken, were frozen in place and stuck up from the surface of the Meadows like broken stakes. The surface was very uneven and pockmarked with shattered air bubbles broken from previous skaters. There were a few children on the north side playing hockey, and to the south, the Meadow's water disappeared around a bend. Myrl pointed to two tiny ribbon marks on the ice that followed around the curve – Marion's trail. We picked up speed. Myrl was excellent on skates. Her long legs served her well, and her movements were like those of a long-distance swimmer: long even strokes, with gliding rests in between. I hastened along next to her, plagued by weak ankles, my arms stiff at my sides, as I continually tried to right myself after every bump in the ice. We came to the bend. Here, the Meadow's water grew narrow and the waterway was only twenty feet or so across. Coming out of the bend we entered a sheet of ice like a small pond, surrounded by fir trees. Myrl stopped and I slowed to a halt next to her.

"What now?" I said, trying not to pant. She continued to look out over the frozen meadows. Then she pointed. "Look there, there she is."

Way across, on the far side, was a fishing shanty, a small wooden structure tacked together, useful to fishermen in winter to keep snow off their backs. Usually three sided, the back faced us, and we could not see if there was anyone inside. But there was Marion. Diminutive, barely a speck on the ice, she was heading toward the shanty a bit hesitantly. She came gliding right up to the side. And then she stopped. Stopped and turned, faltered on the ice and fell. I heard her scream and suddenly a figure all in black, with a black hooded mask, came from the other side and lunged at her.

Myrl and I yelled, and took off. We were probably a quarter of a mile away, close enough for them both to hear our shouts and yet far enough for the attacker to keep pursuit. Marion kicked hard, got back up on her feet, and half running, half skating, went for the woods which lay in front of her.

Myrl gained quickly and I cursed my bad ankles. She came to the shanty, her skates shattering ice in a crystal arch as she skidded to a stop. I came up behind her and nearly fell, grabbing the doorway with one hand.

"Why are we stopping?" I gasped.

I followed her finger. There, sitting with his back to the hut, eyes gazing sightlessly upward, tongue bloated and blood encrusted over his forehead, dripping down his ears, was Hollister McLean. One hand was in his lap, serenely holding a pistol.

"Oh my God. Good God," I said.

I heard a scream in the woods, and saw Myrl lift up one leg, discard a skate, and then somehow run and hobble and remove the other. She slid to the shoreline and ran into the woods. I came barrelling along right after her, floundered on the bank, removed my gun, and fired a shot into the air. I couldn't get my skates off as she had, and so I tramped through the snow and underbrush as best I could. I heard a second scream as I crashed into a small clearing, and there was a sight that will never leave me: Marion French on the ground, on her knees, her neck bent back and the figure in black poised with a knife above her throat. His other hand gripped her hair and when she struggled he just shook her like a dog. Myrl was only a few paces from them.

"You will release her." Myrl's voice was calm. The figure in black did nothing. The knife glimmered electric in the cold air and I held my breath.

"You cannot kill us all and there are more of us than you. Behind me is a woman who is a crack shot. Faye, will you please remove the knife."

In a second, without thinking, her voice as my only directive, I aimed and fired, and the knife flew from his grasp. In a breath he was gone, dashing into thick evergreen. Marion collapsed in the snow and Myrl went to her. I remained frozen, shaking, unable to move. I have never fired upon another person before, and the shock of that power, of knowing what he had been bent on doing, that I and a bullet had stopped him, left me paralysed. I gasped a couple of times, my arm remaining outstretched, the pistol poised for further shots – guarding us all. But he had truly vanished.

Chapter Eighteen

Revelations

My legs were cramping and I was cold. Doubled up I sat crouched in sawdust, in the dark, under the bleachers. Next to me, on my right, was Patrick O'Keefe. To my left sat Myrl and Detective Lorey. In front of me, visible through the bleacher steps, was the carousel. It was very nearly pitch black, and all I could make out were the pale ghosts of white stallions, and even they would disappear if I looked directly at them. To catch a glimpse, I had to shift my gaze slightly off to one side. We had been sitting quietly for two hours. My bottom was sore, and I shifted uncomfortably, trying to shove more sawdust under me. Patrick O'Keefe, not permitting himself to show fatigue or boredom, looked away, but I could tell by his shoulders he was disarming a yawn. He sat cross-legged, his arms in front of him, and he leaned over to whisper in my ear. "At least we're not the ones outside."

He had just finished his sentence when the hall echoed with the hollow, metallic sound of a bolt being thrown open. Moonlight spilled across the floor, fresh sawdust lying white like new snow and then disappearing back into blackness as the moonlight was obliterated by a form, and shadows moved across the floor. For an instant, too, the carousel glittered and twinkled with pale light, the mirrors and metal and glass points reflecting back any light possible. But then the door was shut. A small bull's-eye lantern was lit and the carousel cast back the soft orange light from a hundred reflective points. Boots came close – that's all I could see. Heavy work boots, just a few yards from where I sat. They turned away from me and headed toward the carousel. The person paused. I could not tell for what reason, but they just stopped, fresh sawdust crushed, and it was at this moment that Patrick shouted, *"LIGHTS!"*

The arena was flooded with light, Patrick uncoiled himself from the floor, and I was blinded for an instant. Just an instant, however, and then Myrl and I scrambled out and were standing ankle deep in sawdust only feet from the man with the black knitted mask. Patrick's pistol was pulled and several other men came forward from points on the building's circle. Patrick was nervous, but certainly formidable, and he took hold of the knitted mask in one hand and said, "Don't you dare make a move."

He pulled, and with a crackle of static electricity, the mask was removed.

Giles Wilcox stood before us, suddenly familiar, but different, and at once I felt the flicker of a deep, hammering fear. He looked at us with dark eyes and a cold edge that took my breath away. I was afraid, truly afraid, and I did not want Patrick O'Keefe standing so close to him. I had seen men in Japan disarm others from four paces with a kick. In England the system of self-defence was known as baritsu. I remember the party at Howard's, watching Giles, and the reason why his grace and ease of movement seemed so familiar came to me in a rush.

"You should step back," I said. "Quickly," and before I finished, Giles Wilcox, a man supposedly torn with grief, lashed out, his boot flew, Patrick took a glancing blow to the head, stumbled backward, and fell. A shot was fired. But not from Patrick. Or Detective Lorey. Everyone froze. There, in the doorway, looking stern, were the two gentlemen from the train, the taller one's gun pointing at the ceiling – still smoking.

"The next shot I fire will be at you, sir!" he said, sounding quite British, and Giles Wilcox, after pausing for only an instant, made a lunge toward Myrl. The sound of the second shot ricocheted in the arena and Giles fell, grabbing his thigh. A torrid river of obscenities flew from his lips as he rolled on the floor. Blood flowed into the curled sawdust, matting it crimson. Patrick O'Keefe, trying to determine what had just happened, yelled out, "All righty – everybody just hold on."

* * * * *

Giles Wilcox sat very still and Grace finished tying the tourniquet over his flannel work pants. He was handcuffed and morose, saying nothing, staring ahead at some distant point. Detective Lorey was chatting with the gentlemen from England several steps away from our little group. Patrick had yet to replace his gun, obviously impressed with Giles's agility. He kept the pistol in one hand until Grace was finished, and she then snapped her bag shut and stood up. She glanced at her watch.

"It's two-thirty now, and that will hold him for another hour or so but he needs medical attention."

"Thank you, Grace." Patrick was staring at Giles. Clearly, this time, he was having difficulty fitting fact to personality. He remembered his gun, and returned it to his holster. Three men in uniform were standing in a circle around us at the three exit doors. Several more were stationed outside. I was still nervous.

There was movement by the large entryway and Curran Holt was making an attempt to pass through, flashing his press card, and talking to the officer at hand.

"Let him in," called Patrick and ignored Lorey's grunt of displeasure.

As Curran tipped his hat in our direction, saying "Ladies," Patrick gave him several rules to follow.

"Curran, you are welcome, but you have to stay quiet. No questions, no comments. No exclusive interviews, get it? In return, you can print anything you want. That's the deal."

Curran brought out his note pad. "Done," he said. "Besides, I'm getting the feeling no one's going to believe this anyway."

"It is best to go into these things without prejudice toward any one person," called Myrl from behind. In the aftermath of the shooting, she had retreated to the back of the bleachers, to the very last row, and now she made her way dramatically, step by step, toward the rest of us. She punctuated her descent with more philosophy: "Someone once said, 'Art in the blood is liable to take the strangest forms', Captain O'Keefe. One can never presume. If you do, you set yourself up for delusion. Mr Giles Wilcox, if that is indeed his true name, has deceived this town for four years. It is my conjecture he came here to escape the law in another state, found the town with flavour and atmosphere but little leadership and decided to stay. A notorious person can hide easily in a small town and yet lead an extravagant lifestyle."

"I want a lawyer present," said Giles. It was the first he'd spoken since being shot. "And I don't want anyone yapping off."

"You will not recover from this, Mr Wilcox. You are guilty of the most heinous crime and you will pay very dearly." She stepped off the last bleacher squarely into the arena. Lorey and the two gentlemen came over and stood with us next to Wilcox. The tall, thin man winced slightly as he walked, leaning heavily on his cane. Even so, his height was notable, his thinness one of natural constitution, not illness. His features were very sharp, his eyes grey, and though his hair was a bit thin on top, it remained black with just a little grey at the temples. Seeing him full face, he looked familiar to me now, though I couldn't fathom where we had met. He pulled on his ear slightly, tipping his head forward, and I surmised he was a bit hard of hearing.

"I want you to shut up," said Giles.

"Contrarily, it is my turn to speak and I shall have the floor," Myrl snapped in return.

"Giles Wilcox murdered Alyssa Dansen brutally and with forethought and will suffer the consequences. I also surmise that the presence of these two gentlemen means this situation has a foreign link, and one I would not have foreseen if their appearance this weekend was postponed."

Myrl carried this tone only in class. It was as if she were giving a lecture, speaking irritably, frowning, not caring if the rest of us followed her, offering her listeners bits of illumination out of duty rather than generosity. It was what made her a mediocre teacher. There was little room for creative thought and the pursuit of new ideas – the ingredients which make scholarship exciting – because she had already pursued all the ideas and was merely rehashing them for her students. But in this context, her manner not only worked well, it was necessary.

The elderly man stepped forward and extended his hand. "I would like to congratulate you on such an excellent example of precise thinking and I am keenly interested in everything you have to say, madam." He lifted her hand from the curve of her fingers and kissed it.

The gentleman next to him, who seemed a little taken aback by his companion's behaviour, said, "May I present Mr Sherlock Holmes."

Sherlock Holmes! Never to my dying day did I think I would ever meet the famous detective. Once, in Algeria, when I was nine, my parents attended a party where he was supposed to have been present, and that is how I first heard of him. Years ago, I read one of his casebooks, but I knew of him almost entirely from the celebrity of his name.

"And this is my dear friend, Dr Watson," said Sherlock, dropping Myrl's hand. "Now, Mr Wilcox, what do you have to say in defence of yourself" He did not even deign to glance at the prisoner. "Let me assure you all, Mr Wilcox has murdered many times for greed and fortune, and his apprehension is a service to humanity. You were correct in your assumption – his name is really Thomas Peckering and I had the pleasure of nearly meeting him in 1900 during my involvement retrieving the Black Pearl of the Borgias. He was but a youth then, but a formidable adversary, responsible in part for the initial theft of the pearl and its concealment in a plaster bust. I suspected him only after the case was closed. I began following with keen interest the pilferings of jewels from Europe. His career is littered with the rare, the exotic, the royal jewels – these were the ones Peckering wanted. I always assumed we would one day meet, but I did not foresee our convergence on American soil," said Sherlock Holmes, turning to him.

Thomas Peckering remained impassive. Holmes continued. "In the course of the last five years, you virtually disappeared. I thought you had given up or died until this last foray."

Myrl sat down across from Peckering on the bottom step of the bleachers.

"He did not go underground, he merely changed his interests," she began. "Instead of stealing cut jewels he began smuggling uncut diamonds from South Africa." She said this quietly, without emotion, and I saw Peckering flinch. "The investigation was prolonged solely because of an error in my thinking. I made the mistake of presuming Hollister McLean was re-cutting established diamonds it took me some time before I determined he was cutting new ones. A raw diamond looks much like a dirty piece of rock salt.

"Giles Wilcox, as we all knew him, could not shoot an apple at five paces, let alone big game in the wild. He never participated in friendly shooting matches with his neighbours. In fact, it turns out, no one has actually ever seen Giles Wilcox shoot a gun. No. In fact, he spent his safaris confiscating diamonds and buying skins, probably poached, packing them off to Hollister in shipping crates and hiding the raw diamonds in the rock salt necessary for preservation. Have you nothing to say?" she said to Peckering. She paused for a moment and then went on.

"Peckering, Hollister, and Alyssa were three points on a triangle of deception which was exclusive. Peckering stole and shipped the diamonds, Holister cut them, and Alyssa sold them, presumably to the highest bidder."

Patrick O'Keefe sat down. "I can't believe this."

"Well, you must," Myrl said harshly. "After Hollister prepared the mounts, he would replace the cut diamonds in the throats of the finished animals and send them to Alyssa. We are talking about hundreds of diamonds over the course of four years' work. They needed a system which would be flawless. But from the beginning there was trouble. With the first shipment all three became the sudden victims of blackmail. The blackmailer knew exactly how many diamonds were being shipped, when they were to be picked up, and what their worth would be when cut. All three were hit hard, but not hard enough to find a different avenue for their creativity. They kept performing this rite twice a year for four years when Hollister and Peckering discovered Alyssa was the blackmailer."

"And how did they find out?" Lorey was listening. Carefully listening, and though I know she did not recognise a need for vindication, I was free to revel. It was nice to see him appreciate her.

"It was the telegram Marty McFadden found. Remember what it said: 'Blood on the way. Heart bagged. Let's see what worms crawl out now'." She ticked off each statement with a finger. "These phrases tell quite a story." She grasped her three fingers with the other hand.

"Thomas Peckering would always telegram both accomplices ahead to alert them as to the size of the cache. Hollister, so he would know how many diamonds to look for and the approximate location inside the packed skins – Alyssa, so she could place a few strategic calls and plan her trips. But early last spring, only Hollister received a telegram.

"May I interject," said Sherlock Holmes, sweeping his hand through the air.

"Not yet," said Myrl. "In a moment."

His hand remained open as he dropped his arm. I thought her manner unduly rude, but she continued on without a shred of self-consciousness.

"You see, Mr Peckering here had a moment of weakness. He broke his new pattern and ventured back to his former profession: burglary of the highest order. When the Duchess Royal Ruby was stolen last spring, Peckering was in India. All tickets and passport records confirm this, so he was not the initial thief. But he then murdered or maimed, and by some horrid means got his hands on the Ruby. That telegram was critical. He had to alert Hollister that the Ruby, the 'blood', was on its way and that it would be covered thick with rock salt in the chest cavity, thus the words 'heart bagged.' The reference to 'worms crawling out' was a reference to blackmail, and I believe they suspected Alyssa at this point but had no real proof. This was the proof they needed. Giles then sent the traditional telegram to both parties revealing the size of the heist, number of raw diamonds, and so on. The next blackmail note made no reference to the Ruby and only the diamonds were mentioned. Alyssa's fate was sealed."

"But when and where was she murdered?" Lorey was interested not only in justice but in jurisdiction and he looked weary, clinging to a shred of hope that he would somehow be involved in preparing the prosecution.

"She was shot in her apartment June fifth or sixth point-blank by Thomas Peckering, who then carried her to the tub, slit her throat, and drained the body of blood. He killed her as he killed her onstage – with a bullet behind the left ear. I declare those dates because Peckering returned from India May sixteenth and on June fifth Alyssa Dansen placed a telephone order for a pair of shoes and on the night of the sixth, fires were witnessed behind the tannery. The men hid the Ruby in the throat of the lion's head at the Wheel Club and devised their plan." Myrl looked down at the ground. "You, sir, are an abomination." She cleared her throat. "Peckering left the body in the tub and called Hollister to come and bury it out on his land, or dispose of it in some other manner. When Hollister arrived on the scene they removed the bloodstained rug – either burying it or tossing it out into the woods never to be found – and Hollister moved the body to the tannery. Giles cleaned the bathroom, thus the empty drain. But Hollister was a man on the edge. He panicked. Hollister McLean was a man who lived partly in fantasy, and may have been plagued with a perverted attraction to Alyssa Dansen – who can say at this point. Regardless, he devised a plan to change the time and circumstances of her death and then he did what he does best. He skinned the body, burning the organs and bones in stumps out in back of the tannery. Hollister prepared the skin and stuffed the body. His actions tell of an obsession with Alyssa that is far removed from sanity, and when Peckering was presented with the corpse he was outraged. Am I correct?"

Finally, Thomas Peckering moved. He shrugged.

"Come, man," said John Watson. "Is this true? How could someone be so debased? I've never heard of such a crime." Watson looked at Holmes just as Peckering began speaking.

"He was a bastard. A bastard and touched. I couldn't believe he'd done it." Peckering looked up at Myrl, and spoke the words unhesitatingly. "He kept laughing and grabbing his arms, going up on his tiptoes, saying she deserved it and more. He was insane that weekend. Drinking, blabbing about money. Blabbing about her, about her skin, her hair. He made me sick. He was a madman. And there she was the whole time sitting looking right at us with those black glass eyes. I refused to see him and in fact I very nearly killed him. I should have killed him then, he's such a bastard, but he had a plan and the more I thought about it, the more I realised it might actually work."

Myrl shifted her gaze from him to us. "The most important piece of evidence in a murder is the body. They had effectively obliterated clues to that. The second piece of evidence is the time of death. With the body prepared as such, they could effectively move not just the hour and day, but the month, the season."

"The plan," said Peckering looking down at the ground, "was to say she was very sick, pneumonia or something like that, to get her out of the spring season at the theatre. She's a summer resident almost exclusively, and lives in Northampton most of the time anyway. We tried to get a hold of that boarder, to kill that arrangement – it seemed too dangerous to me – but the girl was in Paris and couldn't be reached, so we had to go along and keep her. Hollister thought it would work well to have the body looking out over the street where everyone could see it –"

"But you rigged up the timing devices, isn't that right?" said Myrl. "After all, Hollister's forte is in fixed items, objects

which do not move, and your passion is for the mechanical –
like your carousel – although the recording of the aria was
one of Hollister's. A simple joke on his part, as he knew
Alyssa hated opera."

Peckering ignored her. "Then we'd bring her up in
December or January, say she's up in Brattleboro on a visit,
get her out on the ice in front of witnesses and have her go
under during a thaw, in the dead of winter. Hollister had
cutting blades and we figured we'd tie rocks around her
ankles. The body would never be recovered and I would play
the distraught fiancée."

"But you weren't engaged to her," I said.

"Right," he answered. "Never was. But to be seen as her
spokesperson, I had to be close to her."

"So you began the charade of a courtship," explained Myrl.

"It was about that time, just before I left on the last trip.
Hollister found her little black box under the bed and
discovered she had done more than blackmail us, she'd
double-crossed us by keeping diamonds for herself, that little
bitch. We figured she had undersold us and kept a third of the
diamonds each time. We had no idea where she'd hidden
either the money or the diamonds, and we knew everything
would go to that ass brother of hers once she slipped under
the ice and was declared dead. So Hollister drew up papers in
secret, vouching to our marriage, I forged her signature, and
we started searching."

"You married her for rights of property."

"Yeah. Hollister's job was to make sure people in town saw
her from a distance every once in a while. We decided we'd
look again for the diamonds when I got back from Africa and
the death certificate was signed. Then I could get into her
safety deposit boxes in case she hid them in there, and get to
her accounts. Then I left for Africa."

"You see," said Myrl, "there were seven letters of
blackmail and eight safaris in all. An important observation.
Simple numbers, but revealing. Had Alyssa lived, there
would have been eight letters of blackmail under her
mattress. But then Hollister met with a crisis, I assume."

"He always had some crisis. And it was always money." Thomas Peckering wiped his nose with his hand. Sherlock Holmes tried to interject again, but Myrl held up a hand.

"Here I shall take the liberty conjecture affords," she continued. "Hollister needed cash, and couldn't afford to wait for winter when Alyssa would have her accident. While Peckering was overseas, Hollister began looking for the diamonds himself, alone, in an attempt to swindle his partner. He became desperate. He searched both homes and her dressing room, fastidiously tidying up as he went along. He even slit the throats of all the stuffed animals at the Northampton home in an attempt to find her hiding place. He did this at night, on several occasions, while Rachel White slept in her bed. Her observations that the animals were moved was accurate. But the diamonds were not to be found anywhere. Pressure on him from his lenders became unbearable. Do I have all this correct?"

"Yeah. Except the fact Hollister's an ass. I never should have left. Or never should have come back."

"This is an important point," said Myrl. "Critical. Hollister McLean played a hand only a losing better would play. Having nothing to lose, he took the greatest risk. He decided to take the Ruby for himself, went to the Wheel Club, and found it was gone. So he had to test his partner. Am I correct?"

"He just wanted to see if I'd come back, that's all, and I stupidly fell into it." I was lost. "I don't understand. Why did Hollister give up the plan? Why did he reveal a murder had taken place?"

Myrl stared at Peckering. "That was the test. He knew, if threatened, you wouldn't chance coming back to Brattleboro. But you did. You returned. You did not trust Hollister McLean much and you had every right not to. After the murder he became even more temperamental and prone to fits of megalomania, and you knew he would bring you down. When you received the telegram from him alerting you that the body had been discovered, you quickly deduced that it had not been by mistake, as he proclaimed, but by design and you had to move swiftly to protect yourself ... and the Ruby."

Peckering flinched again.

"The bait, you see, Faye, was the Royal Ruby. If the Ruby was in the States, Peckering would return. When Hollister received word his accomplice was returning, he began a fever of activity. He had three goals: to find the Ruby, frame Marty McFadden for the murder, and exonerate his own name. Thinking along the same lines as their scheme, he searches Peckering's dressing room, his house, and steals the gun in an attempt to strengthen the case against Marty. He finds the Ruby nowhere and his effort reveals nothing. Grasping, Hollister decided to search the three trophies at the bank, but they are inaccessible."

"So that's why he wanted to get at them so badly," said Patrick. "I heard him moaning about them that night at Howard's."

"Exactly. As did Peckering. Later, when I mentioned the lion's head at the Wheel Club had been tampered with, Peckering, who is no fool, caught on that Hollister was trying to double-cross him and steal the Ruby. I'm sure he also began to suspect Hollister had done more than take his gun while at his house." Myrl turned to Peckering. "But we're a little ahead of ourselves. Initially, you did not suspect Hollister was after the Ruby. He told you of his plan to frame McFadden, and his actions appeared to come from loyalty. You two decided to make it appear as though McFadden was trying to frame you. Thus the stolen gun, the bloodstained knife behind the wardrobe, and the wig. The one unfortunate piece of this was Marion French."

"You mean Marion knew about the diamonds?" This question came from Lorey and I saw Dr Watson wince. Peckering sat very still, not saying a word as Myrl spoke.

"Hollister McLean coerced Marion French to impersonate Alyssa Dansen. Once the body was discovered, people would begin investigating the time of death. If Hollister could demonstrate that he was walking with Alyssa down the street at the end of August, that would throw investigators off any clues which pointed to the murder taking place in early June, and he could exonerate himself."

Patrick, who had been staring at his boots the entire time, spoke up. "But how did he get Marion to do that – to dress up as Alyssa?"

"He threatened to reveal a secret she and Alyssa shared."

"I don't know what it was," said Peckering, "but it must've been good, because Marion hated Alyssa. When I cornered him, he said he told her Alyssa was pregnant – the same story I was supposed to tell when it came time to say we were married and get the property – and she was off having an abortion and didn't want people to know."

"But I still don't understand why Marion did it. Why didn't she just come to me?" Patrick shook his head.

"Their secret shall remain in my confidence. It has nothing to do with this case only insofar as it was a means of coercion. But we must return to the sequence of events. Hollister's final trip to Northampton that Saturday was to frame Marty McFadden, but again greed took hold. He decided to search the house once more for the diamonds and was in the middle of sacking Rachel White's room when she returned home unexpectedly. In his haste, he lost a gold watch chain – the same gold chain he had just recently recouped from Henry in a bet."

She turned to me for a moment. "Thus your observation of Hope Mitchell's anger and resentment at the sight of the missing chain was correct. She knew her husband had been gambling again. Hollister owed Henry quite a bit of money, and the chain represented an offer toward that debt. When Hollister won it back, Hope was outraged." She paused and her attentions were once again on Peckering.

"Discovered in the house, Hollister fled to Alyssa's room where he answered Rachel's questions from behind the door, and had a bit of time to think. In order to incriminate Marty McFadden, he waited until he saw us coming up the path, and then fired the shot we heard in an attempt to disguise the true cause of her death which was, indeed, a bullet to the back of the head. He then ran purposely out the front door where he would be seen by all three of us."

"And people would basically describe Marty McFadden." I rubbed my chin. "So Hollister takes off, without the diamonds, and now the body has been discovered."

"Yes, and he's still in trouble with his lenders, who are not the most understanding group of people. Hollister's involvement with the KKK was no longer a benefit to the group. Peckering is still out of the country, and Hollister sets his trap. He wires or puts in a call to Peckering as to the crisis, blaming McFadden's snooping as the reason he had to force their hand. Peckering responds by saying he will return immediately. This means the Ruby was somewhere in town."

"Hollister was an idiot." Kicking his boot into the sawdust, Peckering glanced at Myrl. "And you were too smart. I should have smelled you coming. My instincts are usually much better. I took you for some eccentric spinster, and I should have known better."

"When you arrived back and overheard Hollister asking about the mounts at the bank, and the tampering with the head at the Wheel Club, you knew Hollister was looking for the Ruby. And I was getting close, very close, wasn't I? When I divulged that I knew Hollister was being blackmailed and that he was involved in covering up Alyssa Dansen's murder, I was one step away from you."

Peckering wiped his hands on his good leg.

"When the attempt on my life failed, you both became even more frantic. By this time, you had to act against Hollister's double-cross – you knew he was searching for both the diamonds and the Ruby, and when it was reported in the papers that the diamonds were found, you knew we were in close pursuit and the stakes were very high. The two people who could reveal unsavoury truths were Hollister and Marion. Hollister, of course, knew the entire operation. All Marion could say was that she had impersonated Alyssa, but with that fact alone, your incrimination would be immediate. If cornered, Hollister would not protect you. If you killed Hollister and left Marion, she would go to the police out of fear, and you would fall into the limelight – and attention is something you cannot afford, given your past. To your benefit, Hollister reads the story about the diamonds and panics. Acting alone, he calls Marion and tells her he will return the incriminating evidence if she will meet him out on the Meadows at the shanty. You follow him out, shoot him point-blank, place the gun in his hand, and then wait for poor Marion. Your plan was to slit her throat, just like Alyssa's, and make it appear as though Hollister killed himself in a fit of madness. His death by his own hand would serve to prove him guilty of both murders. Dear Marion did not know what she was drawing herself into when she told Howard she was meeting us, and slipped on those skates. Luckily, Faye is a magnificent shot."

"Which gets us all here," said Lorey, rubbing his face with both hands. So where's this Ruby? This Royal Duchess Ruby?" said Lorey as Patrick pulled Thomas Peckering to his feet.

"Now I must insist," said Sherlock Holmes, and his voice was commanding. Peckering glared at him. Holmes looked at the man he had pursued over continents and time, and said simply, "Justice is a formidable force."

Myrl sat back, and did not interrupt this time. She watched Sherlock Holmes very carefully and touched her hair, smoothed her hands on her skirts, and I saw her sigh.

"My client, as you can imagine, is from the Crown, and as such I was commissioned to find the Ruby. Following the trail to your modest town, I was amused to find Thomas Peckering and knew him to be a formidable foe. I understand his mind. It works like gears within a clock, with similar indifference to the world. He cares not for others or the consequences of his actions – he is ruthless. He is cold and precise and all that he does is carefully orchestrated. I viewed this murder with the highest interest, but it wasn't until this moment that I understood its complexity. The Ruby is close to Thomas Peckering's heart. He trusts no one. So he would marry it to his other love," and Sherlock swept his hand toward the carousel. "Watson," he called and John Watson helped him up onto the floorboards.

From the corner of my eye I saw Peckering stiffen. His hands turned to fists and then released, his fingers long and white, as Sherlock Holmes walked between the carved figures and found the lead horse – a large, white stallion. Every horse had a bright glass jewel in the centre of its forehead set in a plaster ring painted gold. But something about this particular glass seemed odd. It stuck out too far, and the plaster appeared rough. Holmes suddenly took his cane and with great force struck a blow across the horse's forehead. Plaster crumbled. Reaching up, he picked away a bit more plaster, and then grabbed the red jewel and gave a good wrench. It came off in his hand. Blowing on it he rubbed it against his coat and held it high in the air.

"I present the Royal Duchess Ruby, property of His Majesty the King."

* * * * *

It was nearly three-thirty in the morning but I was far from fatigued. Some of the lights had been shut off and the brilliance of the arena ebbed to a soft glow. Thomas Peckering was being escorted by two officers outside where the Ford waited. Patrick O'Keefe and Detective Lorey were having an exchange of handshakes and discussion. But it was the conversation between Myrl and Sherlock Holmes which I chose to listen to and would never forget.

Holmes stepped forward and spoke with great sincerity, his voice deep and not shrill as I imagined.

"I have great admiration for you – you are an American and a woman and yet" – he glanced at Watson, who was shaking his head ever so slightly – "Oh, I am not putting this well now, am I, and Watson is alerting me to the fact – you have displayed superb wit, on a level I am seldom privileged to witness." He took a step closer. "May I ask how you came to your conclusions concerning this case?"

"It seems you employ the same methods we do," said Watson, and Myrl folded her hands in front of her.

"I use simple rules of logic," she answered, her voice low.

"I did not hear your name, as the opportunity did not arise for us to be properly introduced. May I enquire?" asked Sherlock Holmes.

"This is Faye Martin Tullis, my companion," said Myrl, gesturing toward me. "And you know Dr Watson," said Holmes, waving a hand toward his friend.

"Before I offer you my name, I want to assure you of complete discretion and utmost privacy in all matters." She directed her next comment to me. "Is that understood, Faye?"

"I don't understand." And I didn't.

"I mean no one will breathe a word of this conversation and that is a fact. To no one." And then to me she said softly, "Not even Godfrey." I watched her carefully. Though her manner was calm, I could see her hands shake slightly and the slight quiver of her skirts.

"I am, my name is – Myrl Adler Norton."

There was complete silence. Sherlock Holmes leaned heavily on his cane. Watson gave a sharp intake of breath and looked at Holmes. His mentor reached out, laying a hand on Myrl's shoulder, and I saw them both in perfect profile. It was at that moment I understood the demand for secrecy. And why he had seemed familiar to me. One was the image of the other. She had his height, his sharp features, the same hairline. The same deep grey eyes. Sherlock Holmes was Irene Adler's one indiscretion.

Myrl's voice was soft and I saw her shoulders droop and relax slightly under his hand. "I presume you know who I am?

"I think I do."

"So the ultimate mystery is solved," she said, and smiled at him. A simple smile and very much from the heart.

Sherlock Holmes, unaccustomed to emotion, did not bear it well. He started to speak, his voice trembling slightly. He cleared his throat, looked down at the ground, and then dropped his hand. He glanced at Watson, and then his gaze went back to Myrl. He shook his head slowly.

"And here, my dear woman, I have lived a life in the blackest ignorance. I was not even aware of a mystery to be solved."

Epilogue

We never retired to bed that night. Sherlock Holmes, John Watson, Myrl, and I breakfasted in their room at the Brooks House, where the conversation was not about murder and jewels, but about the meanderings of life. Holmes had retired to Sussex, England to a group of hills called the South Downs, where he had a lovely view of the Channel. Not quite the Connecticut River, he assured us modestly, but sufficient. The air was good for his rheumatism and the quiet of the countryside provided him a serene backdrop for his studies in philosophy. It turns out he first visited Sussex years ago, during his involvement in a case where a man named Robert Ferguson suspected his wife was practicing vampirism. Holmes and Myrl both noted with interest similarities of occult beliefs in small towns. But talk soon turned back to literature, the war, and aspects of travel. Neither ever mentioned Godfrey.

The morning was pleasant, the events of the night before a sorry memory. Though we all had a hand in revealing the truth and laying fertile ground for justice, we could not erase the deed.

When we finally returned to Mrs Howe's we slept without interruption until early afternoon. We were then visited by both O'Keefe and Lorey, who came by to pen our statements. Biggy absolutely demanded a sitting, stealing my pocketbook and keeping it well hidden until six photos were snapped.

Curran Holt also stopped by momentarily, mostly to talk to Myrl, and they sat out on the enclosed porch in their heavy coats, she on one side of the divan, he on the other. They shook hands and I heard Curran thank her for the interview, though his note pad was not to be seen anywhere.

Myrl and I commiserated on how unfortunate it was Forrest Dansen would benefit from his sister's death. Though the diamonds were impounded, Alyssa's savings, if he could ever find them, would all pass to him. Myrl noted with a shrug that she would probably never see her nickel, and I offered one from my pocketbook.

Real brought the buggy around and whisked us to the station around four o'clock so we could bid Holmes and Watson well and good on their trip back to England. As the train pulled in I could see Myrl growing stiff and nervous again.

"I do hope we can afford the luxury of writing one another occasionally," she said.

A courageous suggestion, offered with vulnerability, to which Holmes replied distractedly, "Oh, I am not one for writing." He returned a brief smile and watched as the train rolled up, its pistons grating on the steel rails and steam wafting around us all.

John Watson took her hand, nodded, and said, "Do not fear, my dear. I will see that he maintains correspondence with you and rest assured he will read, with great interest, any letter you may wish to send him. Holmes, really." He frowned at his friend, and walked away from us for a moment to hand their bags to a steward.

Holmes waited until Watson was out of earshot and then turned quickly to Myrl. "I want to give you a gift. It is small, but one I hope you will keep with kind memory." Reaching in his pocket he removed a small leather clip and handed it to Myrl.

She opened it like a book. Inside was a small photograph of Irene Adler in an evening dress, looking lovely, very young, her hair in a loop identical to Myrl's. The photo was worn and the clip had the appearance of a keepsake. I recalled

Myrl's discussion about the link between personal articles and proof, and why people treasure keepsakes. For proof. In this case I chose to believe it was a proof of love.

"Oh no," said Myrl, obviously having the same thoughts, trying to hand back the clip. "I couldn't possibly."

"I have no use for it, really, and it would give me great pleasure to know you have it in your possession."

"But I –"

"I no longer have need for this. Because, well, here you are." With that, he awkwardly cupped her cheek in his hand, and then turned away suddenly to the train. "Watson!"

* * * * *

And that was the closest he ever came to professing affection for her. We were to cross paths with Sherlock Holmes and John Watson again – in the States and in forays to England. When Holmes passed away, we flew to Sussex for his funeral and spent time with John Watson. But I was still quite young then, and failed to recognise how much John and I were alike. As a consequence, years later, when Myrl would pass before me, I was left with few provisions for bearing grief. Looking back, I see now that John's and my roles as friends and caretakers followed a similar path. I should have listened more carefully to what and how he spoke during those weeks after the funeral. But those were the days Myrl and I were immortal, and death seemed far away.

Afterword

What is fact? What is fiction? When bringing history to life, these are the two questions that all 'facts' must be passed through, like a sieve, in order to be evaluated. When I was editing this book, I was aware of competing goals in this tug of war between fact and fiction. Faye's goal was to tell a story of friendship and adventure my goal was to uncover and prove a secret. To accomplish what I had set out to do, I began my quest with a flight to England, to take on the very necessary task of unravelling the puzzle which is at the very heart of *In the Dead of Winter*: the affair between Irene Adler and Sherlock Holmes.

Sherlock Holmes was a man of infinite mystery. What has carried his exploits to the dawn of the twenty-first century is not the intricate trappings of his cases, intriguing though they are, but his strength of character. He was a complicated man, multifaceted to say the least: a person of incredible strength and powerful intellect, a person who battled chemical addiction and depression, a person who could be both gracious and terse. He was born around 1854, the grandson of a sister of the French artist Vernet, and little is known of his early years. He had a brother, Mycroft, with whom he enjoyed a distant but comfortable relationship. He had few friends. He dabbled in science and philosophy. He was an excellent violinist. In his final year in college, he turned what had merely been a hobby into a profession, and in 1878, the world's first consulting detective offered his services. Sherlock Holmes's fame, however, would not have been possible without his friend and companion, Dr John H. Watson.

What John Watson was able to bring his readers in the course of nearly a quarter of a century were the intimate details of his friend's brilliant, if troubled, mind. It is interesting to note that Holmes's pride and sense of privacy were so extreme he could not confide in Watson about his encounter with Irene Adler. It is also proof of Holmes's nature that Watson never even suspected that passion could be accounted for in his friend, for it does not enter into his text at all even though he repeats twice in *A Scandal in Bohemia* that Holmes always referred to her as '*the* woman'.

That woman, Irene Adler, was a person of integrity and great beauty, intelligence, and grace. She was a woman who knew how to protect herself, who gained strength from honesty. She was born in New Jersey around 1858 and was a famous opera star, singing at La Scala and presiding as the *prima donna* of the Imperial Opera of Warsaw. This is where she and Mary Howe first met. In Warsaw, she became romantically involved with the King of Bohemia, a relationship which could not end in marriage as she was an American and not descended from royalty. She received several love letters from the King and had her picture taken with him once. When their relationship dissolved, it was this picture she chose to keep as protection – she could use it to threaten the King if he should decide to harm her good name. The King, of course, was certain she would try and use the picture to ruin his impending wedding plans. Holmes never caught up with Irene Adler. By the time he went to her house to retrieve the photograph, she had left England for the United States with Godfrey Norton. Holmes deduced where Adler had hidden the picture, but it was gone. In its place was a letter which explained how cruelly the King had wronged her and that the compromising photo was only kept to protect herself. In addition to the letter was a new picture, just of her – a picture Holmes would keep for thirty years before passing it on to his daughter.

Because of my background and my access to my Aunt Faye's notes, I suspected long ago that much of what is depicted in *A Scandal in Bohemia* is Holmes's fiction. I spent much time in England, sifting through old marriage certificates in the basement of the registry office. According to Holmes, he witnessed the marriage between Adler and Norton. Yet I never found any certificate of marriage. I then travelled to New Jersey and there in the *Orange Gazette* for April 25, 1888, is the marriage of one Godfrey Norton and Irene Adler. And seven months later, a birth is announced: Myrl Adler Norton. Much of what Holmes related to Watson was therefore fiction, but so well done and so fitting with his own character that Watson never suspected.

Myrl Adler Norton inherited much from her father: her propensity toward addiction, which she fought against her whole life, her bouts with depression, her inability to stay idle. Physically, she was tall like her father and she had his grey eyes. Her hair, however, which my aunt so accurately described as mahogany-coloured, must have come from Irene's side of the family. Though Myrl's analytical mind was a product of her birth parents, her sense of justice and humanity was a tribute to the man who raised her, Godfrey Norton.

When and how Irene and Holmes met remains unclear. I assume they must have met after an opera several years before the affair with the King of Bohemia. Always keenly interested in music, Holmes could have heard her perform many times. At the time the King solicited Holmes's help, Irene was retired from the stage, however. My theory is that they were reunited – that she contacted him upon her return to England just a week or so before the King made his dramatic appearance at 221b Baker Street. While in England, I was able to track down the letters Irene Adler's maid, Helen Boatright, sent back from the United States to her family in Westminster. One of Boatright's letters recounted the fast flight from England to New Jersey and talks about a gentleman caller who arrived at the Adler house just days before. Boatright describes how this man, who was very tall and 'queer', caused Irene, 'an anxiety I have never before witnessed. When he looked directly at her, I saw a blush and when they walked to the parlour, she locked the doors. There was something very amiss. He did not leave a card. He arrived in the morning and left after noon, though she never sent for the midday meal'. Boatright then goes on to say that she never saw the gentleman leave, but that when she entered the parlour again, 'every shade was drawn' and her mistress did not appear until supper. This person, this visitor I am nearly certain was Sherlock Holmes.

* * * * *

Holmesian scholars have often pointed out that Watson depicts Holmes as having no romantic interest in the opposite sex. Or in the same sex. They make the case that Watson paints Holmes as asexual. I disagree. Watson doesn't allude to Holmes's sexuality because sex and sexual attraction just were not discussed and certainly not recorded on paper for an audience of strangers. Dr Watson mentions his own courtship and marriage to Mary Morstan in the driest of terms. Given that, I cannot imagine he would be so bold as to embellish another man's love life. Dr Watson related nothing because there was no interest in telling. Telling did not command the lucrative market it does today.

My aunt was convinced Myrl's father was Sherlock Holmes. And I believe Myrl herself might have had some inkling before their meeting in the Pavilion. The incident on the train when she first sees the two men is most revealing. It is as if she already knows who they are, and by Faye's description she is clearly agitated. In the end, speculation does not really matter. Myrl and Holmes did find each other – a nearly impossible feat given distance, time, and circumstance. It was through a series of coincidences they were united in Brattleboro, and for two such analytical people, the spectre of coincidence must have been quite threatening.

Needless to say, several years later when they were brought together again, control replaced chance, defences were up, and each was able to review the other within the confines of their respectively brilliant minds.

* * * * *

Brattleboro, in the decade from 1910 to 1920, was a town of elegance and opportunity, convention and invention. Like many small New England towns, Brattleboro struggled with a dual nature. With a population of around nine thousand it had all the amenities of the larger cities to the south and wrestled with its identity as a town of cultural worth and rural inclination. It wanted to be progressive and 'citified' but not at the expense of losing its country roots. A reflection on the people who helped shape the town and the institutions which have become a part of Brattleboro history deserves attention.

Mary Howe was born somewhere around 1860, the daughter of a local farmer. She took voice lessons in Boston and Philadelphia, and had little fear of travel. She journeyed by herself to Europe and debuted on stage in Germany. *La Sonnambula* guaranteed her star status. She went on to sing in Wiesbaden by invitation of the Kaiser. From there she travelled to Warsaw and met another American, Irene Adler. The two became inseparable. In 1888 Mary returned to Brattleboro, debuted on stage at the Opera House, and returned that fall to Europe, where she continued to sing until 1905. When she retired from the stage, she returned once again to Brattleboro, and remained active in the arts.

Hayes Bigelow was the nephew of Rutherford B. Hayes. He became a well-known photographer around Brattleboro and shot pictures for the *Reformer*. He also ran the ferry boats out to Island Park. When the park flooded he devoted himself full time to photography in the twenties and thirties and eventually set up a store on Main Street.

Patrick O'Keefe was a person of integrity and honour. He served Brattleboro as police chief from 1923 to 1930. He then went on to become sheriff of Windham County and served until his death in December 1951. He had a fondness for children and a laugh that matched his frame. He was a large man, known for his sense of fairness. The town always knew when spring was officially announced – it was the day Sheriff O'Keefe would stroll down Main Street in his straw hat.

Dr Grace Burnett was the character I found most intriguing. She was, as were Myrl and Faye, a woman outside time. Born in neighbouring West Dummerston in 1886, she left for medical school, returning in 1914 to devote herself to the health and well-being of her town folk. She served as a physician for more than fifty years. She always kept horses, between four and seven at a time, and used them to ride into the hills to administer to her patients. Soft-spoken, slow to anger, and quick-minded – these are among the attributes I heard ascribed to her by her ex-patients, qualities she must have needed as I am sure she must have initially met with formidable prejudice. But she persevered, and went on to found the Green Mountain Horse Association and became active in the SPCA. She was beloved by the town, and was honoured as the Citizen of the Year in 1961. She died in 1963.

These four people were part of the fabric of Brattleboro, a town working hard at establishing a name for itself. In the 1840s and '50s Brattleboro became famous for its water cures, or hydrotherapy clinics. Dr Robert Wesselhoeft's Water Cure and the Lawrence Water Cure were two competing institutions right in town. Brattleboro was also noted for its boardwalks, which followed along the West and Connecticut rivers. The town was picturesque, and even then a large tourist industry brought work to the valley. The trolley, which cost a nickel and ran from Prospect Hill via Main Street to West Brattleboro, was opened in 1895. It was kept busy, carrying more than 2,500 passengers daily. The town was active, with the Opera House, the Wheel Club, taverns and restaurants, hotels, and of course Island Park.

Island Park began as a popular brewery. In 1911, the Island Park Company built a grandstand and opened the Pavilion, a building which housed refreshments, a ballroom, bowling alleys, and a stage. President Taft gave an address at the Pavilion after first meeting with Colonel J. Gray Estey. For nearly two decades Island Park served as a meeting place, an entertainment hall with films and wrestling matches, a place for a good drink, baseball, and ice cream. But after 1920, the park began to deteriorate. More townspeople had cars, and they could drive to attractions elsewhere. Management was poor and did little to adjust for competition. In the end, though, it was the Connecticut River which destroyed the park. The Vernon dam, completed in 1911, caused flooding at Island Park nearly every spring. In 1927, a tremendous flood destroyed the boathouses, the Pavilion, and several private homes. The Island Park Company decided against reconstruction and the remaining buildings were raised.

I am sorry that much of what Faye describes in town is gone. By 1923 the trolley, which I imagine must have been very picturesque, was abandoned in favour of buses. The Opera House was destroyed. The Wheel Club gone. Hayes Tavern is now a parking lot. The springs which gave birth to the water cures are paved over. And, of course, Island Park has disappeared. What remains is the Brattleboro Retreat, Brattleboro Memorial Hospital, Brooks House, and a quaint Main Street. More important, what is constant is a true sense of community, and a vibrancy which reflects the efforts of people today working to shape Brattleboro's future.

* * * * *

I would like to thank the many people who helped me shape this book, constantly checking on the details, coming up with suggestions and words of encouragement: the Brooks Memorial Library and the Rockingham Free Public Library, and the many people I interviewed both in Vermont and abroad. I also want to extend my deep appreciation to those who have lent their time, expertise, critical eye, and seemingly never-ending enthusiasm for the project. I would like to thank close friends and family. To Laura and Edie I offer special thanks and there is Kathy Roberson, my colleague and confidante.

Finally, I want to thank, my children Hannah, Davis, Kira and Joseph – a wonderful group of people who will never understand how incredible they are.

Myrl Adler Norton
will return
in a new adventure

Death at the
Round Table

by

Abbey Pen Baker